W9-AVL-095

# *Praise for Carolyn McSparren*

"All God's Creatures is one of the most endearing and entertaining stories I've read in years. Carolyn McSparren has created a world rich with animals and the people who love them. It's about friendship and family—and the animals—who, without intention, remind us what unconditional love is all about."

*—Sharon Sala*
*author of MISSING, November 2004, Mira Books*

"A great read, even more so for horselovers!"

*—Vickie Presley, Amazon.com*

"Carolyn McSparren delivers all the ingredients for good reading: unique story elements, tantalizing suspense, an engaging subplot and a myriad of well-written characters."

*—Cindy Whitesel, Romantic Times*

"Carolyn McSparren provides the audience with a powerful tale that will evoke feelings from the hard core reader yet does it through humor rarely seen in a sub-genre novel."

*—Harriet Klausner*

"Impressive and original! I can't resist giving a five star review to the talented Carolyn McSparren."

*—Brenda Mott, Amazon.com*

"Carolyn McSparren treats us to a compelling pageturner guaranteed to please the discerning palate."

*—Cindy Whitesel, Romantic Times*

Dedicated to the veterinarians

who treat the animals we love,

and to the animals that so enrich our lives.

# All God's Creatures

Carolyn McSparren

Smyrna, Georgia

BelleBooks, Inc.

ISBN 0-9673035-8-3

# All God's Creatures

This is a work of fiction. Names, characters, places and incidents are either the product of the authors' imaginations or are used ficticiously. Any resemblance to actual persons (living or dead), events or locations is entirely coincidental.

Copyright © 2004 by BelleBooks, Inc.

Printed and bound in the United States of America. All rights reserved. No part of this book may be reproduced in any form or by any electronic or mechanical means, including information storage and retrieval systems, without permission in writing from the publisher, except by a reviewer, who may quote brief passages in a review.

Published by:
BelleBooks, Inc. • P.O. Box 67 • Smyrna, GA 30081
We at BelleBooks enjoy hearing from readers. You can contact us at the address above or at BelleBooks@BelleBooks.com

Visit our website— www.BelleBooks.com

First Edition November 2004

10 9 8 7 6 5 4 3 2 1

Cover art: Monica Van de Meer
Cover design: Martha Shields

# Chapter 1

## *In which Maggie disappoints her mother and chooses a new name*

The day I told my mother I intended to become a veterinarian was the first time I disappointed her by choice. It would not be the last.

The kicker came when I changed my name. Becoming Maggie when I'd spent my entire life as Margaret might not seem like much, but to my mother it was the equivalent of burning my bra and going off to live in an Ashram.

For eighteen years I had attempted to live up to her vision for me, although I knew it was an impossible fit. She held desperately to the forlorn hope that one day I would blossom into a Southern belle with streaky blonde hair. I was supposed to marry a rich planter's son and present her with half a dozen blonde grandchildren. Mother dreamed big.

I never fully understood how she planned to transmogrify all five feet ten and a hundred and thirty pounds of Margaret Evans into a petite size six. The only time I let her bleach my hair—normally the color of the water after you've mopped the kitchen floor—it had come out in tiger stripes—white on the ends, beige in the middle and teint du rat at the scalp.

Mother's given name was Minnatrey—can't get much more Southern than that. She longed to be a member of polite society. In Memphis, Tennessee, where I grew up, that required either a family lineage traceable to General Andy Jackson and his contemporaries, or a sizeable fortune.

The Evans family had neither. We weren't rich. We were solidly upper middle-class. Daddy was a Certified Public Accountant and made a good living, but nothing that could be considered wealth. Mother stayed home or worked on charities. The family hadn't inherited money either.

Mother spent a bundle on genealogy charts. She longed to be eligible to join the Daughters of the American Revolution. Turns out her family fought for the British in 1776.

She would have been happy to join the United Daughters of the Confederacy. Unfortunately, her family fought for the Yankees in what is known in the south as The War of Northern Aggression.

Daddy's family had even less cachet. His great-something grandfather and his great-something uncle snuck into the country from Scotland by way of Canada. They preferred the dangers of the frontier to starving while the Duke of Cumberland hunted them down after the battle of Culloden. Unfortunately for Mother's hopes, they took up stealing and selling horses on the Natchez Trace. They were both eventually hanged. My cheekbones and my nose come straight from one of the Cherokee maidens they married along the way.

Mother's only hope was that I'd marry somebody whose family would shoehorn me into the Junior League, and give her an entry into society as a by-product.

I tried to become a Southern belle, but I was too brainy, too gawky, and much too out-spoken. And I never learned to lie. Successful Southern belles in the 1960s sucked in duplicity with their mother's milk.

Mother had to be content with running the Altar Guild and the Women of the Church at St. Cecilia's Episcopal Church. Both meetings rotated throughout the year from house to house. The week before Mother's turn, we polished every bit of silver we possessed, ironed tablecloths and linen napkins, and scrubbed until we both had housemaid's knee and permanent burn scars on our fingers.

And boy, did we fix food. I have made a million of those nasty little ham horns wrapped around cream cheese. I can still aim and fire a pastry gun of filling into a deviled egg straighter and faster than Wyatt Earp ever shot his .45.

Mother's crowning achievement came when I was a sophomore at Southwestern College in Memphis. She managed to persuade her music club to sponsor a princess at Cotton Carnival. Me. They had never sponsored a princess before. I'm not certain they ever did again.

Cotton Carnival had originally been invented to rival New Orleans Mardi Gras and advertise cotton. Memphians had always called it simply "Carnival."

I don't remember precisely when it lost its association with cotton entirely and became simply "Carnival." For a while it dwindled into a tame and 'inclusive' little party. Lately, it's been enjoying a resurgence, but with less emphasis on *old* money and more on *just* money.

In the early sixties, however, stuffy, staid Memphis turned rowdy and bawdy for one week in May each year because of Cotton Carnival.

Memphis did not allow liquor by the drink in those days. Every time the city fathers suggested regular bars would be good for tourism, the bootleggers and the teetotal preachers joined forces to defeat the proposal. Unless you were a member of one of the country clubs that were exempt from the statute, you brought your Jack Daniels to parties in a brown paper bag and consumed the whole thing during the evening. Not worth carrying home a quarter of a bottle, so most people drank one hell of a lot more than they would have if they'd been buying whiskey sours or margaritas.

During Carnival, however, the secret societies (that were not secret at all), all took 'club rooms' in The Peabody and other fancy hotels, set up twenty-four-hour-a-day bars for their members, and partied down for almost an entire week—Tuesday through Saturday. The married women who were crowned queens of Sphinx or Memphi or chosen as duchesses spent fortunes on their costumes and their parties. I can remember they all had very tall stand-up collars like Dracula's, except as he would have been interpreted by Liberace. I doubt there was a sequin, a paillette or a rhinestone to be had this side of St. Louis for months before the first day of Carnival.

The children of Memphis society were co-opted to act as pages and flower girls for the court. The little girls probably loved the dress-up.

The boys were dressed in elaborate cotton velvet Lord Fauntleroy suits. Since most of them were accustomed either to jeans or Little League outfits, I don't even want to consider the coercion it took to cram a bunch of seven-year-old over-bred tow-headed thugs into short pants and lace. The organizers had learned years earlier that the fewer pockets were available to be filled with live toads and spitballs, the better for everyone concerned.

Sometime during the roaring twenties, the husbands of the duchesses and secret society queens had gotten sick of being ignored for that week, so they invented their own society—the Boll Weevils. They rushed around Memphis in black masks with boll weevil snouts hoo-rawing and courting alcohol poisoning.

The only real fun I ever found in Carnival was in the separate (but equal, right?) Cotton Makers Jubilee held by Memphis's African American social elite. Things were still very much segregated in Memphis and the mid-south at that time, although the cracks were visible in the white monolith. The Jubilee took place down on Beale Street. They had the best jazz, the best blues, the best dancing, and far and away the most awesome parades.

The merry-makers involved in the Jubilee were also polite to white interlopers from Carnival who found their way to the clubs where the jazz greats were playing. I doubt the white secret societies would have been so welcoming to *them*.

Did I want to be a Cotton Carnival princess? Hardly. My parents had struggled to send me to a private school with most of the girls who were princesses of old, established country clubs, that had been sending princesses to Carnival for donkey's years.

I knew most of the boys—those scions of wealth and privilege Mother wanted me to court, but none of them had ever asked me for a date. They thought I was weird, while I thought they were stupid and shallow.

Ditto the girls. But rich and beautiful. Who doesn't envy rich and beautiful when you're eighteen?

Anyway, the one stipulation about the costumes the court had to wear was that they all had to be made of cotton. Not drip dry, not wrinkle free—your basic iron-it-and-starch-it-every-whipstitch cotton.

I'm sure Daddy couldn't easily afford either the day and evening costumes I had to wear as a member of the court, nor the even fancier dress I was supposed to wear to "my party," the ball given by my sponsoring club for the entire Carnival Court. He never complained, bless him.

The other sticking point was that every princess and lady-in-waiting had to be accompanied either by a prince charming or a lord-in-waiting to dance attendance on her. Possibly other Carnival ladies got to pick their own boyfriends. My escort, however, was chosen for me.

He was one of those scions, so Mother tossed me at him the way you might toss a bone to a hungry Rottweiler.

He was not a happy choice. First of all, he stood only an inch taller than I do, so when I wore pumps with heels, I towered over him. Second, poor Giles had been born with no discernible chin and had little piggy eyes set much too close together.

Since he had gone away to college and was four years older than I was, I had never actually met him before. We agreed to meet at the old Fortune's Jungle Garden on Poplar to get to know one another. I intended to make the best of it, I really did.

Within five minutes, I discovered that his political and religious beliefs had been handed down intact from Attila the Hun. Within five minutes of meeting me, he informed me that women were much happier in a subservient relationship to a strong man, and that held true for the "colored folks" as well. Both civil and women's rights were nothing more than a minor impediment to the forward march of history's dominant, preferably Southern, white male.

If not for Mother, I would have walked away and never looked back. But I was still being a good girl. I *did* tell him he was a Neanderthal idiot. We hated each other from that moment on.

One of the few good things about being a Carnival Princess was that for the week I was lent a brand-new yellow Cadillac convertible to drive with a sign across the back that read "Cotton Carnival Princess." The bad thing was that I couldn't remove the sign.

Tuesday afternoon Giles, the Prince of Darkness, and I drove together all the way down to the tip of President's Island on the Mississippi River. He hated having me drive. That was a man's prerogative.

I parked the convertible, and we clambered aboard the gigantic barge that had been fitted up with lights and fireworks for the trip up river to the foot of Beale Street. Once we landed, the Carnival King, an older married man wearing more gold braid than a Paraguayan dictator, declared Carnival open. Fireworks, music, party down.

Then came the first of several parades at which the court got to ride in open wagons called 'tally-hos'. We would wave and throw candy to the peasants who lined the streets. I was about as happy riding the tally-ho as I would have been on a tumbrel in the French Revolution.

After opening night on the float, the prince and I arrived at the staging areas for hospital visits and parades in separate automobiles. It says a good deal for Memphis that I thought nothing of driving home alone at two in the morning in an open convertible with a sign the size of Arkansas across its trunk.

My special Princess party was to be held Thursday night at the Nineteenth Century Club, an elegant old mansion on Union Avenue in the Garden District. Mother wasn't a member, but she had a dear friend who allowed us to use her membership.

There was no place to dress at the club, so I dutifully decked myself out in my ball gown—a white cotton eyelet affair with a Scarlet O'Hara hoop and four crinolines under it—at home. Mother had made me practice sitting down in the hoop. If I didn't smash it flat at the optimum moment it would flip up in front and bare my underwear to the waist.

No matter how warm and sunny May had been to that point, it always rained during Carnival. The night of my party rain was sluicing down in buckets, so Daddy put the top up on the convertible for me. Mother had left hours before to dither about the food and flowers. She expected The Son of Dracula to pick me up in a limousine with champagne and roses. Daddy and I let her think that.

Instead, I squeezed myself into my whalebone corselet, ducked under my crinolines and hoop, fidgeted while Daddy fastened all the buttons down the back of the dress, shoe-horned myself into my convertible and drove north down Cleveland Avenue from our house in the Garden District.

The area of Cleveland close to Union was lined with seedy apartments that rented by the week. I generally drove through that area ten miles faster than the speed limit, but that night I could barely see to navigate. I hugged the right-hand side of the road even though the water was deeper there. The car lights reflected against the curb to provide me an idea as to where I was driving.

If I hadn't been close to the curb I'd never have seen the movement. I have no idea why I didn't assume it was a raccoon trying to cross the street. All I saw was something black and shiny scrabbling in the light my headlights cast.

The gutter was running with water. Whatever the thing was, it was being swept closer to the storm drain. A rat? No, too dark a lump. And two things, not one.

I slammed on my brakes, rucked up crinolines and hoops above my knees, and jumped out practically into the path of an eighteen wheeler. God knows what he thought I was, but I'll bet he went home sober that night.

I didn't consider the rain. I had to keep those things from disappearing down the storm drain.

One was fighting hard to stay afloat. The other was just floating.

I reached down, grabbed one, clutched it to my bosom, and snatched the other just before it slipped out of sight. The one against my chest lay inert.

The one in my hand, however, opened its little pink mouth and gave a pitiful imitation of a howl.

Puppies.

I shook the inert one. No response. Dead? Or unconscious from water and cold? I couldn't tell. The other pup was obviously still alive and fighting to stay that way. He scrabbled against my hand with sharp little claws.

"Oh, no you don't," I said. I clutched both pups with one hand, smashed my hoop flat with the other, dove into my car and slammed the door barely in time to avoid a wall of water thrown up by the wheels of another eighteen wheeler.

As his lights swept across my rear view mirror, I caught a glimpse of my face. God in heaven!

My beauty-shop-arranged French twist was hanging down around my face, and I could barely see for the water running off my eyebrows into my eyes.

My fancy satin pumps squished against the floorboards as I felt for the pedals.

I checked my skirt. The bottom eight inches of my ruffles felt sodden, although the crinolines underneath had somehow stayed dry.

"I'm dead," I said aloud. For one frantic moment I actually considered heading west across the Memphis-Arkansas Bridge and driving across Arkansas until I ran out of gas. I must have been crazy. How could I show up at my party soaking wet? Mother would be mortified.

I would be toast.

The dashboard clock said I had an hour before I was supposed to be presented to the court. Despite the warmish weather outside, I turned the heater on full blast and aimed it straight at my shoes and skirt.

At least one of the pups seemed to love the warmth. He snuggled into my lap.

I couldn't run away from my responsibility, either to the pups or to my mother. Those little critters needed professional help. Fast. I didn't dare take them to the party. I'd never be allowed to leave once I actually showed up.

I'd never had a pet. Mother thought dogs were dirty and stank up the house, and my father was so allergic to cats that one whiff could send him into anaphylactic shock and twenty-four hours in the emergency room.

That meant I had no idea where to find a veterinary clinic.

I turned right onto Union Avenue and wracked my memory. I vaguely remembered the sign for a veterinarian's office east of the Helen Shop where I'd bought my dress. If I found it quickly, I could dump my charges and race to the club in time for Mother to make repairs before the court showed up for my presentation.

I could see it now. 'Your Majesties, may I present Princess Drowned Rat?'

I groaned. Mother would never be able to hold up her head in society again. One mad impulse on my part and the Evans family would be social pariahs forever.

But then again, Mother wouldn't *die*. If I didn't get this shivering little pup some help quickly, it would.

Bingo. I saw the sign. A veterinary clinic. As I looked, the lights that shown through the glass front door flicked off. I peeled into the parking lot, grabbed both pups and sprinted for the door just as someone inside started to turn the key.

"No! Stop! Please open!"

He smiled, but shook his head.

"Look!" I held up the pups. "Help me."

He opened the door and stared at me. "Young lady," he said, "Do you generally dress that way?"

He took both pups. "Brother and sister, I'd say. No more than three weeks old." He held his finger against the bundle that had not moved. "Drowned, I suspect. Where did you find them?"

I poured out the entire story.

"Some bastard probably tossed them out of a car. You see any others?"

"God no. You mean I missed some?"

"No way to tell. Doesn't matter now." The pup wriggled and nibbled at his finger.

"He's a fighter." I pointed to the bundle that was already beginning to fluff in the warm, dry air. "I thought he deserved a chance."

"So he does. Let's see if we can save him."

I glanced at the clock over his head. "Oh, Lord, I have to leave. My mother will kill me."

"He's your pup, miss. I may need your help."

"I have to use your telephone," I said.

"Help yourself. Meanwhile I'll stick this young man in the oven while I get some things ready."

"I beg your pardon?"

"Don't worry. I won't broil him."

When I finally reached her, Mother was frantic.

"I'll be there within half an hour," I said. "Find me some towels and dig out your makeup and comb. I'm going to need some work."

"Cotton Carnival party?" The doctor peered over his bifocals at me.

I nodded and hung up on my mother's hysterics.

"To whom do I send the bill for all this? Or shall I pass him along to the Dog Pound for euthanasia?"

"Euthanasia? I just saved his life. Nobody's going to kill this pup, dammit! Are you crazy?" I'd never spoken to my elders that way in my life.

"Ah, then I shall keep him for you. You can pick him up tomorrow morning."

"About the bill…"

"We'll make some arrangement." He pulled the squirming puppy from the small oven and handed him to me. "Now, first we need to get some fluids into him."

"He's nearly drowned. Fluid is the last thing he needs."

"At what point in your young life did you become a veterinarian? *Intravenous* fluids. You will have to hold him very still. Hard enough to insert a needle into a Great Dane. Finding a vein in a scrap of fur this size requires a genius." He stared at me over his glasses again. "Which, fortunately for you, I am."

So far as I could tell, he was serious. As I came to learn, he was also correct.

He inserted a needle into the pup's left front leg and attached it to a small plastic bag filled with liquid. "Here, hold this bag," he said. "Above the table, blast it, not down by your side. Functions by gravity."

"Yes sir."

He busied himself at the other side of the examining room. His back was to me, but I heard water running, and a moment later, he came back holding a doll bottle. "Let us pray he'll suckle. If I have to shoot the formula down his throat by syringe, he might aspirate milk into his lungs. He doesn't need pneumonia."

He took the now empty bag from me and handed me the bottle. I stared at it until he said, "Young lady, don't you have bat brains? Stick it in his mouth."

Old coot. But I did as I was told, and miraculously, the baby began to suckle. Its tiny little black paws moved in and out rhythmically against the towel on my lap. I laughed. "Look at that. Go to it, little bear."

"He'll need to be bottle fed every four hours around the clock."

"Will he live?"

"I will give him a shot of antibiotics as a prophylactic." He glanced up. "The word merely means protection."

"I realize that. I asked if he'd live."

"That depends on his will to fight, his God, and you." He looked at me over his glasses again. "Who might you be when you're not royalty?" He took the pup from me and began to rub his tummy, which now bulged with milk.

I reached into the beaded evening bag hanging from my wrist and brought out an engraved visiting card. It was a little damp. I can't believe I actually ran through dozens of the things in high school and college. I stuck it out to him. He ignored it and continued rubbing. "What are you doing now?" I asked.

"His mother is not available to stimulate his bowels and bladder. I am in a sense *in loco parentis*."

"Oh."

"Read me what your card says."

I did.

"Hum. Margaret Parker Evans." He wiped the baby's belly and spoke to it. "Good. You'll do, young man."

I wrote down my address and telephone number on the back of the card.

"Leave it on the desk," he said, "and take back your animal while I shoot him full of anti-germ juice. No doubt he's full of worms, but they'll have to enjoy his happy home until he's stronger."

I nestled the now fuzzy baby into his towels, and watched the doctor shoot him with antibiotics.

"Do you intend to raise this pup?" he asked.

I took a deep breath. If I said the words, I could never take them back. "Yes sir."

"Good. When you come to pick him up tomorrow morning, I will set you up with formula, and a schedule for shots and worming."

"Who'll feed him in the meantime?"

"Not your concern so long as he is under my care. As a matter of fact, a young man who is waiting to leave for medical school comes in at ten tonight and stays until eight. He handles such chores."

"Oh." Dollar signs flashed across my brain. The bills for this Cotton Carnival fiasco must have been horrendous. I couldn't ask Daddy to pay a fortune for a foundling, and I definitely didn't have any money. "Uh—can I pay your bill in installments?"

"I assumed from your garb and your automobile that you are rich."

"I'm poor. Extremely poor. Look, I'll work my tail off for you until the bill is paid if you'll let me. I'm free after two in the afternoon four days a week. I'll scrub cages, mop floors—whatever you need. I couldn't do night duty. My mother wouldn't let me."

"We will discuss it tomorrow morning if he's still alive."

"He will be. Oh, Lord, my mother's going to kill me." I ran out without another word.

I checked the sign beside the front door as I ran out. "Hubert Parmenter, D. V. M." The man had asked for my name, but never bothered to give me his. He was rude and arrogant. I didn't care. I was crazy about him. I didn't stop to think why. Maybe it was that heavenly perfume of alcohol and wet dog. I'd never smelled it before, but I knew I preferred it to Chanel No. 5.

Maybe because he didn't know anything about me, but simply accepted me and let me help him. Maybe it was the way he looked at me. He didn't see a soggy, would-be debutante, but an assistant. A stupid assistant, grant you, but an assistant nonetheless. Nobody had ever required anything like that of me.

There are defining moments in every life. Mostly, we don't recognize them, but that night, I knew my life had changed forever. That dingy, antiseptic clinic felt more like home than my bedroom. My life clicked into place like a puzzle when the missing piece finally shows up. I wanted to spend my life smelling that wet fur, holding that little creature whose heart beat so fiercely against mine.

I wanted to *be* Dr. Parmenter.

What I didn't want was to go to my dad-dratted party, but of course I went.

I slipped into the back door of the Nineteenth Century Club and ran straight into my mother in the kitchen.

"Margaret, where have you been?" she wailed. Then she took a good look at me. "Did you have an accident? Oh, Lord, you didn't hurt that car, did you?"

"No, mother, the car is fine. I had to rescue a puppy."

Of course I should have kept my mouth shut. I should have run the car into a telephone pole or off the Mississippi River Bridge. I should have told her I'd been kidnapped by Gypsies. Anything but the truth.

"You what?" For a moment she stared at me blankly. Then she began to simmer. She was swelling toward a full-fledged hissy fit. "I do not believe this. The most important night of my life and you ruin everything! Just the way you always do. Oh, God, I don't know why I try. What will people think? You look like something the cat dragged in. When I think of what that dress cost!"

The Southern hissy fit takes a while to lift off. Mother was fast approaching a rolling boil.

"Mother, we don't have time. You have to fix me up quick."

It was the only thing that could have saved me. Nobody ever said my mother wasn't good in a real crisis. In her estimation, this was right up there with Armageddon.

She went to work. Under her breath and around the hairpins she used to re-pin my hair, she kept up a running commentary. "You do not have the brains God gave a goose. You have never listened to me or your father. Just wait 'til he hears about this! All that money down the drain. We'll be the laughing stock of Memphis. It's no wonder you can't get a date. Nobody in *my* family was ever crazy."

She started scrubbing the mud off the bodice of my dress. "You've never appreciated one thing we do for you. We scrimp and save and what do you do? Pick up some drowned cur. There. That'll have to do." She looked up at me. "You've never loved me. You did this on purpose just to ruin things."

That's when the maitre d' announced the arrival of the court.

Actually, I doubt that anybody noticed there was anything wrong with the way I looked. The entire court was wet from running to and from the buses and cars in which they were traveling from party to party. They'd already been to three or four other parties, so they were fairly soggy. And fairly drunk.

My prince and I welcomed the court and were presented in turn. I whispered to my mother on my way to the dance floor, "Don't worry. They wouldn't notice how I looked if I were stark naked."

She glared.

The court stayed for one full set played by the combo Mother had hired before they dashed off to their buses and limos for the next party.

I was expected to stay for the whole evening and dance with every male there, most of whom were my father's age. Mother kept thrusting me toward my prince.

I was so chastened I only insulted him once. Mostly we danced in stony silence, while I stared over the top of his balding head and prayed to be allowed to go home.

When I finally got to bed, I lay awake until dawn wondering about my pup. I cut my eight o'clock class and drove straight to the clinic.

Dr. Parmenter had been at the clinic late the previous night, so he'd hardly be there early this morning. But there he was. As I walked in the front door, he scowled at me. "Well, Miss Maggie, you here to pick up your dog?"

I started to give him my correct name. A great many Southern belles bear the last names of illustrious ancestors as first names. Mother had tried to have me called Parker, her maiden name, but for once my daddy put his foot down.

Thus I had spent eighteen years as Margaret. Not Meg. Not Peggy. Certainly never Maggie. Why bother to correct him? Besides, I liked it.

"Could I leave him here until Carnival's over?" I asked. "I'll come by to feed him and look after him as often as I can, and next week I'll be here to scrub floors to pay for him." Then what was I supposed to do with him?

With *Mother*?

She had fallen into bed exhausted at three a.m. the previous night. I'd managed to sneak out before she or Daddy stirred, but I knew I'd face the third degree the minute I showed up this afternoon. I had promised Dr. Parmenter to raise the pup, but that had been in the heat of the moment and to keep him out of the dog pound. The only way to avoid a major confrontation with mother was to have a suitable place for the pup to go to.

I couldn't do it. The Chinese say that when you save somebody's life that person is your responsibility forever. This fuzzy, nuzzly, cheerful little black pup was mine forever. He would go to no one's home but mine. Mother would simply have to suck it up.

"Little Bear," I whispered as I massaged his bulging tummy, "You have got me in one hell of a lot of trouble."

He grinned up at me.

"Very well, Miss Maggie," Dr. Parmenter said. "I suspect we can find some lovely cages for you to scrub out next week."

"I'll leave my schedule of classes with your receptionist. Thank you." God knows where I got the chutzpah to do it, but I leaned down and kissed him.

He growled. Dr. Parmenter, that is, not Bear.

I managed to run by the clinic twice on Saturday between visits the court paid to retirement communities and hospitals. By then even Dr. Parmenter believed the pup would live. That meant I had to tell Mother I was bringing a dog into our lives.

But not until after Carnival.

Saturday night of Carnival was the final party called "Last-Nighters," for obvious reasons. After the king and queen declared the official end to the festivities everybody in the court wound up at The Peabody out of costume and ready to party 'til we dropped. The Prince of Darkness escorted me into the room, sat me down at a table with some of my friends from school, set a fifth of bourbon in a paper bag in front of me, and disappeared without so much as a goodbye.

I was amazed that I was asked to dance every dance—and not out of pity either. Being without a stuffy date had its advantages. At seven in the morning, six of us wound up at the Whitsitts' big old house in the Garden District for breakfast.

Then I drove home for the final time in my fancy convertible and collapsed into bed. I never told mother how my prince had deserted me.

Sunday afternoon after I woke up, I convinced Daddy to help me talk to Mother about Bear.

She was horrified. "It goes outside."

"Bear's tiny, Mother, he'll live in my bathtub until he can eat on his own."

Then I regaled her with further piteous details of his dead sister and being tossed out of a car to drown.

Mother was really a pushover. I'd been counting on that.

"Very well," she said, "but only until he's old enough to stay outside in a dog yard."

When I brought him home Monday, she took one look and said, "My God, Margaret's got a rat."

He weighed about five ounces. That evening as I held him on my lap in a nest of towels and listened to him suckle happily from his baby bottle full of formula, Mother walked in. "Humph, ridiculous creature," she said, and touched his little black head with her index finger.

He was in. I knew he'd never live outside in a doghouse.

By the following Sunday none of us could imagine life without Bear.

He toddled after Mother when she charged into the breakfast room at eight o'clock, slammed *The Commercial Appeal* down in front of me and pointed to a photo and story on the society page.

The photographer had done a nice job of hiding the prince's flaws. He stood in the shadows behind a blonde Delta Deb, who had the most vapid eyes I'd ever seen. The story announced their engagement and their marriage in three months.

"If you'd played your cards right, that could have been you," Mother snapped. She picked up Bear and cuddled him against her chest to prove she preferred him to me.

"I can just see our write-up," I said. "'As the highlight of the engagement party, the bride-to-be slit her wrists.'"

"He's been running from matrimony for years. One week with you and he's engaged to another woman. What did you *do* to him?"

"Told him the truth."

Mother started to throw up her hands in despair, realized she was still hanging onto Bear, and stalked out of the room.

Until Bear came into our lives, my father and I had never realized how lonely my mother was. She knew darned well that neither Daddy nor I bought into her view of life, even though we tried. Bear knew at once. He loved us, but he adored Mother and she adored him back. He became her shadow.

After two weeks of working with Dr. Parmenter, I slipped into Mother and Daddy's room to say goodnight, and sat on the end of their bed. "I'm going to summer school," I said.

"You're working too hard," Mother said.

I knew she meant the hours spent with Dr. Parmenter.

"I need some additional credits if I'm still going to finish in four years."

Daddy sat up and looked at me over his bifocals. "I thought you had most of your English credits already."

I had declared myself an English major two semesters earlier. B. B.—before Bear.

"I'm changing my major to biology," I said, not daring to meet their eyes. "I'm going to become a veterinarian."

While they were still gaping at that I scooted. At the door to the hall, I turned back and said, "Oh, by the way, y'all mind calling me Maggie from now on?"

"Margaret! You come right back here this instant!" Mother shouted. I heard her feet hit the floor and knew she was coming after me.

I bolted.

Mother's reaction to my announcement that I was changing my name and planning to become a veterinarian was typical.

"Don't be ridiculous, Margaret," she said. "Girls do not become veterinarians. And Maggie sounds like an Irish washerwoman."

In my previous attempts to break out of the mold she kept trying to force me into, I had meekly gone back to being a nice obedient daughter and relinquished my goals.

Not this time. Mother took to sighing deeply and casting her eyes to heaven every time I mentioned anything about Dr. Parmenter or vet school.

She even enlisted a couple of her Junior League buddies to 'counsel' me.

I never answered back or argued. I simply smiled and signed up for more chemistry classes. Now, that really infuriated her.

By the end of that August I had endured summer courses in biology and chemistry in un-air-conditioned classrooms, and nearly died of asphyxiation. The straight A's kept Mother's disapproval at bay, but only barely. She had retrenched, and was now suggesting that I become a nurse. Then I could marry a doctor.

Dr. Parmenter never questioned me about my plans, although I was up to working four afternoons a week and all day Saturday for him. I had also graduated to doing most of his anesthesia and was learning how to stitch up wounds on old innertubes.

One hot afternoon as he finished neutering a tabby cat, he looked over those glasses at me and asked, "Well, do you really want to do it?"

I nodded. I knew what he was talking about although we had never actually discussed my becoming a veterinarian.

"They won't like it," he said, and clipped the last suture.

"If you mean my parents, they already don't like it."

He pulled off his gloves, balled them up and tossed them overhanded like a basketball into the waste receptacle in the corner. "Goal." Then he turned to me and sighed. "Assuming you get into vet school, and that's a mighty tall assumption, your professors won't like it, your colleagues won't like it, and if you should graduate, a great many potential clients won't like it."

These days more than half the graduating veterinarians in this country are women. But not then. There were women vets, of course, but more up north than in the mid-south. Tennessee didn't yet have its own vet school, so that meant I'd have to vie for a place at Auburn or Alabama or Mississippi State. Against all their native good ol' boys.

"Why should they care?" I asked. Because I spent twelve years in a girls' school environment, I had never worried about competition with males, and Southwestern at that time demanded good brains from both genders.

He lifted one scrawny hip onto the edge of the examining table and clicked off the reasons on his fingers.

"Your professors will not wish to waste their time teaching you as you will undoubtedly get married, quit the profession and raise babies."

I snorted.

"Your male colleagues will dislike you because you are taking a place that should have gone to a man. Your female colleagues will resent you because they wish to be queen bees. Finally, your potential clients will think you're incapable of being as good a vet as a man, particularly if you should decide to treat large animals."

"Why should I want to be as good as a man?" I asked. "I intend to be a damned sight better."

# Chapter 2

## *In which Eli Scheibler saves Maggie's bacon for the first time, but not the last*

Back in the Pleistocene era when I went to vet school, female students were a rarity and not a blessed one. In class I was the invisible woman. The professors ignored my questions. They wrote snide comments on my papers, and graded me harder than any of the male students.

One professor said to me, "You are not precisely stupid, Miss Evans. Go to nursing school. Become a secretary. Teach kindergarten. You don't belong here. You take up time I should be spending with the real students." Meaning, of course, the men.

"I *am* a real student."

"You're a city-bred dilettante. Even if you do manage to graduate, you'll spay toy poodles for a couple of years until you marry and have babies."

"The men will marry and have babies too. Some of them already have wives and families."

"Miss Evans, men have careers. Women have jobs until they become mothers."

Someone slashed the tires of my bicycle. I couldn't afford a car. The male students stole my equipment and tried unsuccessfully to sabotage my lab work. They told endless filthy jokes and cussed extensively whenever I was within earshot. I learned not to react.

They made passes that stopped just short of actual assault. One charmer pinched my rear end so hard I had a bruise on my rump for a week. After I stomped his instep he never did it again.

The book learning was no problem for me, and I certainly didn't mind dissecting dead creatures. I'd been assisting Dr. Parmenter for two summers. I could stitch up an inner tube like a plastic surgeon. Despite the sniping from colleagues and professors, I felt cocky. No—arrogant.

There's an old saying that she who rises fast and far, falls faster and harder.

In theory, I realized that once in vet school I'd be working with every sort of animal—mammals to fish to reptiles. That's one of the so-called joys of veterinary medicine as opposed to human medicine. MD's only have one species to treat.

During my first few weeks, I still entertained some vague illusion of continuing the work I had been doing with Dr. Parmenter—dogs and cats with the occasional cockatoo or box turtle. After all, Dr. Parmenter had already intimated that he'd take me into his clinic once I graduated.

Mississippi State, however, took its role as a producer of veterinarians able to treat livestock very seriously. Most of my classmates were big, strapping men who had grown up on farms and were at ease with everything from guinea hens to Brahma bulls. I did my darnedest to act as though I was ready and willing to castrate every bull that ran in Pamplona without benefit of anesthetic. In reality, if I'd been faced with even one bull to castrate, I'd have been the one needing the anesthetic. Assuming I didn't faint first.

I was not looking forward to working with live critters of the bovine, equine and porcine persuasion. I prayed my first day in the stock barn area I'd be assigned to treat something smaller than a draft horse or a full-grown cow. "Lord," I prayed, "Give me a pygmy goat or a week-old lamb or even a baby pig. I promise I'll get around to the big stuff if you'll just let me start small."

What's that old saw about being careful what you wish for?

Before dawn on one of those December days in Starkville when the fog hung in the air on the verge of turning to ice, my colleagues and I assembled at the stock barn for our first real session. Despite two layers of heavy sweaters and long johns under my jeans and wool-lined parka, I had already lost contact with my toes. I noticed that the guys were all wearing heavily padded khaki jumpsuits and wool John Deere caps with earflaps. Most of them were large to start with. Encased in their jump suits they looked not only monumental but monolithic.

How come nobody told me what to wear?

When little Eli Scheibler, the only other woman in this class, came in, I saw that she hadn't been informed of the dress code either. She looked even colder than I did in jeans and parka.

I caught a snicker from Zach Hitchens, leader of the anti-feminist brigade, and realized that they had intentionally left us out of the information loop.

Although we shared classes and labs, Eli and I weren't yet friends. I knew her real name was 'Elizabeth,' although everyone called her Eli. I knew she lived alone in an apartment across Starkville, an unheard of luxury for the rest of us. We either lived in rented rooms or shared apartments with other people. She drove a ratty truck. I rode a bicycle.

I knew she had been married. Whether she was a widow or divorcee nobody knew. She kept herself to herself.

Eli stood under five feet tall and weighed maybe ninety pounds. She had short brown hair cropped short, wore no makeup on her pointed little face, and seemed to be dedicated to blending into the woodwork.

I couldn't blame her. The other members of the class and the professors all treated her with offhand contempt when they weren't actually calling her names like 'Tinker Bell.'

The professor, Dr. Crawford, a burly, bearded Tweedledum close to retirement age, curled his lip, looked Eli and me up and down, and said, "Ladiiiiiiieees, in future please dress appropriately for this class."

Behind me Zach—or somebody else—snorted. I felt my face flame and started to turn around, but felt Eli's small fingers bite into my arm with surprising strength. "No," she whispered.

I had already learned to dislike Dr. Crawford and knew he reciprocated in spades. This morning, he assigned Eli and me to work together for the first time. He probably thought it was great to segregate the only two women on the rotation so we couldn't get in the men's hair.

"Miss Evans, Mrs. Scheibler," he said and pointed, "in that stall is a sow with twelve piglets born yesterday. They all need to be sexed, examined, their ears clipped, weighed, measured, entered into the registry and given their first shots. Do it." He strode off to deal with what he no doubt considered real students.

I'd never seen even one live piglet. Here I was stuck with a dozen my first day.

"Come on," Eli said, "Let's find one of the treatment carts and set it up."

I followed meekly. "You didn't get the word either, did you?"

Eli cut her eyes at me. "About the stupid jumpsuits? I never wore anything but jeans and a jacket on Daddy's farm. We sure couldn't afford *uniforms*." She made the word sound like an oath. "I'll bet it's not listed as a requisite for this class either. Dr. Crawford's just being a jackass."

"A role he was born to play."

I caught a grin at the corner of her mouth.

Eli and I found the steel rolling treatment cart and set it up with scales, rulers, log book, a dozen worming and antibiotic shots, and alcohol to treat the piglet's umbilical cords. We worked silently, and then congratulated ourselves because we'd gotten the cart set up properly without once referring to Dr. Crawford's checklist.

One up for us.

We walked over to look at our patients. The pen that held the sow and piglets stood waist high with a three-foot wide gate of lumber with metal strapping.

Pigs have a reputation for being dirty. They are, in fact, extremely clean. Given sufficient space in their enclosure, pigs will choose one corner in which to wallow, another to use as a latrine. The rest of the pen will remain dry and clean.

All my life I have heard my daddy say, "I'm sweating like a hog in August." In actuality, pigs do not sweat. That's why they need their wallow, to cool off and to coat their bristly bodies with mud to lower their body temperature and avoid fly bites. Pigs are also extremely intelligent. So intelligent that they regard human beings with suspicion and generally refuse to do anything we ask of them unless they see the sense of it for themselves.

Eli and I leaned over the edge of the pen and peered at the sow. "She a Yorkshire," Eli said.

"Same as an American White?" I asked.

"Uh-huh. And a big one."

In theory I knew what I was supposed to do with the babies. I simply had never done it. Eli seemed to be familiar with live pigs, rather than pigs in books. Was I the only city person in the class?

Then I looked down at those piglets. One baby pig might be cute, but a dozen was twelve times cuter. All my fears about my inexperience evaporated in sheer lust to get my hands on those babies. They looked like small bundles of pink velvet with wiggly snouts and fat little bellies, and they made soft little snuffling sounds as they nursed. Occasionally they'd squeal tiny little bat squeaks. How could something so cute be a problem?

"Momma's asleep. Good." Eli sounded very professional. I was beginning to feel like a real dude. If I couldn't *sound* knowledgeable, I'd have to *act* like an expert.

The pen in which the new mother nursed her piglets was large enough to provide separate areas for food, wallowing and toilette. It was bedded with straw and wood shavings. At the back left hand corner hung a triangular trough for Momma to root around in when feeding time came. It would be some time before the piglets would eat solid food, but when they did, they'd fight to be first to get their noses into that trough.

The sow lay propped against the back wall of the enclosure with her eyes closed. She snored softly while the piglets rooted around her belly searching for a teat to latch onto. Since she didn't have a dozen nipples, somebody was always on the outside butting in, but she didn't seem to notice.

Even Eli was making cooing noises at the babies. We must have looked like a pair of dotty matrons at the window of a hospital nursery.

Eli got her senses back first and turned away, once again all business. "I'll roll in the table."

I decided not to wait for Eli to bring the cart. She might have some experience of pigs, but she was itsy-bitsy. She wouldn't be able to hold more than one or two of those piglets at one time.

I, on the other hand, could gather five or six in one armload. I'd go in to the pen, sweep up as many as I could carry, deposit them in the empty pen to the right, and return for the rest. Before Eli had the cart in place, I'd be set to bring the first piglet out for processing. We could do our thing and return each one to Momma as we finished, thereby avoiding the necessity of handling the same piglet more than once. Fast and efficient and impressive as hell.

"Piece of cake," I said.

I opened the gate to Momma's pen, stepped in and shut it behind me. Momma opened one eye and stared at me, but didn't move. She seemed completely serene.

As I took a step toward mother and young, I heard Eli whisper,

"Lordy, Maggie, back out. Fast."

"I'm fine," I said.

The sow surged to her feet. Piglets clung to her teats and hung on for dear life.

Eli yelped.

I froze.

"Nice piggy," I crooned.

She stood her ground and glared at me.

"Go back to sleep like a good girl."

She opened her mouth to reveal three-inch tusks she must have inherited from a prehistoric wild boar.

"Oh, shit," I whispered.

That's when she charged. She rained piglets into the shavings like hailstones.

If she hit me, I'd go down.

That was blood lust in those piggy little eyes. Once she got me down, she'd eat my liver.

I didn't hear the gate behind me open, but I felt somebody yank me backward into the aisle so hard I toppled over backward.

"Quick. Kick the gate shut," Eli wheezed.

I kicked with both feet and felt the gate connect with the sow's snout. She screamed in rage and backed up. I kicked again and heard the gate latch an instant before she hit it for the second time.

The safety latch held, but the sound of hog against steel and wood echoed through the barn like a mortar round. She hit the gate three more times before she gave up and sauntered back to her piglets. She'd made her point.

"Get off," Eli wheezed. "I can't breathe."

I hadn't realized I'd fallen on Eli.

I rolled off to the side, pulled myself to my hands and knees, and reached down for her. "Are you all right? "

"Assuming she can still breathe." A male voice spoke from behind me. I looked up to see Dr. Crawford, hands on broad hips, scowling down at both of us.

The rest of the class was hanging out of their respective pens laughing their guts out.

I started to gabble about having done this many times with Labrador Retrievers, but Eli brought her knee up into my gut. I shut up.

"If you have quite finished your comedy routine, Miss Evans, Mrs. Scheibler, may I suggest you complete your assignment?"

I saw the glee in his nasty little gray eyes. This was a damned setup.

"Certainly, Professor," I said through clenched teeth. How the hell were we going to do it?

"The normal method is to begin by leaning over the side of the pen from *outside* the fence, snubbing a line around the sow's neck and hauling her up tight. One of you can then go into the pen and tie all four legs together. That, my dear Miss Evans, is why it is called hog-tying."

I could have killed him with my bare hands.

"You have so far successfully avoided her teeth. Take care that you avoid her hooves as well. They are sharp. She is quick. I would prefer not to risk having those piglets hurt by another show of irritability on her part. A distressed sow will eat her own babies."

Well, great. Now I was going to be responsible for porcine cannibalism.

"Thank you, Professor," Eli said quietly. Without another word she walked away to get the chains and rope to hold the sow.

Eli and I worked well together. Once the sow was immobilized, she simply went back to sleep while we treated her piglets.

We watched her after we released her to check her reaction. She showed no signs of mistaking her babies for lunch. Thank God. She probably weighed two hundred and fifty pounds. We couldn't have stopped her.

As we were trundling the cart back to the staging area, I asked, "How did you know what would happen when I went into that pen?"

She shrugged. "Daddy used to raise hogs when I was little. Not to sell, just to smoke hams for us and the relatives at Christmas. Sows and boars are mean as water moccasins."

"So if I'd waited for you... I am so sorry. You saved my life."

She grinned up at me. "No, just your bacon. I'm not so sure about your grade."

I later found out that Dr. Crawford had paired the male members of the class so that each twosome weighed, measured and registered one lamb with one hundred pound ewe apiece to deal with, while Eli and I were assigned a mighty hog and a dozen piglets.

"The old bastard did it on purpose," I said as Eli and I left the barn together.

"He'll do it again too. The next time we'd better be ready to do the job he gives us without screwing up."

I felt my face flame. "You didn't screw up. I did. I have never been that close to a pig in my life. Or a cow, for that matter."

"Then you'd better stick close to *me*," she said and looked me over. "I can use your brawn."

"And I obviously can use your brain." She didn't deny it. "At least I owe you lunch."

From that time on, Eli and I have saved one another's bacon innumerable times. After a while, we stopped keeping score.

# Chapter 3

## *In which Maggie loses a mouse, but a gains a man*

Those first two years of vet school I remember only that I was exhausted all the time, but I kept up a four point average. The summer before my senior year my grades landed me a really plumb assignment.

A private corporation in Olive Branch, Mississippi, just south of the Tennessee State line from Memphis and Germantown, had been conducting a long-term study on the effects of obesity on rheumatoid arthritis. They were searching for a combination of vitamins and minerals that could alleviate both the obesity and the arthritis. I don't think they had much success. Two years later they closed that lab and moved the entire operation to Arizona to start another study on hanta virus.

Despite some of the horror stories to come out of animal labs in the 1960s, most reputable labs treated their animals with kindness. This lab treated the monkeys and white mice they used in their tests like royalty. Once their part in the experiment was finished, they were sent to zoos or retired to live happy lives—not that mice live that long.

That's where I learned to distrust monkeys. They may be cute, but they are dirty, noisy, and prone to bouts of viciousness against one another and any human being in the vicinity. We had to be extra careful not to let them bite the hand that fed them. I darned near got carpal tunnel syndrome the first week chopping fresh carrots and apples and cabbage for the little dears. They didn't appreciate my efforts and delighted in firing the remains of their meals back at my head with amazing accuracy.

The best assignment was supposed to be with the mice. Mice were relatively clean, quiet, and they didn't throw things at you. Unfortunately, as a temporary employee, I got stuck with the monkeys.

Then, the first of July the mouse person quit. She said flipping burgers was preferable to shooting syringes full of vitamins into the mouths of mice. I took over her job.

I *knew* mice from all my lab work at school. When I opened the sound-proofed door to their holding area, I realized that a great many mice all squeaking at once reached a much higher decibel level than I had anticipated. They also smelled worse.

Across from the door hung a large sign that read, "Please do not throw mice on floor."

Why on earth would anybody throw a mouse on the floor?

There were wire cages floor to ceiling on three walls and a desk and cabinets for supplies along the back wall. Soft artificial lighting left the corners of the room in shadows, but the room was air-conditioned. Blissful. Monkeys hate the cold, so their big room was hot and stuffy. After playing Jane to dozens of Cheetahs (okay, I know Cheetah was an ape and not a monkey), I really looked forward to my first day with the mice.

I checked my list for my first subject and found the corresponding cage number. The sole inhabitant was a spectacular mouse twice as big as any mouse I had ever seen. I was supposed to shoot a syringe of vitamin mixture down his fat little throat. According to my predecessor, the stuff tasted like cherries. The mice loved it.

I opened the cage, took out the mouse, held him in my left hand, and poked at his mouth with the syringe in my right.

"Hey," came a baritone voice almost at my shoulder. "Know where I can find Royce Williams?"

I jumped a foot and loosened my grip. The mouse snapped his teeth hard into the ball of my thumb.

I yelped. Without a conscious thought I side-armed that mouse straight at the wall with the force of Arthur Ashe returning a serve.

Now I understood the sign that said, "Do not Throw Mice on Floor."

The mouse slid down the wall completely unhurt, tossed me a satisfied look and scurried under the supply cabinet at Mach 1.

"Oh, God, I'm sorry. I hope it's not rabid or carrying tetanus," said my visitor.

"Listen, you..." I said, and swung around ready to deck him.

"It bit you," the man said, and came out of the shadows with a fresh white linen handkerchief in his hand. He took my thumb and wrapped it quickly and efficiently. Then he looked up at me.

Up to that point I had considered Juliet was the sappiest of Shakespeare's heroines. Really stupid to fall in love at first sight with a thug from the wrong side of town. That day changed my mind. The French call it a *coup de foudre*—a blow of madness. It happened at a most inconvenient moment.

The man holding my hand had the bluest eyes I'd ever seen. They were full of concern, but they crinkled at the corners with good humor. He looked as though he laughed a lot.

"Do you need to sit down? Should I try to recapture the escapee?"

I shook my head and probably said something like 'urk.' Then I remembered I was annoyed at this jerk, snatched my hand back, and said, "The mouse is perfectly healthy. You can't possibly catch him."

"If that sign by the door is any indication, I suspect he will join his compatriots who have successfully escaped to freedom."

"At least I didn't actually throw him at the floor."

He took back my hand and carefully unrolled his handkerchief from around my thumb. "Little bastard."

"Huh?"

"The mouse."

"Oh. I might need to sit down after all." Not because I was faint at the sight of my own blood. After two years of vet school I had seen plenty of my own and everybody else's. I was weak at the knees. "Who *are* you and why did you scare the hell out of me that way? This area is off limits to visitors."

"I'm Morgan McLain. I work in a bank and I'm looking for Royce Williams to get his signature on some papers. One of the secretaries told me he might be out here."

"I have no idea where Mr. Williams is. I haven't seen him all morning."

"Look, the least I can do is to walk you over to the main building so you can get that hand looked after, then buy you a cup of coffee, maybe lunch."

I started to tell him not to be ridiculous, that I was perfectly capable of bandaging my own hand, but for some reason I didn't want him to walk out of my life. "Yes, all right. Damn, I'll have to type up an accident report. I'm going to have to account for the one I side-armed. It's my first day with the mice. Mr. Williams will scalp me."

"No, he won't. It's my fault." He put his hand casually on the small of my back. "Shall we go?"

I've never believed in jolts of sexual electricity either, but I swear I jumped a foot when he touched me. As we walked out the door into the heat, he said, "I wish I had you on my soft-ball team at the bank. We'd be leading the league with a pitching arm like yours."

This guy wasn't exactly handsome, although he had plenty of chin, unlike the Prince of Darkness. He did have a wonderful voice, deep and warm and friendly, but who falls in love with a voice? He was about six feet one, which meant I could wear heels when we went out, and had the kind of burly figure that would be called portly by the time he was forty. I guessed he was probably five or six years older than I was. Maybe over thirty.

He wore an air of casual authority that said 'man,' rather than 'boy.'

But it was those bright blue eyes of his that got me and held me.

I was not looking for a serious relationship, much less marriage. I had all I could handle with my last year of school, passing my board exams, and starting my internship with Dr. Parmenter. Unfortunately, no life-changing experience ever seems to come at a convenient time. Not in *my* life, at any rate.

# Chapter 4

## *In which Maggie marries Morgan*

I gave Morgan my virginity on a rainy Saturday night in a Starkville, Mississippi, Holiday Inn.

Sex with him was incredible. When he reminded me that I had no frame of reference, I assured him I wasn't about to acquire one. My entire last year of vet school I was torn between elation that I had him and terror that I'd lose him.

Starkville isn't just over the hill from Memphis—it's a three-hour drive if you speed. I certainly didn't have time to come home to Memphis to see him, so he dutifully commuted to Oxford to see me.

That's where our lives became permanently entwined with Eli's.

It started as a way to save money—Holiday Inns in Starkville aren't cheap, particularly on weekends when the Mississippi State football team is playing at home.

At Eli's little apartment we could be together. Thanks to Eli's kind heart we could often be alone as well. When she gets to heaven, her crown is going to glitter like a crystal chandelier from all the stars she accumulated during those months. She'd camp out at the library so we could snatch a couple of hours of passion. One day she remarked that my skin had never looked clearer. I seem to recall I smacked her. Not hard. Since she weighed under a hundred pounds, I might have broken her.

No, that's wrong. She had already taken more hard hits than most women experience in a lifetime. She hadn't broken. We'd known one another for nearly four years. She knew just about everything about me, but I still knew only bare facts about her life. I didn't know what had forged her into the person she'd become. Her father ran a commercial cattle farm outside of Pontotoc, Mississippi. Eli had four older brothers, and her mother died young. I knew Eli was a widow.

One night over pizza and too much red wine she finally opened up.

My youth had been relatively privileged. Hers should have been at least comfortable.

"I guess the family genes for bulk petered out before they got down to me," she said. "Momma died of a heart attack two days after my twelfth birthday. Only way she could get any rest."

Having met Eli's four enormous older brothers a time or two, I could see that death might be an appealing alternative for a wife, but hard on an only daughter. Her father, a fireplug of a man with the soul of an armadillo, believed that women were put on this earth to make the lives of men pleasant, to provide them clean houses, good food and plenty of it, and to stay the hell out of their way when they went drinking and whoring. "He believed Momma ought to be able to handle all his needs on butter and egg money," she said.

As is so often the case, one magnificent teacher opened Eli's eyes to the possibilities of the world and discovered that this underfed waif with the circles under her eyes was not just bright, but brilliant.

"Not that being smart would cut much ice with Daddy," Eli said. "He didn't believe in more than a high school education for females, and he only put up with that because the truant officer would have fined him if he hadn't. I'd have settled for marrying some good ole boy and having a passel of kids and dying young like Momma if Josh Scheibler hadn't come along."

She leaned back against the ratty old couch in her apartment, but I could tell from the dreamy look in her eyes that she was seeing Josh Scheibler the day he walked into her life.

"Here I am, four feet ten, and here comes this long, tall, drink-of-water veterinarian that must have been about six-six. Came into the kitchen to warm up before he went back to Tupelo where he was a partner with a small animal vet. He'd been treating one of daddy's bulls. I fixed him the damndest, richest cup of hot chocolate man ever had this side of Paradise."

"He came back, I take it?" I asked.

She smiled sheepishly. Eli was seldom sheepish about anything, but just thinking of Josh Scheibler made her blush. "I already knew I wanted to be a veterinarian. I also knew there wasn't a chance in hell I could do it. Daddy would never pay for college, much less vet school.

He planned to hold onto his housekeeper and cook as long as possible."

"So how did you wind up Mrs. Josh Scheibler?" I asked.

"One day Josh came by and found me crying, because Daddy had just refused for the umpteenth time to consider even sending me to junior college. I sure didn't have the money to pay for myself, even with my part-time job at the Dairy-Queen. I had graduated from high school in June and turned eighteen in July. Here it was August and I was fit to be tied. Josh picked me up, slung me into his truck and drove off with me. When we were out on the highway, he told me that if we could make it to Tunica before the court house closed, we could get blood tests, a marriage license and be married before dark."

"Wow! Romantic."

"Terrifying. Took me nearly halfway to Highway 51 before I said yes. He bought me a ring and a dress at Shainberg's, and enough jeans and underwear to last until we could get home to tell Daddy what we'd done. We were married that night."

At that point in my friendship with Eli, I was already talking about the wedding that Morgan and I would have—bridesmaids and flowers and a big reception and showers and all the hoopla that is usually associated with society weddings. When I looked at the light in Eli's eyes, I understood what weddings were all about for the first time. "What happened when you went home?"

Eli laughed. "Daddy had a cat fit, said he'd disown me, and in the next breath said he supposed that meant he'd be getting free veterinary service from then on."

"What about Josh's people?"

"East Tennessee farmers from outside of Cookeville. He was an only child. Nice enough folks, kind of quiet. Very religious. I don't think they ever approved of Josh's marrying me, certainly not without a preacher."

Her tone told me that was another subject I shouldn't pursue.

"We had four glorious years," she said. "Poor as church mice, but we managed to get me through college. He had some buddies on the faculty, and of course he was a Starkville alum, so he was pretty sure we could get me into Mississippi State. Being a woman and four-foot ten I needed all the pull I could get. Grades alone would never have been enough.

"We'd been saving every penny so I could get through school, then we were going to go open a practice together back in Cookeville in East Tennessee where everybody knew him.

"Josh joined the National Guard to make a little extra money. I mean one weekend a month and two weeks in the summer. How bad could it be? Even when his unit was called up, we both thought he'd be sent to someplace like Fort Campbell, Kentucky. Who on earth would need a veterinarian overseas? I'd received my admission to vet school as soon as I finished my B.A. I planned to spend the summer with Josh wherever he went, then come back to school in the fall. When he came home, he'd rejoin his old practice and we'd have weekends until I qualified. It all seemed so simple."

"What changed it?"

"Believe it or not," Eli said, "Viet Nam was just hotting up, and that's where they sent him—lonely veterinarian and all." She tried a little laugh, but I saw her slide her finger under her eye to catch the tear.

"What on earth would they do with a veterinarian in Viet Nam?"

Eli shrugged. "He said it was boring, but beautiful. He sent me pictures of the big tent camp where he was assigned. It was right on this gorgeous beach. Mostly he inspected meat for the army to make sure it wasn't diseased. Then they started going out to some of the villages to try to help some of the native livestock. Completely safe, he said." She looked away, much farther than the walls of the little apartment.

I didn't want to breathe. I didn't want to hear the rest of the story, either, but I kept my mouth shut.

"I don't know how they do it now, but back then, they sent two soldiers in dress uniforms—white gloves and all. I was outside our apartment in Tupelo. It was Saturday morning. Funny the things you remember. I was changing the spark plugs on our old truck. Did you know I can change sparkplugs, Maggie? I can change oil, too, if I have to. Josh taught me. At home my brothers did all the work on the tractors and stuff."

Now I really couldn't breathe. She sounded so matter of fact, so casual.

"I looked up when the car stopped. When the doors opened and they started to get out, you know what I did? I bolted right for the front door. When I got in I slammed it behind me and put the chain on. Isn't that crazy? As though if I didn't let them in it wouldn't be real." She shook her head. "One of them was a woman—a big woman, bigger than you are, Maggie. She kept talking to me nice and easy through the door. Not saying the words, just talking to me, trying to get me to let them in. Finally, I did."

I could feel the tears sliding down my cheeks just listening to her, but Eli's eyes were dry. Her face looked like one of those death masks—caved in and lifeless.

"You know, I don't remember a thing after that until they handed me that folded flag at his memorial service a month later at the old National Cemetery in Memphis. I must have gotten through it. I'm here, after all. But it's like I had a stroke or a heart attack that wiped out all those days." She shook her head at me. "Isn't that weird?"

I wanted to go put my arms around her and rock her the way my mother used to rock me after I'd hurt my knee, but I was afraid to move. She was still speaking, but I knew she wasn't even aware that I was still in the room.

"I got the usual letter from his C.O. about how he'd died a hero. When his sergeant got back to the States he called me. They'd been out on one of those perfectly safe trips to one of the villages, and on the way back, the jeep hit a land mine that somebody had just planted. He and his driver were both killed instantly. But they always say that, don't they? Instantly? At least he didn't suffer? For all I know he lived minutes, hours, all that pain and the blood..."

That's when we both lost it. We clung together and just sobbed. When we had hiccoughed and gulped ourselves into silence, I said, "I can't believe you kept on."

"What else was I supposed to do? Go home to be a free maid and cook? Betray everything we'd hoped and dreamed for? Not on your life. His G.I. insurance pays for school and this apartment, and when I get out, it's going to help me set up in practice right back in Cookeville where he wanted to be." She looked me right in the eye with her head high. "Keeping on is what you *do*."

That night over pizza in Starkville, I sympathized with her, but I didn't understand a thing about losing the other half of your soul.

Eli and I graduated together, took our boards together, then Eli packed up the few things she'd accumulated in the back of her old pickup truck and drove off to Cookeville. She was planning to stay with Josh's parents until she could find a job with one of the vets in the area.

I didn't see her again until she drove down for my wedding to Morgan.

The wedding itself was a far cry from what my mother wanted, but Morgan and Daddy and I had ganged up on her. We refused to have twelve bridesmaids. I told her I didn't actually know twelve girls I could force to buy a dress and shoes. Eli was my matron of honor, and I paid for her dress. I swore to her that was traditional. I doubt she believed me, but she let me do it anyway. I knew what a hard time she was having financially, and both Morgan and I wanted her to stand up with us.

We had a morning service with champagne and wedding cake in the parish hall of St. Cecilia's Episcopal Church afterwards. A friend of Mother's did the flowers, which were lovely but simple. We hired a single harpist instead of the string quartet Mother wanted, and one of the vestry of the church took photos.

On our way to The Peabody for honeymoon night, I asked Morgan why on earth he'd married me. He said, "Because, my dearest heart, you are an eagle among canaries. You were born to soar. I was born to hold the cage door open for you."

*He* might see an eagle. I saw myself as a badger or a possum, nose to the ground, plodding along.

Eli and I didn't really have much of a chance to catch up either before or after the ceremony, but from the little she said, I got the idea that moving to Cookeville to stay with Josh's parents hadn't been the world's greatest idea.

Eli was working part time for a small animal hospital—not her thing. Her boss treated her like a half-witted servant because she was a woman. Too reminiscent of the way her father treated her.

I had fitted seamlessly into Dr. Parmenter's practice. He was fun to work with. I was learning a great deal. So long as I worked on small animals with the senior partner there to keep tabs on me, the clients were willing to let me treat their pets, but many of them treated me like a veterinary technician rather than a full-fledged vet with D.V.M. after my name.

Then I started having some successes on my own. Dr. Parmenter talked about my talents as often as he could. That didn't hurt. The first time a client actually asked to see me specifically, I went home and split a bottle of Spanish champagne with Morgan and had a God-awful hangover the next morning.

Eli, on the other hand, was miserable. I simply didn't know what to do about it.

Morgan and I had moved into an apartment in midtown Memphis largely furnished with Late Relatives and Early Attic. It wasn't plush, but for us it was spacious and comfortable.

Eli was confined to a furnished bedroom in a house that wasn't even hers. At least in Starkville she'd had her ratty little apartment.

Dr. Parmenter didn't have a job to offer her, neither did anyone else I knew. Morgan ached for her as much as I did.

I felt as though I was flaunting my happiness in the face of her misery.

But what could I do about it?

# Chapter 5

## *In which we meet Patsy and Maggie learns a lesson*

Dr. Parmenter was only in his mid-forties when I joined his practice in the late sixties. To me that was middle age. He hadn't hired a full-time associate for a while, but had made do with young vets who were between jobs or hadn't yet passed their boards.

If anything, he was a better surgeon than he'd been the first day I met him. He was also crabbier. He put me in my place on the average of twice a day for the first six months.

At school I had worked with the newest equipment, cutting edge meds and diagnoses, and superb surgeons. But school is not life, and a multi-million dollar university vet clinic is not your average cat and dog hospital. Despite my summers spent working for Dr. Parmenter, I had lost sight of one half of any vet's responsibility, the human being that pays the bills for his animal and who agonizes over him and loves him. Sometimes the dog or cat is the only creature a human being has to love him back. In the clinic at school we never met the client directly, so I had missed out on seeing the joy of an owner when his cat or dog miraculously recovered.

I had also avoided seeing the desperate grief of losing one or having to say goodbye. At school I never had to worry what a procedure would cost a client. I didn't deal with quality of life issues for elderly and sick animals. I simply did the job I was assigned, so, despite all the state-of-the-art qualifications I brought to the job and the time I had spent with him before, Dr. Parmenter still had plenty of real-life experience to impart.

He began by handing over after-hours and weekend emergency

calls to me as the low man on the totem pole. Besides, he liked his Sundays free.

I didn't mind. I was still so thrilled by the D. V. M. after my name that the idea of being called at two in the morning gave me a sense of pride. So when the telephone rang close to midnight one Saturday evening, I grabbed it quickly before Morgan waked and sat on the edge of the bed with the light off.

"Dr. Parmenter?" a throaty female voice asked.

"No, ma'am. This is Dr. McLain. I'm on call tonight. How can I help you?"

"This is Patsy Dalrymple. I don't believe we've met."

"No, but I've heard about you." You bet I had. Patsy Dalrymple had grown up in Hattiesburg, Mississippi, and had married one of the richest planters in the Delta. She lived in an enormous antebellum mansion outside of Red Banks, Mississippi, and also kept an apartment in Memphis on top of the Kimbrough Towers, Memphis's first and fanciest high rise apartment building. She raised and trained horses almost as successfully as her husband raised soybeans and Black Angus cattle.

The Mississippi state line is just south of the Memphis metro area, and Arkansas is just across the Mississippi River bridge. Dr. Parmenter had clients in all three states then, as do Eli and I today. He looked after Patsy's small animals, and when he was available, her horses. He always said he enjoyed the drive down to Red Banks. It got him out of the office. There weren't quite so many country vets back then, and none with Dr. Parmenter's skill and reputation. Mrs. Dalrymple wanted the best. She was a valued client—meaning she spent a bunch of money with us.

When I heard her voice on the phone, I snapped to attention.

"I'm just real sorry to wake you up like this, Dr. McLain," she said in a voice that could have warned barges away from sandbars in a Mississippi River fog. "My German shepherd had a close encounter of the skunk kind a few minutes ago."

"Oh, boy. Did it get him in the eyes?"

"Apparently not, but it definitely got the rest of him. And there is a big ole bundle of dog there to stink, believe you me. What on earth can I do? He's smelling up the whole barn. By morning all my horses are going to smell like road kill."

Thank God this was an easy one. "The standard de-stinker, Mrs. Dalrymple, is tomato juice. You have any tomato juice?"

"Well, Lord, yes. I'd heard that some place. I just never believed it."

"It's the chemicals in the tomatoes. If he's a big dog, he's going to take plenty of juice."

"Oh, that's okay. Dan loves the stuff—Dan, my husband? If I run low I'll just open a few cans of tomato paste and add some water. I just rub it in?"

"And rinse it out."

"Thank you. I swear I will be forever grateful. Come on, Robespierre, let Mommy give you a nice bath."

She hung up without saying goodbye, and I went back to bed.

The telephone rang again at nine o'clock the following morning. "Dr. McLain? This is Patsy Dalrymple again. I know it's Sunday morning and all, but I've got a filly down here that cut her rump on something in the pasture—God knows what. I found her when I fed the horses this morning. It's going to need stitches. Can you drive down?"

Of course I could. "Oh, and Mrs. Dalrymple, how did the tomato juice work?"

"Well, it did take the smell out of Robespierre's coat..." She sounded hesitant.

"Is he all right?"

"Oh, he's fine." I heard something in her voice, but I couldn't quite decide what. So I told her I'd drive down to Red Banks at once and stitch up her horse after I cleared it with Dr. Parmenter. He told me to go ahead.

I found the back road to the Dalrymple Farm easily, then drove alongside a mile of three-rail black creosoted fence before I found a set of ornate iron gates under a sign that said, "Dalrymple Farms, Farm Entrance." So they had a separate entrance that led to the farm buildings and not the house? Like the tradesman's entrance in England. Kept the workers away from the quality.

I wasn't all that certain Mrs. Dalrymple and I were going to get along. She was probably one of those languid Delta darlings in riding britches and jangly bracelets.

I stopped my truck in front of the fanciest horse barn I had seen up to that point. As I climbed out, a round little woman not much taller than Eli bustled out of the barn. She had red hair, but she hadn't been born with that particular shade. Nobody had. It bristled around her head like copper shavings. I wondered how she ever dragged a comb through it.

From the look of it, she didn't often try. She wore an oversize man's blue workshirt over a pair of threadbare jeans that barely covered dusty brown work boots. She was about my age or a little older. I figured she was probably the head groom.

"Good morning," I said. "I'm Dr. McLain. I'm looking for Mrs. Dalrymple."

"Oh, good," she said. I knew that voice. She might sound like a Delta Darling, but she sure didn't look like one. She stuck out a hand with neatly manicured short fingernails, and shook mine long and hard. I could feel calluses on her palms. "Come on, I cross-tied the fool horse on the wash rack. I hosed the cut out real good, and she's quiet, but you better give her a shot before you try to stitch her up."

The cut on the little bay's fat little bottom was about three inches long and fresh enough so I could stitch it without trimming off dead tissue. "Looks as if it went through the skin and the fat," I said, "but doesn't involve any muscle tissue or major blood vessels. She up to date on her tetanus shots?"

"And everything else."

"I'll give her a local so she won't feel the stitches." Much better than having her kick my head off when I stuck the suture needle into her.

"Good. That way she can go straight back out into the pasture."

I looked around me. The elegantly varnished stalls were all empty. She caught my gaze.

"Horses belong outdoors as much as possible. I only bring them in to train them or feed them and when the weather's really nasty."

Maybe we would get along. I had already seen too many barns where the horses were only allowed outside for a few minutes a day. Most of the show Walking Horses could endure that treatment without losing their minds, but a good many show hunters, dressage horses, and even cutting and reining horses went quietly crazy.

They took up what I can only call autistic behavior. They would walk the same path in the stall endlessly until they wore grooves in the clay floors. Or they'd stand at the front of the stall and weave back and forth—elephants in the zoo do the same thing.

Or become cribbers. That was bad. An unbreakable habit once established. They would grab hold of the edge of a stall—or anything else they could get their teeth into—pull back and suck in as much air as possible. Not only did it wear down their teeth, it gave them gas pains.

Some of them simply went psychotic from boredom and loneliness so that they became dangerous to work around.

This mare, however, seemed normal. She stood quietly with both sides of her halter clipped to the cross ties of the wash rack, and didn't even react when I shot her to deaden the area around the wound.

It was a fairly straightforward suture job, although I glowed when Mrs. Dalrymple remarked on how small and neat the stitches were. Good old inner-tubes never let me down. "She shouldn't even have a scar," I said.

"May I put her back out in the pasture?" she asked when I had finished.

"Sure."

I expected her to attach a lead rope to the mare's halter, unclip the lines that held her in the wash rack, then lead the mare to the pasture.

Instead, she took off her halter, hung it on a hook, and walked off.

The mare followed her docilely. As a matter of fact, she kept her nose as close to Mrs. Dalrymple's right shoulder as she could without stepping on her heels. I watched them walk to the pasture gate. The mare waited patiently until the gate was opened, then sauntered through and trotted off to find her buddies.

When Mrs. Dalrymple came back up the hill, I asked, "How did you do that?"

"What? Oh, you mean Sally. All my horses are trained that way. The trick is to get away from them. Can't be done."

"So how do you bring in a horse you want to ride?"

She grinned. "I'll show you." She walked back down to the pasture gate. I followed.

She leaned over the gate and shouted in that rough Jack Daniels voice, "Soldier!"

I could see a group of ten to fifteen horses grazing at the top of a hill a half mile away.

Instantly, a chestnut gelding lifted his head, detached himself from the herd and trotted across the pasture toward us. When he reached the gate, Mrs. Dalrymple opened it, waited for the horse to go through, then shut it again and walked back up the hill to her barn without even looking back to check that the horse was behind her.

He was.

"Pretty astonishing," I said.

"Not really. A number of trainers condition their horses that way. It's fairly simple. You just become the leader of the herd. The Plains Indians did it, the horse whisperer types can do it. Most people don't bother. It takes time and effort, but I think it's worth it."

"Anybody ever get fractious?"

She leaned against the gelding's shoulder and scratched his ears. He bent his neck and sighed in ecstasy. "Shoot, yeah. There's not a horse born that won't lose it given the right circumstances. I have a mare that is a saint unless a horse fly bites her. At that point she rivals any bucking bronco in any rodeo you ever saw." She grinned at me. "Want to see a trick?"

"Sure."

She turned to the horse. "Soldier, treat."

The horse wriggled with pleasure. She reached into the pocket of her jeans and came out with a sugar lump, which she held out to Soldier. He took it gently between his lips. Big deal.

"Watch," Patsy said.

The horse held the lump of sugar motionless.

"Okay," Patsy said, and handed him another. He added it to the first.

She kept feeding him lumps of sugar until his jaws pooched out so far he looked like a pocket gopher.

"Doesn't he like them?" I asked.

"He loves them. Soldier, eat."

The horse munched contentedly and swallowed with a beatific expression on his face.

"He knows that if he eats the sugar immediately, he won't get any more. If he holds it in his mouth, I'll keep feeding him. At last count, we were up to twenty-two before he ate them."

I realized this woman knew more about horses than I was likely to learn in a lifetime of equine practice. It would behoove me to let her teach me if she would. I was trying to formulate a way to ask her as we walked back to my truck.

"You ride?" she asked.

"I was crazy about horses when I was growing up, and I guess I still am, but the closest I ever got to a real riding horse was pony rides at the zoo when I was three."

"You better learn."

"I'm not certain how. I don't have much time."

"Make time. I'll teach you. I have a lighted outdoor arena and an indoor arena for bad weather. If you have to come at night or on weekends, that's fine. Besides, I could use somebody to trail ride with. My husband Dan never seems to have time."

"I don't have riding clothes or boots or..."

"You can start in jeans. I have everything else including the horses. Well?"

I nodded, absolutely elated.

"Good, I'll call you next week and we'll set up a time. Aren't you married to Morgan McLain?"

I nodded again.

"I've never met him, but Dan knows him. Bring him along. Dan says he can ride."

More than I knew. And he was my husband.

As I climbed into my truck, the biggest German Shepherd I had ever seen trotted from the shadows at the back of the barn. I hadn't even been aware he was there. He must be as well-trained as her horses.

"God," I whispered.

"Dr. McLain, meet Robespierre."

Robespierre was a delicate strawberrry pink.

"Last night I forgot to mention that Robespierre is white." She started to laugh. "Or he was."

I began to stammer apologies, but Patsy Dalrymple leaned over, put her hands on her chubby knees, and guffawed.

I turned beet red. So much for my casual handling of the skunk in the night incident.

"Next time, Dr. McLain, maybe you should ask a few more questions before you recommend a course of treatment."

"Please let me stay and bathe him. I have some shampoo in the truck that ought to take the color right out."

"That's okay. Robespierre thinks it's fetching, don't you, darlin'?" The dog wriggled and barked.

"I promise it's not permanent."

"Good thing." She laughed again and scratched the dog's ears. She was still standing there when I drove around the corner of the driveway and out of sight.

That was my introduction to Patsy Dalrymple. I've tried never to forget the lesson she taught me.

# Chapter 6

## *In which Morgan makes dreams come true*

Even before we married, Morgan and I spent long hours outlining plans for the McLain Clinic, a full-service veterinary clinic that we would open one day outside the suburbs of Memphis. I would be the vet, he would manage the business end.

For me, the clinic was a dream that might come true twenty years in the future when we had substantial savings.

My accountant father had always counseled caution. Always hedge your bets. Never sign a contract without an escape clause. Never risk more than you can afford to lose.

Some people might consider marriage a risk. I didn't. Not with Morgan. I assumed he was every bit as fiscally conservative as my father. He was a *banker,* for pity's sake.

A darned good thing he wasn't so conservative, or the McLain-Scheibler Clinic wouldn't exist today.

Morgan was born to organize, manipulate, and thrust me into risky situations I'd never have considered without him. I'd had to be tough as nails to become a vet, but I was just as insecure as the next person about when it came to other areas of my life. Most of the time, I didn't allow those insecurities to show.

A year after we were married, he came home one Wednesday night, dragged me into his car, and drove me out southeast of Memphis, past Germantown, past Collierville, and into Fayette County just far enough north of the Mississippi State line to still be in Tennessee. We turned off the highway, bumped down four or five miles of gravel road, and turned into a dirt road that led into somebody's overgrown pasture.

"What on earth are you doing?" I asked. "I've had a long day and so have you. The people who live here aren't going to be pleased to have us show up at suppertime."

All he did was grin and lift his eyebrows.

We rolled to the top of a rise and into the front yard of a perfectly dreadful house. One of those amorphous ranch houses, it was painted a ghastly shade of mustard yellow and looked to have maybe twelve hundred feet inside if you included the garage.

"Who are these people?" I whispered. Then, "Look, nobody's home. They're probably at Wednesday night prayer meeting. Let's get out of here before they come back and set the dogs on us."

"Nobody's living here," he said and took my hand. "Come on." He had a key.

Inside was worse than outside. The carpet was the color of day old vomit and rotting away at the doorways. The kitchen was tiny. Three separate patterns of orange wallpaper covered the walls above orange counter tops. The two little bathrooms were completely done in tile and fixtures the color of *fresh* vomit, as opposed to day old. The three bedrooms were barely long enough for beds, and to finish up, there was a gigantic wood burning stove sitting on the carpet in the middle of the living room floor with black pipes disappearing up the chimney.

"This place is hideous," I said.

"It'll be fine once we fix it up."

"Say what?"

He grabbed my hand. "I will build you a house in the future, my love, but until I do, this place isn't much worse than our apartment, now is it?"

"You have lost your mind."

"Come on." He dragged me through pastures knee deep in uncut weeds. I nearly impaled myself on four-inch thorns that covered the bark of the black locust trees that infested the pastures like alien predators.

At the back a large pond filled a declivity. "That's where they breed the water moccasins, right?" I asked.

The only other structures were a couple of decrepit lean-to's that still bore the unmistakable odor of hog.

By this point the legs of my jeans were wet and festooned with cocklebburs. "I am being bit to pieces by chiggers," I said grumpily. "Can we please go back to the car now?"

Once in the car, he waved a hand at the disaster in front of us. "It's perfect, isn't it?"

"For what? A prison? A hospital for the criminally insane?"

"Our clinic."

"Morgan, do you need to go to the emergency room? Have you had a stroke?"

"It's not even on the market yet. The people who lived there have moved into town so their children can go to city schools. It's cheap as dirt—"

"Of course it is. It *is* dirt."

"And it's in the path of growth. In another twenty years we'll practically be in suburbia. Right on the cusp." He turned to me and laid both hands on my shoulders so that I had to face him.

"Maggie, pay attention. We live in the house while we get the land in order—I'll need a tractor. God, I've always wanted a tractor. We can paint and do a few things to it to make it livable in the meantime."

"In the meantime to what?"

"We bring in a double-wide trailer to serve as your clinic until we acquire enough capital to build a building. I can get a great construction loan. We can put up your house over there behind the present house at the same time we build the clinic building and covered by the same loan. There are a few minor considerations—fencing, of course, and some kennels behind the double-wide."

"Morgan, you have lost your mind."

He took my face in his hands. "If we don't do it now, love, we will put it off and put it off. You'll be a hundred and five and still working on kittens and puppies for Dr. Parmenter."

"Who will be as old as Methuselah. There's nothing wrong with Dr. Parmenter."

"The thing is, this is chancy, but doable. Now."

"It didn't occur to you to consult me first?"

"There wasn't time."

Most women of my generation and economic background have been taught to embrace their husband's dreams. You work as a secretary or a nurse so hubby can become a bigtime lawyer or a doctor or an engineer. Then you sit back and play bridge. If I'd wanted that kind of life, I'd have tried to seduce The Prince of Darkness.

I had already departed from the norm by becoming a veterinarian, but since falling in love with Morgan, I had begun to retrench.

We weren't rich, but we were making enough to enjoy ourselves. We were comfortable. Sooner or later Dr. Parmenter would retire. By then, I could probably afford to buy his practice.

Morgan was going to rise at the bank. I would gladly play corporate wife and entertain (with my mother's help) to push him along his way.

Eventually, we could sell Dr. Parmenter's practice and move to the country. But not yet.

I was happy, in love, and safe. Even if something happened to my job with Dr. Parmenter, we wouldn't starve. We might have to scrimp, but our lifestyle wouldn't change appreciably.

Now, suddenly I had to fish or cut bait.

I could deliver a calf, sew up a gaping wound in a Brahma bull, and go nose-to-nose with any redneck farmer who questioned my skills or my diagnosis, so long as somebody else billed clients, ordered supplies, kept track of inventory, and paid the bills on time. I hated dealing with money, and I was lousy at keeping records. Morgan would help me with the logistics, but the final responsibility would be mine alone. "I'm terrified," I admitted.

"What? You don't think you're good enough?" Morgan knew that was the hottest button he could push.

"Of *course* I am good enough," I snapped. "I am a fantastic vet. But working for somebody else is different from opening my own practice. What if nobody hires me? It won't matter how good I am."

"They'll hire you."

"Oh, right. Can I think about it?"

"Sure." He sounded deflated and I felt like the biggest party-pooper on earth. He sighed and put the car in gear. "I shouldn't have sprung it on you like this. Hey, if we renege on the contract, all I'll lose is a thousand bucks earnest money."

"You've put down a bid on this place?" I swung around to gape at him. "Without asking me?"

"Didn't want it to slip through our fingers." He sounded chastened.

Dammit, he *should* sound chastened. "Morgan, of all the high-handed..."

"Just drop it."

We barely spoke the rest of the way home. As we pulled into the parking lot, I said, "What's the worst that can happen? We go bankrupt. Big deal. I can always get another job."

He grabbed me. "That's my Maggie!"

Next day, I talked to Dr. Parmenter. I was fighting second thoughts. "The house is horrible."

"How many acres?"

"Morgan says fifty. He says if I can't make a go of it, he'll turn it into housing plots and become a construction tycoon."

"I have taught you all—no, most—of what I know, and you have Morgan to handle the business side of things. Much better than my business manager, I assure you. Hadn't you planned to leave?"

"Not yet. What if nobody hires me?"

"Fight for business."

When I came home that afternoon I found an envelope from Eli in Cookeville among the bills and circulars. I hadn't heard from Eli for a month or so. I'd meant to call, but I'd been so busy. I felt terribly guilty as I tore the letter open.

After I read it, I tossed it to Morgan. "And I thought *I* had worries."

Poor Eli. Josh's parents disliked her. She didn't like them much either. Although she was a Methodist, they kept demanding she go to their hard-shell church and disapproved of her clothes, her makeup, and her attempts to help around the house. She had finally stopped trying to be accommodating.

She had just moved out into a single room in a rooming house with rats that didn't come in cages. She was still working only part time, and her boss ordered her around like a flunky instead of a colleague. She hadn't treated a cow or a horse or even a goat for three months. She'd been stuck looking after small animals exclusively—not Eli's cup of tea.

Morgan read the letter carefully, the way he did everything (except put earnest money down on Tobacco Road), then picked up the phone and dialed the number Eli had given us in her letter. Apparently the telephone was in the hall of the rooming house. Morgan had to fight through a landlady and wait a good five minutes before Eli answered.

I only heard his half of the conversation. I assumed he'd pass the phone to me after he'd exchanged pleasantries with her.

Instead, he said, "How much money can you get your hands on?"

I sat straight up. "Morgan, my word! What a question!"

He flapped a hand at me to shut me up. "That much? Quickly?"

He listened. "Fine. Give me directions to Rat Central. Maggie and I will be there to help you pack before dark tomorrow. If we need to rent a U-Haul trailer, where's the closest place? Nashville?" More listening and nodding. I gaped at him. "You can stay with us. I have just bought fifty acres of pastureland in Fayette County just this side of Rossville. Are you interested in affording half a practice?" He nodded and smiled at me, then winked. "It's going to be tough for the next few years. You may end up living and working in a trailer... No, a nice trailer. I promise you can come into our house if there's a tornado. Eli, you are part of this family. I try not to let members of my family suffer." He handed me the telephone. "Tell her."

"Eli," I asked, "you don't really want to stay in Cookeville, do you?"

"Hell, no. Are you serious about this?"

"You bet." I looked at Morgan, stared at the telephone, and suddenly my soul was light and full of joy. "I've been telling Morgan he was a lunatic. You always say I have about as much ESP as a watermelon, Eli, but I swear this is right. I can feel it."

So the McLain-Scheibler Clinic was born. *Without Morgan*, the dreamer in the stuffed shirt, the believer in miracles, to push me, none of it would have happened.

# Chapter 7

## *In which Maggie and Eli start a practice*

The process by which any new veterinary practice starts up is fairly standard. In our case it was complicated because we were women and one of us was the size of a twelve-year-old child.

We advertised in the local suburban newspapers. We spoke to every club meeting from the Dressage Association to the 4-H club to Rotary. We handed out hundreds of business cards to everybody we met who might not actually be practicing vivisection secretly in his basement.

We talked to the farriers who shod all the local horses and called on all the boarding barns and breeding facilities.

We haunted the cattle sale barns in Collierville and Somerville. We schmoozed at every church supper we heard about. Most of the time Morgan was right there beside us, telling the good ol' boys what geniuses we were.

We hung around horse shows and handed out cards to the participants. We sponsored classes at horse shows for the walking horse people and the hunters. We did the same for cat shows and dog shows just so our name would be announced. Maybe the next time Rover had a cough they'd think of us.

We offered to handle weekend and night emergencies for all the other vets who didn't necessarily want to be called out to the home of the local serial killer at two in the morning.

We bought a used house trailer for Eli and moved it onto the far side of the property. We bought another and moved it into the center between Eli and the Hideous House. That became the first McLain-Scheibler Clinic building.

Morgan worked a full day at the bank, then came home in the evenings to cut fifty acres of pasture with his newly acquired John Deere tractor and bushhog, both of which had been built sometime around 1940. We also painted The Hideous House inside, pulled *up* the carpets and *down* the orange wallpaper.

Miles of new fence had to be built around the property, and a new kennel and boarding facility to be built behind the clinic trailer. I drove metal fence posts in clay so hard it would have made bricks even without baking. Eli and I learned to screed concrete for the kennel flooring.

Even my mother and father grabbed paintbrushes. My mother, with Bear along for the ride, scoured yard sales looking for office and reception area furniture, then made slipcovers to cover the spots and tears. She found appropriate animal pictures for the walls and ancient cabinets to be repainted for medical and file storage.

Daddy set up the accounting system and helped Morgan work out payment schedules and a business plan. Established veterinary practices are billed monthly or even quarterly for the drugs they order from pharmaceutical houses. New practices must pay up front until they've established credit. That was tough. We certainly had no cash flow.

We needed equipment such as mobile x-rays and fluoroscopes. We had to stock both our elderly pickup trucks with cabinets and supplies.

Morgan surprised us by having the first McLain-Scheibler logos designed and painted on the doors of our used trucks. Both Eli and I broke into tears when we saw them.

After the first month, Morgan refused to allow me to see the bank statements. "Frankly," he said, "I prefer your monthly PMS to your monthly fiscal hysterics."

Either we ate take-out or my mother brought dinner out for us.

We were so tired we were bleary-eyed most of the time. Looking back, I don't think any of us has ever been happier. We—the five of us—became a family.

Eli lost that pinched look she'd had that awful day when we drove up to bring her home from Cookeville. Morgan lost twenty pounds and the beginnings of his paunch. I developed biceps like a super hero.

Little by little we made advances. We acquired some small-animal clients, mostly people who didn't want to drive Fido or Kitty all the way into town for treatment.

Still, it was a hard row to hoe and one that looked like we would be hoeing for a long time.

Then we got lucky. Well, sort of.

In the village of Williston, Mike Rasmussen ran a small logging operation using Percheron draft horses. Many people don't realize that logging with draft horses has never gone out of style. At the time I first met Mike, his was one of three groups in the area using Percherons and Belgians for logging. At present there are six groups operating. Every one of them has a waiting list.

Big logging companies preferred to clear-cut and buy an entire stand of timber. If a man had forty or fifty acres of old growth woods and needed a little money for next year's seed, he might only want to sell a few trees to the local sawmill. He did not want to lose his woods, nor create erosion.

The solution was a pair of intelligent draft horses and a wood skid. Once the tree was dropped and cut into manageable lengths, a team of draft horses could maneuver it through the woods, around trees, over stumps, and through underbrush, all without disturbing the environment except for the occasional pile of manure. And that's fertilizer.

I've watched teams work at the logging contests at fairs and field days. Most of the time the team only needs to be shown how to find the logging truck up on the highway at the start of the day. Thereafter, the logger loads the logs and tells old Sam or Patch or Bob to 'git on up there to the truck.' Then he goes back to cutting up the next tree while the horses make their way to the highway completely on their own. Once they are unloaded, they take the skid back down to the logger, also without supervision.

So Mike Rasmussen and his ilk have always taken extremely good care of their horses.

When he called our service one hot August night, he sounded desperate. "Hey, doc, my young stud Jake's down and I can't get nobody else to come. He's real bad. Can you come on out here?"

I later learned I was the fourth vet he'd called. The others were either not on call or didn't want to roll out at one in the morning for a thirty minute drive into the back of beyond. At that point, I would have driven to Arkansas for a job, and I had heard enough about Rasmussen to know he generally paid his bills without a quibble.

Morgan woke up when he heard me dressing. When I told him

where I was going, he offered to ride along, but I knew he didn't really want to. This was my country now. If I couldn't drive alone around here in the middle of the night, I might as well move back to an apartment in midtown and work for Dr. Parmenter. Eli and I had no car phones yet, so we both carried two-way radios. Most of the time, however, they didn't work where we did.

The temperature that night still hovered around the eighty-five degree mark, and the humidity wasn't much better.

Mike's directions only got me lost once before I found the gravel road that led off into the woods towards his farm.

He had opened the gate for me, so I drove straight through into a grassy paddock in front of an old barn. Light seeped out between the slats that comprised the barn's sides—a dead giveaway that it had originally been used to hang tobacco.

Rasmussen opened the door of my truck before I could. "'Preciate this a bunch, Doc," he said. "Can I tote something for you?"

"That's okay, Mr. Rasmussen. I've got an emergency bag with me, and whatever else we need in the back of the truck."

Under the lights in the barn aisle, I had my first good look at Mike Rasmussen. He was two or three inches taller than Morgan, and downright cadaverous. He was wearing a plain white undershirt and dusty jeans and looked as though somebody had stitched him up from a worn out pair of leather boots. From the bridge of his nose down, his face was as red and lined as the side of an eroded ditch beside a Delta creek. From there up, his forehead was dead white where the brim of his hat must have shaded his face while he worked. I couldn't tell whether he was thirty or eighty.

As he led me down the wide center aisle of the barn, I asked, "What do you think it is? Colic? Founder?" Those were the two most frequent causes of distress in horses. Draft horses with their slow metabolisms were prone to overeat and get belly aches that sometimes killed them.

"Don't seem like that."

Rasmussen had turned the old tobacco barn into a first class horse barn with a broad wash area and stands along the walls holding immaculately polished leather harness for half a dozen horses.

"See, Ma'am, Jake, he's my stud horse. Ain't but five year old. Don't want to lose him."

I followed him down to the last stall on the left—a big double stall fit for a king.

And that's what Jake was. He stood well over eighteen hands high at the withers, the beginning of the back. A 'hand' is four inches. You do the math.

At that point, however, he wasn't standing at all. He was stretched out flat in his stall on his right side with all four hooves pointed straight out. The whites of his eyes showed and his tongue lolled.

If this was colic or founder, both of which are life-threatening gut problems, this was far advanced. My heart sank. My first big horse case, and I was probably going to lose the patient.

"Look at him, Doc. Look there at his side."

I had already knelt in the bed of clean shavings in the stall and pulled back Jake's lips. His gums were still pink, but not as red as they should be.

He lifted his head, then flopped back down. I ran my hand down his flank. At the moment his pelt was so wet he looked as though he were carved from ebony, and his mane lay tangled against his shoulder.

"Stay with me, baby. Mr. Rasmussen, hand me my bag." I gave Jake a shot of tranquilizer and started an IV drip of electrolytes on him at once. The way he was sweating, he needed to replenish the electrolytes in his body.

Rasmussen hunkered down beside me. "What the Sam Hill's wrong with him, doc? I come out to check on one of my mares a hour ago and found him down in his stall. He don't act like he's colicking. He's got plenty of room to stand, but I couldn't get him up. Sorry to drag you out in the middle of the night like this."

I ran my hand back to Jake's loin and then leaned over and put my ear to his side. The gut sounds were good. But his whole side was pulsing. I had never seen a case like this, but I'd read about them. I wracked my brain. Took me a moment to remember the name for what Jake had. "Mr. Rasmussen, what your horse has is a tympanic diaphragm. Pretty rare."

"Is it fatal?" He sounded desperate.

"It certainly can be. His heart is beating in time with his diaphragm. His diaphragm is just a big band of muscle like a drumhead. Somehow his heart has kicked that drum head into beating at the same tempo."

"That ain't so bad, is it, doc?"

"He can't draw in a deep breath to get enough oxygen to his lungs." I pulled back Jake's upper lip. "See here? His gums aren't white, but they're paler than they should be."

Mike turned frightened eyes on me. "What causes it?"

"Nobody knows for certain. Did you work him hard today?"

"No more'n usual. He come in, had him some supper like always."

"I'd say it's a combination of this heat and humidity. Not much breeze in the woods, is there?"

"Shoot, hottern' the hinges of hell." Rasmussen reached down and stroked the stallion's shoulder. "Poor ol' boy. Is there anything you can do?"

"We need to get him up on his feet somehow."

"Doc, that horse weighs all of two thousand pounds." He looked me up and down. "You're a big woman and I'm no lightweight, but it'd take the Tennessee linebackers to haul that horse up."

"If we can get ropes under his belly, we can use your tractor to winch him up."

Mike rubbed his stubbled jaw. "Well, maybe." He hawked and spit into the dirt across the aisle. "Got a couple of old ropes we use on the bulls."

"Get them, and get your tractor. Fast."

Mike left the barn at a run.

I turned to Jake and slapped his shoulder. "Pay attention, damn you." Jake looked up at me. Horses in pain will frequently simply turn their faces to the wall and die. It's important to keep them focused on something outside themselves. Now that I had Jake's attention, I wasn't about to lose it.

"Mary had a little lamb, little lamb, little lamb," I sang. "A horse is a horse of course of course." I tried to think of other nursery rhymes or nonsense songs, but my mind went blank.

So I crooned, "Jake, if you die, sweetie, I will barbecue your good-for-nothing hide. You'll never raise your big feet up to breed another pretty little mare. You hear that, horse? No more nookie." I slapped him again, harder this time. "Jake! Listen to me!"

Jake groaned.

"No way, horse!" I kicked him hard in his fat rear end. "Get up and fight for your life. You're just a big ole wuss."

He rolled over onto his belly and heaved himself to his feet.

"Good boy." I threw my arms around his nose. I couldn't reach any higher. I couldn't see over the top of him, much less reach around his neck. "That's it, baby." I called, "Mike! He's up." Now if we could just keep him up. I knew there was another treatment I should be giving him, but for the life of me, I couldn't remember what. What kind of a vet was I if I couldn't remember how to treat animals? Okay, so this was extremely rare. That was no excuse.

He was up, all right, but just barely. He swayed on his platter-sized hooves. The tranquilizer should be taking effect.

I thought the pulsing in his diaphragm had slowed, but couldn't be certain. I put my stethoscope against Jake's belly and leaned down to listen.

Without warning, Jake sat down on his rump like a donkey with his front feet in front of him. He looked surprised. I certainly was. I'd never seen a horse do that except in trick shows.

"Mike!" I yelled. "Hurry!"

The tractor stopped in the aisle and Mike said, "Godawlmighty! Get up, you fool horse, you look like a damn mule."

"Grab his halter," I said. "Keep his head up."

"Sweet sufferin' Jesus."

I reached the aisle outside Jake's stall and bent over with my hands on my knees. "You all right?"

"Fine."

Suddenly, it hit me. I remembered what to do for Jake. "Wait a minute, Mr. Rasmussen." I ran back to my truck, filled a syringe and ran back. "You get on out of there. This is going to happen fast if it happens at all."

He obviously didn't believe me.

I wasn't certain I believed me either. I'd never done this before. I'd seen it work with cows, but never with horses.

I said a silent prayer and pushed the syringe of calcium straight into the throbbing vein in Jake's broad black neck.

He grunted.

Then he pulled his long legs under him and surged to his feet.

Rasmussen had to jump away to avoid being stepped on.

"God a'mighty, woman, what did you do?"

I stroked Jake's black nose, pulled his upper lip back and smiled. "His gums are turning red as a Brownsville peach. He's breathing normally."

"That fast?"

I nodded. "Look at his side." I leaned down and listened. "Perfect. He's fine."

"It's a doggoned miracle."

Jake took a mouthful of hay and eyed me suspiciously.

"If you ever try to die on me again, horse, I'll take you out, you got that?" I started to giggle. A moment later both Rasmussen and I were sitting on a bale of hay in the aisle laughing our heads off.

As I drove out of his paddock, I checked the dashboard clock.

The whole episode had lasted under an hour. The quarter moon was already down, leaving only stars so thick that they really did look like milk pouring from a jug. I rolled down the window of my truck and drank in the scent of Delta dust. Somewhere to my left a barn owl screamed.

I was fine. The horse was fine. I could climb back in bed, cuddle against Morgan, and thank God I remembered in time about the calcium shot. No one knew precisely how it worked or why, but it did, both on cows and horses.

I was a miracle worker.

At least Mike Rasmussen told everybody I was. Before the week was out I had two whole hunter-jumper barns to worm, and an entire hunting pack of Penn Marydel hounds to vaccinate. That was the first month the McLain-Scheibler Clinic ended up in the black. All thanks to Big Jake and Mike Rasmussen.

# Chapter 8

## *Eli turns a cow into a bowling ball*

Eli and I scrimped and saved any way we could. Pharmaceutical companies were happy to give a line of credit to most veterinary services, but they were hesitant to grant much leeway to a pair of crazy women who were living in the country and expecting to build a practice in a used double-wide trailer.

We couldn't work without drugs. So everything else in life ran to peanut butter sandwiches and make-do. When Eli's Wellington boots—knee-high black rubber boots that she wore while slogging across pastures—developed a split along the sole, she tried first to fix them with duct tape. Didn't work.

Eli wore a size nothing, so she took a child's size in Wellingtons, but even those weren't cheap. We shopped yard and estate sales for things like used file cabinets, and at one house, Eli found a pair of canary yellow rubber children's rain boots that fit her for only fifty cents.

I snickered.

"I am trying to live within our means," she said huffily.

I didn't mention the boots again.

We still hadn't broken through to the big beef cattle ranches, but we did get the occasional call to a dairy farm. I suspect that in most cases the farmer had already tried several other vets before he called us, but we never asked. We simply prayed that every odd call we took would lead to an ongoing relationship with a new client.

We didn't have enough business to divide our calls, so we often went out together. One rainy dawn, our answering service took a call from Roy Wilson, who owned a dairy farm thirty minutes away if I drove and forty-five if Eli drove. So I drove.

Mr. Wilson said he had a cow that was having trouble calving. Cows have a great facility for picking the worst possible weather in which to calve.

Eli and I hoped Mr. Wilson would have his cow up in his barn and under cover, so we could work on her in relative—or at least dry—comfort.

"I just pray the calf's still alive," I said. Cows can spend eighteen hours calving and still deliver a healthy calf and recover.

Now horses are a different matter. Once a mare's water breaks, she'd better have a live foal on the ground in twenty minutes. When a vet is called to a mare that's having trouble foaling, she can seldom save the foal, and sometimes not even the mother.

Eli preferred cows. Not nearly so fragile as horses.

When I pulled up in the morass of mud in his paddock, Roy Wilson sauntered out to meet us with the rain running off the brim of his elderly Stetson. The man acted as though we had all the time in the world.

"I hate to wear these stupid boots," Eli whispered. "Maybe I can wear my sneakers."

"And catch pneumonia and leave me all the work? Forget it, Miss Eli. What do you care what he thinks about your boots?"

Eli opened the passenger door and looked down. The mud in the paddock looked as thick as oxtail soup. She jammed her rain hat on her head, reached behind the seat for her rain jacket and pants, struggled into them, and pulled on her yellow boots.

The rain suit was nearly as yellow as the boots. "You look like a canary," I whispered.

The look she gave me would have peeled paint.

"She in the barn?" Eli asked Mr. Wilson.

"Down in the pasture. Won't move. Gonna have to take your truck to get to her."

"Hell," Eli whispered.

He came around to the passenger side and scrunched in beside Eli. He was not a small man, and he smelled of wet wool and chewing tobacco.

"Is there a road?" I asked.

"Track's good most times, but could be a tad slick in this mess. Back out, turn right and follow the road around to the left."

"What are we looking at?" Eli asked.

"Cow's an old hand at this. Usually drops 'em where she stands like squirting ketchup out of the bottle. Calf's still alive, or was last time I checked. She's been straining about five hours now. Must be breech. Have to pull it."

Pulling a live calf with the block and tackle was vastly preferable to cutting up a dead one in its mother's uterus and pulling it out piece by piece. "Let's hope it's still viable." I said.

"Big sucker. Fine Guernsey. Don't want to lose it."

"We'll do our best. Shit!" The truck hit a deep puddle and slued sideways.

I managed to straighten it and plowed on. This was more a cow track than a road. Apparently, generations of Guernseys had used this path to come from the pasture to the barn morning and night for milking. Their hooves had dug ruts much deeper than the roadbed. I prayed the undercarriage of my truck would survive intact. McLain-Scheibler could not afford to have an oil pan replaced.

"Stop. We're here."

I patted the brakes. The rear end threatened to slide away, but came to a shuddering stop. I heaved a sigh of relief. "Where is she?"

"Yonder." Wilson pointed out the passenger side window.

Silhouetted against the rainy early-morning sky on the very top of a hill stood a lone cow. While we watched, she strained and lowed in obvious discomfort.

Wilson was already out of the truck and trudging up the hill. Several times he had to catch himself on his hands to keep from sliding back down again.

Eli and I each stuck four pairs of shoulder length obstetrical gloves into one of our pockets, a stethoscope into the other. I slid a coil of rope over my arm.

"We can't work on that cow up on that hill," I said. "I don't care what Wilson said about moving her. We have to get her down to the truck somehow."

Eli dashed the water out of her eyes. "Please, Lord, let it stop raining."

We struggled up the hill. I slid down on my hands and knees once. Eli had to shove my rump to get me moving again. She was always much more agile. Even so, Wilson had to pull her the last couple of feet.

"Hey, doc, them's some fine rain boots you done got on," he snickered as he hauled her upright. "Never did see no *yaller* gumboots."

Eli ignored him and walked to the uphill side of the cow where she could brace herself against the cow's flank. She listened to her vital signs, felt for the calf, and said, "There's a second heartbeat. Calf's still alive."

"We've got to get her down to level ground," I said, "We're going to have to use a block and tackle."

"She ain't goin' nowhere. I done tried." He smacked the cow. "Damn fool cow! Move! Cows are dumber than dirt."

We wasted ten minutes trying to move the cow. She simply dug all four cloven hooves deeper into the mud and refused to budge.

"Okay," Eli panted. "You're going to have to go back down to my truck and get the block and tackle out of the back."

I sighed and prepared to slide down the hill.

"Don't need but one of us," Wilson said. "You dirty enough already. I'll bring up what we need."

"You know what to get?" I asked.

"Don't teach your Granmama to suck eggs," Wilson said. "I been doing this for nigh onto forty year." He looked up and squinted. "Dang. I do believe the rain's lettin' up a tad."

"Thank God. Now, go."

Both Eli and I stayed on the upside of the cow, but I had sense enough to move back a ways. I have never had the fondness for cows Eli has. I prefer not to be impaled on horns, even short ones, nor stomped with cloven hooves or lashed across the face by a tail.

The cow didn't seem to resent having Eli braced against her. She continued placidly chewing her cud, unconcerned about the enormous bundle of flesh and bone trying to work its way out of her. For the moment at least, the contractions seemed to have stopped.

Then, without warning, she swayed once and toppled over straight-legged, with all four feet pointing down the hill. Her bloated body landed on top of Eli.

I screamed.

Eli screamed. Actually, she wheezed as though somebody had just sat on a whoopee cushion. "Maggie! Get me out of here!"

The cow lay across her thighs and hips so that her legs and feet stuck out on the downhill side of the cow's belly. She could breathe. "Ow!" she yelped. "Fool cow! Maggie, her hipbone's gouging my liver out."

I grabbed the cow's head and tried to drag her down the hill and off Eli. Eli wriggled backwards for a moment, then sank back into the mud.

"Wilson!" I shouted. "Get back up here."

Eli opened her mouth to shout just as the heavens opened and dumped a torrent of rain into her open mouth. She gurgled and spat.

"Damnation, Eli, with all this mud, you ought to slide out like a greased pig."

The cow lifted her head and bellowed. "Oh, shut up," Eli said and smacked her on her shoulder. "Move!"

"Wilson!" I hollered. What was keeping the man?

Then from the downhill side of the cow I heard laughter. Not chuckles. Guffaws. Roy Wilson was laughing!

"Cut that out and help me drag Eli out of here!"

He appeared around the tail end of the cow, block and tackle over his shoulder, a broad grin on his face. I decided to beat him senseless with it the instant he got Eli out from under the cow. He leaned on the cow's flank to brace himself and reached down to grab Eli under her shoulders.

Without warning, the cow slid straight down the hill in the mud.

Eli's legs popped free. She raised up on one elbow. All three of us watched the cow turn slowly with all four legs in the air, then continue her slide head first, picking up speed as she went. We watched in fascination until she fetched up against the side of our truck.

"Gawd," Wilson breathed.

"Amen to that," I whispered.

"Come on," Eli said. "Dammit, Maggie, get me up."

We all slipped and slid after the cow. I went most of the way on my bottom. Eli used her fancy new yellow rainboots like skis. Somehow she managed to stay on her feet.

When we were about five feet away, the cow struggled to her feet, turned to stare at us, bellowed once, and spread her hind legs.

By the time we reached her, the calf lay on the ground behind her.

"Doggone," Wilson breathed.

"Put the block and tackle back in the truck and hand me a stack of towels out of the rear cabinet," Eli said. She dropped to her knees beside the calf. It blinked at her.

In this downpour the calf couldn't be dried off, but the rough towels would stimulate it. Eli checked the calf's vitals. "Perfect." She nodded with satisfaction. Its toboggan ride seemed not to have harmed it in the least.

The calf was already struggling to its feet. Its mother watched Eli with narrowed eyes, bellowed once, swung her head and slammed Eli into the side of the truck.

Wilson slid into the passenger seat and held the door open for Eli. "Y'all best leave her alone and get your tails in here fast. She tends to be a might ill-tempered if you mess with her calf."

"Now you tell me." Eli pulled herself up by the side of the truck, accepted a grubby hand from Wilson, slid in beside him and slammed the passenger side door.

I bolted for the driver's side, as the cow noticed me and started after me, bellowing at the top of her lungs.

I jumped in, slammed the door and started the engine just as Momma's heavy head landed hard where my shoulder had been a minute earlier.

I rolled down my window and punched her smack in the middle of her forehead. "Get out of the way." I leaned forward. "Wilson, is there room to turn around?"

"Nope. Better back up. You got about five feet between you and the calf."

I twisted to look back over my shoulder as the cow butted the tailgate.

"Shee-ut!" said Wilson.

"Move, cow, or I swear I'll back right over you!" I shouted over my shoulder. Then I threw the truck into reverse. The cow moved.

I was forced to back most of the way to the farmyard before Wilson pointed out a gravel area where I could turn around without getting stuck in the mud.

When we reached the barn, I glanced over at Wilson. He was still shaking with glee.

"All right, dammit, what's so funny?"

He didn't answer until he was safely outside the truck and leaning in Eli's window. "Doc," he said to Eli, "when I started up that hill, all I could see sticking out from under that cow's belly was the soles of them yaller rain boots of your'n."

"And?"

"Ain't you never looked at 'em?"

"My soles? Of course not."

"Doc, the soles of them boots got fat yaller and red duckies painted on 'em big as life."

Eli closed her eyes. "Wilson," I said, "if you ever tell one soul..."

"Shoot," he said as he climbed out of the truck. "I'm gonna be too busy tellin' the good ol' boys down to the sale barn 'bout this fancy new technique y'all lady vets done invented to deliver stuck calves."

"Wilson," Eli warned.

"Darn sight easier than a block and tackle." He grinned. "Just take ol' cow up top of the nearest hill, then roll her down like a bowlin' ball." He hunched against the renewed rain and waved at us over his shoulder as he raced through the downpour to his barn. His shoulders still shook.

Neither Eli nor I spoke a word for several minutes. Once we were safely off Wilson's gravel road and onto paved county road beyond, Eli said very quietly, so quietly that I knew she was close to a major explosion. "I do not care if new black Wellington boots cost more than the national debt. I do not care if we have to deliver twenty cows to pay for them. I do not care whether we meet the mortgage or the car payments or our salaries. Tomorrow morning I intend to call State Line Tack and order the finest children's Wellington boots they have and get them mailed to me overnight." She took a deep breath. "And you better not say one word."

"My lips are sealed."

"Maggie, by the time Wilson tells this story to all his good ol' boy friends, you and I will have arrived to deliver his calf wearing pink polka-dot tutus and toe slippers. We'll be stuck with kittens and puppies for the rest of our lives."

"It's not that bad."

"The hell it's not." She turned to look out her window. "I'll never be able to show my face at the Monday morning cattle sale again."

# Chapter 9

## *In which Eli discovers the power of publicity*

Farmers and cattlemen have always been notorious gossips. They all start their days before dawn, then long about eight o'clock a good many of our local farmers repair to the Wolf River Café or some other local cafe for a late breakfast and another cup of coffee. They swear business is transacted at those coffee klatches, but I discovered as a young vet that the 'business' in question was usually somebody else's and none of theirs.

The story of Eli's boots would have made the rounds within twenty-four hours. I figured she'd want to keep a low profile until the laughter died down some. I planned to attend the cattle sales in Collierville without her for the next few weeks.

At ten-thirty the following Monday morning—a blessedly sunny day—she stuck her head in my office and handed me a cup of coffee.

"Come on or we'll be late," she said.

"Huh?"

"The cattle sale in Collierville starts in thirty minutes."

"Oh. Yeah. Wouldn't you like to stick around here and handle the small animal cases?"

She glared at me. I shut up and followed her out to my truck.

She climbed into the passenger side, clipped on her seatbelt, and drank some of her coffee as we backed out and started down the road toward town.

Finally, she turned to me and said, "If you think I intend to let some gossipy old farmer keep me from doing my job, you got another think coming."

With that, she kicked off her sneakers, and pulled on the rubber duckies.

Eli was endlessly patient with animals, even those that stomped and bit her. And with children. Eventually, however, the steam built up and she blew. Until we both mellowed, she and I generally had one big battle per year, usually over something silly. No matter who was at fault (never me, of course) I apologized. I knew she simply couldn't.

By the time we pulled into the parking lot at the sale barn among the mud-spattered stock trailers and the big diesels that pulled them, I was sure she'd commit mayhem on the first man that snickered. We'd probably get ridden out of town on a rail.

We climbed out, and Eli strode off toward the nearest group of cattlemen. Her chin was so far in the air she could hardly see where she was walking. Around a sale barn, watching where you put your feet was important. Cow patties were wet, nasty, slippery and stank.

"Morning," she said airily and tossed her hair. In the early '70s she wore her brown hair shoulder length, so there was plenty to toss.

One especially grizzled old geezer grinned at her and tipped his battered Stetson. "What's up, Doc?"

"Everything's just ducky," Eli said.

He cut his eyes at his buddies, who covered their mouths to conceal their answering snickers. He glanced toward her feet. "Mighty nice boots you got on."

"Indeed they are. Yellow's my favorite color. What's yours?"

They jostled and punched one another's shoulders. I had visions of Eli's punching them out and landing us in jail. I had started forward to intervene when the geezer said, "Gonna buy me a bunch of calves this morning, Doc. Want to do the brucellosis checks on them?"

"How's about checking on a bull I'm thinking of biddin' on?" asked his neighbor. They stood aside to include me in the group. "Y'all both gonna work this morning? If I was a bettin' man, I'd bet y'all are gonna be full up with work today." He started laughing. A moment later his four buddies joined him.

"Whoa!" I said. "Don't joke. I swear we'll bill you and expect to be paid."

A lanky, fortyish man in clean chinos and polished brown boots walked up from behind the crowd. "No'm, we're all dead serious." He stuck out a lean hand. "I'm J. L. Maxwell." His hand was rock hard and so callused it felt like badly tanned leather.

I knew who he was although I had never met him. He had one of the largest herds of purebred Brahman cattle in the mid-south. Now I was really suspicious. If they were playing a practical joke, I'd be punching jaws right beside Eli. "I don't get it," I said. "You've been ignoring us for the last six months."

"Shoot, honey," one of the other geezers said, "Didn't know who you was 'til we saw them boots." Snicker, snicker.

"Like hell you didn't," Eli said. "How many four foot ten female vets you got in this neighborhood?"

"That was before we heard about what a fine job y'all did with that cow, mud and all. Ol' Roy said both of y'all come out to the pasture in the middle of the storm. Some vets around here done got above their raisin'. Don't fancy pulling calves in rough weather in the mud."

"Yeah," said the heretofore silent member of the group. "And Mike Rasmussen told me you done saved his Big Jake's life." He nodded at me almost imperceptibly. "If y'all can handle cows *and* horses, you'll do 'til something better comes along." With that, he spit a stream of tobacco juice about six feet into the nearest manure pile.

"Come on, sweet thang," J. L. said, hooking his arm through mine. "Sale's starting. Got you some work to do."

We packed over fifty vials of blood to be sent off to Nashville to the lab for Brucellosis tests before the sale ended. When at last we climbed back into our truck about four in the afternoon, dirty and exhausted, Eli leaned back. "Who said any publicity is good publicity?"

"In this case he's right."

Eli wore those yellow boots until they literally fell off her feet. She tried to find another pair, but never could. She still has them wrapped in tissue paper in a box in the back of her closet. She says they're like the baboons on Gibraltar. As long as they're there, we will be too.

# Chapter 10

## *In which we meet an extraordinary dog*

Despite the cattle sales and Mike Rasmussen's praise for Jake's miracle cure, we were far from busy our first couple of years in practice.

Small animals came to us in dribs and drabs, but they paid more than their share of our bills. We could see a dozen in the time it took to drive forty miles to somebody's farm to treat a sick cow. And we saved gas in our elderly guzzlers. We thought gasoline cost a fortune, although it was a pittance compared to today.

We gave out our cards at dog and cat shows and at obedience and agility classes. We also schmoozed at the Jack Russell and Dachshund ground races. Little by little we picked up a few dog and cat owners like Mayrene Carteret.

She lived so far out in Fayette County that we were more convenient than vets in suburban Germantown and Collierville. Her rough-haired miniature Dachshund, Snooper, always placed in the go-to-ground races in which the little dogs had to find their way through an underground maze to a caged (and perfectly safe) rat at the end. Eli and I both liked Dachshunds, and Snooper was one cheerful little guy and fast as greased lightning.

I learned in my first year of practice that a veterinarian treats not only the animal, but the owner. For a great many people, their pets are the most important creatures in their lives. There's proof that petting a cat or dog lowers blood pressure. Elderly people who own pets stay healthier longer both in mind and body. Seeing eye and other helper dogs don't simply assist with the physical problems of the disabled, they keep them psychologically healthier as well.

The corollary is that when a beloved pet dies, the owner may simply give up and give in to death or disease.

But nobody wants to watch a beloved creature suffer. We don't always pay attention to quality of life issues in human beings, but we certainly do in the animals we love.

Mayrene carried Snooper into the clinic just before closing time. In the early '70s we wouldn't have thought of making the clinic smoke free. Most of our clients smoked, although Eli and I didn't. Mayrene lit one non-filtered Camel off the end of the last inch of the one she'd been smoking when she brought Snooper in and put him on the examining table without a word. He was always a cheerful little critter, and that day was no exception. Except that he didn't wag his tail. His rear end collapsed.

Unfortunately, long-bodied dogs like bassets and Dachshunds are prone to spinal injuries. In a human being, a disk slips out of place, presses on nerves and causes horrendous pain. When a dog slips a disk, however, ninety-nine times out of a hundred the disk presses *in* on the spinal column. Suddenly and without warning, a perfectly healthy dog's back legs will simply cease to function. The dog often feels no pain, but he can't move his rear end at all.

In many cases surgical fusing or removal of the offending disks can restore movement. Sometimes the disks slip back into place on their own and the dog recovers as suddenly as he went down. The problem, however, will recur. Age and what my grandmother used to call 'the rheumatics' get us all sooner or later.

Plenty of dogs don't ever recover from that first horrendous paralysis.

I asked Dr. Parmenter to come out to assist in the disk surgery. If anybody could fix the problem, he could.

Snooper recovered from surgery beautifully, but showed no sign of regaining the use of his rear end.

After two weeks, Eli and I sat down with Mayrene.

"I can't bear to let him go," Mayrene said. She was no lightweight, and the bell bottomed jeans she wore strained across her tummy and stretched tight across her thighs. She had made a towel nest for Snooper in what little lap she possessed. When she bent over him, her long straight hair fell across him like a black curtain. I could see the light brown roots in the part. I guess she'd been too worried about Snooper to worry about touchups.

"He's pretty young for this to happen," Eli said. She reached over and stroked his long ears.

"There is one thing you could do," I said. "It's not a great solution, but it may be harder for you than for him."

"Who cares about me? I'll do anything—send him to specialists. I don't give a darn how much it costs. I'll take out a loan if I have to."

I shook my head. "Dr. Parmenter's as good as anyone in the world."

"Then..."

"Look at Snooper. He certainly doesn't seem put out by being half a dog, now, does he?"

"I can't stand to see him drag himself along. Don't you dare tell me that's a solution." Mayrene began to cry. "I'd rather you put him down right this minute. It may not hurt *him*, but it sure as shootin' hurts *me*."

"I wasn't suggesting that. There are two companies that make little carts for paralyzed dogs."

"Carts? I'm supposed to roll him around in a cart?"

"Mayrene, listen to me, honey. You buckle Snooper's hind end into his little cart, and the wheels act as his back legs. I'll guarantee you that after he gets used to it, he won't pay the last bit of attention to it."

"I've seen a couple of those things on television for dogs that lost a leg," she said. "I never really believed they could work."

"Works on dogs like Snooper that are paralyzed too, except the legs are still there. They simply don't touch the ground any longer."

She stroked Snooper's ears. "I don't know. Let me think about it."

She thought about it for about twenty minutes, before she agreed to try the cart. We measured Snooper and ordered one that afternoon.

When it arrived, Mayrene carried Snooper into the clinic in her arms. She looked haggard. "I don't know how much more of this I can take," she said. "It's eating me alive watching him."

"Don't give up until we try the cart," Eli said. "Come on, Snooper, old boy, let's see if we can get you mobile."

Snooper fussed about being buckled in, and he kept turning the cart over behind him when he tried to turn, getting himself tangled up and having to be righted. We adjusted and adjusted. Finally, Mayrene said she'd take him home and work with him there. She agreed to bring him back in a week.

I climbed out of my truck the following Monday morning, and Mayrene rolled into the staff parking area right behind me.

"Hey," she said as she opened the door. "I'm early, but I didn't want to take a chance on Snooper going after another dog. He'd take on a Great Dane."

"How's he doing?"

She opened the rear door of her van and grabbed Snooper before he could launch himself, cart and all, out of the car. The minute his forefeet touched the tarmac he trundled toward me. Mayrene clopped behind him. With every step her wooden platform sandals threatened to fall off and dump her onto the pavement. At that point Snooper seemed much better coordinated than his mistress.

"My Lord, Mayrene," I said as I intercepted him, bent over and petted him while the fore portion of him wriggled with pleasure. "This dog belongs on the Nascar circuit."

"Sure does." She turned, trotted to the far side of the parking lot, turned and clapped. "Come on, Snooper, come to Momma."

His little wheels practically burned rubber when he turned and raced across to Mayrene. If anything, he was faster than he'd been before. He certainly didn't seem the least bit put out by having a wheeled vehicle holding up his backside. We both stood there laughing while he did wheelies around us.

"Never tips over now," Mayrene said. "He's figured out just how tight a turn he can make before he winds up in a pickle. Ought to take him to the disco Saturday night. He's a darned sight better dancer than those *Saturday Night Fever* wannabes."

"He's this good in a week?"

"In twenty-four hours." We started toward the clinic. We could hear Snooper's little wheels rolling behind us. "The second day he ran off down the sidewalk. Damned near broke my neck trying to catch him. Thank goodness he's easy to track."

"Because of the noise the wheels make?"

"Lord, no." She looked back and pointed. "I guess he'll never have control of his pee-pee again. Whenever he disappears I just follow the Yellow Brick Road and voila, there's Snooper at the end of it." She shrugged. "I just have to remember to keep him off the carpets."

# Chapter 11

## *In which Eli receives an unusual Christmas present*

Christmas for the young McLains and the young Scheibler usually spiralled out of control. I'm not talking about your garden-variety stress—last minute shopping for the unobtainable toy, battery envy and the like.

Add the problems of the beasts of the field, the aquarium, the aviary, the barn, and the zoo, to human problems.

By our first Christmas, the inside and outside of The Hideous House had been painted off-white. The carpet had been replaced. I picked the color by bringing a handful of west Tennessee dirt from my back pasture to the carpet store and telling the salesman to match it. That way, the mud that we tracked in wouldn't show as much. We had even acquired a cat, known only as That Cat. It liked people, and had probably been dumped by its owners, may they rot in hell. It refused to come inside The Hideous House, but graciously allowed me feed it on the back door step and rub its belly.

In vet school Eli swore that no matter how bad things got she would never live in a house trailer. She was, however, doing precisely that three hundred yards south of The Hideous House and a hundred yards south of the double wide house trailer that was the first incarnation of the McLain-Scheibler Clinic.

All in all, we were well content, despite the fact that we didn't have much money. Morgan made a fair to middling salary at the bank, but it was barely enough to cover our bills for equipment, pharmaceuticals, and general supplies. Eli and I were hard pressed to cover frivolities like food, utilities, telephone and gasoline.

Three days before Christmas Morgan brought home a Charlie

Brown Christmas tree that he swore was being given away by the Boy Scouts. My mother lent us some strings of her old lights, big fat multicolored bulbs that refused to light if even one bulb went out. Morgan swore, but he finally got every light to work.

Eli and I made wreaths out of pine boughs cut on our property, and spent an evening stringing popcorn and cutting out paper stars. My parents even donated a few extra ornaments from their big tree.

God, we were happy.

That year started a tradition we've followed ever since. I am no domestic goddess, but I am what my grandmother called a 'pretty good plain cook,' and I can read a recipe. We splurged on rib roast—the simplest cut of beef to cook. I made roasted veggies and Yorkshire pudding, also extremely simple and practically foolproof. I did make a trifle for desert. Again, simple. Whipping cream is tough to screw up.

Just Eli, Morgan and me, my mother and father and Morgan's father. After a couple of glasses of wine even *he* loosened up.

Morgan and I finished cleaning up the kitchen and climbed into bed around midnight, too tired to make love. Fifteen minutes later the phone rang.

"Not tonight," I wailed as I picked it up, dreading to hear of a horse that was impacted or a cow that couldn't calve.

"Maggie McLain, you get yourself out of that bed and over here right this minute!"

"Eli?" I rubbed my hand across my eyes. "What is it? A burglar? Are you all right?"

"I will expect you in twice no-time." She hung up.

I knew Eli well enough by that time not to ask questions. I dressed and flew across the intervening area, across the parking lot of the clinic, and into Eli's back door. She was standing in the kitchen in an old nightshirt with her hands on her hips.

"You better have a broken leg or something equally dire," I said.

"It's dire, all right." She stepped aside. "Look at your damned cat."

Unlike most American Domestic Shorthaired cats (what most people call alley cats), That Cat talked all the time. I think from the look on her face that the world bewildered her. She was constantly trying to explain it not only to us but to herself.

I disapprove of pet cats being allowed outside—there are too many dangers lurking, but That Cat never ventured inside The Hideous House. From time to time she would pay me for food and tummy rubs by leaving a fat dead mole on the back steps. I managed to get her into a cage long enough to spay her and give her all her shots. She wasn't precisely a pet, but she was the closest thing either Eli or I had. We felt we were too busy at the moment to give a dog or cat the attention it deserved.

That Cat had different ideas. The little tabby huddled beside the hot air register in Eli's trailer. She had something in her paws, and I could hear her purr across the room.

"Why'd she come to you? Is she hurt?" I asked, going to her. "What on earth is that? A dead bird?"

"That," Eli said, "is a newborn puppy. Very much alive. She has obviously stolen it from its mother."

"Oh, good grief." I dropped to my knees. Cat looked up at me, and for the first time, I thought she had figured out the universe in a way that suited her. She looked radiant and incredibly proud of herself. "What are we going to do?"

"Do? You are going to take your cat and its puppy home with you and try to locate the owner."

I sat down. The little critter was obviously hungry. It was scrabbling against Cat's stomach, but of course, Cat had no milk.

"She brought it to *you,* Eli. She obviously doesn't trust me."

"For good reason. You spayed her."

"She doesn't know that." I tried to pick up the pup. That Cat bared her teeth and hissed at me.

"It's her baby," Eli said. "She's not going to give it up without a fight."

"If we don't feed it, it'll be dead by morning. Oh, hell, I'll go get some puppy formula from the clinic." I stood up. "But I am not taking this baby to raise. You are."

As I trotted across the lawn to the clinic, I heard Eli behind me. "I can't raise a dog. Did you see the size of those paws?"

So Christmas morning Eli, Morgan and I tacked up posters about a lost puppy on every utility pole within a five-mile radius. We put ads not only in the *Memphis Commercial Appeal* but into the Fayette County papers as well. We also knocked on the doors of our few neighbors. None would admit to having a new litter, and no one called.

Surely That Cat wouldn't have gone far astray to find her pup. She had to carry it to Eli's, after all, and it was darned near as big as she was. We decided Cat must have discovered a feral dog's late litter and snatched a pup while the mother was away hunting. We were afraid she'd go back for another, but she never did, nor did we ever see signs of a feral dog on our property.

Eli was stuck with the little creature whether she liked it or not.

It was a little male. It grew to be about the size and shagginess of an unclipped Irish Terrier. That Cat never realized it was not a kitten, and I doubt the pup ever caught on either. Of course, he was known as "Son of Cat" shortened to "Son of."

Eli had grown up with her Daddy's hunting dogs, but she'd never actually owned a dog herself. Eli swore Son Of was the best Christmas present she ever got.

Maybe That Cat wasn't so dumb after all.

# Chapter 12

## *In which we discover that even we have limits*

One afternoon in early spring we had a call from a Mrs. Benson, who told us that her Arabian stallion had cut his belly and needed stitches. After I agreed to come out, Eli shook her head. "Bad move."

"Why?"

"I've heard about this Benson woman. She's weird."

"Some people might consider *us* weird."

"I mean it. Why are there so many nut cases breeding Arabians?"

"They don't have a lock on *weird,* Eli. Plenty of sensible people breed sensible Arabians. If you want to come along to help, go get in the truck."

On the way to Mrs. Benson's stable, Eli said, "Beats me how supposedly intelligent people can take a hot-blooded Arabian stallion, spoil him rotten and never bother to teach him any manners, just so they can turn him loose in a show arena and have him act crazier than the other crazy stallions. Then they find a sociopathic mare who hates not only human beings but other horses as well..."

"And because nobody dares ride either the stallion or the mare, what do they do?" I joined in.

"They breed them to each other, of course."

"Then they're stunned when the resulting foal makes Charles Manson look like Mother Theresa." I said. "Real Arab horses aren't crazy. A Bedouin would no more put up with the shenanigans some of these horses get up to than I would if a child of mine started misbehaving."

I said that before I had children. When my own two became teenagers, I realized that a rank Arab stallion was the soul of sweet reasonableness beside your average fifteen-year-old.

"Here we are. Ziggarat Farm."

"Fantastic. That barn looks as though it came straight out of the Arabian nights."

The barn must have cost a fortune. It was some kind of sand-colored fake stone on the outside. Each stall had its own door to its own small paddock. The doors were onion-shaped and surrounded by wood painted in bright Arab designs—or at least I assumed that's what they were. I glanced up and punched Eli. On the roof, instead of the usual running horse weathervane, was a tiny minaret.

"Oh, my God," Eli said. "What does this woman do for a living?"

"Something that makes a bunch of money."

Sylvia Benson ran out of the barn to meet us. She seemed frantic, literally jumping from one foot to the other. Eli and I glanced at one another. Was the poor horse stretched out in his stall with his guts hanging out?

"Please, hurry! Oh, my baby! I can't bear to see him in pain." She actually wrung her hands. We followed her into the shady interior of the barn. Inside, the stalls looked like regular wooden stalls with metal bars on top of them. Apparently either Mrs. Benson had gotten an attack of practicality when she got to the inside, or more likely she'd run out of the gew-gobs of money the outside had taken.

We heard the stallion at the end of the aisle on the right. He was yelling his head off.

Then we saw him.

"He's gorgeous," Eli whispered.

He was pure white with a mane that would hang all the way down to his knees when he stood still. He was, however, not standing still.

He was alternately rearing and striking out with his front legs and kicking with his hind. I didn't see how the heavy 2 x 6's that made up the lower portion of his stall could survive under an onslaught like that for long.

"Sounds like front row at a Stones concert," I whispered.

Mrs. Benson grabbed my arm and dragged me over to his stall. "There! Look! He's wounded! He can't have a scar, he absolutely can't."

He had a doozy of a cut, all right. Halfway back along the underside of his belly a six-inch gash oozed blood much more freely than it would have if he'd simply stood still and given the blood a chance to coagulate.

"He'll definitely need stitches," I said. "How'd he do it?"

"My stupid neighbor two pastures down has a Walking Horse mare in season. Can you believe he had the effrontery to turn her out while Ajax was in his paddock? The nerve of the man."

"I see." I glanced at Eli. The poor man probably wasn't even aware that two pastures away lived a crazy woman with a sex maniac stallion. He had a perfect right to turn his mare out, but I wasn't about to say that to Mrs. Benson.

"Poor Ajax just went mad trying to get to her. He kicked through the fence and got his belly caught on a broken board." She dropped her face into her hands and sobbed.

"Don't worry," I said. "We'll stitch him up clean. When the hair grows back, you'll never see he was ever cut."

"Thank God. A scar would count against him in the show ring."

"Would you halter him, please, then bring him out here into the light where we can see what we've got?" I had no intention of entering that stall nor allowing Eli to. Ajax knew his owner. He was less likely to kick her brains out.

"What?" Mrs. Benson looked stunned. "You want *me* to halter him and bring him out?"

"Yes, Ma'am."

"Can't you do it?"

"He's pretty upset. He needs somebody he trusts. Oh, and you better use your stallion shank just to be on the safe side. Put the chain across his nose."

She stared at me in horror. "Oh, I couldn't do that! It might leave a mark."

I had assumed Mrs. Benson handled her own stallion. Obviously, I was wrong. A surprising number of owners never touch the horses they own. Some, like Mrs. Benson, are afraid of them. They are simply trophies like Georgian silver teapots or old masters. Unlike old masters, however, they are not inanimate. They have feelings and personalities.

"Mrs. Benson," I asked, "who walks Ajax from his stall to his pasture and back again every day?" Surely she had a groom that could handle this little thug even if she couldn't.

"He's only two years old. Manuel just opens the stall door to his paddock and lets him run out on his own."

"He's not halter broke?"

"Of course he is." She sounded affronted. "He wears a halter. Just not often."

"Where's Manuel?"

"Gone for the day."

Eli and I stood silent. After a moment, Mrs. Benson gave up. "Oh, very well. If you refuse to halter him, I will."

She flounced over to an elaborately cast brass hook beside the stallion's door and removed a fancy leather halter set with silver lozenges. She clipped on a long leather lead shank that shone with fresh oil. She gave us a look that would roast meat, squared her shoulders, and opened the stall door. "Come on, Ajax, sweetie, Mommy's here. Holy shit!"

If she'd been a pace slower, he'd have scalped her with those flashing teeth. She jumped back, slid his door closed with a crack, leaned against the wall and panted. "Uh, he's a little upset."

"Oh, hell," I said, "Give me the damn halter." I hadn't been born on a horse, but I'd learned a great deal about them since I started vet school. "Get back, you little gangster. Reach for me with those teeth and you'll be wearing dentures the rest of your life."

The stallion whipped his butt around. I smacked him hard with the lead line. "Don't you dare turn your back on me."

He was too stunned by the discipline even to kick, although I was poised to avoid his hind feet if he tried. He wheeled to face me. A moment later, I had the lead line around his neck and the halter over his ears. I ran the long chain shank through the halter ring, across his nose, and yanked down hard.

"Don't!" Mrs. Benson screamed.

The stallion was obviously intelligent. He recognized *force majeur*, and like a badly behaved toddler who longs for discipline, he quieted instantly.

I dragged him forward. He strained back. I held the line taut. He took a step. I released the line. After four steps he understood that the line only pulled when he didn't come at my request. He moved with me more or less willingly into the center aisle.

"Here," I said and handed the shank to Eli. At that point neither of us trusted Mrs. Benson. "Keep this taut while I shoot some tranquilizer into him to settle him down."

"Tranquilizer?" Mrs. Benson might have used the same tone had I suggested cyanide.

At the moment, I would have liked to use cyanide. On Mrs. Benson, not the stallion.

"You mustn't tranquilize him. We never allow harmful drugs of any kind to enter our horses' systems."

"You're kidding, right?" Eli asked. "He needs antibiotics as well as tranquilizer." Ajax swung his head and nearly knocked her off her feet. She yanked. "No, you don't."

"For pity's sake, stitch him up right now. Can't you see, he's still bleeding."

I ran my hand gently down his flank. He was shivering with fear and pain. He had never learned to trust or rely on anyone, except possibly Manuel. He definitely didn't trust Mrs. Benson, but then, who would?

As my forehead came about even with his groin, he reared and pawed. I sat down hard, and scrambled quickly to my feet.

His front hooves narrowly missed Eli's head. She hung on gamely and hauled him back down to earth.

Mrs. Benson had fled to the far end of the barn. I talked to Ajax and stroked him until he calmed down a bit, as Mrs. Benson sidled back. She was poised to run at the first sign of trouble.

"It's obvious what your problem is," Mrs. Benson said indignantly. "Ajax doesn't *like* you."

Eli and I gaped at her. Then we looked at one another and nodded.

I took the lead shank from Eli and handed it to Mrs. Benson. "Come on." Eli and I walked toward the front of the barn.

"Wait! Aren't you going to stitch his cut?"

Ajax was now dragging Mrs. Benson after him, following us. He probably thought we were the only sane people he'd ever met in his young life.

"Stop, please!"

"Ma'am." I turned to face her and held my hand up so that Ajax could see it. He stopped. "You have several choices. The only way either of us is going near that cut is if Ajax there is so stoned on tranquilizers that we can lay him flat out in the aisle and tie his legs up so he can't kick even if he tries."

"But…"

"Second option. Call your regular vet."

She refused to meet my eyes. "Rodney was busy. He gave me your number."

Oh, really. I didn't blame Rodney for fobbing Mrs. Benson off on us—well, I didn't blame him *much*. "Mrs. Benson, only a lunatic would try to dig a suture needle into that son of a bitch's belly without tranquilizers and topical anesthetic."

Mrs. Benson opened her mouth to protest. Ajax swung his hind end and tossed her against the wall. She yelped and skittered away.

"Third option," I continued. "Do nothing. The way he's thrashing around, by morning he will literally be wearing his guts for garters. Now, which will it be?"

"Well!" she huffed. "I wouldn't call your attitude professional."

"Neither of us is a professional *suicide*. Take your pick."

"Oh, very well." Ajax yanked her arm nearly out of its socket. "Shit. Take this thing," she said, and handed the line to Eli.

"Fine." He pulled. Eli pulled back. He relaxed enough for me to get a needle full of tranquilizer into him. We walked him back to his stall and waited until he sank onto his side. We supported his body with bales of hay. Then I cleaned and sutured the cut. It was a lovely job.

Mrs. Benson watched from the other side of the stall door in safety. "I must admit, doctor, you do beautiful work," she said. Once she had accepted the inevitable, she calmed down nearly as much as the horse. If I had been her people doctor, I would have prescribed Valium in a heartbeat.

We stayed with Ajax until he threw off the tranquilizer and struggled groggily to his feet. He leaned his beautiful white head on my shoulder for twenty minutes, until I felt safe in leading him up and down the barn aisle to get his feet back under him.

"Are you sure he won't have a scar?" Sylvia Benson asked. She kept a safe distance from her horse, although he was too zonked out to pose much risk.

"I do *not* leave scars." We put him back into his stall, left him to sleep off his tranquilizer, picked up our things and walked out to the truck.

While Eli stowed the gear, I leaned out the driver's door and said to Mrs. Benson, "Let me give you some free professional advice. At the moment that horse is a menace to you, himself, your grooms, other horses, and the entire western world. It's not his fault. It's *yours*. You're terrified of him, but you won't teach him manners. He's spoiled and rank, but he's intelligent and still young enough to understand and accept discipline. Send him to a conscientious professional trainer. If you don't, the first time you try to breed him, he'll hurt his handlers and savage his mare. Worst case scenario, he'll wind up killing somebody and you'll have to put him down. And if you decide not to breed him, for his sake and yours, geld him." I left her sputtering.

"Well," I told Eli. "Cross Mrs. Benson off the client list."

"She'll never call us back after that diatribe," Eli said.

"God, I hope not. That poor horse. Maybe I scared some sense into the woman. I wouldn't go near her again to pay off the mortgage on the clinic."

Hah. After the stallion recovered, the woman called us every time one of her babies had so much as a sniffle. Of course we went. Over the years we even convinced her that the word "drug" didn't pertain exclusively to raw opium straight from the pusher.

Six months later she gelded Ajax and sent him to a good trainer—a real horse whisperer. The teenager who bought him from the trainer rode him to plenty of championships.

Maybe I saved his life that day. I'm sure I saved his sanity.

# Chapter 13

## *In which Maggie discovers for the second time that life changes aren't convenient*

The first time I threw up I decided I was reacting to the fresh paint in the bedroom of The Hideous House. The second time, I thought I was reacting to the chemicals in the examining room. The third time, I decided I had the flu. Eli said my temperature was normal, but sent me home to bed while she handled the afternoon small animal clinic alone. Not much of a stretch. We were still struggling. We'd been open less than a year.

I perked up in time to fix dinner for Morgan. I put on an Italian pork loin with plenty of garlic and rosemary and oregano. Again, a very simple recipe. After all that throwing up I felt as though I'd starved for a month. I planned to eat at least half that roast by myself.

One minute the kitchen smelled like heaven. The next I was clinging to the toilet bowl like a teenager after a doobie and a fifth of whiskey.

I was certain I'd be fine by morning, and I was. Fine, that is, until I started for the kitchen and smelled the fresh coffee Morgan had put on. I barely made it back to our bathroom.

Morgan always acted as though my relatively minor and infrequent illnesses were a personal affront to him. My family doctor had retired, and I hadn't bothered to find another since my pre-marital exam. We really hadn't needed medical attention since we'd been married. Whatever I had, I assumed I'd get over in due time without medical intervention.

Over my protests, Eli cancelled the morning's appointments and drove me to Moscow to a GP she'd found in the Yellow Pages. She had to stop once so that I could upchuck by the side of the road.

Dr. Wheeler was a general practitioner of the old school. I had never met him before, but Eli had talked to him at several cattle sales. He raised Herefords on his family's land near Middleton as a hobby. She said he came across as one of those tough old coots, but it was an act. He was really a pussycat.

He was four inches shorter than my five ten, about the same weight as I was then and almost totally bald. Mr. Clean with a paunch. He had warm hazel eyes and an engaging smile. I had glanced at the diplomas in his waiting room. He might be a country doctor, but he'd gone to med school at Johns Hopkins and was a diplomate in OB-Gyn and rheumatology. Maybe other things as well. I didn't get around to the other walls of the waiting room before his nurse set me up in an examining room.

He and his nurse did all the usual blood and urine tests and left me lying on the table for what seemed an eternity.

When they walked back in, I sat up so quickly I felt dizzy for a moment.

"I'm fine," I said. "I haven't thrown up for an hour. I must be getting over it."

"Nope. Don't think so." He picked up my chart. "Put your clothes on and come on in my office at the end of the hall. We need to talk."

I could feel the adrenaline rush. Something I caught from the animals? Tetanus? What were the symptoms of rabies anyway?

When I slunk into the chair in front of his desk, he leaned back and templed his fingers.

"You're one of those intellectual woman, aren't you?"

"What?"

"Smart as a whip. Lots of book learning."

"What's wrong with that?"

"Not a darned thing, but sometimes you need to toss out the books and listen to your instincts. When the time comes, I don't plan to do much except catch."

"What?"

He leaned forward and patted my hand. "Girl, you are six weeks' pregnant. Enceinte. Gravid. With child."

I couldn't have been more surprised if he'd slapped me. "That's ridiculous."

"When did you have your last period?"

"I don't really..."

"Weren't you suspicious? Wasn't your husband? I always know when Nancy is a week late."

"We use birth control. I don't keep track."

"Not but one foolproof method of birth control. Abstinence ain't a whole bunch of fun."

Morgan and I definitely had not been practicing abstinence. I had a diaphragm. It came in a little blue plastic zipper case, and I loathed it. The thing acted like a greased pig. Just about the time Morgan was ready to go from foreplay to play, I would have to get up, go into the bathroom, pull out the diaphragm, stretch it over the prongs of its applicator, fill it with gooey stuff, and insert it. Half the time it sproinged and stuck on the ceiling over the toilet. I'd hear Morgan's lustful entreaties while I was trying to peel the thing off.

But we had been faithful about using it. We had agreed we couldn't possibly afford a baby yet.

"I don't intend to have a baby for three or four years," I said.

"Not a good time?"

"An impossible time. You must be wrong."

"Honey, Nancy and me had our first when I was an intern. Worst possible time, but we managed. If men and women waited until the right time to have a baby, this old earth would have been empty of human beings by the second generation after Adam and Eve. It may not be convenient," he said, and pointed at my stomach, "But it's there."

I sat and stared at him. How could I tell Morgan? Worse still, how could I tell Eli? Before long I'd be Maggie the Elephant. She was already shouldering more than her share of the large animal work. Now she'd have to look after even more. "How long can I keep working?"

"Honey, strong as you are, you can drop that baby at the end of the row and finish the plowing." He leaned forward. "Seriously, you'll know when it's time to cut back."

"But I'm already exhausted from all this barfing."

"That goes away after three months or so."

"Three months?" I wailed. I was an only child with no girl cousins and no aunts. By the time my college buddies started having babies, I was hip deep in cow manure. I could detail the process of gestation in a hundred sorts of animals, but I didn't figure I needed to know all that much about human beings.

"Yep. It's natural to be tired all the time too. You need to stretch out like an old momma cat in the sun every chance you get."

"I don't have time to stretch anywhere. This is horrible."

His face went serious. "No, it is a miracle. It's a miracle you see at least as often as I do. You ever think a newborn foal is horrible? Or a calf? Or a kitten?"

"No, but..."

"Honey, you got a new life growing in you, and it's not going to appreciate all that stomach acid you're churning out."

A new life. There's a quote from a Broadway musical about "a whole new person suddenly is that never has been before." I'd always thought it a charming sentiment. Suddenly the full force of the words hit me right between the eyes. A total stranger was growing inside me.

I listened to his rules and regulations, took the folder of stuff for new mothers-to-be, made an appointment for a month hence, and took a paper sack full of vitamin bottles with me.

When I walked out into the waiting room again, Eli stood up and came toward me with her hands outstretched. "Maggie, honey, what is it? You look like hell." She followed me out to the truck and helped me in as though I were an invalid. When she climbed in to the driver's side, I put my face in my hands. "Oh, Eli, I am so sorry. I'm pregnant."

"Say what?"

"I know, I know. Isn't it awful?"

"Awful?" She grabbed me, swung me around and hugged me. "Awful! You idiot, it's wonderful! We're having a *baby*! Morgan is going to have kittens."

"But the practice..."

"We'll manage. I'd go get a bottle of champagne."

I worried all the way home while Eli babbled happily about what colors to paint the baby's room, and how delighted my parents would be.

"I'll bet it's a boy," she chortled.

I hadn't gotten that far. Had never babysat as a teenager. All I knew about babies was that they screamed and pooped a lot. And never slept and ate all the time and seriously encroached on your freedom.

I knew a few things about girls, being one myself. I knew nothing about boys. Who would it be? Would it like me? Would I like it?

Would I live up to my duties?

"Maggie, honey," Eli said as she pulled up to my front door. "You're not in this alone. Stop worrying. You have Morgan and me and your parents. You always think everything is your sole responsibility. It's not. Smart as we are, we ought to be able to raise one baby."

Morgan had demanded I call him at the bank the minute I got home from the doctor's office to tell him what was wrong with me. I didn't.

When he called me I hemmed and hawed so badly he probably thought I'd come down with acute leukemia. When he came roaring in an hour later, he found me asleep on the couch in the living room.

"Maggie," he whispered as he sat on the couch beside me. He put the back of his hand against my forehead. "You feel cool. Did the doctor give you antibiotics?"

I sat up and clung to him. "Drugs won't help."

I felt him tense. "Maggie, what is it?"

"I'm going to have a baby."

He sat perfectly still for a long moment, than he said quietly, "Well, you didn't do it alone." Then he whooped, dragged me up, spun me around and only stopped when I threatened to throw up on his nice navy banker's suit.

"Why is everybody acting so cheerful about this?" I asked.

"Because it's joyful."

"It's more work for Eli, less money coming in just when we need more. And once it gets here, it's twenty some-odd years of responsibility for a total stranger."

"Maggie, you said you wanted children."

"But not now!" I bolted for the bathroom.

That night I fell into bed exhausted before eight o'clock. Morgan and Eli were both sworn to secrecy. I refused to tell my parents or his father. Birth equated to complete lack of control over one's body, and what if I sucked as a parent?

I woke before dawn, crawled out of bed expecting to start my morning barf, but actually made it into the kitchen to start the coffee without feeling as though I was on the Titanic as it rounded Cape Horn in a gale.

The morning was clear and warm and tender. With no warning, I felt a startling rush of love for this creature inside me. My knees went so weak I had to sit down at the kitchen table.

Somehow we would manage. Other people did it. If I was a lousy mother, both Eli and Morgan would take up the slack so this child probably would not turn out to be a psychopath.

Up to that point, I had not touched my stomach. Now I sat on the couch and patted my belly. It was still flat, although I realized that for a couple of weeks I had fastened my jeans with difficulty. Nobody ever tells you that you lose your waistline way before you begin to pooch out in front.

"Okay, kiddo," I whispered. "We're in this together."

Dr. Wheeler saw no sense in ultasounds without a good reason, so we didn't know which sex the baby would be. Over the next months I decided the kid was punishing me for my lack of initial enthusiasm. You name it, I got it. I was exhausted and headachy. I cried if you looked at me cross-eyed. I barfed and had gas and swollen ankles.

I also ate everything that was not actually nailed to the floor. When I finally told my mother, she said I was 'blooming.' I was actually *ball*ooning.

I kept working full shifts and taking my share of night calls, although both Eli and Morgan tried to dissuade me.

Patsy gave me a baby shower. The baby would have enough stuff for an English princess.

I wore men's extra-large lab coats because we couldn't find any actually made for pregnant women. The military had only recently come to terms with creating uniforms for pregnant soldiers. Most maternity clothes were made either for stay-at-home moms or for corporate lawyers who could afford to spend a fortune on outfits they would wear for only a few months. Maternity shops did not cater to pregnant women who wrestled sheep.

One night in my fifth month Morgan took Eli and me out to dinner at an inexpensive restaurant. When I went to the ladies' room, I discovered that I had spotted.

That was the moment when I realized how much I wanted to meet this little person, this baby. Not *some* baby, but this particular one. I didn't think I could endure a miscarriage.

The spotting stopped spontaneously and never occurred again, but after that I tried to rest more. For a little while, anyway, until I stopped being scared.

Dr. Wheeler told me that first babies are generally late and take a long time to be born after labor starts. At eight and a half months, he told me that I wouldn't have the baby for at least three weeks.

Good thing. We were a week away from Christmas. Having been

born in January myself, I knew that a child born close to Christmas was shorted on presents. One actually born on Christmas day would be short-changed even more. Besides, I had plans for this Christmas that did not include labor and delivery. I wasn't anxious to plunge into a job I knew nothing about and was afraid I couldn't do.

I've seen enough momma animals to know about the nesting instinct and that burst of energy and euphoria that precedes labor. Dr. Wheeler didn't mention that it happens to human mothers as well, and I was too dumb to notice that, all of a sudden, I felt as though I could lick my weight in wildcats. Morgan never ate such fancy dinners before. I tried new recipes nearly every night.

My cabinets were never cleaner. My lab notes were never before so complete. Our first year in The Hideous House we'd decorated a pitiful tree. This year I bought ornaments we couldn't afford and struggled to make not only a wreath for the front door but a pine garland for the fireplace.

Christmas was on Tuesday that year, so Eli was at the Monday cattle sale when Patsy called. "I just sold a filly," Patsy said without preamble. "It's a Christmas present for a kid. You up to doing a pre-purchase exam this morning? Nothing fancy. No x-rays."

"Sure."

"I'll fix you lunch afterwards."

"You're on. I've got one cat with ear mites, and then I'll be out to your place."

By that time we had hired a lovely grandmotherly lady named Mildred to look after the office. I told her where I was off to and promised to check in regularly. Then I waddled my fat body out to the truck.

Hoisting myself into it had become a major chore. I had to turn around backwards, slide my rump onto the driver's seat, hold onto the steering wheel and swing my legs up and around. The driver's seat had been pushed back to the maximum. If the kid grew much more I'd have replace the seat with a kitchen chair the way I'd seen some of the farmers do.

I had worn black slacks, the only ones I could still fit in even with the belly cut out, and my Paul Bunyan size lab coat. When I climbed out of the truck, Patsy walked out of the stable and said, "My Lord, it's Moby Dick."

I did not laugh.

The filly was a three-year-old Arabian, a lovely chestnut. "She's a good, quiet girl," Patsy said.

"I know you wouldn't let me near a spooky horse, Patsy," I said.

"Hardly." She raised her eyebrows at my belly.

The filly passed her exam with flying colors, so I drew blood for an EIA test and walked out to the truck to put it into the box to send to the laboratory.

As I leaned over, Patsy put her hand on my shoulder. "Um, Maggie, I hope you have another pair of slacks with you."

"What?"

"You've wet your britches."

"I have not," I said indignantly. "Don't you think I'd feel...Uh oh. I think my water's broken."

Patsy's hand flew to her mouth. "You said you had three weeks."

"Dammit, I do. Or I did." The sense of unreality overwhelmed me. Patsy took care of calling Dr. Wheeler. I refused to let her call either Eli or Morgan. First baby—no rush, right? I refused to have this baby until at least the day after Christmas.

When I told Patsy that, she just looked at me and shook her head. "Two and a half days in labor? No doctor in his right mind would allow that."

No woman in her right mind would want to do it. "Okay. Christmas Eve is better than Christmas."

I wanted to drive myself to the hospital, but Patsy wouldn't let me. It took more than an hour to drive from her place to the hospital in Somerville where Dr. Wheeler examined me.

I had still not effaced or whatever they call it. "Kid's crossways. Hasn't dropped into the birth canal yet," he said.

He gave me a POP shot to increase the contractions. Oh, lovely. "May have to do a Cesarean," he said and walked out. "See you in a few minutes."

Two minutes later a black LPN walked into my room. She stood by my bed and put an enormous hand on my belly. "Dr. Wheeler's a fine doctor," she said and sniffed. "For a man."

"Ow!" I replied.

"Ain't nobody never tole you havin' a baby hurts?"

"Not like this."

"Now, you listen to me, girl. You don't want no Cesarean. You got to turn that baby."

"I beg your pardon?"

"You do like I say. You get yourself up on your hands and knees and you start to rockin' that baby."

"I think I'll wait for Dr. Wheeler, thank you."

"Hush. I got me four boys and six girls and all but one of them breech. I turned every last one of them. Now roll over."

Anything to get this crazy woman out of my room. I rolled, although my belly barely cleared the mattress. With her instruction, I began to rock back and forth. She rubbed my back, and after a minute, I realized she was humming. "Go down Moses," it was. I'll never forget it. She hummed it over and over. I swear she hypnotized me. The pains didn't seem to come so sharp or so often.

I have no idea how long I kept it up because time seemed to collapse on itself.

I heard the door open, and Dr. Wheeler's voice. "Well, Taisie, I see you got her turning that baby. Let's us see how far she's got."

My decision to go natural—no epidural—suddenly seemed the dumbest decision I had ever made. And where the hell was Morgan? Patsy told me she'd call him and Eli whether I liked it or not. This was all Morgan's fault. When he showed up I planned to rise up off this bed and strangle him with my bare hands.

Dr. Wheeler and Taisie helped turn me back over. I felt like a turtle on its shell with all four feet in the air.

Dr. Wheeler looked between my legs. "Whoo-ee! Taisie, help me get her on the gurney or she's gonna have this baby right in this bed."

"Cesarian?" I managed to enunciate.

"Baby's right side up now," he said.

Taisie said. "Didn't I say, child?"

I've been told that some mothers take hours, days, even weeks to bond with their children. Some never do. I certainly had never expected to feel anything except exhaustion when they laid Sarah Elizabeth McLain on my belly thirty minutes later.

My first thought was that I wouldn't have to teach a boy to stand up to pee.

Then I felt a great rope of love as thick as a hawser holding her against my heart. I might not be the world's best mother to this little mite, but I intended to give it my best shot.

# Chapter 14

## *In which Maggie has another Christmas baby*

Two years later, I was pregnant again and expecting another Christmas baby. This time we did an ultrasound, and it came up a boy.

Nathan-to-be was two weeks from his due date. I could barely see past my belly. I had carried Sarah all over. Nathan sat in a tight ball right in front of my navel.

Except when he heard music. I finally had to stop playing the radio in my truck on my way to calls. The instant the radio came on, whether to PBS classical, jazz, rock or country, Nathan started doing the Conga. One, two, three *kick*!

It's hard to keep a truck on the road when your belly keeps trying to knock the steering wheel out from under you.

This would be the first Christmas Sarah would actually be a little girl instead of a baby, and all of us were looking forward to watching her face the first time she saw what Santa had left her under the tree.

I should have known better than to count on anything where Christmas was concerned.

I did not want another Christmas baby. This time, however, Dr. Wheeler warned me that Nathan could come any time. I had effaced, I was starting to dilate, and the baby was in position to be born normally, unlike Sarah. Since Nathan was the second baby, I could expect labor to be much shorter. Much less time to get to the hospital. I planned to leave for the hospital at the first sign of labor.

Christmas Eve is usually a dull time for vets. The pre-purchase exams on the new horses and ponies that will be Christmas presents for children and grandchildren have been completed. The Christmas puppies and kittens won't come in for their first shots until a couple of days after Christmas. Most cows aren't calving yet, and no foals are scheduled to be born for several weeks.

Our traditional Christmas Eve dinner was a success, although we missed Morgan's dad, who had died of a massive stroke the previous September.

Even little Sarah enjoyed the party. Morgan removed her the minute she started getting fussy, so the adults could have a pleasant evening, despite her grandmother Minnatrey's pleas that she be allowed to stay. My idea of a company dinner did not include a two-year-old who felt she must kill her roast beef before it was safe to eat and drew pictures with her mashed potatoes.

I had been nesting for several days. This time I realized what was happening the minute I started scrubbing out the kitchen cabinets. Thus I wasn't completely surprised when I started labor as we were finishing our coffee and trifle. Not surprised, but really annoyed.

My mother caught on immediately. She took one look at my grimace and asked, "Margaret? Is it the baby?"

The woman still called me Margaret.

I puffed for twenty seconds. "It sure as shootin' something."

"How close?" Eli asked.

"Who the hell knows?" I snarled. Labor tended to have that effect on me.

"Minatrey," Morgan asked my mother, "Could you and Will stay here with Sarah while I take Maggie to the hospital?"

"Of course, dear. What are grandparents for? You go on. I'll call the doctor."

"Want me to come?" Eli asked.

"Absolutely," Morgan said before I could answer. "You sit in the middle and keep Maggie from clocking me on the jaw."

I sniffled and wailed all the way to the hospital. "I don't want another Christmas baby. Send it back."

"Maggie," Eli said. "Shut up unless you can say something sensible. You're not drugged yet."

At that time a few doctors were beginning to let fathers and friends come into the labor area with the mother. My doctor wasn't one of them. I was wheeled off alone and left lying on a gurney in the corridor of the hospital and completely ignored.

Finally, I lost it. I swung my legs over the side of the gurney and stood up. I wore only socks. My feet slid out from under me, the gurney starting sliding the other direction, and only the intercession of a massive orderly kept me from hitting my tailbone on the tile floor.

"Get my doctor," I snapped without even thanking him. "Hell, get me somebody!"

"It's all right, Mother," he said soothingly.

"Damnation, I am not your mother, but I am one step away from throwing the mother of all hissy fits. Get me a nurse."

He took one look at my face and backed off.

Before the nurse could get down the hall to the crazy woman, my doctor finally showed up. It was now one-twenty on Christmas morning. I did not wish good will to all peoples. As a matter of fact, I couldn't think of one single person to whom I wished even an iota, a soupcon of good will.

They hooked me up to monitors and left me again. Eventually, the nurse came in. "You're not in labor, Mother," she said in an accusing tone.

"Well, what the hell am I in?"

"You are having Braxton Hicks contractions. Not all that unusual in a second pregnancy. You may have them off and on until the onset of *real* labor."

"And I tell the difference how?" They felt like labor to *me*.

She smiled at me. "If they stop, they're Braxton Hicks. If the baby arrives, you'll know, won't you, Mother?"

She turned to the door. "Oh, you can go home."

"Where's my doctor?"

"He left an hour ago."

Damn.

"Merry Christmas," she said, and pushed through the door.

False dawn was lightening the east by the time we rolled into the driveway at the clinic and dropped Eli off at her house. I was still simmering. "Braxton Hicks," I snapped. "Horses don't have Braxton Hicks. And it only takes them twenty minutes to have a foal."

"Calm down, Maggie," Morgan said.

"You can say that. Christmas or not, I've decided I want this baby *out*."

My mother and father were waiting. Morgan had called them with updates, so they knew no baby was imminent. My mother put me to bed as tenderly as she had when I was Sarah's age and told me not to get up until I woke up on my own.

That's when we heard Sarah from her crib. I staggered out of bed and followed her downstairs to see her Santa presents, but I don't think I was sufficiently joyful. She swears she still remembers how disappointed she was in me. I think that was the first time I disappointed her. I've been disappointing her ever since.

Nathan was born without incident the day after Christmas. When I brought him home, Sarah took one look at him, said "Yuckie," and demanded to move in with her grandparents.

# Chapter 15

## *In which a very small dog saves the day*

One afternoon in early March, however, Dr. Parmenter called me. "Maggie," he said, "I have a problem."

To admit a problem must have cost him. To admit it to *me* must have cost him dearly. I glowed to think he trusted me to that extent.

The glow faded quickly as he continued. "Elvira Sanderson's Irish Wolfhound Gladys is in the process of delivering a damned sight more pups than she has any business having."

He didn't need to say anything else. I had helped one of Elvira's bitches deliver three pups several years earlier while I was still working with Dr. Parmenter. We nearly lost her that time, although we managed to save all the puppies.

"Even if I can manage to get all eight of them to breathe," Dr. Parmenter said, "And even if I could manage to bottle feed some of them, they won't be socialized properly."

"How can I help?"'

"Find me a wet nurse and come get at least two of these pups tonight."

Right. Just like that.

"I don't..."

"Doctor," he said. That meant he was dead serious. "You have two packs of foxhounds in your neck of the woods plus at least two packs of rabbit beagles. Somewhere in all that crowd you should be able to find a bitch to raise these puppies. Now do it."

He hung up before I could say a word. I yelled at Eli to come into my office, and the minute she got there I unloaded. "What does the man think I am? A miracle worker? Even if I can find a bitch who's just whelped, she probably won't accept those puppies."

"Uh-huh."

"Besides, it's too early in the year. The hound packs aren't whelping yet."

"Better start calling. I'll handle Three Oaks Hunt—Jack Foster's the huntsman. I know him from the cattle sales. You call Pete Dimwitty. He's the whip for the Money Market Hunt."

Unlike hunts in Great Britain, American foxhunts never kill anything except by accident. The people and hounds chase either fox or coyote until the prey get tired of the game, then everybody goes back home to eat and drink and boast. The coyotes and fox seem to enjoy the sport nearly as much as the riders and hounds. The huntsman is the guy who handles hounds—not 'the' hounds, by the way. A 'whip' is one of the hunt staff who rides along with hounds to keep them in order. And hounds are counted not as individuals but as couples. If you have twenty hounds, you have ten couple of hounds. I have no idea why. If hounds should chase after anything other than a fox or coyote—a deer, for instance, then they are "running riot." Interesting the way hunting terms have made their way into general usage.

Unfortunately, when Eli and I finally spoke to both huntsman and whip, they had no bitches that might foster a pair of newborns.

Jack Foster, however, had a suggestion. "There's a woman named Helen Weatherbee out past LaGrange that raises beagles. I think she has a fair-sized kennel, although hers are mostly show dogs, not rabbit dogs. You might try her." He gave us her number.

Although she was not a client of ours, and we had never met her, Eli and I both knew her by reputation. Small hunting breeds like beagles lend themselves to puppy mills, but Weatherbee's Kennel was noted for producing well-bred dogs that went only to a few carefully selected homes.

Weatherbee's was just past LaGrange, twenty miles farther east into Fayette County from the McLain-Scheibler Clinic. It was at least fifty miles from Dr. Parmenter's clinic in Midtown Memphis.

LaGrange, a charming old cotton town, escaped being burned by General Grant as he retreated from the battle of Shiloh. The story is that they bribed the soldiers in charge of the arson.

Many of the mansions in the village were built before 1860, and until recently were falling into decay. Lately, however, a number of FedEx pilots had bought and restored them with fresh white paint and dark green shutters. Banks of azaleas ranging from bright orange to palest pink rioted in the spring gardens. The town was once more becoming an ante-bellum gem. I loved driving through it.

After half a dozen tries, I finally got Mrs. Weatherbee on the telephone and explained Dr. Parmenter's problem. I didn't have much hope she could help us.

"Honey," she said in a voice nearly as deep as Patsy Dalrymple's. "You have called at the pure-D perfect time. Champion Weatherbee's Jenny Lind delivered last night. Only had one pup."

That was unusual. Beagles generally have large litters.

"And that one faded. Lost him this morning. Poor little Jenny is just miserable. She keeps hunting for him and crying her little heart out. She's dripping with milk."

"Thank you, Jesus," I whispered the minute I hung up. "Come on, Eli, get some towels and fill a hot water bottle. We're off to Memphis."

"You think a beagle can foster Woofies?" Eli asked as we drove through the early evening toward Dr. Parmenter's. "She'll take one look at them and know darned well she couldn't have produced anything that big."

"Newborn puppies don't look that much different breed to breed."

"They sure won't stay the same long."

She was right about that. Irish Wolfhounds, or IW's as their breeders like to call them, are the tallest domesticated dog, although some Mastiffs outweigh them and Great Danes are nearly as tall.

Despite their giant size, they are kind, gentle, good-natured dogs who make wonderful pets except that they break your heart by refusing to stick around and let you love them for years and years. Your average Jack Russell terrier can live to fifteen or sixteen. Your average Irish Wolfhound will be lucky to see seven.

They also present some unique problems as house pets. They can sweep a coffee table clean with one tail swish. Standing up to check the pots on the stove poses no problem. Neither does turning over a pot of boiling stew onto their heads.

Even pet quality Irish Wolfhound puppies could cost over a thousand dollars. Show quality dogs jumped up sharply from there, but a prospective owner with all the money in the world might be turned down by a breeder. They were extremely picky about the homes and the human beings that took their pups.

Waiting lists for puppies were common, so every healthy pup

represented not only a great deal of money to Elvira, but a new puppy to a prospective owner who might have been on the list for a long time.

When Eli and I walked into Dr. Parmenter's clinic, he stuck his head out of the whelping room, looked over his glasses at us, and said, "About time."

I glanced at Eli. She merely grinned in return.

"She's had all eight," Dr. Parmenter said. "These are the last two. Take them and make sure they live." He handed me the pups. I gave them to Eli who wrapped them in towels and snuggled them against the hot water bottle.

"Well, what are you waiting for?" he asked. "Shoo. Go. Call me tomorrow morning."

We shooed. I settled Eli with the pups warm in her lap with the hot water bottle, and started the fifty-mile trip to the far side of LaGrange. I didn't even bother to grumble. I ought to be used to the man by now.

Eli ran her index finger over one of the small gray heads. "I hope Champion Weatherbee's Jenny Lind is near-sighted."

"I hope she's maternal. Those two can't fight back if she snaps at them."

Eli knew how I rescued Mother's Bear. "We could only save one of the pups that night," I said. "With luck, maybe this time we can save them both."

"Has Dr. Parmenter always been that grumpy?" Eli asked.

"He's not grumpy. He's like Dr. Wheeler. Gruff, but a sweety at heart. Look what all he's done for me. I'll never be able to pay him back."

"Can't you drive this thing any faster?" Eli asked. "Shoot! I don't need you in my armpit, you little squirmer."

"I'm breaking the speed limit now."

"You always break the speed limit. This hot water bottle is barely tepid. We should have refilled it at Dr. Parmenter's."

"Who had time? Put the pups inside your shirt."

"That's where they've wound up anyway." She looked up. "Maggie, I think that was the turn."

It was. By the time I'd found a driveway to turn around in to retrace our steps, we'd wasted ten minutes. By now the night was dark and moonless. I turned the heater up to high while Eli snuggled those pups inside her shirt and close to her heart.

We nearly drove past the small sign for Weatherbee Kennels. I backed up and drove up the rutted driveway in the pitch black dark until we turned a ninety-degree corner and saw the long, low house ablaze with light.

The moment we stepped out of the truck we heard a chorus of barks and yips from half a dozen beagles in the kennels beside the house.

Instantly the front door of the house opened and a lean shape stood silhouetted in the light. She looked to be taller than I am and a darned sight thinner.

"Come on in here with those babies," she said in a husky voice. "Y'all made good time." We could barely hear her over the beagles.

She stepped aside and led us down a narrow hall to her kitchen. "Don't need an alarm system," she laughed. "Got my own and then some." She stood over a badly scarred but obviously antique butcher-block table in the middle of her kitchen. "Now, let me have those babies."

Eli shot a glance at me. We were about to lose control of this situation. Not unusual. Breeders frequently think they know more than the vets. When it comes to whelping problems, they often do.

At that moment I felt my hair stand on end. The wail that came from the den sounded human.

"That's Jenny. She's so full of milk. I'm sure she's in a lot of pain. Now y'all just leave this to me," she said. "When you called, I went and got the dead puppy." She took a shoebox off the kitchen counter and tenderly unwrapped the dead pup from its towel. "I figured if we rub this pup all over these babies, maybe we can convince Jenny. She ate the afterbirth, so I don't have that to use." She turned to her refrigerator. "I did get some milk from her to rub all over them as well."

We worked with both puppies until we had them covered with scent and their little faces white with Jenny's milk. They were obviously ravenous.

"Keep your fingers crossed," Helen said as she took the two pups into the den and knelt beside Jenny's whelping box.

Beagles come in twelve and fourteen inch sizes. Jenny was fourteen inches tall and obviously deserved her championship in the show ring. She was a perfectly marked tri-color with eyes that would melt your heart.

We let Helen manipulate the pups for Jenny to see and sniff.

After only five minutes we felt safe in putting them down into the nest Jenny had made for the baby that had not survived.

For a long moment, I thought we'd failed. She stood over them with the hair raised along her spine. We held our breath, and Eli and I shifted back on our bottoms so that Helen's face was the only one Jenny could see.

A moment later we heard a small thud. A moment after that Helen gave us a thumbs-up sign. Eli and I slid back to peer over the rim of the box. Jenny lay with her spine pressed against the side of her box and her tummy exposed. The babies were working away at her teats with their little paws kneading in time to their slurps.

I called Dr. Parmenter at once. "Mission accomplished. Although God knows what mother and pups will make of one another in two months."

A month later when Helen brought mother and babies in for their first baby shots, the pups were already more than half as large as their mother. Jenny waddled over to lick my hand with both pups hanging off her like Romulus and Remus from their wolf mother in that Roman statue. She could barely walk.

I caught her looking at them quizzically a time or two, as though wondering if she could have forgotten a close encounter with some kind of giant canine alien that produced these monsters.

"I've supplemented them since they were a week old," Helen said. "And I'm really throwing the food to Jenny. She simply doesn't have enough milk for those critters."

By the time they were six weeks old they were eating solid food as well as supplement. "I'm weaning them early," Helen said. She put them all down on the floor of the examining room. The two pups were already as big as their mother.

As pups do, the two little ones immediately started roughhousing. Jenny looked on patiently until they rolled into her. Instantly she snapped at them. Both pups scurried under the examining table.

"She's definitely socialized them," I laughed. "Dr. Parmenter will be pleased. So will Elvira, the owner."

"I can't bear to send them back." Helen said, scooping up both pups, one in each arm.

"Helen, be sensible. What are you going to do with a pair of Irish wolfhounds?"

"I know, I know. The thing is, I think they're both show quality. All that good beagle milk, I guess."

"Can you afford to buy them?"

"Lord, no. And it wouldn't be even remotely possible if Gladys hadn't delivered more pups than the names on the waiting list. But I've been talking to Elvira. She and I have known one another from dog shows for donkey's years, but you know, different breeds, different class times at the shows. We never really got friendly. Anyway, she's come out to my place a couple of times to visit. We're going into partnership on them. I'll train them, she'll show them, and we'll split the expenses. Then whoever champions out first, she'll get pick of the litter on the first litter."

She leaned over the examining table. Both pups could already stand on the table and put their paws on her shoulders while they licked her and whacked me across the chest with their tails.

While she took Jenny out to her truck on her lead, I carried the pups and slid them into their travel cages for the ride home. Jenny hopped into the front seat beside Helen and was fastened into the seat belt of her traveling seat. "Just like a baby, aren't you, good girl?" Helen crooned.

She turned on her ignition and leaned out her window. "I've had to buy bigger cages, and my food bill has gone sky high, not to mention having a pair of bull moose to raise. Next time you ask me for a favor, remind me to say no."

# Chapter 16

## *In which Mr. Poochie gets his comeuppance*

Finding a wet nurse for wolfhounds wasn't the only trouble Dr. Parmenter got me in.

At that point the clinic had been open several years, but Morgan, Sarah, Nathan and I were still living in The Hideous House.

Morgan's father had left him a sizeable inheritance, plus trust funds for the children's educations. We decided to use the inheritance as collateral for a construction loan. Morgan arranged a loan for Eli at the same time and the same interest so that we could build her a house south of the clinic at the same time we built our own house north of the clinic. In the meantime, we had invested in a state-of-the-art kennel and boarding area behind the doublewide we were still using for the clinic. I said it was crazy to build from the back to the front, but Morgan said that being able to board animals and have good care facilities to care for animals who were hurt would generate enough income to pay for a good part of the clinic construction.

As usual, he was right.

With the kennels open, we needed a someone to clean and care for the area and the animals. Roy Wilson recommended a kid named Duane Goodpasture. He was kind, good-natured, competent, liked animals, but couldn't function in a complicated world. He learned the job quickly and fit right in.

One early May in the late seventies, Dr. Parmenter called. "Maggie," he said without preamble, "I want a favor." He cleared his throat. "That is the Memphis Zoo wants a favor."

"The zoo? Are you working at the zoo?"

"No indeed. I am, however, on the board of directors. This particular chore has fallen to me. I need you to house twenty monkeys for two weeks."

"What?"

"You'll be paid for their care. The zoo will deliver them and pick them up. They'll be there in two hours."

"Whoa! Dr. Parmenter,we can't handle monkeys. We don't have the facilities, for one thing, or the expertise for another."

"You handled monkeys in school and after, Doctor," he said. When he called me Doctor I always knew I was in big trouble. "These monkeys are not diseased, they are simply homeless for a couple of weeks."

"How..."

"Some idiot threw a lighted cigarette into a trash can in the monkey house and started a fire."

I froze. Animals do not mix with fires. Especially caged animals that can't get away.

"There was some minor smoke inhalation, but those monkeys will be kept under observation in the zoo hospital. The monkey house, however, must be repainted inside and out. The monkeys do not react at all well to the odor of new paint. They must be moved and the zoo does not have the space available."

"So you want to send them out here? Dr. Parmenter, I'm afraid..."

"Doctor, I am asking you to take twenty of the creatures. I am taking six, several of the other local vets are taking a dozen or more. It is your civic duty."

"Dr. Parmenter, I don't even live in Memphis."

"It *is* your local zoo, dammit."

"We can't handle twenty. We don't have the cage space. What kind of monkeys anyway?"

"Spider monkeys. A Colubus or two. A couple of squirrel monkeys. Nothing terribly exotic."

"Nothing like a mandrill? Nothing big and ferocious?"

"Small monkeys. Monkeys with which you had experience during the summer before your senior year."

He knew darned well he'd recommended me for that internship, and that I might not have met Morgan without it. That was playing dirty.

"I'll have to ask Eli."

"Tell her. The monkeys will be there this afternoon."

"A dozen, all right?"

"Good. That's what I'd planned to give you anyway." He went on to describe the monkeys, their reactions to the paint, their needs, and their schedules in detail. Then he hung up.

Old fox. Scare me with twenty to get me to house the number he'd already selected. I went to find Duane, Eli, and our receptionist, Mildred Wilkins, to tell them we'd would be a bit more crowded than we'd expected for the next couple of weeks.

"Apparently the stink of the new paint bothered them," I said.

"How on earth do you tell if a spider monkey, one of God's most hysterical creatures at the best of times, is upset?" Eli asked.

"They aren't eating, and instead of grooming one another the way they normally do, they're attacking one another and pulling out gew-gobs of fur. The staff decided the only way to get rid of the smell is to totally repaint the inside of the building."

"Oh, fresh paint will certainly smell lovely. They'd love that," Eli said.

"Right. So they decided to move the monkeys until the painting was finished and dried so they wouldn't get sick."

"Why on earth would they call you?"

"Dr. Parmenter is on the board of directors at the zoo. Look, food is furnished, transport to and from the zoo is furnished. The keepers will put them in the cages for us and take them out when they go home. We won't even have to look at them except to give them their fresh fruit and monkey chow every day."

"Two weeks?"

"At most. Probably three or four days," said I with my fingers crossed.

"Lord help us."

Mildred was delighted at the prospect of 'cute little monkeys.'

Wanda Jean, our new surgical assistant who was fresh out of vet tech school, was horrified. She'd been around monkeys when she worked as a docent at the zoo as a teenager. "Those things are demons from hell. Just wait until they start to throw things at you—and I'm not talking about their food."

Duane was calm as usual. "If all I have to do is hose out the cages and feed them thangs, I can do it."

The zoo van arrived an hour later.

When the keepers opened the rear door, Mildred's dark eyes grew huge. "Jesus and all the saints, listen to those things." One of the keepers jumped out of the van holding a wire carrier in which a large brindle male monkey rode. He clutched the front of his cage, rolled his lips back from vicious incisors, shook his mane, and screamed.

Mildred yelped and ran back into the building. Duane, Eli and I watched until all the monkeys were safely locked in our cages.

Within an hour the monkeys discovered that if they worked carefully with their clever little hands, they could unhook their water dishes from their cages. They spilled the water on the floor, of course, but that hardly mattered when they could create such a pleasant cacophony by banging the empty dishes on the wire and the concrete floor.

"Mildred," I said, "keep everybody—and I do mean everybody—out of that room. If possible, don't even let the clients know we have visiting monkeys. Closed door at all times. Got it?"

She nodded. Her opinion of cute little monkeys had altered drastically in an hour. "They look so cute," she said sadly. "I know they train monkeys to help people with disabilities. I saw it on television."

"You may have also seen a horror movie where the helper monkey takes over the guy's life and murders all his friends," I said. "These guys don't just hurl water dishes and banana peels. The big males can be regular Mickey Mantles with monkey poop."

"Yukk."

By their second day, they had grown bored and had settled down somewhat. Despite my command that none of the clients should be told about the monkeys, everybody who came in had heard about them and wanted to see them. Mildred had her hands full keeping them from 'just taking a little peek.'

She did fairly well until the morning of the third day. She scurried into my office and closed the door. "Mr. Poochie Gamble's out there. He wants to see the monkeys."

"He can't."

"Are you kidding? You try saying no to Mr. Poochie."

The door behind her opened and Mr. Poochie stuck his snow-white head inside. As the largest breeder of Santa Gertrudis cattle in north Mississippi and a big client of the clinic, Mr. Poochie usually got the red carpet treatment as a matter of course.

"Hey, Maggie," he said. "Hear tell y'all got some monkeys. I come by to see 'em."

"Now, Mr. Poochie, we're not letting anyone in the room with the monkey cages. They are very easily upset. You wouldn't want to upset them, would you?"

Mildred slid around him and fled back to her office.

"Honey, if the IRS don't never say no to ol' Poochie, you don't think I'd let a pretty little thing like you get away with it, now do you?" His smile was brilliant, but there was a hint of crocodile in those white teeth.

I came around the desk. "Mr. Poochie, you know I can't let you in there and not let every other Tom, Dick, and Harry in as well. Why, if one of those monkeys was to get out, they might eat you alive. I can't afford to have you sue me. The insurance company would cancel my liability insurance in a heartbeat."

"Sweet thing, if ol' Poochie can handle one of them big ol' bulls, ain't no problem handling a tee-ninesy little monkey. I ain't gonna sue you, no matter what happens." He leaned over and called down the hall to Mildred, "You hear that? Whatever happens is on my head."

"Yes, sir, Mr. Poochie," Mildred said.

"Come on, Miss Maggie, let me in there."

"All right. I'll let you in and shut the door on you. Look to your heart's content, although you better be quick at ducking. You will not, and I mean this, not so much as crack the door of one of those cages."

"Anything you say, sweet thing."

"If even one of those monsters gets out, you're on your own. I won't lift a finger to rescue you."

Mr. Poochie merely grinned and patted me on the butt.

I let him into the monkey room with a dire warning of consequences. He waved me off.

I went to the reception area. I'd be willing to bet Mr. Poochie would try to open one of those cages. I prayed he wouldn't be successful.

"How come a grown man is called Poochie?" Mildred asked. "Does he have a real name?"

"I have no idea. He's older than Methuselah, and I've never heard a soul call him anything but Mr. Poochie."

"Maggie, help!" Mr. Poochie ran out the door to the monkey room and slammed it behind him. He wiped his face with an immaculate linen handkerchief. "One of those imps of Satan is running around loose trying to open all the other cages."

"I warned you not to open the cages."

"I just cracked one door a teensy little bit, swear to God. Honey, either I ain't as fast as I think I am or them monkeys is faster than a rat snake chasing after a bullfrog. You got to get him back in his cage."

"No, I don't. You let him out, you put him back. I'm not about to get bitten over your foolishness."

"How the hell am I gonna do that?"

"Come on." I went into the storeroom and brought him a capture net plus a couple of towels. "Enjoy yourself."

I kept my ear to the door listening for human screams. I planned to help him, but he deserved a little punishment first. Mr. Poochie used words even his mother wouldn't have understood. The monkeys went insane.

After five minutes when I was ready to give him a hand, I heard a cage door slam. By the time he staggered out I was halfway down the hall.

"You come right on back here, young lady," he gasped and wiped his face with an immaculate linen handkerchief.

"Yessir?" I turned a bland face toward him.

"Here's your dad-blighted net and your consarned towels. That's no monkey, that's a miniature gorilla." He stalked past me, then came back shaking his finger at me. "If you ever let me do something that dad-blasted stupid again in this lifetime, I swear I'll take my bid-ness elsewhere." He thought a minute. "And after I die, I'll come back to haunt you, see if I don't. My family is notorious haunters."

"Yessir, Mr. Poochie." I managed to keep the grin off my face until he grinned first.

"Oh, hell, I got to go home and get the monkey stink off me." He walked out without another word.

From then on, I never had a minute's trouble with him. If he started getting fractious, I only had to mention monkeys and he'd quiet right down.

# Chapter 17

## *In which Sarah displays her gift*

By the time my daughter Sarah turned seven in 1981 I knew that she was one of those rare people with an almost spiritual ability to communicate with animals. Considering that she had precious little patience with the foibles of human beings, I found her talent surprising.

She'd complain when she had to ride along on one of my calls, but if she went with me to Patsy Dalrymple's place to worm all Patsy's horses, I'd find Sarah in the pasture rubbing noses with one of Patsy's skittish young foals when I was done. They nibbled Sarah's fingers and blew in Sarah's nose as if she were simply another small horse on its hind legs.

Morgan had built me my house—a simple two story Georgian, but a palace compared to The Hideous House. Eli had moved into her new cottage, and the clinic was housed in its first permanent building.

One glorious April morning, I walked out onto the patio behind our new house to check on the pink azaleas I had planted before I walked across to the clinic for morning surgery.

I nearly jumped out of my skin as a yellow streak flew across the lawn twenty feet away to disappear into the trees. At first I thought it must be a bobcat, but bobcats don't have long, furry yellow tails. Theoretically, there were no panthers or cougars or mountain lions remaining in Fayette County. I knew that was untrue, however, because I nearly ran over one on a misty morning in the Wolf River bottoms. This animal, however, wasn't large enough to be what the old farmers around here called 'a painter.'

I never expected to see the yellow critter again, but the following morning it streaked across my field of vision the same way. I didn't get a good look at it for at least a month. Then one afternoon in early May when the weather was still cool enough to sit outside and the mosquitoes weren't yet large enough to carry off small children, I fell asleep on my patio chaise longue after a God-awful day handling one emergency after another.

I woke suddenly feeling somebody was watching me. Thirty feet away the biggest, ugliest yellow cat I had ever seen glared at me.

That glare said I was the interloper.

We stared at one another for what seemed like hours. I must admit I looked away first. When I looked back this thing, whatever it was, it stalked off straight down the middle of the pasture toward the back of the property.

As a general rule, cats do not walk down the center of any open stretch. They skirt. They slink. They skitter. Occasionally they run like hell. This guy sauntered off as cocky as an African lion. He must have weighed thirty pounds at least, but he didn't look fat. He looked like a heavyweight boxer in training for a title bout. His *skull* probably weighed as much as the average house cat. But he wasn't a bobcat or a lynx. He had plenty of tail and no tufts in his ears.

I called a buddy in the Fish and Wildlife Service and described the cat.

Kent broke out laughing before I'd even finished detailing the faint tabby markings on the yellow coat.

"Dr. Maggie, you have got yourself a bona fide Tennessee Feral Cat. You're damned lucky to have seen one at all. They're extremely rare."

"I never heard of a Tennessee Feral Cat. You're putting me on, right?"

"Not at all."

"What you're saying is that this cat is the second or third generation of some escaped alley cats."

"I mean nothing of the sort. The Tennessee Feral Cat is a real breed. If you go down to the Pink Palace Museum in Memphis, you can see a stuffed one—pretty ratty and probably eighty years old. They originated from English tabbies that mated with local wild felines and evolved. Any wild cat tends to revert to that solid yellow with tabby points after three or four generations. These have been around a lot longer than that. They're pretty shy."

"Shy? Listen, Kent, that sucker sat twenty feet away, then turned and ambled straight down the center of the pasture. He was practically daring me to go after him."

"I wouldn't if I was you. Ever hear of a Scottish wild cat?"

"I've seen pictures. They look like a plain gray tabby, but apparently they have the temperament of a Tasmanian devil."

"I've heard your average Tennessee Feral Cat does not take kindly to human beings either."

"What am I going to do about him?"

"Why should you do anything about him?"

"That thing is a tomcat, Kent. It needs to be neutered and given its shots."

"I wish you luck neutering it, Dr. Maggie. You're about as likely to catch that cat as I am to stick my head into a rattlesnake's mouth."

I was bound and determined to snare that cat. It was just as bound and determined not to get caught. I left food for it on the patio every night. Every night I watched until my eyes were too heavy to see, and every night it outwaited me before eating. I borrowed a humane trap from Kent—one used to trap beavers and skunks that were making nuisances of themselves under porches and in attics. Every night that cat would manage to snitch the food and spring the trap, but without going inside. I still don't know how he managed that little trick.

My family thought I had a screw loose. Sarah didn't see why it should be a problem. The first time she saw the cat, she named it Vercingetorix.

She'd been watching a TV show on the history of the Roman Empire. She said Vercingetorix, the barbarian, beat the stew out of a bunch of top-notch Roman legionnaires and ripped off some of their battle flags.

She said she just liked the name. I got the feeling I was the Roman legions, and that she was telling me I was getting the stew beat out of me.

She was right.

I noticed that every evening when the weather was nice, she went walking back toward the pond.

Then one evening in September just after school had started, I looked out the kitchen window. Sarah was walking up the new road to the back of the property. Trotting beside her for all the world like a big puppy was Vercingetorix. I couldn't believe it.

I definitely couldn't believe it when she stooped and scratched behind his plug-ugly tattered ears.

But I didn't say a word when she came into the kitchen. Sarah was always touchy about her accomplishments. Mentioning her conquest would most likely result in her ignoring Vercingetorix from then on.

I couldn't ignore her, however, the Saturday evening in October when she walked up on the patio with Vercingetorix lying on his back in her arms and purring like a lawnmower.

"You can pet him, Mommy," she said. "He likes it."

I reached out a tentative hand expecting to draw back a nub, not to mention having to put a tourniquet on my daughter's arm after he ripped if off. He didn't move. He merely screwed up his ruined boxer's face and purred even harder. It was though he'd discovered what he'd been missing during all his years of anti-human behavior and had decided to make up for lost time.

In the end I gave him his shots, but decided not to neuter him. I don't approve of unneutered feral cats, but he was one of the last members of a dying breed. He had a right to preserve his gene pool. He never became a house cat, but he certainly became a member of the family. He tolerated Eli's border terrier and held long conversations with my indoor cats through the kitchen screen door. He lazed on the patio and sat on all our laps for as long as we'd have him.

If he ever reproduced, we never saw any of his offspring. I like to think, however, that somewhere deep in the Wolf River bottoms at least a few big, ugly yellow cats are maintaining their territories and stalking straight across open fields in defiance of all the world.

Eli, Morgan, and even Kent from fish and wildlife told Sarah how remarkable socializing a thug like Vercingetorix was. She would only shrug and turn away in embarrassment. As with many innate talents, she saw no value in that particular gift.

I, on the other hand, would have given at least a couple of toes for even a tiny portion of her talent. I'm certain that she still has it, unless her refusal of her gift has resulted in atrophy.

# Chapter 18

## *In which Maggie learns a lesson about elephants*

Dr. Parmenter had usually been point man for the circus when it came to Memphis. That year he said he didn't feel up to it and recommended us. I was thrilled. I adored the circus, especially the elephants.

So Dr. Murchison, the vet who looked after the animals in their winter quarters, called me to check us out. "Heard good things about you," Dr. Murchison said. "Vachel Carey is a golfing buddy of mine."

I almost choked. "How is Vach?"

"He swears you have second sight."

"Oh, lord. If you golf with Vach, you know how he can be. I never know whether he's making fun of me or is deadly serious."

"In this case, I think he is deadly serious. He has told me numerous times about your extraordinary abilities with ultra-sound."

"Why me, Lord?"

"Listen, for a man who raises the most expensive Paint horses in the world to have a vet who can read ultrasounds the way you can is miraculous."

"You do realize what happened, don't you?"

For the first time Murchison chuckled. "You took an ultrasound to see if his foal was healthy. He asked you what color it was. You said black and white. The foal was born black and white. Therefore you have the sight."

"I meant the *X-Ray* photo was black and white."

"I know that and you know that, but we will never convince Vach."

I had tried to persuade Sarah and Nathan to go with me when I had to go down to the circus staging area.

Ten-year-old Sarah wrinkled her nose and said that was for babies.

Nathan, only eight, was thrilled. He'd been talking lately about becoming a vet himself, which thrilled me, even though he said he wanted to go to Africa or South America to practice.

So there I was a bona fide circus vet wearing spiffy new jeans and a snowy white lab coat, and showing my fancy badge to the security guard at the Memphis Coliseum where the circus had stopped for the week. He peered down at Nathan, then shrugged, passed us through and pointed us down the aisle toward the head elephant keeper, a Mickey Talbot.

Talbot had the look of a man who had spent his life around trains and sawdust. Whipcord thin, in disreputable jeans and a worn flannel workshirt, with a two-day growth of black beard, he looked me up and down with rheumy eyes. He reeked of tobacco smoke, and spoke with the sandpaper voice of a man who smokes and drinks as much and as often as he can manage.

"Who's the kid?"

I introduced Nathan who stuck out his hand. Talbot raised his eyebrows, but shook it. "Watch yourself, kid." Then he looked me up and down. "Lose the lab coat."

"I beg your pardon?"

"Lose it. What you got on under?"

"A turtleneck sweater."

"What color?"

"Blue." Behind him, I could see a dozen or so elephants each chained loosely to a single picket line by one front foot. Dr. Murchison told me that circus elephants were all Indian and female. I was dying to meet them. I knew Nathan was too.

But this Talbot guy was starting to piss me off.

"Go take that white coat off where they can't see you and come back," he said. "Leave your medical bag here. Kid'll be okay. They like kids."

"Why should I do that?"

"Doc, take a look behind me. That's Rosie on the end. Watch her."

Rosie was the biggest and most formidable animal I had ever been close to. This elephant and several past her were shifting from foot to foot and swinging their trunks rhythmically. Their beady eyes, however, were on me. I didn't read welcome in them.

Then Rosie reached over to the pile of hay next to her. A large hay shovel, big as a snow shovel but concave, stood on end in the pile.

With the delicacy of a surgeon selecting a scalpel, Rosie wrapped her trunk around the handle of the shovel, picked it up from the hay, and laid it gently in front of her on its face.

She swung her head to look directly into my eyes, then slowly and deliberately set her left front foot on the back of the shovel.

I couldn't see any movement, but the metal screeched.

When Rosie removed her foot, the shovel was completely flat—a pancake looked like Mt. Everest compared to that shovel. I gulped.

"Mom," Nathan whispered. "Did you see that?"

"See, Doc, they recognize that coat," Talbot said. "They know you're a vet and they don't like 'em. Vets mean pain, and they don't like pain. So if I was you, I'd go where they can't see you and lose the coat."

I lost the coat. In my blue turtleneck and with Talbot's help, I carefully edged past the rhythmically swinging trunks down to the elephant on the end. Nathan stayed close on my coat tails. He pretended not to be scared, but I could hear him breathe.

"That's Helen. She's the one with the arthritis," Talbot said. "Has to have her shots every month like clockwork whether we're on the road or in Sarasota for the winter."

"Hello, Helen, I'm Maggie. I'll try not to hurt you."

She shifted. I held my ground. To his credit, so did Nathan.

Dr. Murchison had explained in detail how to get the heavy needle through the elephant's hide. Once it was in place I shot vial after vial of hyaluronic acid into Helen's shoulder. Talbot took the used vials from me. Helen seemed to understand that I was trying to help her. She stood stock-still and made no attempt to snatch the vials out of my hand or knock me down with her trunk.

After I finished and turned away, Helen touched my hair gently, then slid her trunk down and patted my shoulder. I froze, uncertain whether to be flattered or terrified. The others watched her.

"Sir," Nathan said, "Can I touch her?"

Talbot scowled down at Nathan. I was certain he was going to say no. Instead, he nodded. I wanted to say no myself, but I kept my mouth shut.

Nathan reached out and stroked her shoulder. "Nice Helen," he whispered. She ran her trunk over his head and down his shoulder.

He giggled. "I can feel her breath. She tickles."

"Yeah. Come on, Doc, next patient."

As we followed Talbot back down the picket line, the elephants swung their trunks, but made no attempt to stomp us. The moment we were out of their sight, I wailed, "But I love elephants."

"Sorry, Doc." He shrugged. "You did good introducing yourself to Helen that way. See, elephants really do remember everything. They don't forget and they don't forgive. You mistreat an elephant and sooner or later you'll pay for it. Maybe twenty years later, but you'll get yours." He sat on a bale of hay and lit a cigarette.

"Can you smoke in here?"

"Nope. But I do. I got more sense than to set the hay on fire. Hell, I been with the circus nigh onto forty years. Been doing elephants for thirty. Them's my girls in there. Don't nobody treat 'em bad."

"According to you, they can take care of themselves."

"If they get the chance. Chained up on the picket line, they can't stampede." A wreath of smoke encircled his grizzled buzz cut. He raised his eyebrows at Nathan. "That is unless they're in musth."

"I thought only male elephants went into musth," Nathan said.

"So you done your homework? Good for you. Females go into musth too, but lighter. Makes em cranky. Like PMS only bigger and meaner. I remember once…" he broke off and cut his eyes at me. Apparently my next patient could wait.

I suspected he was showing off for Nathan. I also suspected he was a master raconteur. I smiled and settled on the bale of hay opposite him. Nathan leaned against my knee. What else did we have to do on a beautiful October day?

"Back when I joined up and got put with the elephants, all this stuff about kindness to animals was just starting," Talbot said. "Folks said you had to hurt 'em before they'd respect you. If they don't respect you, you better pray to God your insurance is paid up.

"Anyway, the head elephant man at that time was a real bastard—" He cut his eyes at Nathan. "A real bad character when he was drinking. He'd cry and apologize to his girls afterwards, but I found old infected sores under their armpits from the elephant hooks…" Talbot shook his head. "Made me cry. I'd treat 'em, and try to keep 'em safe. They appreciated it, but I wasn't always there and I couldn't go up against the man without losing my job. He really had a hate on one big old bull name of Pauline. Said she reminded him of an old girlfriend. I finally reported him to the management. They read him the riot act, but let him stay. He didn't change.

"Anyway, he finally got hisself fired all on his own for being drunk and near about burning the tent down, and I got his job. Heard he took up being a keeper at some two-bit private zoo. Forgot all about him. Got my girls happy and healthy. In the winter they got this whole big pasture, and when they get too old to work, we know some elephant sanctuaries where they retire happy." He stubbed out his cigarette on the palm of his hand without evident discomfort, then began to field strip it.

"Then about five years ago, we was playing St. Paul, Minnesota. Afternoon show. Got time for the grand parade at the end. I don't go into the ring with the girls. Ain't dressed for it. The clowns and the roustabouts do that. Not that they need 'em. They know what they're supposed to do—carry the show girls around while they wave at the crowd.

"I'm in the back, see, standing at the exit watching. I always do that just in case. I see some fool come running down to the edge of the arena shouting and waving. The guards are after him, but they're a long way off.

"I didn't recognize him for a minute, then I saw it was old—well, I won't tell you his name. Still drunk. Still yelling at his girls.

"*Jesus Christ,* I says, and starts running. Pauline was the third elephant in line. I saw her drop the tail of the elephant in front of her, stop for a second and look around like she recognized his voice. I didn't know what to do. If he ran back up the stairs to get away from her, she was liable to climb into the audience after him.

"Didn't get the chance to make a decision. She swung out of line, trumpeted, and lashed out with her trunk. She knocked him out of the stands and onto the tanbark."

"What happened?" Nathan demanded eagerly. If there is one thing I have learned about little boys, it is that they are born bloodthirsty. Nathan was no different.

Talbot shrugged his shoulders. "Know how an elephant goes after something it really wants to kill? None of this stamp-on-the-shovel stuff like Rosie pulled on you. That was funning. Rosie does have a sense of humor.

"Pauline smacked him flat with her trunk. Everybody was screaming. The showgirl riding Pauline was holding on for dear life, and the other elephants were heading for the exit at thirty miles an hour. I could see his eyes. He knew what was coming. Pauline went down on her knees and laid her forehead against his chest. Then she pushed down with all her weight."

I felt my gorge rising and looked at Nathan. His eyes were the size of Rosie's hooves.

"Gross," he said. "Did he pop?"

"Nathan!"

Talbot grinned. "Nope. He flattened. By the time I got to her with the hook, she'd finished. She got to her feet, gave his body one flick with her trunk, way you'd kick a bug out of your way, then she walked on around the ring toward the exit like nothing happened."

"What did they do to her?" Nathan asked.

"Please don't tell me they shot her," I begged.

"They wanted to. Bad publicity, they said. Scared people off coming to the circus, they said. We had kind of a trial. I told 'em what all he'd done to Pauline all those years ago. They finally decided to send her to one of them sanctuaries free of charge." His eye took on a faraway look. "Heard she died a couple of years ago. Real peaceful. Good ol' Pauline." He glared at Nathan. "So, you see, boy, don't never mistreat a elephant."

I never knew whether Talbot's story was true. It didn't really matter. Legend or not, the inner truth was there laid out for any human being to read. Don't muck with the elephants.

I exhaled. The last thing Nathan needed was more of Talbot's gory stories, although Nathan was loving every minute of it. "Who's our next patient?"

He stood up and eased his back. "We got another Rosie. This one's a hippo. She's got glaucoma. Have to take the pressure on her eyeball once a week and put drops in every day."

"Mr. Talbot, I can certainly take her pressure, but I don't have any idea what's normal for a hippo."

"That's all right. I do."

Rosie was a pgymy hippo who stood no higher than my waist, but still weighed at least a ton. Either she still had some vision, could smell Talbot or hear him, because she swung her head in his direction when we were still a good distance away. Then she opened her mouth.

I stopped dead. She might be a pygmy, but that maw was plenty large enough to hold me, and her teeth were eighteen inches long. She could bite me in two. "Stay well back, son," I told Nathan.

"Uh-huh," he whispered. Even he was impressed.

"It's okay, doc," Talbot said. "I'll keep the carrots and lettuce going down her gullet while you take her pressure. She's used to it."

He was as good as his word. I reported the pressure on the eyeball to him. "Good? Bad?"

"Bout the same." He tossed Rosie another cabbage and walked back toward the front of the arena.

"I'll give Dr. Murchison the results in my report to him. Now, if you don't have any other patients for me, I need to get back to my regular clients. Call me if you need anything."

"Will do. Thanks, doc." He grinned at Nathan. "You ought to see some of those big tough vets we get. Scared to death of my girls. You did good, boy."

Nathan talked non-stop all the way back home and was still driving Sarah crazy when I walked over to the clinic.

Eli had already finished for the day.

"There you are. Was it fun?"

"I'll tell you sometime. All I can say is, you better pray that their *big cats* stay healthy until they leave town. Elephants are dangerous enough. I am not playing Androcles to anybody's lion. If a lion gets a thorn in its paw, *you're* going to be the one to take it out."

# Chapter 19

## *In which we meet a spaced-out Terrier*

Within ten years after we moved to the country, suburbia began invading us. The road that had been gravel was paved, and traffic increased. We installed a wrought-iron gate with a code and an electric gate opener at the road so that we could close ourselves in at night. We put up new PVC fences along the road frontage. We were still in the country, but we weren't nearly as country as we'd been when we started.

Nathan and Sarah were growing up. We couldn't keep them chained in their rooms, although there were times it sounded like a great idea.

Sarah had begun taking riding lessons with Patsy when she was six, and began bugging us for a horse of her own shortly thereafter. By the time she was eleven, Morgan and I agreed she was ready for her own horse, but we didn't see how we could afford to give her one. It's true that a hundred-dollar horse costs the same to keep as a million-dollar horse, but a million dollar horse is generally more talented. Sarah wanted a competitive show jumper. Not cheap.

We did notice that her young friends with horses seemed immune to a lot of teenaged problems. We figured we could save up for a year or so, then try to find her a horse that fit her needs when she turned twelve.

One fall morning, Morgan was reading the paper at the kitchen table at six-thirty in the morning, while I was splitting the can of Cat Chow among three cat bowls. I was hoping for an easy day in the clinic after I got Nathan and Sarah off to school with Morgan. It had begun to drizzle during the night. With luck I wouldn't have to leave the clinic all day.

When the telephone on the wall of the kitchen rang, I said, "Oh, foot."

"Dr. McLain? It's the answering service?"

"Yes?"

"Ma'am, we just had a call from the police?"

"I beg your pardon?" Eli and I had discovered that this particular young answer-service lady invariably spoke as though every remark were a question. Disconcerting.

"A detective MacDonald?" she said.

"What did he want?"

"I gave him your number? I hope that's all right?"

The phone clicked. "Must be him now. Thanks." I switched lines.

"Ma'am? This is Detective James MacDonald with the Collierville Police Department. I've got kind of an emergency here, and I know you take care of our drug dogs like Amos..."

"That's right. Good grief, it's not big Amos, is it? He hasn't been shot or anything?"

From the timbre of his voice, he was speaking on a cell phone. In the background I could hear the blat of a siren.

No, the siren was down at the highway just outside the front gates. "Are you here?" I asked.

"Yes, ma'am, right outside, but the front gate's locked."

"I'll buzz you in and meet you at the clinic." I hung up, kissed Morgan, yelled at Nathan and Sarah to hurry up and not to forget their books, and lit out for the clinic.

I arrived puffing, but the squad car still beat me. I bent over and put my hands on my knees. "Whew! I'm in worse shape than I thought."

"You look in great shape to me," said the driver. He was dressed in T.A.C.T. team black with high top combat boots, was shorter than I am, and looked as though he did a thousand pushups before breakfast.

"Is Amos all right?"

"He's fine, ma'am. It's not one of our dogs." He opened the back door of the car, which, I saw, was separated from the front by a grill. It probably had no inside door handles to prevent escapes. Was this man bringing me a prisoner?

The man who climbed out didn't look dangerous. He was near my own age, a couple of inches shorter and built like the proverbial fireplug with a beer belly that hung over his jeans. His mass of gray hair looked uncombed. Bristles of white beard stuck through the tanned skin of his jaw. He was fiercely clutching a white towel wrapped around something that squirmed and growled and squealed and thrashed.

And probably bit, given the opportunity.

"Come on, MacDonald," he said. "I can't hold Willie Nelson much longer."

I ran up the steps in the rain, opened the front door, ushered both men in and led them quickly to the first examining room. I dashed the rain out of my eyes and off my eyelashes.

"What have we got here?" I reached to take the bundle from the man's arms.

"I gotta hang onto him. He's done gone plumb crazy!"

Rabies? There hadn't been a case of rabies in this part of Tennessee in ten years. "I do have to examine him, Mr. uh?"

"Cletus Monroe, Ma'am." He ducked his head.

"Detective MacDonald, if I need help, can you weigh in?" I asked.

"Before you go doin' that, you better hear the story," MacDonald said.

"Let's get Willie into a cage first," I said. I ran next door to the storeroom and returned with a pet carrier. Cletus shoved the bundle, towel and all, into the carrier. I slammed the door. The bundle inside immediately unwrapped itself and began gnawing frantically at the towel.

"It's a Jack Russell terrier!" I said. "No wonder. They're a twelve pound rhinoceros on speed."

"Yeah, well," Jim MacDonald said. "The problem is that this one really *is* on speed."

"I beg your pardon."

The dog hit the front of the cage snarling. I jumped.

"My God, my God," Cletus crooned. "Poor baby, poor baby."

He burst into tears.

"Come on, Mr. Monroe," MacDonald said, "The doctor can't hear us with all that yapping going on." He took the man's arm and led him protesting into the hall.

Monroe kept shaking his head and looking back over his shoulder until I shut the door.

"Tell me fast before he goes into convulsions."

"Okay," said MacDonald. "Here's the deal. We busted a couple of gang bangers yesterday evening out in a shack on Highway Fifty-Seven. We knew they were cooking and distributing crystal meth, but we didn't know where. They had enough stuff in their van to hop up most of West Tennessee."

Mr. Monroe wrung his hands.

"Anyway, we worked on them most of the night about where the lab was."

"Please, talk fast," Mr. Monroe begged.

"I'm getting there."

Not fast enough to suit Mr. Monroe or me, but it seemed as though nothing could keep MacDonald from regaling us with all the details.

"Long about four a.m. they decided the best way to lighten their load was to snitch on somebody else. They told us they'd been buying from a couple of guys who had set up a meth lab in a motel six blocks from where we picked them up. As far as they knew, the guys were still there."

"A motel? As in a room surrounded by other rooms?"

"Yeah. Happens all the time. Never know who's doing what in the room next door. Blow you up right along with them and half the motel."

"I'll never stay in a motel again," I whispered.

"We get there about six in the morning, give one quick 'police' and hit the door with the ram. That's where Mr. Monroe comes in."

"You hit the wrong room?"

"Right room, but the bad guys had skipped. Mr. Monroe here is an over-the-road truck driver. Checked in about ten last night. Innocent civilian."

"Scared to death," Mr. Monroe said resentfully.

"He travels with…"

"Willie Nelson. Goes with me everywhere."

"See, this Willie is bouncing off the walls. I had to go put Amos in the van. I swear Willie would have taken him on."

"He's been like that most of the night," Mr. Monroe said. "I just thought he wasn't getting enough exercise. It got really bad when somebody knocked on my door at three this morning saying he'd left something in the room and needed to get it. Hell, I know better than to open my door. I told him I was armed and he could come get his property after I checked out."

"At that point we started searching for the lab stuff they must have left behind," MacDonald said. "We found the stash behind some ceiling tiles in the bathroom. I thought we'd found everything there was…"

"Then just as they were getting ready to leave Willie Nelson had a seizure," Mr. Monroe said. "It was awful! He was over by the bed flopping around with his eyes rolled back in his head."

"So I yanked the bed away from the wall." He grinned. "Cookers, hot plate, everything you need to cook crystal meth. And some powder spilled on the rug."

"Willie Nelson must have slid under the bed after his ball and gotten it on his paws," Mr. Monroe said.

"Oh, God," I whispered, and started back to the examining room. "I'll give him as much barbiturate as I dare, get him on a drip."

"Then what?" MacDonald asked.

"We pray."

"Jesus loves me," Monroe whispered.

"Did he bite anybody?"

"Me while I was trying to get that towel around him," Monroe said and shook his head. "Not bad. I put a Bandaid on it. He's up-to-date on his shots. Didn't know what he was doing. He was plumb hopped up like some kind of motorcycle freak."

"Will he live?" MacDonald asked as I prepared my syringe. The dog was still snarling and barking and squealing.

"If I can manage to get this into him, maybe," He'd already bitten the man he loved. He was unlikely to be enamoured of a fat syringe and needle headed his way in the hands of a woman he'd never seen before. I'd need help to get a muzzle on him, and I wasn't certain I could count on Cletus.

Without warning the door to the examining room slammed open. "What in the Lord's name is going on *now*?"

"Eli, it's not even seven o'clock."

"Sirens, squad cars, and you don't expect me to come running? Who died?"

"Nobody—yet." I filled Eli in much quicker than MacDonald had done. Mr. Monroe stood by the cage crooning to Willie. Didn't seem to be doing much good.

"I'll grab the dog and get a muzzle on him. You shoot him. Make it fast," Eli said.

I was fast, but nobody could touch Eli's reflexes in an emergency. Willie was muzzled, shot, and back into his carrier before he had time to do more than snap once.

We watched him for five minutes as he settled down on the motel towel.

"Can I touch him?" Mr. Monroe whispered.

"Give it another ten minutes, then we'll get the muzzle off and let him sleep it off."

"Can I stay here, watch him?"

"Absolutely. I'll bet you haven't had a bite of breakfast, have you?"

"Nobody has," MacDonald said.

"I'll get the coffee pot in the storeroom going. Eli, call Duane and ask him to pick up a dozen Krispy Kremes and a quart of o.j. on his way in. Can you wait another twenty minutes before you go back to work?" I asked MacDonald.

"Unless I get called." He turned to Monroe. "Mr. Monroe, is there anybody you need me to notify you'll be starting late? Your trucking company?"

"I'll call them."

"You let me know when you and Willie can leave and I'll send a car to get you back to your motel."

"Thanks, MacDonald." He looked a question at me. I smiled and nodded. He opened the carrier door carefully. Willie slept on his chest with his pointed little brown nose neatly aligned between his white paws. Monroe scratched the little dog's ears and gently removed the muzzle. Willie sighed softly and whimpered in his sleep.

Monroe jumped. "Is that normal?"

"I believe so. Listen, did you all clean his feet off?"

"As best we could," MacDonald said.

"Okay, I'll really clean and sterilize his feet between the pads. I didn't know you could absorb crystal meth through your skin. That's scary."

"Yeah." MacDonald touched my arm. "Listen, Dr. McLain, I'm not kidding about this. Don't you ever go barefoot in a hotel or motel room. Last thing you want is to step on a used crack needle or absorb leftover crystal meth through the soles of your feet."

"You're scaring me."

"I mean to."

By ten o'clock I felt comfortable letting Mr. Monroe take Willie with him. He paid his bill without a murmur.

The little dog was still sleeping off his overdose, but his pulse and respiration were normal, and he hadn't developed any temperature. "He shouldn't have any long-term effects from his seizure, Mr.

Monroe," I told the man. "If he seems to be having any recurrence, you get him to your own vet fast. Tell him to call me for his chart."

"Yes, ma'am," Monroe said. Willie slept in his arms, his body snuggled in the white towel so that he looked like a little brown and white baby with a funny nose and ears. "I'll put him in his bed behind me in the cab. He can sleep it off there. I sure am grateful." He bent and rubbed his nose against the little dog's face. "Don't know what I'd do without Willie Nelson."

After I saw him into the squad car that would return him and Willie to his truck, I shut the door to my office and called Morgan. "I'm going to talk to Patsy about finding Sarah a horse right now," I said.

"What's all this about, hon?" he asked.

"I've just had a lesson in drugs. We can't vaccinate the kids against them, but maybe if we keep Nathan in soccer and Sarah on a horse, we'll have a chance."

# Chapter 20

## *In which Sarah looks a gift horse in the mouth*

There is something surreal between horses and little girls. The horses know it. They take advantage of it, as a matter of fact. Sarah collected horse statuettes and models, devoted a corner of her bedroom to her pretend stable with all of her pretend tack, and began angling for her own horse in the first grade.

When she began showing Patsy Dalrymple's horses over fences at the local horse shows, even that put a strain on our budget. By the time she was twelve, she was as tall as I am, slim and coltish, and showed signs of becoming a beauty. She was a superb rider with absolutely no fear. I'd watch her at horse shows as she cantered down to a humongous four-foot fence with that zoned out look in her eye. I knew at that moment she wouldn't feel it if somebody cut off her foot.

*Better than motorcycles,* I told myself. *The horse wants to survive. The motorcycle doesn't care.* There is an optimum moment to give a girl her own horse. Morgan and I knew that moment had come.

Once we decided to bite the bullet and buy her a horse, Morgan and I scouted for suitable horses all summer and fall with no success. The ones we could afford, Sarah didn't want. The horses that were competitive were so far outside our price range as to be in another galaxy far, far away.

Patsy came up with the solution. She had a five-year-old warmblood gelding—barely out of his own teens as warmbloods grow—with all the jumping talent in the world. He was a little squirrelly, but nothing Sarah couldn't handle. Patsy offered us a lease for a year to be renewed as long as we liked. We would basically pay the expenses for the horse and treat him like our own, but we wouldn't have to pay Patsy's asking price, which was well over fifty thousand dollars even at his age. His value would increase dramatically as he gained experience. It was a good deal for both Patsy and Sarah.

Sarah really loved the horse, and he seemed fond of her.

All fall we kept the secret that we planned to lease him for her. That was to be her great Christmas present, and her twelfth birthday present as well.

Morgan and I were splitting child-transporting duties as much as possible. Nathan was playing soccer and lacrosse after school every afternoon, so Morgan could pick him up on his way home.

Patsy picked up a gaggle of teenaged girls most afternoons to take to her barn to ride. Sarah was among them. Then I'd pick Sarah up at five-thirty or so, unless I was out on an emergency.

On those rides home alone together, Sarah and I came closer to understanding one another than we had before or have since. She never mentioned my practice, but prattled on happily about horses and girlfriends. I listened and kept my mouth shut. That was Morgan's suggestion, and as always, it was a good one.

We signed the lease for Patsy's Pride, known as Pride, on the 20$^{th}$ of December. Morgan took special delight in finding just the right box to house the lease papers, and then had it wrapped beautifully. He was so proud when he put the box under the tree for Sarah.

Eli, Morgan and I waited for Sarah to reach that box. Nathan was already giving ineffectual swipes with his new lacrosse stick and threatening to break every lamp in the living room when Sarah finally opened that box.

The way her face lit up when she saw the paper and read "Patsy's Pride" on top of it made my heart jump. She began to read while Eli, Morgan and I sat there with dumb grins on our faces.

Then she looked up. "This says lease."

"That's right, honey," Morgan said. "We've leased him for you."

"I don't want a dumb lease," she said and threw the paper down. "He's still Patsy's horse. He's not mine. He'll never be mine." She ran up the back steps and a couple of seconds later we heard the door to her bedroom slam.

I took one look at Morgan's face and felt as though someone had stuck a knife in my stomach and twisted. How dare she toss his gift in his face?

"Mom, Sarah's being a butthead again."

"Don't call your sister a butthead," I said.

"I'll talk to her." Morgan stood up wearily. So did I.

"Let me go," I said grimly and started for the stairs. I was strongly considering tossing her out her bedroom window. Maybe she'd land on her head. It might knock some sense into her.

"Maggie, let me. If you go you'll wind up screaming at each other."

"I sincerely hope so."

He shook his head. "It's all right. It's Christmas, remember?"

Morgan could always reach her. I slumped on the couch and watched the tree until Eli reached over and took my hand. "Don't, Maggie."

"No matter what we do, it's never right," I whispered. "How could she hurt her father that way? Doesn't she know we can barely afford the lease? Not to mention show fees, riding britches, tack, transport and all the rest of it. Ungrateful little…""

Eli smacked me on the hand she'd just been holding. "Margaret Evans McLain, you knock that off. It's not your problem if Sarah goes through life seeing only the portion of the cup that's empty."

"I want her to be happy. Most of all I want Morgan to be happy."

"Happiness takes an effort of will, one that Miss Sarah chooses not to make. We will not allow this—brat—to spoil Christmas. Get over it."

By the time Sarah and Morgan came back downstairs, Sarah's eyes were suspiciously red and swollen, but she seemed perfectly fine. "Thanks, Mom," she said and hugged me. "Can I go ride him this afternoon?"

"How about 'I'm sorry I behaved like a total jerk?'"

She opened her mouth, probably to say something jerky, then she thought better of it. "I'm sorry."

Later I asked Morgan what he'd said to her. "I told her that she had a choice. Lease Patsy's Pride or sit on the sidelines and watch her friends ride. I also told her that she'd damned well better get over her feeling of entitlement. We're not rich, we'll never be rich, and if she wants to be rich, she'd better start learning how to make her own money. And change her attitude." He shrugged. "She shed a few tears, but she's okay."

"Why did she act that way?"

"One of her friends told her we were actually buying her the horse. She was surprised, that's all. She still got her dream horse, just not the way she thought she would."

I escaped to the clinic as soon after breakfast as I could, ostensibly to check on the few animals we were boarding over the holidays. Morgan took Sarah and Nathan and Eli out to Patsy's.

At that point I didn't even want to look at Sarah. I didn't mind for myself, but I knew how hard Morgan had worked on that lease and how thin we were stretched financially. I don't believe in using violence against children, but that day I wanted to smack her. There. If that makes me a bad mother, then so be it. The important thing is that I didn't do it.

By dinnertime that evening, all four of them came in aglow and Sarah bubbled about her horse until she went to bed.

I cried myself to sleep, because I realized that although I loved my daughter, I didn't like her very much.

# Chapter 21

## *In which a tragedy strains a relationship*

By the time Sarah turned eighteen, she and Patsy's Pride were winning junior jumper championships all over the southeast. I couldn't always travel with her, but Morgan was usually at ringside to cheer her on. Since the horse shows were on weekends and Nathan's soccer matches were mostly on weekday afternoons, Eli, Morgan and I could be there to cheer him on as well.

When the horse shows were in Germantown, Eli or I was generally on call as the veterinarian on site. That suited me fine. I could watch Sarah ride without feeling guilty that I was avoiding work.

The McLain Scheibler Clinic had started by marketing our services to horse shows and still found them a good revenue stream, as did any new large animal vet who moved to the area. Although horse shows officially started on Friday and ran through Saturday, riders and horses nearly always moved to the showgrounds to school over the fences Wednesday and Thursday. Eli and I were seldom on call for schooling days.

Patsy's Pride had made a remarkable improvement in Sarah's attitude, especially toward me. Nathan had always understood when I had to leave one of his soccer matches to treat an animal emergency. He'd been born easy-going and self-sufficient.

Sarah, on the other hand, still had not forgiven me for the time I walked out on her piano recital to rush to an emergency when she was only halfway through *Clare de Lune*. Sarah had been nine at the time.

Now, for the first time, she seemed to accept my professional commitments. She'd always loved animals, but she was jealous of the time I spent with them. Now, I was actually employed by the show, so she could count on my being there. I loved cheering her on, but I could also comfort her when she or Pride screwed up. Losing was hard for her, but she was learning that one loss was only a blip, not a major disaster.

Sarah was a truly talented rider. She'd always made good grades, but they meant nothing to her. Now, her self esteem soared with every blue ribbon. She was even thinking of attending one of the colleges where she could take Pride and continue to ride.

In the early nineties, the first show of the season in Germantown took place in early April. Wednesday, the first schooling day, I was dipping a herd of sheep outside of Oakland, while Eli held down the office.

A new young vet named Kevin something-or-other was on call at the schooling. He had been hired by Rodney Armbruster's practice and had been in town a month. I had met him only once at a meeting, and he seemed competent enough. He was good-looking and tall, so all the female junior riders were tripping over their own feet to get his attention.

Sarah was no exception.

I was really looking forward to getting back home that Wednesday afternoon so I could hear how the schooling went. Patsy called me on my new car phone when I was about twenty minutes from the clinic. I knew it wasn't good news from the tone of her voice. "Is Sarah all right?" I asked. "Was she thrown?"

"Pride's dead," Patsy said.

I gasped. "Sarah?"

"Sarah wasn't riding him when he died."

"How? What?"

"Just come, Maggie."

By the time I reached the show grounds, the grounds keepers had removed Pride's body. Not a good idea to have competitors see dead horses.

Patsy was waiting for me when I drove up, and opened my door before I'd shut off the ignition.

The atmosphere around the stables was much too quiet. Several of Sarah's friends ran up to me in tears to say how sorry they were.

But where was Sarah?

Horses do have strokes and heart attacks, just like people. I figured that's what had happened to Pride. I'd have to explain that to

Sarah and give her what comfort I could. I knew she'd be devastated.

"Maggie, she got in her car and drove off," Patsy said. "She didn't say anything to anybody. She didn't speak. She wouldn't even look at Pride. You know how sensitive Sarah is. I expected her to cry, scream—something. Maggie, I'm frightened for her."

The last place she needed to be was behind the wheel of her car. I dialed her car phone and got that horrible message about the caller being out of service.

Patsy's normally ruddy face was ashen except for the red rings around her eyes. "She was completely calm. Dry-eyed. She just walked away." Patsy spread her hands.

"She must have been in shock. Patsy, what happened?"

"Pride had the sniffles this morning. He hadn't improved by this afternoon, so when I couldn't get you, I asked the show vet—that Kevin person," she spat his name. "That Kevin person to give him a shot of penicillin…"

I closed my eyes.

"That's right, Maggie. He pushed a whole syringe of penicillin straight into Pride's vein. He was dead before he hit the ground."

I leaned back against the truck. One of the first lessons any vet learns is always to pull up a syringe to check for blood before pushing medicine that should be given in the muscles. If there's blood, you're into a vein or an artery, and penicillin in a vein will kill a horse before you remove the needle.

"Call Eli and Morgan," I said. "Call Nathan's school and get him to call me. He'll know where to look for Sarah."

"Where are you going?"

"To find my daughter!"

I finally found her two hours later standing by the pond on the back of our property. I tried to put my arms around her, but she shrugged me off. I would have preferred hysterics.

"I'm never getting on a horse again," she said as she walked away from me and back toward the house.

"You'll change your mind, baby," I said as I followed her. "I know this is a tragedy, but…"

As she stepped up onto the back deck, she turned to look at me.

"You're always there for everybody else," she said. "Why weren't you there when *Pride* needed you?"

A moment later the door to her bedroom slammed. I sank onto the patio. I was still there when Morgan and Nathan came home and found me.

The young vet fled after he realized what he'd done. Rodney's clinic tried to avoid responsibility, but in the end they paid Patsy for the loss of Pride.

Nobody and nothing could pay Sarah.

# Chapter 22

## *In which Maggie has another sow problem*

Sarah withdrew from everything and everyone except her friends at school and her studies. Eli, Morgan, and even Nathan tried to convince her she needed to get back on a horse again, if only to keep from losing her nerve.

Every time I tried to talk to her, she insisted she was fine, she had no intention of taking up drugs or alcohol or prostitution. She was simply moving on with her life to more adult pursuits. She informed us that she had been accepted at the University of Southern California. With her grades, she could have been admitted to Harvard or Yale, and with the trust funds Morgan's father had left for his grandchildren's education, we could have paid her expenses to an Ivy League school.

She preferred USC. It was as far from home—and by extension from me—as she could get.

Morgan and Eli both counseled me to give Sarah some time. I tried to talk to her about seeing someone—a psychologist. I knew she was in pain. Lord knows I was. She refused. Every time any of us tried to talk to her about Pride's death, she said, "I'm fine."

I did what I always do in times of personal crisis. I worked. And as much as possible, I worked in the field rather than the office. I tried to fall into bed exhausted. I volunteered to see clients who were on the outer fringes of our area, or who had the largest herds.

At that point we still had some substantial pig farms in Hardeman County, the next county over from us. Even now that the agricultural conglomerates have driven most of the small pig farmers out of business, some still raise hogs to show and to butcher for country ham.

Country ham is not Smithfield. It is not cured with sugar. It is nothing like the canned variety from Denmark or from Virginia or the spiral cut hams. We are talking salt cured, smokehouse-hung hams that mature over months, not days, that come out encrusted with salt and looking on the surface as though they died sometime in the previous century.

Country ham is never injected with water to plump it up. It may not be pretty, but a slice of real country ham served with red eye gravy and hot biscuits is as close to heaven as breakfast can come. Red eye gravy, by the way, is pan drippings with a little coffee added.

Pork is big in Memphis, which is home to the granddaddy of all barbecue contests, held down at Tom Lee Park on the banks of the Mississippi River over a weekend in mid-May. Two out of three years it rains, but the contest so far has never been cancelled. Sometimes the cookers and visitors have to run for cover to get out of the way of thunderstorms that roar across the river straight at the Memphis bluffs. We've even had the occasional tornado warning that sent everybody scurrying. But the cooks go right back to baby-sitting the coals on their cookers. If we ever did have a tornado hit during the contest, the cooks would probably stay at their cookers until they were sucked up like Dorothy and Toto and be plumped down in Oz still holding their sauce mops aloft.

We do not barbecue beef. The country folks still barbecue the occasional possum or squirrel, but to the rest of us, barbecue is pork, pure and simple.

I like pigs for their intelligence and their 'screw-you' attitude. You can train a pig to do tricks, but only if the pig sees some benefit in taking orders. They give affection the way cats do. If they like you, they like you. If they don't, watch out.

At that point, the best country hams in our part of the world came from Lynn and Doug McCabe. They raised long, lean Derbyshire whites and Durocs so red they made the ladies in Titian's paintings look drab. I met them first at the Mid-South Fair where they often took home multiple blue ribbons for best sow or best boar. I hung over their pens and lovingly scratched the ears and backs of their exhibition pigs. We got to talking, and I wound up driving forty miles a couple of times a year to do their testing and vaccinations. Not only did they pay their bills on time, but Eli and I both wound up with the lagniappe of country ham to go with our biscuits.

Doug volunteered at the local animal shelter in Brownsville three afternoons a week, while Lynn still worked full time as a nurse anesthetist. I knew my way around their farm whether they were home or not, so when Lynn called me to say that they had a sow that had been attacked and had her tail bitten off by another sow, I was happy to go take a look at her.

The trip would take me most of the afternoon and keep my mind off Sarah.

"She's close to farrowing," Lynn said. "We were planning to move her from the gestation barn to the farrowing barn this evening after Doug gets home. Then this morning she gets into this ruckus with one of her own daughters that's also close to her time. You know how sows get when they're close to farrowing. Real bitchy."

"Did you isolate her?"

"Sure did. She's in a separate pen closest to the door to the paddock. You know her. It's Peaches. She's a good ol' girl."

She was indeed. An experienced brood sow, she weighed over two hundred pounds, and was intelligent and friendly.

"I'm sorry to hear about her tail," I said.

"We should have separated her last weekend, I guess. Just didn't get around to it."

"I'll drive out, clean up her wound and give her a shot of antibiotics."

"If you have time, you mind moving her to the farrowing barn?" Lynn asked. "It's just across the yard."

"Sure. No problem."

"Just open the door of her pen. She'll follow you over to the farrowing barn like a dog. She's done it often enough."

I always enjoyed the drive out to Lynn and Doug's place. It was close to LaGrange down narrow roads with trees so thickly planted on either side that they had interlocked arms through the years.

I pulled into the McCabe's yard and parked beside the gestation barn. Everything was immaculate as it always was. No mess, no odor.

I found poor Peaches in her stall in the gestation barn quickly. Her tail had ceased to bleed and looked clean. She let me treat it. Unlike most animals, she seemed to realize I was there to help her.

If you've ever been around pigs that are used for show and breeding, you'll have seen little notches cut into their ears. One notch stands for three—so a pig with one notch in its ear was the third piglet born in his litter. Two notches—the piglet was the fourth, fifth or sixth, and so on.

Peaches had been born in a large litter. Instead of clipping half a dozen notches into her ear, Doug had simply popped a red ear tag through the ear itself. Sort of like a woman with pierced ears wearing a red plastic tag for an earring.

After six months or so, the ear tag fell out, leaving a small hole. As Peaches grew, the hole grew with her. It was currently half an inch across. As the sunlight hit her ear, a small dot of light would be reflected across her pen and onto the wall. As she flapped her ear, the dot would move back and forth like a wobbly laser pointer.

She wasn't thrilled when I stood over her and shot her with the antibiotic, but she merely waved those ears and snorted.

I opened the door to her pen and stepped back. "Come on Peaches. Time to move house."

She wrinkled her snout at me, but she trotted out cheerfully and followed right at my heels. I closed the door to the gestation barn behind me, walked across the small grassy area between the barns, and opened the door to the farrowing barn. "Okay, girl, inside you go."

Peaches walked up to the door and stuck her snout inside. Farrowing barns are kept relatively dark and quiet so the sows won't be disturbed. This one was no exception.

Peaches stuck her head in, looked around into the semi-darkness, saw no other members of her own species, and decided there must be monsters inside instead. She backed out, turned around, walked half a dozen steps, and began to nibble grass.

"Peaches, doggonit, come on. Git in there."

I gave her a hefty shove toward the door. She trotted up to it and walked her front half inside before she stopped, sniffed, and backed out again.

I looked at my watch. I was and am fond of pigs, but I had dinner plans that evening. Barbecue. Pork.

"Peaches, honey," I wheedled, "Go on in there unless you want to be tonight's menu."

She blinked up at me. She didn't trust me. I was attempting to force her into the Black Hole of Calcutta, and she was entirely too smart to fall for that gimmick. She wasn't annoyed. She simply had no intention of doing what I asked.

"All right for you," I said under my breath. I had two choices. I could go back to the gestation barn, find some rope and drag her into that barn. That would take time and a bunch of energy.

Or, I could stick my index finger through that hole in her ear and pull her into the barn in about six seconds flat. I had no doubt she'd come willingly once she felt the pressure.

I reached down and pushed my index finger through that hole.

I realized I had just forced my finger into a Chinese finger cuff at the same time she realized I had my finger through her ear.

The more I pulled with my right hand, the tighter that hole clamped down around my finger.

I had also transgressed some piggy rule of privacy about which I was unaware until that moment. She didn't mind my pushing and shoving her. I could not, however, put my finger through her ear.

She snorted, squealed, bucked, and ran straight across in front of my legs in a body block worthy of Refrigerator Perry.

I struggled to keep my feet as she galloped in a tight circle around me.

I had to keep twisting with her. If I didn't I'd either dislocate my shoulder or tear my finger off. I didn't dare fall. I tried to concentrate on her snout so that I wouldn't get dizzy.

It didn't work.

For a sow in the last stages of pregnancy, she was a real sprinter. She dug in with her piggy little hooves and corkscrewed around me again and again while she squealed at the top of her lungs. I revolved with her and kept yelling for her to stop. I yelled some other things, too. I used cuss words I hadn't used since high school.

I'd stopped counting revolutions when without warning she sat down and fell over.

I fell over *her*. My heart was racing and my head was spinning. I didn't think I'd been that drunk since I graduated from vet school.

For a moment I was scared she'd had a stroke or aborted. Then I realized she was as winded and probably as dizzy as I was. I collapsed against her bulging belly with my right index finger still trapped in her left ear and her fat little trotters sticking straight out on either side of me.

We both panted. I reached over with my free hand and popped my finger out of her ear, but neither of us moved. We were companions in exhaustion. She raised her head once to look at me as though to say, "This is your fault, sister," but then she lay back down and panted some more.

Finally, I struggled to my feet and walked back to the gestation barn for the rope I should have used in the first place.

By the time I came back, Peaches was up and breathing normally once more.

The door to the farrowing barn had stayed open all this time. There were no other sows in residence at the moment, so we hadn't had any breaks for freedom.

I reached out to loop the rope around her head, but she shook me off, trotted up to the door and walked inside. She turned her head, tossed me a single contemptuous glance, and disappeared into the shadows.

I shut the door on her, put the rope back where I found it, left Lynn and Doug a note, and drove back to town.

In every encounter I have ever had with pigs, the pigs invariably make me feel like the biggest doofus on the planet. Maybe I should stick to sheep. They make earthworms look like Einstein.

On my way back I started laughing. I had about as much chance of changing Sarah's mind about where she was going to college, about seeing a psychologist or riding again as I did of dragging that pig into the farrowing barn. Morgan always told me to pick my battles. Maybe Sarah belonged at USC. Maybe God planned a better career for her than professional riding.

Maybe I should butt out.

# Chapter 23

## *In which we meet Lanier and Susan*

Until I finished school and qualified in the state of Tennessee as a full-fledged vet, Dr. Parmenter carefully kept me out of his personal life. The little I knew came from staff gossip overheard while I was cleaning cages after my classes at Southwestern, or during the summers when I worked for him.

I knew he had married his wife, Irene, just after he finished vet school at Auburn, and that they had no children, although I gathered there was some tragedy in the past. He had Irene's picture on his desk in a silver frame, but she never even came to the office parties at the clinic. Dr. Parmenter had them catered. I never knew whether the choice was hers or his.

I actually met Irene Parmenter in the reception line at my wedding. Yes, we had a reception line. My Mother would have had a cat fit otherwise.

I recognized Irene from her picture. She was shorter than Dr. Parmenter, maybe five two or three, and partridge plump where he never seemed to have an ounce of fat on him. She had kind hazel eyes and a ready smile, and a wreath of hair. She must have been in her late thirties or early forties, but already her hair was so white she looked for all the world as though she wore a halo.

She definitely deserved one. As I got to know her, I found that she was the financial brains behind the clinic, and smoothed Dr. Parmenter's way much the same way Morgan did for me. She had one other characteristic that I found fascinating. She had that politician's talent for giving everyone she spoke to her whole-hearted attention. Unlike politicians, however, she didn't forget they existed the moment she moved on. She could work a room with the aplomb of Alice Longworth Roosevelt. She was Teddy Roosevelt's daughter, and lived well into her eighties as the doyenne of Washington Society. She is said to have remarked, "If you have nothing good to say about somebody, come sit by me."

Irene Parmenter was much kinder. I liked her immediately, and I think she liked me back.

Morgan and I invited them to dinner in our first apartment—the one furnished with Late Relatives and Early Attic. They reciprocated, and for the first time I got to see where Dr. Parmenter lived. Very, very nice. A twenties-vintage mock Tudor cottage right on Galloway Golf Course, a public golf course in Memphis, but a lovely one. The house was decorated with antiques and oriental rugs.

It was obvious from the first moment I caught Dr. Parmenter's eye on Irene that he adored her.

As is a requirement in Southern houses, she took me on a house tour after dinner while Morgan and Dr. Parmenter talked golf over coffee in the living room. Not the den. The living room—an actual separate room that was used for living, and not simply kept pristine in case the preacher made an unexpected call.

We looked all over the upstairs, but she passed one door without opening it. As we started down the stairs, she said quietly, "That was our daughter Mindy's room. Hubert has never let me turn it into a study for him, although he could use one at home."

So this was the tragedy. The loss of a child. But whether the child had died, or run away, and when, I had no idea. So the next day I called Patsy Dalrymple, who knew everything.

"Real sad," Patsy said. "If there ever were a woman cut out to be a mother, it's Irene."

"What happened?"

"Cystic fibrosis. Doesn't usually happen on the first child. Of course they didn't do gene testing in those days. She died when she was twelve. It nearly killed Dr. Parmenter, and I thought for a while it would break up their marriage. The loss of a child so often does."

"How awful for them."

"Irene is even busier than I am. She takes art classes and volunteers at St. Jude and I don't know what all. Runs herself ragged. I guess it's how she stays sane."

Plato was right—children should bury their parents, not the other way around. Although Dr. Parmenter had never given me an inkling that he considered me anything remotely like a daughter, I wondered if that was the reason he had mentored me so assiduously. And why he kept me at arm's length. Must be terribly hard to trust yourself to love somebody the same age as the child you lost.

What with growing the clinic and a pair of pregnancies, Morgan and I didn't get together much socially with the Parmenters. It was one of those relationships that disappear like an underground river, only to reappear just as healthy when least expected.

Irene called me one day out of the blue.

My heart leapt into my throat when I heard her voice. Being Irene, the first words out of her mouth were, "He's fine. We both are. This isn't bad news."

I relaxed, and we chatted about getting together more often. She commiserated with me about Pride's death, but I didn't burden her with Sarah's reactions.

Then she said, "Maggie, I need a favor, and if Hubert finds out I've asked he will fry me for supper."

"Anything."

She let out of a deep sign. "Good. Hubert is hunting for another junior partner."

I laughed. Dr. Parmenter's search for junior partners had become legendary in the local vet community and probably across the country. They would come, fresh from vet school, stay six months or a year, then leave abruptly or be sent packing because they couldn't come up to his standards.

"This time it's serious. He'll kill me for telling you this, but the doctors have told him he has to cut back. His eyes aren't as strong as they were, and he's developed some arthritis in his fingers. Since we don't have any children to leave the practice to, we need someone to buy at least a portion of it and take up the slack until he retires completely."

I was afraid she was going to ask me, but she knew better.

"We've been advertising and writing back and forth to several candidates for the last two months. We've narrowed the choice down to three possibles."

She had said 'we.'

"The next couple of weeks we have scheduled each of them to come into town to interview, see the practice, and look at the city—each on a different day, of course. None of them knows about the other."

"How can I help?"

"I told Hubert we needed to take them out to dinner the one night they were in town after the interviews. He says if they can't feed themselves in a strange city on their own, he's not interested in them. He says he'll be sick of them by dinnertime anyway."

"You want Morgan and me to entertain them?"

"Not Morgan. Just you. Take each of them out to dinner, really get into the nitty-gritty of why they want the job, and give me a report. Verbal, of course. Hubert must never know we've done it."

"Of course. Just give me the dates, names, and how to get in touch with them."

"I'll write each of them and tell them to expect your call. Thank you so much, Maggie."

"Just me? Not Eli?"

"Just you, if you don't mind. Eli's lovely, but I don't know her well enough to ask a favor of her."

When I picked up Dr. Steve Lansing the following Thursday, I decided that he had given up a career in the movies for vet school. The man was gorgeous. Six feet five of pure hunkdom with a degree from LSU and excellent grades and recommendations. I was worried he'd be an arrogant jerk, but he didn't seem even to be aware that the parking lot attendant (female) nearly drove my truck into a retaining wall because she couldn't take her eyes off him. We had a delightful time.

The next morning I reported to Irene. "Sorry. He's not your guy."

"Oh, why?"

"On the surface, he's perfect. And I mean puuuuur-fect. His wife is a dental technician, so she has a portable career that makes enough money to sustain him until he builds a practice. He's knowledgeable about veterinary medicine, he loves small animals, and the old ladies in Dr. Parmenter's practice would drool over him."

"So what's the matter with him?"

"Daddy. Daddy is a big-time contractor in Shreveport who has promised to build Steve a clinic and set him up in practice after two years in the hinterlands of Tennessee."

"No chance Daddy would consider Memphis?"

"None. Daddy wants to be close to his not-yet-born grandchildren and is willing to pay for the privilege."

"Well, nuts."

"Absolutely."

I must admit that when Dr. Marcia Callahan, D.V.M., Cornell, walked into the lobby of her hotel to meet me, I did something I rarely do. I took agin' her. That means I didn't like her. She was my height, slim, well groomed, a little horse-faced with a couple too many teeth, but her smile was pleasant and her grip was firm. She seemed nice, but some intangible struck me the wrong way.

We had a pleasant enough meal, although she didn't eat red meat or drink anything with alcohol or caffeine. We didn't have dessert, because she didn't eat sugar either. Okay, so she wasn't a hedonist like me. She was also thinner. She was unmarried, thirty-four years old, and looking for a new challenge.

"What was your last challenge?" I asked. I tried to keep my voice even, and either I succeeded, or she didn't have a sense of humor.

"For the past six years I've been working with a pharmaceutical company doing research."

Nothing wrong with that. I'd done the same thing the summer I met Morgan.

As she began to speak about her research, for the first time her face became animated. Within ten minutes I knew what I'd picked up on instinctively. The woman did not like animals. That sounds strange for a veterinarian, but there are medical doctors out there who don't like human beings and dentists who don't like teeth. I doubt that she was intentionally cruel to any living thing, but I wasn't certain she had enough empathy to know whether she was causing pain or not.

She would certainly not empathize with Dr. Parmenter's clients or their charges. She might splint little Suzi's broken paw perfectly, but fifteen minutes later she wouldn't be able to tell you whether Suzi was a Dachshund or a Corgi. She wouldn't see the point in answering questions from worried clients or reassuring them when they needed it. She would be highly productive and see lots of patients. At least once. I didn't know how many would return.

In short, I didn't think she appreciated the role pets play in their owner's wellbeing.

Working for Dr. Parmenter, she would be miserable and would lose him half his client base in six months.

I spent the next hour discouraging her from private practice and suggesting she might be happier going back to research. We parted amicably. As a matter of fact, she thanked me profusely for my guidance.

When I drove away from her hotel I realized I hadn't relaxed my shoulders in over two hours.

"No way," I said to Irene the next morning. Then I told her why.

"Oh, dear." She sighed. "I don't have much hope for the last one either. I think she may have psychiatric problems."

Lovely.

When I picked up Lanier Polman from her hotel, I could see why Irene might think that. She was dressed in a shabby denim skirt and a white blouse slightly frayed at the collar. Probably she was still paying off student loans. It was late October in Memphis. The temperature was running in the fifties after dark. She could have borrowed a coat, surely. She had to be freezing.

Her color was high, and it wasn't simply the Florida tan she must have gotten living in Ocala. Her hands were constantly in motion, moving through her brown hair that could have stood a good cut, down her skirt, hugging herself.

Her first words were, "I'm sorry to keep you waiting, but I have to call my mother. She's looking after my daughter while I'm up here and the phone's been busy." I waited while she found a pay phone and talked for about five minutes. When she came back, she seemed even more agitated.

"Something wrong at home?" I asked.

She shook her head. "Everything's fine."

I looked at the set of her jaw and heard the quiver in her voice and didn't believe her. I said, "Why don't we go have a glass of wine in the bar?"

"Won't we be late for our dinner reservations?"

"On Monday night? I didn't make reservations. We won't have any trouble getting in."

She smiled, but she came with me, and when her wine was delivered, she took a single hesitant sip before she put it down and began to twirl the stem between her fingers.

"Is your daughter all right?"

"What?" She shied as though I had asked her whether she'd dismembered her mother before she left Ocala. "Susan, my baby, requires a lot of care." She took a deep breath. "You're really nice to do this, but it's not necessary. I could just have a sandwich sent up. I know your family must be waiting for you."

"My family? They're at home with their father. They don't need me."

She stared at me and then she burst into tears.

I didn't have the first notion what to do. She grabbed the napkin off the table and buried her face in it. I could hear her choking on her sobs.

"Stay right here," I said. "Don't you dare move. I'll be right back." I grabbed the nearest pay phone and called Eli. "I know you weren't supposed to be included in these little *tete a tetes*, but something's changed. Defrost a couple of pizzas and throw them in the microwave. We'll be there in thirty minutes."

I strode back to the table and nearly dragged her to her feet. "Come on. This is no place for hysterics."

"I'm so sorry."

"Don't be. I'm taking us someplace where you can have hysterics in peace."

I turned up the heat in the truck and offered her my spare windbreaker from the back seat. She shrugged into it gratefully.

"I didn't think it would be this cold," she said.

On the way out to Eli's, I kept up inane prattle about Memphis. Most of it was supposed to be funny. I could hear Lanier gulping and sniffling beside me, but she didn't seem in the mood to laugh.

Eli, accompanied by Sweet Pea, her current Border Terrier, met us at her front door. "Pizza should be done in five minutes. Hey, Lanier, I'm Eli."

More stammers.

Sweet Pea gamboled around Lanier's ankles demanding to be petted. Lanier knelt, rubbed his ears and cooed to him.

*Aha,* I thought, *this one likes animals.*

"Sit down, have another glass of wine, and tell us what's the matter. I might eat you alive," I said, "but Eli will protect you."

It took some more prodding, but eventually her story tumbled out.

"Your children have a father who cares about them. My Susan's father wishes she'd never been born," Lanier said.

A single mother? A father who refused to admit paternity? "Surely not," Eli said.

"That's what my mother said on the phone tonight." She dropped her head into her hands. "Susan has cerebral palsy."

Eli and I exchanged glances.

"The doctors weren't sure there was anything wrong until a couple of months ago, but I knew she wasn't normal. Geoff, my soon to be ex-husband, couldn't handle it. He walked out and is living with someone he met at Wellington at the winter horse shows."

Once she started talking, she couldn't stop. "Geoff's a large animal vet." Her shoulders heaved with the effort of her breathing. She was close to tears and probably even closer to exhaustion, physical and mental. "The bills are piling up, and I can't find anybody to look after Susan except my mother who has osteoporosis and shouldn't even be picking her up, and I've got to get out of Florida where I keep running into people who—"She shuddered. "People just look at me with all this pity as though Susan were some kind of vegetable, and she's not. She's my baby and I love her and why can't he see that and love her too?"

"Surely he does," Eli said.

"He told my lawyer that he doesn't see why he should have to pay child support when the state looks after kids like her in nursing homes."

We both caught our breath. "Bastard," I whispered. She didn't appear to hear me.

"The doctors say Susan's CP is very mild—motor function, not her intelligence at all. I can't stick her away in some horrible home!"

"Of course you can't," I said. "He's an S.O.B. Let your lawyer deal with him."

She ran her fingers under her eyes and along her cheekbones. "I'm so sorry to dump this on perfect strangers. Dr. Parmenter doesn't want a basket case." She gave us a wintry smile. "I am definitely a basket case."

"But how good a doctor are you?" I asked. "That's what he cares about. What are your qualifications for this job?"

She stared at me as though I had lost my mind. Then she rallied, sucked in a deep breath, clasped her hands in her lap, and answered my question. "Degree and vet school at University of Florida. I worked for Sea City in Ocala as a marine vet."

"Wow!" Eli said, shoving another piece of pizza at her. "I don't think I've ever met a marine vet. What made you choose that?"

Lanier relaxed a tiny bit. Eli and I exchanged glances.

"One of my professors told me that of every ten women vets who want an equine practice, nine will fail. I had been considering equine, but those seemed like bad odds. I figured there wouldn't be that many women going into marine. I'm certified as a general vet, of course. Otherwise I'd never have put in for the job with Dr. Parmenter."

"Did you like marine?"

She shrugged. "I got picked for an internship at Sea City, probably because they couldn't tell from my name I'm a woman. When I showed up, they were not pleased. They would have preferred a man."

"Tough," Eli said. "How did they handle it?"

"How do they always handle it? They tried to run me off. Stuck me with the penguins, theoretically one of the worst jobs they had." She actually grinned. "I loved it. I had a blast."

Eli and I leaned forward. "How do you treat penguins?"

"There wasn't that much treatment, but I did get to swim with them. That was fantastic. You know they mate for life? I had a couple of big male Emperors who were bound and determined they wanted me to have their babies—or at least produce their eggs. They used to wait for me, and then swim circles around me and bump into me and do all this courting behavior."

"Sounds like fun."

"Oh, it was. Then the management switched me to the dolphins. If I thought the penguins were fun, the dolphins were fabulous."

Her face glowed under its tan. Her eyes glittered with enthusiasm. For the moment, at least, she'd forgotten her personal situation. Good.

"I've heard they're dangerous," I said.

"They can be. They're big, although not nearly as big as the killer whales. You have to wear a really thick wet suit so that if they grab you, they won't grab skin. And of course we had air tanks, so we didn't have to worry about being under water with them." She hunched her shoulders. "They really do have a sense of humor. They loved to sneak up behind me under water until I could feel their sonar tingling off the back of my neck. Then they'd blow as hard as they could." She laughed. "I was supposed to turn around, take out my mouthpiece and blow air from my tank straight into their faces. I swear they'd laugh. And then sometimes they'd grab hold of an arm or a leg and drag me around the pool underwater as fast as they could. It was great."

"Why on earth did you quit?"

Instantly every trace of animation dropped from her face. "I fell in love."

"Oh."

"Sea City made it clear I'd be stuck where I was if I stayed with them. Geoff convinced me to marry him and said I could make more money working small animals until he could get established with the big racehorse breeding farms around Ocala."

"But you must miss it, surely."

"The dolphins? Of course I do, but I'm a realist. Somebody had to support us while Geoff was building his equine practice. And I do like small animals. Large too come to that. I just didn't expect—"

"You don't have to go on," Eli said. "Have a little more wine."

"No, please. I don't usually drink at all, and I certainly didn't mean to dump all my problems in your laps." She gave us a watery smile. "I can't really talk to my mother and the doctors openly."

"Hey, if you can't talk to a pair of colleagues who are old enough to be your mother—well, nearly old enough," Eli said. "Who can you talk to?"

"Please don't get me wrong. I wouldn't give Susan up for all the dolphins and penguins in the universe. I just feel so helpless."

"You ought to feel damned mad," I said.

"That too. But mostly I'm scared."

"If you got the job with Dr. Parmenter, would your mother move up here with you to look after Susan?"

She shook her head. "My dad's heart is bad. They can't move."

"Who would look after her?"

"She's a little over a year old, and she's no more trouble than most babies right now. Actually, she's so sunny, she's better than most. I planned to put her in a nursery. Dr. Parmenter has good insurance..."

"Even for a pre-existing condition?"

"They can't turn her down if she's on my plan. That's one of the reasons I want this job so much."

"How much care will she need down the line?"

"That's just it. The doctors don't think there's anything wrong with her mental capacity. But I don't know yet whether she'll ever walk, ever speak, ever feed herself. She's going to need therapy and ongoing medical treatment. I'm just beginning to find out what I'm up against."

"You ought to get help from the bastard who fathered her," I said.

"My lawyer says he can afford to pay decent child support now, but even if he's conscientious about that, I'll be all alone."

"Maybe not," Eli said, and patted her hand.

At that moment while we were all sitting around sniffling, the telephone rang. Eli took the call in the kitchen, while Lanier and I got ourselves ready to go back to her hotel.

"Don't go anywhere," Eli said. "That was Roy Wilson. He's got a cow down with a prolapsed uterus. He needs somebody quick." She turned to Lanier. "It's really a two man job. You mind riding along? Either that or we can call you a cab. The practice will pay for it."

"Don't even think about that. Hey, I don't have anything to do tonight except watch the late news and worry about Susan. I'd like to ride along. I've handled my share of prolapsed uteruses in school. Maybe I can help."

On our way out the door, I asked Eli over my shoulder, "Is that cow in the barn or up the side of a hill?"

"He swears she's inside."

"Good."

On the way to Roy's, Eli and I regaled Lanier with the story of Eli's yellow rainboots. I made Lanier put my heavy windbreaker back on before she climbed out of the truck at Roy's and was introduced.

In the barn under the lights, the cow was standing up and looked to be in fairly good shape except for the massive uterus hanging out behind her. Prolapse of the uterus is fairly common in cows, and if it can be popped back in quickly, it's not that serious. If not, or if it's torn, it can be a death sentence for the cow. So speed was essential.

"Got another problem," Roy said as he opened the stall door. "She won't have nothing to do with that calf. Been trying to kick the fool out of it. Finally had to tie her hind legs together to keep her from stepping on her uterus and tearing it out while she was kicking at the calf."

The calf still lay in the hay. If it had been trying to stand and nurse, it had apparently given up, and now looked up at us with worried brown eyes.

"We need to get that calf out of here and into someplace warm," I said.

"It needs some milk," Lanier added.

"Don't I know it."

"Mr. Wilson?" Lanier asked, "Can we move that calf into your kitchen? We could turn on your stove and warm it up. I can get it to nurse and help it to stand so you can help the doctors out here."

Roy looked at her through narrowed eyes. "Got a couple of old blankets we could put down on the kitchen floor."

"Do you think you can carry it that far?"

Roy drew his bony shoulders up. "Doc, I been toting newborn calves since before you was born." He snorted. "Can I carry a calf, huh." He reached down and levered the calf halfway up. We could tell he was struggling. Between the four of us we got it up into his arms and across his chest. He walked out of the barn with immense dignity, but I suspected he'd have a heck of a backache come morning.

Lanier followed him.

"Lanier? You okay with this?" I asked.

"Sure."

I turned back to Eli who was already positioning the cow's uterus to push it back inside. It was like trying to shove an enormous bowl of gelatin through a small funnel—frustrating and annoying and time consuming. Once the uterus started to go back in, however, it disappeared like a rabbit down a burrow. The cow never seemed to feel any distress. As a matter of fact, that particular cow never stopped munching her hay.

When I checked my watch after we had treated the cow, I saw that it was after midnight. Despite the chill October air, Eli and I were drenched with sweat and blood. We hadn't given a thought to Lanier and the calf.

We rinsed off as much as we could under Roy's barn tap and half staggered up his back steps and in the kitchen door.

Roy had been a widower for over ten years. He kept a bachelor kitchen. Clean, but with a minimum number of gewgaws and decorations.

What few there were had been knocked off the lower shelves. The small kitchen table lay on its side. Lanier didn't just look disheveled, she looked as though she'd been battling a dozen Sumo wrestlers at the same time.

Milk dripped from her eyebrows and the end of her nose. It ran down the front of her shirt and her denim skirt. Her arms were sticky with it.

She knelt at the edge of a woolen blanket that had been spread in the open space in front of the stove as she tried to hoist the little black and white calf to its feet. Every time it struggled half way up, its hooves would spread out the blanket and it would start to slide.

Splat. All four legs at four points of the compass.

Roy tried to hold it around its belly, while Lanier made stabs at its mouth with the nipple of a large nursing bottle half full of milk.

The baby would reach out, grasp the bottle, take a few good pulls, then slide back down. Calves, unfortunately, learn to nurse standing up. This one wanted to eat the proper way.

"Dang it, Maggie, grab this fool calf!" Roy wheezed. "I can't hold her up by myself."

"Pull the blanket out from under her feet, you doofus," Eli said.

"Tried that. Floor's even slipperyer. She don't make it halfway up without the blanket."

I expected Lanier to look frustrated or annoyed or even apologetic, but the face she turned up to mine was radiant. "Hey, Maggie, Eli," she said. "We got a whole bottle into this little girl already and she's warm as toast. Come on, Mr. Wilson, how about we let her take a little nap?"

"Whew!" Roy released his hold. The baby slid to the blanket as gently as a Boston matron taking her seat at the symphony. Apparently she decided that nourishment was more important than standing as she was supposed to. She grasped the nipple in Lanier's hand and suckled noisily and contentedly for a minute, then let go the bottle, struggled to curl her legs under her, put her head down on the blanket and went to sleep.

Lanier got up off her knees and looked around. "Guess we made kind of a mess staggering around until we worked out the blanket routine."

"Don't matter none," Roy said. "We got us a warm calf with a full belly. I can clean up tomorrow morning." He looked down at the sleeping calf. "Think maybe I'll call her Lanie. You mind, doc?"

"I'd be honored, Mr. Wilson," Lanier said. "How's mamma doing?"

"She's fine," Eli said. "Can't say the same for us. Come on, Lanier, I've got a perfectly good guestroom with it's own bath. I can lend you p.j.'s and a robe. We'll toss your clothes into the washer and dryer, and you'll be good to go by morning."

"Oh, I couldn't."

"Sure you could," I said as I marched the two women out to the truck. "Call your hotel and give them Eli's number in case your mother calls. We can stop by and pick up your stuff tomorrow when I take you to your plane. What time do you leave?"

"Not until ten-thirty in the morning. You can't take time off to drive me."

"One of us will make time. We owe you. Right, Mr. Wilson?"

He held me back as I followed Eli and Lanier to the car. "That's a game little gal," he said. "She comin' to work with y'all?"

"No, sir," I said. "If I have my way, you just met Dr. Parmenter's new junior partner. I bet she'll be moved into Memphis by Christmas."

And she was.

# Chapter 24

## *In which we meet a cold hound and a warm shepherd*

Sarah was in her junior year at USC and interning with a small independent film company. She wanted a career in what she said everyone in Los Angeles called films, not movies.

Nathan was a freshman at Brown. He planned to follow his father into something to do with banking or investments. He was aiming for Wall Street where, he said, the action was.

I had come to terms with the fact that neither of my children would become a vet. As a matter of fact, if one lived in New York City and one stayed in Los Angeles, neither of them would live within driving distance.

Because the children were home, Eli agreed to take emergency calls so I wouldn't have to. Then, of course, the children, as college kids do, spent most of their time seeing all their hometown friends.

For the first time in my memory, we had a white Christmas. Boy, did we ever! The Mississippi River froze all the way across. River traffic stopped because of the danger of icebergs. A couple of big ones bashed into bridge peers north of St. Louis and caused enough damage to keep the bridge closed for a week.

In west Tennessee we did not, nor do we yet have snow removal equipment. The best we could manage was trucks that threw ashes and rock salt onto the bridges and overpasses.

People around here weren't used to snow and hadn't a clue how to drive in it. School was cancelled as the first snowflake stuck to the first schoolbus windshield.

Because animals still got sick and hurt, Eli and I had snow tires on our trucks, carried chains, flares, blankets, candles (to stay warm under the blankets until help came if we got stuck on a back road), cell phones, snow shovels, and kitty litter to put under spinning tires.

Not only was the snow fifteen inches thick—unheard of in this neck of the woods—the temperature was down in the teens. Memphis and the surrounding counties all opened heated shelters for the homeless and indigent, and crews worked twenty-four-seven to keep electricity and gas flowing.

The clinic, our house and Eli's house all had generators in case the power went out, but thus far it hadn't. We were warm, we were safe, and we prayed we wouldn't get any calls.

We had closed the clinic on Christmas Eve, but about four in the afternoon Eli called me at home.

"Sorry, Maggie, we've got a new client coming in. I may need some help. Can you come over to the clinic?"

"What's the problem?"

"He says his dog is dying."

"I'll be there half an hour. I have to put the roast in the oven or we won't have any dinner tonight."

I put on the roast, shrugged into my heavy parka and stuffed my feet into my heavy rubber boots. Nathan and Sarah and Morgan were playing Scrabble in the den. They didn't even notice when I left.

The day was semi-dark already. The gray clouds felt like a soggy woolen blanket pressing the life and the breath out of every living thing. Morgan had scraped the driveways and parking lot with his tractor, but I had to slog across virgin snow to get to the clinic.

I saw that the client had already arrived as I slipped and slid up the front steps. If his car was any indication, he was a rich prospect. He was driving the first Lamborghini I'd ever seen. Even in the dusk its scarlet pelt gleamed like the breast of a bluebird.

I pushed open the door and heard Eli's voice and an answering baritone coming from the closest examining room.

He had his back to me, so all I could see was a heavy leather sheepskin jacket with the collar pulled up.

"Hi, what's up?" I asked.

He turned.

I blinked. I probably gaped. Why do men grow better looking as they age? This one was fiftyish, with a mass of iron gray hair, a lock of which had flopped down on his forehead. He had wide gray eyes and the chiseled facial bones of one of those Greek statues. He was drop dead gorgeous.

Not tall. Probably no more than five feet ten—my height. But even under the heavy coat he looked slim and fit. The kind of guy who models in GQ.

On the examining table a greyhound bitch lay stretched out stiff. And I do mean stiff.

"She's hypothermic," Eli said. "I've got hot packs in the microwave."

I fetched them. When I came back, we wrapped them and packed them around her.

"Is she dead?" the man asked. His voice was as handsome as his face, a low baritone with the rich accent that only comes from generations of Southern wealth and privilege.

"Not yet," Eli said, "But I don't guarantee anything."

We covered the brindle dog with more heavy towels and rubbed her feet and ears.

"How did this happen?" Eli asked.

The man sank into the client's chair in the corner of the room and dropped his handsome head into his hands. "I didn't know. They didn't tell me."

"Who? What didn't you know?" Eli snapped.

He sighed deeply and stared at the greyhound. I was afraid he was going to cry. I turned away and kept rubbing the blood back into the hound's extremities.

"I should never have agreed to dog sit," the man said. "What do I know about animals? Zip. But it was only for a week. Nobody knew they'd get stuck in New York because of this storm."

"Okay," Eli snapped. "She's not your dog. Start at the beginning."

He took a deep breath. "A couple of my friends flew to New York to shop and see some shows. Greta, here, retired off the dog-track and hates to be cooped up in a cage. She's a sweet dog, and I know her well, so I said I'd be happy to check on her. She has a dog door so she can come and go to their yard to run. All I had to do was look in on her morning and night, make sure she had food and water. Until it got so cold I took her out to Shelby Farms to run every morning, although she gets plenty of exercise on her own. Most of the time she lies in her bed in the kitchen and sleeps. A real couch potato."

"So what happened?" Eli asked.

"Sometime last night the power went over there. I couldn't get out of my driveway or through the streets until an hour ago. The house was frigid! I found her lying on her bed like that. She was barely breathing. Her eyes were rolled back in her head."

"Why us?" Eli asked as she kneaded the dog's rib cage over her heart and lungs. "If you live in town, why risk the drive to the country?"

"You were the fifth service I called. You called me back. None of the others did. Even the Memphis Emergency Clinic seems to be closed." He turned to me. "And I've met Morgan at several luncheons. I figured his wife would be good at her job. Morgan would have to be married to an extraordinary woman."

Eli stuck her stethoscope under the toweling. "Heart's stronger."

I nodded. "She's starting to move her legs."

"Thank God," the man whispered. "I don't know how I'd ever face Jack and Peter if I killed Greta. They dote on that dog."

I glanced at Eli. She'd heard the names the same as I had. Oh well. Somebody that age and that gorgeous and without a ring on his wedding finger was bound to be gay. Too bad for single women.

"Look," I said. "There's a coffee pot in the room next to reception. You know how to operate a Mr. Coffee?"

He nodded.

"Then make a pot. We're a long way from done here. We have to make certain her kidneys are working and that there's no brain damage. Greyhounds can't take extreme heat or extreme cold. They have very little hair, very thin skin and no layer of fat at all."

"I know she's sensitive, but I didn't realize *how* sensitive."

"You couldn't have foreseen the power outage, Mr. —?"

"Shepherd Fischer. Shep." He held out his hand to me and smiled for the first time. Then he went to find the coffeepot.

"Damn shame," I whispered as soon as he was out of earshot.

"What?"

"He's obviously gay."

"No, he's not."

"Of course he is. His two friends, Jack and Peter?"

"Bet you twenty he's straight."

"How do we find out? Ask him?"

"He's going to ask me out before he leaves," Eli said. She sounded very smug.

"He is not."

"Trust me."

We worked over the dog for an hour until finally she could walk without stumbling. Apparently her kidneys hadn't been damaged because she piddled in the snow outside the back door. Eventually she ate a bowl of dog food. Shep stuck with us the whole time.

"How does she do around other animals?" I asked.

"Fine. Greyhounds are the sweetest dogs in the world," he said as he stroked Greta's long, narrow head. She stared up at him adoringly.

"She get along with cats?"

"I think so, why?"

"Because I have two Maine Coon cats and a Siamese. It's already dark outside and the roads will be like glass. Do you have plans for Christmas Eve?"

"A large glass of Glenfiddich and a salami sandwich, actually," he said with a deprecating grin. "You two probably have families to go to. If Greta's okay to travel, I'll take her home with me. I have power, or I did when I left home this afternoon."

"I'd like to keep an eye on her overnight," I said. "Why don't you join us for Christmas Eve dinner?"

"Oh, I couldn't barge in."

"You wouldn't be barging," Eli said. "There's plenty for a whole army of extra guests if I know my Maggie."

"No Glenfiddich, but I can offer you a glass of wine. A guest room as well, if you decide to get blotto," I said. "I'm serious. We'd love to have you, and I'd really prefer to watch Greta sleeping in front of my fire tonight. No cages."

He glanced at Eli. "If you're sure..."

"Absolutely, positively."

So he stayed. By the time we'd finished the roast, he had already asked Eli to an evening of jazz at a new Memphis nightclub down on Beale Street.

"Cool jazz, you swear?" Eli asked. "Modern Jazz Quartet cool? I'm not overly fond of honkers."

"Marsalis-cool," he replied. "Decent food and we can hear ourselves talk. You game?"

"Sure. Why not?"

Morgan and I left them arguing about whether Charlie Parker ever descended into honkerdom. Eli said yes. Shep said no.

In the kitchen I asked Morgan about Shep.

"Straight as a die. He has no end of lady friends who'd like to snare him, but he's never been married. Some kind of lost love a long time ago."

"Nuts," I said. "I just lost twenty bucks."

# Chapter 25

## *In which we meet Vickie*

The only place that veterinarians generally meet one another is at local meetings. We are in a sense competitors, and from time to time one of the guys turns cutthroat, but usually encounters are pretty amicable. That was especially true among the women.

By the time Vickie Anderson came onto the Memphis scene in the late nineties, Eli and I counted as old campaigners.

Vickie moved to the Memphis area to follow her husband, Herb. Big mistake. I had one unbreakable rule about my friends' husbands. "If he makes you happy, I'll love him like a brother. If he makes you miserable, I will put voodoo hexes on him."

Herb Anderson was a corporate lawyer. The multi-national company that transferred him from Kansas City to Memphis without a moment's consideration of his wife's career shall remain nameless. In this case, Momma made more than Daddy, so she needed a job. Herb's company couldn't have cared less.

The first time Eli and I met Vickie was at a Christmas party for the local DVM society. She came alone. Her husband, she said, was working on a big case for his company. Eli and Lanier came with Morgan and me. The moment Morgan realized Vickie was alone and didn't know anyone, he adopted her, sat her at our table, and brought her into our group to share our rubber chicken.

If I had been the jealous type, Vickie would have set off my green-eyed monster. As a matter of fact, Vickie's eyes *were* green. Her hair was a real mahogany red (as opposed to Patsy's red hair, which varied from strawberry blonde to Lucille Ball henna depending on her moods).

Vickie was a runner and a gym rat, so she had a wonderful figure on that five foot nine frame of hers. Her two sons, Adam and Jason, were in high school.

Vickie was working as many shifts as the local veterinary emergency clinic would give her, but she was searching for a partnership in a going small animal practice that offered both boarding and grooming.

"That's where the money is," she said. "I was close to closing a deal on a partnership in Kansas City. Now I'm back to square one until I can build a client list."

Dr. Parmenter had died two years earlier, and had left the practice to Lanier. She didn't have room for a partner, but she did call me to say Vickie impressed her. "She's concentrated on opthamology. If you have a tricky eye case, you might consider bringing her in."

That was where we left it. We had liked one another at once, but our orbits didn't coincide. One late afternoon in June, I was finishing up a string of straightforward small animal cases at the clinic.

A scarlet macaw that shouted obscenities at me in Spanish needed its wings and beak trimmed. According to its owner, it called every female *puta,* Spanish for prostitute. The bloody bird nearly impaled me twice, but I managed to avoid losing a finger.

A half dozen Labrador puppies needed dew claws removed and baby shots.

A lilac-point Siamese queen needed ear mite treatment. She was highly incensed when I put the oily stuff down her beautiful ears and let loose a string of Siamese howls that made *puta* seem like an endearment.

Standard stuff.

I ushered my last client of the day, Lilly Padmer, out to the waiting room after she picked up her Shih Tsu. "Lula Mae's ulcer should be fine in a week or so," I said. I wanted to wring Mrs. Padmer's neck. She'd fed Lula Mae General Tsao's chicken, a Hunan specialty loaded with hot peppers, because Lula Mae liked it. It's a miracle the little dog had any stomach lining left.

"Thank you so much," Mr. Padmer simpered. "Come on, Mommy's sweetheart. I've got some lovely liver for you."

"Mrs. Padmer," I said, "Remember, bland food. Preferably out of a can of dog food and not from the takee-outee. And don't forget her medicine."

"Oh, yes, of course." Mrs. Padmer smiled vacantly and left.

"She'll have that dog back on tortilla chips and salsa before the week is out," I said.

Suddenly the door burst open. One of our older clients, Wilfred Grantham, stood there with his silky terrier, Elly, in his arms. "Maggie, for God's sake, help me, please. Oh, God."

The terrier's head lolled.

"Ew!" said our receptionist when she saw the blood. New receptionist. Very young. Mercifully, I have forgotten her name. For obvious reasons she didn't last long. It didn't do to react that way to blood in a vet's office.

"Give her to me, Will," I said. "What happened?" I rushed back to exam one and laid the terrier gently on the table, still wrapped in the bath towel in which the man had carried her.

"My grandchildren were swinging in the back yard. It's a new swing set and Elly is fascinated by it. Kept running up and barking. I should have put her in the house, but you know how she loves those kids." He dropped his head in his hands.

"The swing hit her."

"Right on the temple. Look at her. All that blood! And the eye!"

I had already begun to check the terrier's vitals. She had a goose egg nearly as large as her small head. Her left eye hung completely out of its socket. I couldn't tell whether the eyeball had been ruptured for all the blood.

"Maggie?" Eli said as she stuck her head in my door. "Oh, my God."

"X-rays first to check for skull fracture, then we drain the hematoma." I touched the little dog. She whimpered and tried to turn her head, but didn't try to bite me. "Then we put the eye back in."

"Can you do that? Will she be blind?" Wilfred ran his hand down his face. "Tina and Tommy are hysterical. My wife's trying to calm them down."

"You left them at home, didn't you? They're not outside, are they?"

"No, I left them. I just bundled her up and came right over. Elly's been awake, but groggy."

"I'll bet she is," Eli said.

I nodded to Eli. "Call Vickie Anderson. Tell her we've got a bad eye case. Ask her if she can come out here stat."

"Right."

"Can't you do it?" Wilfred asked. "You've looked after her since she was born."

"I can and I will if I have to, but we have a new vet in town that specializes in opthamology. She's had better and more recent experience that I have. If we can get her quickly, I recommend we do it."

"Anything. I don't care what it costs."

A good thing since Vickie—or any specialist for that matter—wouldn't come cheap.

I picked up the little dog and headed to X-ray. Eli met me in the hall. "Vickie's leaving right now. She should be here in half an hour if she drives like you and forty-five minutes if she stays under the speed limit."

By the time Vickie rolled in twenty-five minutes later—talk about *my* driving—the little dog was prepped, shaved, and ready for surgery. We hadn't anesthetized in case Vickie needed to test reactions.

Miraculously, despite the hematoma—the goose egg—the x-ray showed no skull fracture, and there seemed to be minimal bleeding into the skull.

Eli handled anesthetic while I assisted Vickie.

She was good. She sewed up the rip in the little dog's eyeball, then stitched the eyelid shut with stitches as fine as any I had ever done.

"What do you think?" I asked.

She shrugged. "There was a small tear in the retina, but it wasn't completely detached. Despite all the blood the vitreous was intact. With luck we'll save not only the eye but most of the vision."

When she told Wilfred that, he burst into tears.

"Call your family," I said, and handed him the telephone off the reception desk.

"It looked much worse than it was," Vickie said.

Eli and I glanced at one another. The injury was every bit as bad as it looked. Either of us could have done the surgery, but we might not have saved the eye, and certainly wouldn't have been able to reattach the retina as well as Vickie did.

"You'll never know how much this means to me," Wilfred said. "I have to get home and reassure the kids." He took Vickie's hand in both of his. "Thank you so much." He leaned over and kissed me on the cheek. "Thanks, Maggie. I knew I could count on you."

The three of us stood in the front door of the clinic and watched him drive away. "Funny," I said, "I was thinking what a boring day this has been."

Eli said, "You do good work, doctor."

"Who's here to check on her during the night?"

"We are," I said. "Eli or I will check on her every hour all night."

"You mind if I stick around until she's out of the anesthetic?"

"Love to have you. How about some dinner?"

"I don't expect you to feed me," she laughed. "Herb's off at some meeting. The boys can feed themselves. I'll pick up something on the way home later when I'm sure little Elly's out of the woods."

"Nonsense," I said. "I'm on my own tonight too, so it's just Eli and me anyway."

Over soup and sandwiches at Eli's, she asked Vickie how she got into the vet business in the first place.

"Mom bred and showed dogs all my life. I was a junior handler when I was eight."

"What breed?"

"She started with Borzois—Russian wolfhounds." Vickie shook her head. "They are beautiful but can be dumb as dirt. And the grooming! After she got rid of the Borzois, she fell in love with Irish Terriers."

"Not stupid, but definitely high maintenance."

"Tie a dozen Irish terriers on a treadmill and you could generate enough electricity to light New York. After another couple of years she got sick of all the coat-stripping and clipping and went to basset hounds. She stuck with bassets until Dad died and she moved to Florida. The money I planned to use to buy a partnership comes from the dogs." She sighed. "If I can keep Herb's greedy paws off it."

That was the first time Vickie joined us for dinner and the first time she ever said anything about Herb. I suppose it was the start of what eventually came to be known as Maggie's Militia. I didn't name it, mind you. Through the years other local female vets have come and gone, but the core has remained. We meet once a month at my house for dinner, and we are in some ways closer than family.

# Chapter 26

## *In which Maggie and Morgan enjoy their empty nest*

The first Christmas without the children—the empty nest Christmas—was meant to be our first truly laid back, do what we wanted to, grownup Christmas. Sarah was sailing to Catalina with some friends who had a big sailboat, and Nathan was going skiing with the family of a girl named Lisa he'd met at Brown.

"Sounds serious," Morgan said after he'd talked to Nathan.

"He's much too young to get serious," I said.

"He graduates in June, my love, and he's got a job lined up in New York already. He's a grown man."

"You didn't get married until you were over thirty."

"I didn't meet *you* until I was thirty. Remember Romeo and Juliet?"

I cuddled deeper against his back. This was not difficult to do since we were smack in the middle of our new king-sized bed. "Romeo and Juliet were lousy planners," I said sleepily. Morgan simply grumbled.

Morgan and I should have felt lonely and abandoned. Not a chance.

We invited Lanier and her daughter Susan, Vickie Anderson, and several other vet friends to join us for our usual Christmas Eve dinner. Adults only. Morgan bought champagne to go with my trifle. Eli played carols on the spinet in the den and we all sang. We even danced to music that Nathan and Sarah would have found antediluvian. Morgan always was a good dancer—one of the skills that any Southern gentleman must possess.

We had told the answering service not to disturb either Eli or me for anything less than an apocalypse in the animal kingdom.

After midnight, and therefore on Christmas morning, Morgan and I were drowsy from making love and I was curled against his chest playing with the increasingly gray curls of hair when the phone rang.

"Apocalypse?" he whispered sleepily.

"Damnation." I realized it was our private line and not the line from the answering service. Immediately I saw Nathan and Sarah in the midst of some horrible disaster. Nathan had run into a tree on the downhill slopes in Vermont, or Susan had fallen off the sailboat. I stared at the telephone until Morgan picked it up, listened a moment, then handed it to me.

"It's Bernadette Coleman."

"What?" I took it from him.

"Damn it, Maggie, Bella's about to foal." Bernadette Coleman sounded personally affronted.

I brushed my hair out of my eyes. "Did I or did I not warn you to wait another month last year to breed Bella just to be on the safe side?"

"Don't you dare rub it in. Can you come? She's a week early. I'm here by myself. She seems to be having a tough time."

"The water hasn't broken, has it?"

"No, but she's sweating and biting at herself. She keeps lying down and getting up again. Her teats have waxed and are dripping already. I don't like the look of her, Maggie. It's gone on too long with nothing happening. I know It's Christmas, but I'm scared. We can't afford to lose that foal."

I hung up the phone, kissed Morgan lightly, and swung out of bed. He swung out of the other side. "What are you doing? Go back to sleep. I'll be home before morning," I said.

"You have enjoyed wine and champagne, and need I remind you, some pretty good sex. You do not need to be driving alone tonight."

"You enjoyed some pretty good sex too," I said.

"But nowhere near as much champagne and wine, and I had coffee."

I started to remonstrate, then nodded. "Okay. Thanks."

I napped against Morgan's shoulder on the thirty-minute drive to Bernadette's farm.

Being born just before January first seriously handicaps a racing thoroughbred. Although he'll be listed as a yearling on New Year's Day, he'll actually be only a couple of weeks old, and far behind the

January foals that won't be considered yearlings until *next* New Year's Day.

I prayed Bernadette was mistaken, even though it meant a wasted trip in the middle of the night. Foals born even a week or ten days early have a bad rate of survival. A late foal is better.

Victor and Bernadette Coleman's foaling barn lay in semi-darkness except for the spotlight and heat lamps suspended above Bella's stall. Bernadette met us at the stall door. "Maggie, I'm sorry about this. Oh, hello Morgan. I'm glad you came."

"You said you're alone? Where's Victor?"

"Lying in bed with a torn ligament in his ankle. One of the yearlings stepped on him. He'd try to hobble down here if I asked, but he wouldn't be much help." She hugged herself. "Besides, I knocked him out with a pill earlier."

"Okay, let's check the mare."

I peered through the door of the stall. Bella, a professional broodmare with a number of stakes-winning horses to her credit, looked miserable. "Doesn't get any easier, does it, old girl?" I whispered to her.

She raised her head and pinned her ears as another labor pain hit her.

At that moment her water broke.

"Show time," I whispered.

Morgan stood by looking fascinated. He didn't usually ride on calls with me, so he hadn't seen but a couple of foals born.

The white bubble, as the bulging placenta is called, protruded from the mare. In a normal birth, the two front feet protrude first with the baby's nose lying flat on top of them. The mantra for successful birth is thus "foot, foot, nose."

I stood close behind Bella as she went down on her side and began to push. "Foot, nose... Damn! She's got a foot caught behind her pelvis. We've got to get her on her feet. Morgan! Help. Grab Her halter and haul."

The last thing the mare wanted to do was to stand up. She wanted that baby out of there, and nature had not notified her that there was a problem. We heaved, and finally she surged to her feet.

I used both hands to shove the foal, whose eyelashes I could see fluttering through the white bubble, back down into the birth canal. Then I reached in, found the bony length of leg, and popped it free of Bella's pelvic bone. "Let her go, Morgan."

He did and jumped away as she collapsed practically on his new sneakers. The mare wasn't young, and she'd been in labor a long time. I bent down, grasped the foal's ankles, and began to pull gently as she pushed.

"Can I help?" Morgan whispered over my shoulder.

"Thanks, dear heart, but you're too strong."

"Maggie has to exert just the right force every time Bella pushes," Bernadette said. We were all whispering.

Finally with one great heave the mare delivered the foal. It slid out like toothpaste out of the tube, and before it hit the ground it was fighting to free itself. I cleaned off the face, made certain that the nose and mouth were clear, that the foal was breathing normally, then stood up and stepped away. I was a bloody mess; so was the hay.

No matter. We moved out of the stall and watched the two of them as Bella turned her head and nickered softly to her new baby.

"This part always makes me cry," Bernadette said.

"Looks like a big strong baby, even if it is early," I said.

At that point we heard a crash and an oath from the aisle behind us. Victor Coleman, retired jockey and now a breeder of racehorses, hobbled toward us on crutches. He wore pajamas under a down jacket.

"Dammit, Bern," he swore, "You gonna let me miss this?" He turned to me. "Colt or filly?"

"Victor, I have no idea. I haven't had time to check. Get yourself back to bed before you catch pneumonia. Morgan, give him a hand."

"I'm staying," he said. Morgan could probably have picked him up and carried him into the house bodily, but one look at that tough face and we all gave up.

"At least sit down," Bernadette said and pulled up a bale of hay. "God, I married an idiot."

We turned back to the foal, which looked at us through wide, liquid, and slightly worried eyes. His front legs pawed at the straw as he struggled to get up.

"A December foal," Victor said with disgust. "Exactly what we need."

"Maggie warned us," Bernadette said. "But Bella's always gone over her due date. We were so sure we were safe."

The mare stood up with the remains of the placenta still dragging behind her.

Bernadette turned to look at the foal, already fighting to organize its legs. "You got time to dance the New Baby Waltz?"

"Wouldn't miss it," Morgan said happily. If he was tired from the party or the romance he didn't show it. "What do we do?"

"It'll never stand on its own with those legs. It'll need help to find the spigot under Bella's belly."

Bernadette switched off the flood lamp. The heat lamp bathed mare, foal, hay and human beings in soft red light. We leaned against the wall and watched Bella nibble all over her baby. Occasionally she would raise her forefoot and thump the baby gently on its side.

"She is a good mama. How old is she now?"

"Only twelve. She's got some stakes winners in her yet."

The baby flailed, kicked, and managed to get his front legs stretched out in front of him. He strained to raise his butt, then collapsed into the hay. Bella kept up her baritone encouragement.

After a few minutes, I stepped into the stall, reached my hands under the baby's bottom, and heaved him up. "It's a colt," I said. "Ow. You little troll. Caught me with a hind hoof. I'll have a bruise the size of Pittsburgh."

"Hush," Morgan said and stepped into the stall. "Like this?" He wrapped his arms around the baby's middle. Halfway to a standing position the baby flopped and both Morgan and I landed in the straw with two hundred pounds of baby wrapped around us.

Berndadette put her arms around the foal's shoulders. This time we managed to get him all the way up, but a moment later he subsided tail end first against me in a semi-sitting position. I heaved. He stood, rocked and shook, then steadied. A moment later he took a tentative step forward.

"How about that?" Morgan said. He still held the baby's waist.

The baby took faltering steps forward, its little pink tongue already searching for its mother's nipple. After a dozen attempts to suckle on her belly, her knee, and Bernadette's thumb, the baby finally found the milk. With Morgan still supporting its little body, it latched on and began to suck noisily.

"Is he up?" Victor asked, struggling to regain his own feet.

"He's up and suckling," Morgan said.

At that moment the mare released the placenta. I checked to be certain it was complete. Retained placenta would cause infection.

"Mission accomplished," I said. "Get some sleep. That's what Morgan and I plan to do. I'll be back tomorrow morning to do shots and test the baby for antibodies." I rubbed my calf. "I'm too old for this."

As we walked side by side down the quiet aisle of the foaling barn with Victor hobbling behind, we listened to the snuffling and occasional snores of the broodmares. "I love a horse barn at night," I said.

"Hey, doc," Victor called. "How about we call him Maggie's Christmas?"

As we drove away, Morgan laid his hand on my thigh. "We're not old, love, but if we keep putting off seeing the world too long, we will be. I don't fancy the Spanish steps on a walker."

"This year I promise we can see Europe," I said.

"Florence, Rome. The hill country. Lots of sunshine and good food."

"Right now sunshine sounds marvelous," I said sleepily.

"I'm glad I came."

"Me too," I said sleepily. "Joy to the world. I do love you."

# Chapter 27

## *In which Maggie's world changes*

My life changed forever last January the third when Morgan had a fatal heart attack. He'd never shown any symptoms of heart problems. His blood pressure was good. His bad cholesterol was low and his good cholesterol was high. He was a few pounds overweight, but he didn't drink much and had never smoked. He worked out at the gym at his bank religiously three times a week. I would have bet he was in much better shape than I was. His doctor gave him a clean bill of health a month before he died.

Morgan collapsed on the front steps of the bank. The EMTs said he was probably dead before he hit the concrete. One moment he was fine. The next he simply wasn't there any longer. His doctor called it a sudden death episode. He offered to do an autopsy, but what was the point?

I was stunned; I was scared. Mostly I was furious. I remember after my father died that my mother told me that for years she would watch elderly couples walking hand in hand and feel angry with my father for dying on her. I know that's irrational, but human beings aren't always rational.

One moment I was cleaning out a basset hound's ears and the next, a single telephone call had plunged me into the logistics of death without a chance to catch my breath.

Those logistics were necessary to keep me functioning and to keep the pain of loss at bay.

I have a good friend who piled her entire family, children and grandchildren, onto an airplane and flew them to Disney World for a week the day after her husband's funeral. In retrospect, I probably should have done the same thing, except that nobody would have gone along with me. I was so busy assuaging Nathan and Sara's grief that I didn't have time to grieve myself. I felt as though I had walked into a brightly lit room and suddenly someone turned out the lights and plunged the world into darkness. I stuck out my hand and felt no answering touch. I knew that if I took a single step forward I'd fall into that darkness and keep falling forever.

At first I was simply stunned and unbelieving. I told myself the whole episode was a mistake. I kept turning around expecting Morgan to walk in the door.

When Sarah arrived from Los Angeles, she seemed incapable of coherent thought, much less action.

Nathan flew down from New York with Lisa, his new bride. He had been married to her less than a year. She didn't know us very well. Besides, she'd never experienced the death of a loved-one, much less a *Southern* loved one. Lisa, raised in wealth in Massachusetts and Connecticut, didn't have a clue what needed to be done. Nathan certainly didn't.

At a time of disaster, women bond together. Eli, Lanier, Vickie Anderson, and little Heather, a newly-qualified vet who had joined our group only a year or so earlier, banded together to look after everything. During that time, Lanier's daughter Susan, just turned thirteen, named the group of us "Maggie's Militia." In my book they were as good as General Forrest's best cavalry.

Those dear women knew what needed to be done and went to work without guidance from me. They manned both our house and the funeral home so that callers would be welcomed, they kept logs of who brought food and what, they answered telephone calls from as far away as the Netherlands where Morgan's bank had a branch. They arranged to put off most of the clinic's scheduled clients. Those that couldn't be put off, they handled themselves.

And a week after the funeral, we sat around my dining room table eating take-out Chinese while we faithfully wrote thank-you notes to everyone who had helped or come by the funeral home.

Nathan, Lisa and Sarah stayed four days. After I saw them off home, I went back directly to the clinic and worked a full day from "kin to cain't", as my grandmother used to say.

Then I walked across the lawn and into the back door of my house. Eli had offered to come with me, but I knew I had to face that emptiness sometime. "Might as well be now," I said to her with a bravado that I did not feel.

I slept in our big bed—but on my side. I turned the television on the moment I came into the house and left it on until I went away again. Most of the time I remembered to eat three meals a day. I demanded to handle all the night calls. Eli refused at first, but compromised by coming with me as often as I would let her.

After a month I considered I was adjusting pretty well. I was lying. One morning I was walking across to the clinic when it hit me. Certainly the death of a horse didn't equate to the death of a husband, but I realized that the total emptiness I felt, the cold void at the center of my being, must have been what Sarah experienced after Pride's death. I didn't want to talk about Morgan. Hell, I didn't want to *think* about Morgan. I was like a badly wounded animal that is careful not to bump the wound for fear the pain would be unendurable.

I wanted no sympathy. I focused on work, work, and more work.

Monday morning the second week in February I walked into the back door of the clinic as usual at eight-thirty, despite a sleepless night in that blasted king-sized bed. I poured myself a cup of coffee from the never-ending supply in our break-cum-supply room, and called good morning down the hall to our current receptionist, Tonesha. I thought I sounded pretty normal.

"Morning," she answered. Tonesha was taller than I, young, beautiful and smart, with skin the color of mocha latte. Unfortunately, she didn't suffer nitwits gladly. We'd been working on that, since a great many of our clients were nitwitted about their animals.

She walked down the hall and lounged against my door. "We've already got folks in the waiting room. You ready to start?" She had learned quickly not to peer at me as though I were about to collapse into hysterics.

I nodded, took a long pull on my coffee and slid the uneaten bagel into my desk drawer. "Who's first?" Same ol', same ol'. I was *not* on the raw edge. No way.

In retrospect, I'm sure the staff, Eli, and our clients were watching me to make certain I didn't implode.

In the next hour, I treated Mrs. Crane's Llewelyn setter for ear mites, and gave annual shot updates to two coon dogs.

Tina Kessler's demonic black cat, Moose, twenty pounds of muscle and determination, needed his toenails clipped. I called our assistant, Wanda Jean, to help on that one. Eli stuck her head in the door of my exam room when she heard the yowls, but withdrew quickly when she saw Moose.

As Tina walked out with the cat glaring at me over her shoulder, Tonesha whispered, "I bet that thing's daddy was a bobcat."

"Or a cougar," said Eli, who had come out after her last client.

I leaned on the edge of the steel examining table. Suddenly even standing erect was enough to wear me out. I wanted to go home, climb into bed, hug Morgan's pillow and sleep until the pain of loss went away. But it wouldn't, and I couldn't. I pulled myself up, took a deep breath, and walked down the hall to greet the next patient, whoever it might be. God, I needed a challenge to force me to focus on something outside myself.

Behind Tina the front door to the clinic opened, and a tall, gray-haired man rushed in. "Are you the vets?"

Tonesha pointed. "That's them."

"Look, I've got a problem, and I'm late for a meeting." He spun on his heel and ran out. Eli and I followed. "Never a dull moment," Eli whispered.

"I hit him on the way to work," the man said. "Couldn't just leave him there. I think he's dead, but if he's alive—well, I pass this place every day, so I grabbed him up in some newspapers and put him on the back seat and brought him to you." He opened the back door of a shiny new BMW sedan.

Stretched on newspapers on the gray leather upholstery lay a red fox.

"Tonesha!" Eli shouted over my shoulder. "Tell Wanda Jean to bring the biggest roll of vet wrap she can find. Fast!"

"Is he dead?" The man asked. Without waiting for an answer, he glanced at his watch. "Can you get him out of there? I really have to go. I'll pay you for whatever he costs. Here's my card."

I stuck the card in my pocket without looking at it. Wanda Jean ran down the steps and thrust a thick roll of tape into my hand. Well, I'd asked for a challenge. A wild fox certainly qualified.

"Maggie, be careful, for God's sake," Eli whispered.

I leaned into the car and gently wrapped the fox's muzzle five or six times with the tape, then took a turn around the back of his head. Then I wrapped his legs.

"God forbid he should come to," Eli said.

"That ought to hold until we can get him into the clinic."

"I hope so, for all our sakes."

"Wanda Jean, call Duane."

"He's not in yet."

"Well, then, dammit, get a blanket. Something to slide him onto."

"He's not dead, then?" The man asked. "I mean, one minute I was driving along, and the next, here's this—this thing—practically under my wheels. I don't think I actually ran over him."

Eli turned to the man. "Most people would just have left him."

"I couldn't—my daughter'd never forgive me. You think he'll be all right?"

"No idea."

"No chance he's rabid, is there?"

"We haven't had a rabid fox in this part of Tennessee in twenty years. He didn't bite you or scratch you, did he?"

"No, I'm fine. I put on my driving gloves to handle him. Now, I really have to go. Have somebody call me and let me know how he is."

Tonesha and Wanda Jean arrived with a horse blanket. I slid the still unconscious fox off the seat, then we carried him into the clinic.

I turned to the Good Samaritan. "What you did was kind, but I have to tell you, you took one hell of a chance. If he'd waked up while you were driving, you and that upholstery would have been in bite-sized pieces in about a minute and a half."

The man blinked. "I never—I mean, I thought it was dead." He glanced at his pristine leather upholstery and shuddered. "I guess I *was* lucky."

I ran into the clinic to find Eli and Wanda Jean. The five people left in the waiting room clutched their dogs and cats, and in one instance a lop-eared rabbit, closer to their respective bosoms. The cats were hissing and clawing, Mayrene Carteret's Dachshund, Snooper the Fourth, was barking frantically, and the rabbit was trying to turn invisible.

"Is that a fox?" Mayrene Carteret whispered.

"A real fox. A live one, I hope." I headed for the first examining room. *Please, God,* I thought, *no more death.*

"B'rer Fox, here, has a concussion," Eli said, "But I don't think his skull is fractured. He just got his chimes rung pretty good."

I ran my hands along his body. "He is so beautiful."

"He's a dog fox. Probably out hunting to feed his family."

I stroked his gray ticked pelt all the way down to his bright red brush of a tail. "Stupid, guy, really stupid." I slid my hand down his foreleg. "Uh-oh."

"What? I hadn't gotten that far."

"He's dislocated his shoulder. I don't think there's a break, but we need an X-ray."

"I'll set it up. Wanda Jean, where *is* Duane?"

"I'm right here, doc," said a gruff voice. Duane, our man of all work, stuck his grizzled head around the corner of the room that housed the kennels.

"Help me roll in the X-ray."

"Might as well give him a rabies shot while we've got him," I said. "We'll need to fill out the paperwork and report this to the wildlife people anyway." I walked over to the drug cabinet in the corner of the examining room, took out my key, unlocked it, and filled a syringe, all the while thinking, *he's going to be fine. He's going to go home safe.*

"Here we go," Eli said. "Oh, hell!"

I heard the thud and spun around in time to see the fox bound down the hall toward the waiting room. Despite his strapped muzzle, in the few seconds that my back was turned, he'd waked up and gnawed through the bandages that held his legs. The tatters flew behind him like banners.

The clients in the waiting room screamed. So did Tonesha.

For a moment my mind went blank, then I grabbed the empty metal garbage can from the corner of the examining room and raced after him.

Clients stood on the chairs and sofas. Tonesha climbed onto her desk. Dogs and cats and rabbit tried frantically to escape the clutches of their masters and mistresses.

"Where is he?" I asked.

"Under that chair in the corner," Mayrene said.

"Gone to ground. Good. Stay where you are, people. Duane, get me a carrying cage. Wanda Jean, stay out of the way."

"Maggie, he'll tear you up," Eli whispered.

"No, he won't. He's still muzzled, and I can avoid those claws. He's just scared." Suddenly, the exhaustion was gone, replaced by a surge of adrenaline.

"I'm scared too," Eli said.

"Hold a cushion against the side of the chair so he can't get out that way. He won't be able to go anywhere but into the garbage can." I slid the garbage can along the floor in front of the chair with its open end toward the cowering fox. "Come on, sweetheart, come to Maggie."

"I got your cage, doc," Duane said from behind me.

"Good. Put it down and when I tell you, bang on the seat of that chair."

"Yes'm."

"Now."

Duane banged and Eli pushed my cushion. The fox bolted straight into the safe darkness of the garbage can. The instant I heard him inside, I tipped the can on its nose and sat on it. The fox scrabbled frantically against the metal. "Now, all we have to do is transfer him to the cage, sedate him, treat him, give him his shot, drive him back to where he came from and let him loose."

"He was running on all four legs," Eli said. "He must have popped his shoulder back in when he jumped off the examining table. We can give him enough tranquilizer in a bit of dog food to get the muzzle off. As for the concussion—if you think I'm going to shove an aspirin down this thing's throat, you have another think coming."

"Is it safe to come down?" Mayrene asked. Snooper the Fourth was still in attack mode. His ruff stood straight up while he barked non-stop.

"Go back into the examining rooms and shut the doors. B'rer Fox is not going to get loose again, but just in case..." Decanting the terrified fox into the cage wasn't as easy as I had made it seem, but he gobbled up the dog food with his muzzle still on and settled right down five minutes later. I clipped the muzzle carefully, then Duane carried the cage back to the kennel area at arm's length.

"Tonesha," I said and tossed Tonesha the card the Good Samaritan had given me. "Call that man and ask him where on the road he hit the fox. And tell him everything's fine. I'll drop him about where he got hit. Old Foxkin can run on home to his wife and family, assuming he has one."

"And call the wildlife people," Eli said to Tonesha. "Tell them what happened and what we plan to do. Should be all right, but better be certain."

"Okay," Tonesha said. "I swear, this place is a zoo!"

An hour later Duane carried the groggy fox out to my truck and slid the carrier into the back seat. The good Samaritan had hit him less than five miles from the clinic. I knew we had foxes and coyote around, but I'd never been lucky enough to see one on our property.

I pulled my truck onto the shoulder approximately where the fox had been hit. I carried the cage across the shallow ditch beside the road to the edge of a cotton field. I stood well back when I opened the cage door. For a moment nothing happened.

Then B'rer Fox bolted out as though he'd been scalded and took off running across the field, his bright red brush like a knight's banner behind him.

I watched him until he gained the shadows of the trees in the first hedge row. The moment he disappeared, the old, cold emptiness struck me again. And the exhaustion. I had to force myself to load the cage back into my truck and drive back to the clinic.

Was his vixen pacing back and forth in front of her den worrying about him? Was she afraid he'd gone forever? If he had died there beside the road, would she have grieved? Animals did grieve.

But they also seemed to accept death. Why couldn't I?

As I walked in the back door of the clinic, Eli stuck her head out of her office.

"Maggie, Nathan's on the phone for you."

I froze. Nathan never called me during the day. He wouldn't call me simply to chat, would he? I didn't think I could bear any more bad news.

# Chapter 28

## *In which Nathan's birth certificate starts a chain of events*

"Hey, Nathan, how are y'all?" I fought to keep my voice normal, but no doubt I sounded shrill. My hand on the telephone shook.

"We're fine, Momma," he said.

"Lisa?"

"Fine. How are *you*? That's what's important."

"Fine. I'm doing fine." God, we sounded like a pair of strangers. But what good would it do to blubber and scream and tell him that I wasn't fine, that I'd never be fine again, that I was empty and frightened and wanted to go curl up in a corner and die? The least I could do was to protect him from my grief. He had his own to deal with. We continued the banalities until he got around to telling me why he was calling.

Eli listened to my end of the telephone conversation, which consisted mostly of "uh-huh." When I hung up, she asked, "So? Lisa's pregnant? He's been busted for insider trading? Disaster or good news? What?"

I shrugged and tried to act nonchalant. Eli had seen my panic, however.

"No, Lisa is not pregnant and Nathan is not under indictment—or if he is, he didn't mention it. Lisa is going to put off having children until her eggs are too old to recognize a sperm, much less blend with it. They may never get around to grandchildren."

"If we're not talking disaster, what did Nathan want?"

"He needs the original copy of his birth certificate."

"Whatever for?"

"He and Lisa are bringing their wills up to date."

Eli nodded. "Since Morgan died he's feeling his mortality."

"I'm sure that's it exactly. He's setting up some kind of trust for Lisa. Apparently the good old bureaucracy in Nashville has not ambled from the nineteenth into the twenty-first century and will take ten days to get it to him. He wants me to FedEx it."

"Oh. Why are you looking like that?"

"He told me exactly where it is. Good thing, since I haven't a clue. He says it's in Morgan's file cabinet in his office over at the house."

"So?" Eli narrowed her eyes. "Do not tell me you haven't been in Morgan's office since he died."

"I never went in there when he was *alive*. That was his sanctuary. He kept up with all the paperwork." I looked away and refused to meet Eli's eyes. "And I let him."

"I'll bet you haven't opened his closet either, have you?"

"I've been busy. Besides, I don't need any more closet space. Morgan's stuff can stay where it is."

"Get up. It's lunchtime. You can fix us a sandwich, then I'll go up to the office with you and get that birth certificate."

"That will not be necessary."

"Bull hockey. Come on, tough guy, the least you can do is fix me a chicken salad sandwich."

I opened the door to Morgan's office, took two steps and stopped so quickly that Eli bumped into me. A moment later, I said, "The cleaning crew dusts and vacuums in here every week. I don't know why I had visions of cobwebs hanging everywhere like Miss Haversham's wedding reception in *Great Expectations*."

"So find the birth certificate and let's get back to the clinic." Eli pointed to the three-drawer walnut file cabinet in the corner of the room. Morgan didn't stint on his comfort either at home or at his office in the bank. The walls were paneled, the dark wood floor was covered with an antique Heriz that Morgan had inherited from his parents. He'd inherited the mahogany partner's desk from his father.

The big computer with its twenty-one inch monitor seemed at

first glance to be the only modern piece in the room. I sucked in a deep breath. "I was hoping that I could still smell him, but all I smell is Murphy's oil soap." I strode purposefully to the file cabinet and yanked open the top drawer as though I actually wanted to.

Eli curled up in the big blue leather wing chair in front of Morgan's desk.

"Go on back to the clinic," I said. "I won't slash my wrists."

"Fine," she said and started to pull herself out of the big chair.

"No, wait. Please. Tonesha will call if there's an emergency."

"So you want me to stay?"

"Dammit, all right, yes, I want you to stay."

She nodded. "Okay, but you need to do the actual work." I'm sure she heard my cavernous sigh because she said, "Maggie, trust me on this. I've been through it. Starting is horrible, but it gets easier."

I did not believe her for an instant, but I began to thumb through the folders. "Nathan said the personal family papers were in the first or second drawer," I said. "This seems to be stuff on private clients and general correspondence." I checked to the end of the drawer. "No birth certificates."

"Try the second drawer."

There they were. Thick hanging files for each member of the family. Next all the official papers from mortgages to tax forms for what looked like the last twenty years. I pulled out a copy of my marriage license to Morgan.

"Morgan always said he felt as though we'd been married forever, and at the same time, just married yesterday." I pulled out Nathan's folder, opened it, and said, "Here's Nathan's birth certificate. Just where he said it would be." I put it on the corner of the desk, replaced the folder and slammed the drawer. "Okay, time for work."

Eli didn't move. "What's in the bottom drawer?"

"No idea."

"No curiosity either? Come on, now that you've started, keep going at least a few minutes more. I promise I'll come over Sunday afternoon. We'll get a real start on cleaning out the debris—file cabinets and desk drawers."

"Oh, hell, all right." I did not want to go on a moment longer. I wanted to go back to work where I could safely hide from this room, so full of Morgan and yet so completely empty. I bent down and pulled open the bottom drawer. A moment later I sat down on the floor in front of the cabinet. "It looks like a scrapbook." I said over my shoulder, "Weighs a ton." I held it on my lap and heard my heart thud in my throat. Like many busy families, we rarely took photographs. The ones we did take were shoved away in boxes waiting to be mounted. Or at least I had supposed they were. "If Morgan put all our pictures in here, Eli, I'm not sure I can bear to look at them."

Eli was beside me in a flash. "Of course you can. Here, let me."

Wordlessly, I handed her book.

Eli opened it across her knees. "I always told Morgan he was too anal-retentive for his own good." She opened the book and caught her breath. "It's your wedding pictures and your honeymoon. Lordy, were we thin!"

"Put it away." Eli turned a page. "Eli, put that thing away right this minute!"

"Morgan looks so cute in his striped pants and cutaway. And the way he's staring at you..."

"Damnation, Eli!"

She glanced up then and saw my face. "Sure, Maggie. It's okay, honey." As she began to close the book, a shower of brightly colored brochures spilled out onto the floor.

Next came old airplane tickets, stubs, receipts, notes in Morgan's handwriting. I grabbed at a cascade of still more loose brochures. "Help!" I set the book down and began to scrabble at the brochures and pieces of paper on my knees. I was suddenly frantic to get those bits of paper safely shut away into that scrapbook again.

Almost against my will, I stared down at the brochure in my hand. Across the front Morgan had written: "Booked Alaska Cruise, June 84." Underneath was another note: "Cancelled, August 84."

Still stacking loose notes and brochures, Eli slid the book across the floor. "Don't drop anything else."

I began to leaf through the pages. After the pictures of our honeymoon I found neat, orderly pages on which Morgan had mounted photos, old airline tickets, brochures for side trips to Gatlinburg.

I could trace every moment of the week we spent together in New York when Sarah was a year old. Eli had looked after her because Morgan said I needed a break. Everything—theater stubs, old theatre programs, brochures from the Frick and the Museum of Modern Art, even hotel receipts and restaurant menus. Morgan had not only kept every scrap of paper, he'd lovingly built this scrapbook. Why had he hid it from me?

The leaves at the front of the book were thick with keepsakes, but I found more and more blank pages, some with brochures still stuck loosely between them. I'd cancelled our trip to Tuscany to go to the International Veterinary Congress in St. Paul.

The following year Morgan had tried to take me on a cruise down the Seine on a barge, but I'd gone to a course at Colorado State to learn about embryo transplants in horses instead. The opening at State had come so late, I'd had to cancel France at the last minute.

I told Morgan to go without me.

He told her there was always next year. Or the next. After the children left. After they went to college. After they graduated and moved away from home for good. Or after he retired.

He planned to retire in August of this year.

"Maggie , here's your passport," Eli said. "Yours and Morgan's. I wonder why he kept them here." Eli flipped open the pages. "It's out of date."

"After…I forgot." I bristled. Morgan would have reminded me. Except that he no longer could.

"I guess he planned to do them both at the same time. You wouldn't be able to leave the country even if Morgan could finally have persuaded you to actually go someplace instead of just promising and reneging."

"I didn't always renege, dammit!"

"Sure you did. I don't think you've taken a real vacation with Morgan since we built the clinic. The Militia and I ran an annual pool on the day you'd cancel."

"Was I that bad?"

"You know you were."

"Why didn't he let me know how important it was to him?" I swept a hand at the papers on the floor around them. "Look at all these things. It's like I told him year after year he'd get a pony for Christmas and year after year I didn't deliver. What kind of a monster am I?"

"You're not a monster. You're simply afflicted with tunnel vision where your work is concerned. Morgan understood that. He was perfectly willing to wait…"

"Until he keeled over dead eight months before he was due to retire." I surged to my feet and began to pace. "He never saw the pyramids or the Mona Lisa or the Great Wall of China. Hell, he never even saw the Grand Canyon."

"He wanted to see them with *you*. You haven't seen any of those things either."

"Not yet I haven't."

Eli scrambled to her feet. "Calm down. Morgan wouldn't want you to…"

"He's not here to express his current needs. All I can see are the ones I failed to meet in twenty-seven frigging years of married life. He was always there for me. I was supposed to be there for him too. Half and half. Only my half was a damned sight bigger."

"You're shaking. It's all right."

"It is not."

Eli's pager beeped. "Lord." She picked the phone off Morgan's desk and clicked into the office. "Yes, Tonesha? Yes, all right. I'm coming." She hung up the phone. "Dog hit by a car. I have to go."

"I'm coming with you."

"No, you're not. You stay here." She touched my shoulder. "I'll be back as soon as I can. Morgan loved you."

I heard Eli footsteps recede down the hall. "And I loved him. Maybe not enough."

I slid out of the chair onto the floor and crawled over to the file cabinet. I went through the scrapbook page by page, carefully fitting the brochures into the blank pages in the order the trips would have taken. Every note of a cruise or a trip booked and then cancelled tore into me. He gave me so much—his financial support in the early days, his child-rearing skills when mine proved to be minimal, his sense of humor, his kindness, his patience…

He'd made my dream for the clinic *our* dream. Without him to push me I'd never have had the nerve to try it.

I hadn't been able to cry since he died. Suddenly I leaned against the file cabinet and howled like a banshee. "Damn you! Damn you, Morgan! Damn you for dying on me and leaving me the whole rest of my stupid life to live without you!"

I don't know how long I wailed. Eventually I hicchoughed into silence. I lay down on the floor the midst of all those brochures. I was so tired, and my life without him had just begun.

Was the old dream, the one we had shared, empty now without him? Was it enough to get me through my leftover life? If Morgan had given up so much for me, then somehow I had to make the rest of my life without him count.

# Chapter 29

## *In which Maggie and Eli perform an unusual surgical procedure*

In the past when faced with a career choice, I had consulted Dr. Parmenter, but he was dead too. So I did what I usually do when faced with a life-changing decision. I mulled, I puzzled, I ruminated.

And I worked even harder.

One morning in early March, Eli and I had just finished pinning a cat's broken leg when Tonesha walked into our exam room and said, "Y'all, the weirdest thing just happened. This guy drove a fancy horse trailer into the paddock, unhooked his truck, drove around front, ran in, threw some papers on my desk and tore out like a bat out'a hell. Whatever's in that trailer is doing some heavy duty kickin'."

"Duane!" I called. "Come take this cat to recovery." Then I started toward the back door with Eli on my heels.

"Maggie?" Tonesha called. "These papers—they're releases for surgery. The guy says he needs a orchidectomy. I know what that is. It's gelding a stallion. But what on earth is a *saddle-ectomy*?"

My eyebrows climbed. "What now?"

"Rodney Armbruster called me at breakfast," Eli said as I followed her through the clinic. "Said he'd be here before noon."

Rodney was one of our colleagues. He owned the clinic where the young vet who had effectively killed Patsy's Pride had been working when my Sarah was eighteen and still riding. We stayed on good terms, but like most of the vets in the area, we snickered at Rodney's pretensions.

"He sure didn't mention a saddle-ectomy, whatever that is," Eli said. She opened the back door to the clinic and started across the parking lot to the paddock. "You know how he thinks he can ride the hair off of anything with four legs."

"Which he can't," I added.

"He's got this Danish Warmblood two-year-old-stud colt. Been out in the pasture with nothing but a goat for a companion since it was weaned at six months. Not even good halter broke. Some crap about not wanting to break his spirit until he's older."

"Better wait until he weighs fifteen hundred pounds, stands seventeen hands high and produces enough testosterone to grow beards on the Rockettes, then it's a real treat to drag him into the barn and toss a saddle on him."

"Rodney said he saddled and bridled the colt in his indoor round pen last night, and tried to get on. He hit the dirt, and the colt spent the night in Rodney's round pen."

"Good grief," I whispered. Inside the paddock gate, Rodney's shiny silver two horse trailer rocked to the rhythm of the horse's hooves as they kicked the inside of the back door.

I pulled myself up onto the side of the trailer. "Eli, he's still got his saddle and bridle on. That's what Rodney meant by a saddle-ectomy. Damn!" I jumped down. "The little bastard tried to bite me. He's not even tied, and I can see about three feet of leather reins hanging down. He must have broken them in the round pen."

"Rodney said he was afraid to tranquilize him for fear he'd fall down in the trailer, so they just herded him into the trailer and shut the door on him."

The horse landed a solid blow with his hind hooves against the inside of the tailgate. The trailer rocked. "We have to get him out of there before he turns the thing over," Eli said. "God knows how we can do it safely." She pulled herself up on the side of the trailer to peer in the opening, but kept well out of biting range. "I can't believe even Rodney would leave a horse standing in a trailer unattached to a truck. It's a miracle he hasn't broken the front axle and fallen on his nose. Lordy, Maggie , he's the size of a bull moose! He must be over seventeen hands." She dropped to the ground. "Shut the paddock gate. That way if he gets away from us he can't get out of the paddock."

I ran back into the clinic and came back with a pair of heavy cotton lead lines, each about ten feet long with snaps on one end. I closed the paddock gate on my way by. "We're going to have to clip these to the bit rings on his bridle. We'll never be able to halter him until we can get him out of that trailer and calmed down enough to get a shot of tranquilizer into him. Think we could inject him in the rump with some tranquilizer while he's still in the trailer?"

Eli rolled her eyes. "I don't think I'd try it. We might hit a vein instead of muscle. The way he's jumping around I might miss his rump entirely and tranquilize the front window."

"One of us is going to have to attach those lines to his bridle without being bitten. The other will have to drop the tailgate and stand by to grab the other line when he backs out."

"Draw straws?"

I grinned and handed the lines to Eli. "Eli, darlin', you took Rodney's call, so it's your stallion. You get to clip the lines to his bridle. I'll drop the tailgate when you give me the signal."

I stood by the rear of the trailer.

At the front, Eli shouted, "Horse, you bite me, you die! Damn it, settle down!"

After an eternity, Eli turned from the front of the trailer. Her short gray hair stood in sweaty points around her head. "You're going to have to reach in and undo the butt chain before you open the tailgate," she said. For a moment her upper body disappeared inside the trailer. "And fast!"

The instant the horse felt a human touch on its rear, he began to buck as well as kick. I managed to pull the pin that held the chain across the rear of the trailer in place, loosened the hasp on the trailer door and prepared to let it down slowly.

Wham! Black hooves flashed within a foot of my forehead. The kick wrenched the tailgate from my hands.

It hit the ground like dynamite.

A millisecond later seventeen hands of angry stud colt exploded backwards.

I dove into the azalea border.

The colt spun past me with Eli clinging doggedly to one of the two lead lines.

I struggled to my feet and grabbed for the second lead line.

It was like playing 'crack the whip' with Godzilla. Both of us landed back in the azaleas.

"Shit!" Eli snapped. "Why didn't you hold him?"

I gasped. "You're kidding, right?"

The stallion reared and pranced and tossed his lead lines in triumph. Then he turned around and kicked the side of the trailer with both hind feet. The metal buckled in a pair of identical hoof-shaped depressions.

"Rodney won't like that," Eli said.

"Screw Rodney," I gasped.

At that moment Tonesha opened the back door. "Uh-oh. Y'all hurt?"

"Get the capture pistol," Eli said. "It's in my top desk drawer. Make sure it's loaded."

From the neighboring azalea bush, I gasped, "I thought you didn't want to shoot him with tranquilizer."

"You got any better ideas?"

"You're sure the dart's loaded with the correct dosage?"

"At this point," Eli said, struggling to her feet and rubbing her bottom, "Ask me if I give a damn."

We stood close by the gate ready to dive over if the colt came at us, but he had discovered the clover, and was contentedly munching, still wearing the head stall of his bridle, two lead lines and a saddle.

Tonesha handed the pistol to Eli without taking her eyes off the colt. Eli checked the dosage in the tranquilizer dart, slammed shut the cylinder, and took aim on the colt's rump.

"For all our sakes," I whispered, "Don't miss!"

# Chapter 30

## *In which we meet a sensible stallion owner (with a very strange friend)*

When I walked into the clinic waiting room the following morning, Tonesha pulled me over to the reception desk and whispered, "We've got another one."

"One what?"

"Another weird guy with a stallion." She pointed over her shoulder. "He's out back."

The truck in the parking lot was held together by rust, and the two-horse trailer had probably carried more cows than horses in its day, but both were as clean and dust free as though they had been washed that morning.

A man sat in the passenger seat, but beyond him the man I assumed was my client had taken his colt into the paddock. The horse grazed quietly at the end of his lead rope. When he saw me, the man walked over. I realized instantly what the colt's problem was.

Behind me, I heard the door of the truck open, and a man's deep voice said, "Gotta get me a R-uh-C Cola."

I glanced over my shoulder. The passenger was very tall, cadaverously thin, with tanned leather skin and a few wisps of white hair. He might be as young as sixty or as old as ninety. He and his companion both wore bib overalls with no shirts. The passenger's were three or four inches too short for his long legs, revealing gigantic feet in aged tennis shoes. No socks. His bony shoulders and ropy arm muscles ended in hands the size of soup plates.

"Ma'am," he said, ducked his head and wandered toward the

back door to the clinic with his big hands thrust deep into the pockets of his coveralls. They too were old and frayed around the cuffs, but clean and pressed.

"Now just you behave yourself, Eugene," the other man called. He picked up the lead line and brought his colt over to the fence. "Mornin', ma'am," he said. "Can I please see the doctor?"

"I'm the doctor."

He ducked his head and sighed. "Oh, my. Don't y'all got no men doctors?"

"No sir, I'm afraid I'm it at the moment." I hadn't met this kind of blatant chauvinism in a while.

He was as small as his friend was tall, and his shoulders and arms were still muscled from years of hard work. He smiled up at me diffidently. "It's like this, ma'am. I don't rightly know just how to tell no lady about Sunny's problem."

The colt had wandered up to stand beside his owner. He stood less than fifteen hands high, but was a superb specimen of a quarter horse, with a sorrel coat so brilliant it hurt the eyes. "I don't know if you done looked, but—oh, my—he's done been in some pain for two, three days now." The old man looked away, but pointed between the colt's rear legs.

"Yes," I said. "I see."

The old man sighed deeply. "He's a fine stud colt, gonna sire him some extra good babies, so I don't want to cut him. I done throwed him out in the pasture with my mares the day he was weaned. Them mares'll teach a youngster manners right fast. He's been running with them until I brung him up to the barn last week to start breaking him."

He looked close to tears. "I been workin' him pretty hard, and he ain't had his mares. Then a couple of days ago, I looked back there and he is so swole up—well, it hurt me to see it. Hot compresses seemed to help some, but this morning he is swole up even worse, so me and Eugene brought him up here—'cause y'all got a good reputation when it comes to horses. See, what I think is, all that work I been doing with him, them balls o'his has just been a'jingling and a'jangling together, wham, bam, for a whole week. Done swole 'em up." He made a back and forth motion with his hands.

I gulped.

"And then, him getting took off his mares—well, ma'am, he's been used to gittin' him some anytime he wanted it. Could it be that all that gizzum done backed up in there?"

I cleared my throat and fought to keep a straight face. "How is he around people? Will he kick?"

"No, ma'am, I gentle my horses when they're borned. Why, a colt that acts up ain't worth nothin' but to be a yard dog. He ain't eatin' *my* grain, no ma'am."

"I wish there were some other people who agreed with you," I whispered as I leaned down close to the stallion's horribly swollen scrotum. I touched it gently. Hot. The stallion shifted his weight, but made no attempt to avoid my fingers. After a short examination, I came up smiling. "Mr. uh?"

"Dockery, ma'am, B. K. Dockery. Farm's down this side of Pontotoc."

"Mr. Dockery. It's not the—uh—friction or the celibacy that caused…" I glanced back at the colt.

"Doc Juke's Sunny Morn, ma'am, call him 'Sunny.'"

"Yes, well, you've been doing the right thing with the compresses, although you need to alternate warm with cool—not hot and cold."

"No, ma'am." He grinned at me. I was amazed to see his teeth were in excellent shape, and definitely his own. "Sunny's a good sort, but I wouldn't want to put no real hot nor yet no ice on them balls."

"He's also going to need a course of antibiotics. Sunny has been bitten by a spider. I don't think it's a brown recluse or a black widow. There'd be more necrosis, dead tissue. It was a large spider, but probably only mildly poisonous."

"Then how come…"

"That spider must have been munching some really foul stuff and had infected pincers. Sunny has a nasty case of cellulitis. If you want to wait here, I'll give him a shot and a bottle of pills to take home, and you can load him up. I wouldn't work him until the swelling goes down."

"Can I put him back with his mares? He's a sight happier."

"Sure you can. I think his activities are going to be self-limiting for a while. He's not going to feel like breeding anything."

"Yes, ma'am. That is a load off my mind." He patted the colt's neck. "Yessir, Sunny. I was afeared I'd done done it to him what with working him and all."

"Uh, Mr. Dockery, we usually require payment for services from new clients. Will that be a problem?"

"Shouldn't be. No, ma'am. How much?" He reached into his

pocket and pulled out a roll of bills the diameter of a quart of milk.

I gave him a figure. He popped the rubber band off his wad and peeled off several twenties. So far as I could tell, the whole roll was comprised of twenties. So much for the poor country farmer.

"If you want to load Sunny, I'll go get the shot and your medication, and bring your change. Do you need your Eugene to help you load?"

"Shoot." Dockery led the colt to the back of the trailer. "Get on up there."

The colt jumped instantly into the trailer. Dockery fixed the butt chain and started to close the door.

"No, leave it open, please, Mr. Dockery. I'll give him his shot in his rump."

"Yes, ma'am. Would you tell Eugene to come on out? I got thirty mares yet to feed and hay this morning."

Whew, thirty mares. I 'd learned the first year in vet school that you couldn't tell from a Southern farmer's clothes whether he sharecropped or owned twenty thousand acres of black Delta dirt. Generally, our trucks gave away our status, but Mr. Dockery's truck should have belonged to a poor man, not a multi-multi-millionaire, which was probably what he was.

Getting his business would be a nice chunk of change for the McLain-Scheibler clinic.

As I started back toward the parking lot, Tonesha grabbed me.

"I told you they were weird," I whispered. "Get that old man out of here before I call the cops."

"What?"

"Just look at him."

I leaned around the doorjamb and smiled at Eugene. He sat propped between the back of his neck and his tailbone in one of the straight client's chairs. An empty Coke can sat on the table beside him. He smiled back.

"What?" I hissed. "He's just sitting there quietly twiddling his thumbs."

"Maggie! Are you blind? That is *not* his thumb he's twiddling."

I looked again. I had heard that the size of a man's feet and hands could be a measure of his more private appendages, but had never before seen the equation so aptly demonstrated. Eugene was what my mother would call 'some lady's kind friend.'

As I tried to decide how to handle the situation, I heard steps behind me, as little Mr. Dockery walked up.

"Eugene! You stop that right this minute and high-tail it out to the truck, you hear?"

Eugene turned a beatific smile on the group huddled in the hall. Tonesha shrank back into the office as Eugene carefully rebuttoned his coveralls and sauntered out behind Mr. Dockery.

By the time I had assembled the medication and my shot, Eugene was safely stowed inside the truck.

"Sorry about that, ma'am," Mr. Dockery whispered with a shake of his head. "Eugene's a good boy, but he ain't never been quite right. Good with the stock. Don't mean no harm, wouldn't hurt a fly. Just forgets where he is sometimes."

I tried to think of something—anything—to say.

"Thank y'all," Mr. Dockery said as he took the medication. "Done been hearin' 'bout this clinic for years. Y'all willin' to drive down to my place?"

"Of course."

"Good. I'll holler at ya if I need ya."

He climbed into the truck, waved and drove sedately out of the parking lot. I walked back into the clinic.

"I quit," Tonesha said.

She threatened to quit regularly, but this was the first time I ever thought she might actually go through with it. Took me twenty minutes to convince her to stay. If I went to Mr. Dockery's place to work with his horses, I'd make certain Mr. Dockery kept a close eye on Eugene while I was there.

# Chapter 31

## *In which Patsy asks a favor that turns into a disaster*

A week or ten days later, I had barely climbed out of the shower and gone downstairs to feed my current cats, Beer and Teasy, the Maine Coon cats, and Bok Choy, the sealpoint Siamese, when Tonesha called from the office.

"Patsy Dalrymple needs to speak to you right this minute."

"I'll be there in ten minutes."

"She's on the phone."

"Oh, Lord, Tonesha, can't Eli handle it?"

"She's spaying a King Charles spaniel. Besides, Patsy asked specially to speak to you. You can tell that woman no. I am not about to." Tonesha clicked the line through.

"Maggie! Thank God I got you!"

"Hey, Patsy, what's the problem?"

"I'm calling for a friend. She needs a really big favor."

"Friend? That mean she's not a client at the clinic?"

"She lives in the Garden District. One of those huge old mansions on Belvedere. She uses Lanier Polman."

"So why call me? Don't tell me it's a horse."

"No, actually—" Her voice faltered and dropped an octave. "It's a wolf."

"I beg your pardon?"

Now Patsy's words tumbled out as though she was afraid I would hang up before she finished. "Don't ask me why, but eight months ago she bought this little wolf puppy someplace in Arkansas—cutest itsy bitsy ball of fluff you've ever seen. And so precious! Just a little sweetheart. Loved to cuddle up in Marion's lap. Great with her children too. The children were all for it, of course, but then they're both in college and only home for vacation. I really think she did it because she felt 'empty-nesty.'"

"That's a dangerous way to fill it."

"Her husband Humphrey was a little hesitant at first—Marion can go off half-cocked sometimes—but he got to be just as crazy about little Loba as she is."

"Loba?"

"That's the female of *lobo*. It means wolf."

"I know what it means, Patsy. Couldn't she come up with anything better than that?"

"Just hush and listen. They don't just have this huge house, they've got half an acre of back yard and trees that were there before the War of Northern Aggression. You just have to come see her garden, Maggie, you really do. In May..."

"Patsy."

"Oh, sorry. Anyway, they built Loba a palatial outside doghouse—I swear you could get an F.H.A. loan on the thing—and an enclosed outside run big enough for a pack of wolfhounds, but of course Loba was a puppy. She stayed in the house at night. Slept right beside Marion and Humphrey's bed."

"So she's now, what? Eight months old? That's nearly full grown for a she-wolf, certainly old enough so that she could start coming into sexual maturity."

"I don't think Marion thought much beyond the cute little puppy stage, and I guess when you live with an animal day by day you don't notice so much, but I swear, Loba must weigh ninety pounds. She is absolutely the most beautiful thing you ever saw, but my word, she is enormous."

"And less good natured?"

"Oh, no, she's still a sweetie at least with Marion and Humphrey and the children. But she's protective. I guess she believes they're her pack. Marion started having to keep her on leash when she answered the door, and the maid swore she'd quit unless Marion put her in her outside kennel while she was working. Poor Loba wasn't too happy about that. She took to howling when they locked her outside."

I could almost hear the howls of affronted she-wolf reverberating through one of the fanciest neighborhoods in Memphis. "The neighbors must have loved that."

"Well, at first I don't think they realized she wasn't just some big

German Shepherd, but you know how servants talk. There was some grumbling and a few nasty phone calls, but Marion swore she'd keep Loba as quiet as she could."

"Get on with it, okay, Patsy. What favor?"

"Hush. Just let me tell it. You have to know the background. Loba went into season a couple of weeks ago, and by the time Lanier gave her a shot to bring her out of it, she'd about worn Marion out. They couldn't leave her outside because every male dog in the neighborhood—and you know those people let their darlings run loose half the time—came sniffing around. Loba was not happy about that."

"I don't imagine the owners of the dogs were overly thrilled either."

"For the first time I think Marion was a little frightened of her. So the minute the shot Lanier gave her brought her out of her 'interesting condition,' Marion started putting her out in her kennel during the day and leaving her in her indoor crate at night and only letting her out to play when she could devote all her time to her and when Humphrey or somebody was home in case she got fractious." She took a deep breath. "Sooner or later there was bound to be a disaster."

"She bit Marion?"

"Two days ago, Loba managed to drag the fence loose from the bottom of her outdoor run and got out. I was there when we discovered the hole and started hunting for her. Marion took her spray gun and Loba's leash, thank God. It was awful!"

A full-grown she-wolf loose in a neighborhood full of elderly people and young children with their nannies? Talk about disaster. "Don't tell me she savaged a child."

"Please lord, not that! She tried real hard to eat a standard poodle. She didn't growl or anything. No warning, no bared teeth. One minute she was standing there staring, the next she went straight for that poodle like it was an elk. If Marion hadn't had her spray…well, the poodle got away with twenty-some-odd stitches. Once Marion got Loba's leash on she was fine again."

"Good grief, Patsy."

"The neighbors wanted to call Animal Control right then, but Marion agreed to pay them a bunch to let her handle it. They'd have shot the poor thing, you know they would. It's not Loba's fault."

"It's the fault of your friend Marion and all the other nitwits who think raising a bear or lion cub will be so much fun because they're so cute."

"Don't lecture me, Maggie McLain. I didn't buy the damned wolf."

"Sorry. But that sort of thing makes me furious."

"Good. So you'll help."

"Help? Help what?"

"Take the wolf."

"Are you crazy? What would I do with a wolf?"

"Now, calm down. Marion's found a refuge in north Minnesota that will take Loba, but she couldn't make arrangements to ship her until Thursday. In the meantime, she has to get her out of the neighborhood, and since you're out in the country and have that huge place and those wonderful kennels, I told Marion I was sure you'd be happy to have Loba."

"No way!"

"Please, Maggie. It's only two days. Call Lanier if you want to see what a sweetheart she is. A rhinoceros couldn't escape from your dog runs, and I know she'll be well taken care of. She'll be picked up first thing Thursday morning. Marion is out of her mind with worry. She gulped half a bottle of Zanax. Wolves are endangered, Maggie, and she'll be a perfect reproductive specimen once she gets up to Minnesota. You don't want to lose her gene pool, do you?"

Patsy had moved from emotional blackmail to a weird kind of logic, not an unusual step for Patsy. I could, however, see what she meant. After all, I hadn't neutered the feral cat, Vercingetorix. "Let me talk to Lanier, run this by Eli and call you back. You promise she'll be out of here in two days?"

"Cross my heart and hope to die."

I hung up the telephone and called Lanier Polman.

"Garden District Animal Hospital," a voice said.

I asked for Lanier, and told her about Loba.

"There's a sucker born every minute, Maggie. I have to admit I'm the one who suggested calling you. You need a new challenge."

"The last thing I need is a challenge. I can barely keep my head on straight as it is. And two days is hardly a significant challenge. You understand this means you're out of my will?"

"Seriously, Loba really is a sweetheart. I've given her shots and wormed her and looked after her general care since Marion picked her up in Arkansas and brought her home."

"Why on earth did you let her do it?"

"Did she ask me ahead of time? I've been telling her for months she needed to find a sanctuary for Loba. She came up with one so fast she'd probably already gotten information on the one in Minnesota."

"So, do you recommend I take her?"

"All I can tell you is that I doubt Loba will be any trouble, and it is only two days. I'd have her here except it's only a couple of blocks from Belvedere. Even if I had an outdoor run tough enough to hold her, she'd howl so loud we'd have the animal control people down on us in a heartbeat. It would be cruel to keep her inside the building in a cage for that long."

The minute I hung up the phone, I called Eli.

I used all Patsy and Lanier's arguments to convince Eli with semi-success.

"Maggie McLain, you are crazier than Cooter Brown! A wolf? Do what you like, but it's your problem. I'm leaving to do a pre-purchase exam on a hunter pony. We don't have anything scheduled this afternoon in the clinic, but if we do, you'll have to handle it alone, plus play Sergeant Preston of the Yukon. It's Duane's day off, so you'll have to clean her run."

"I've scrubbed down my share of dog runs. One more won't hurt me. I'm going to do it. Eli, it's Patsy. She doesn't ask favors."

I called Patsy back and agreed to help her friend for a hefty fee.

"She'll pay anything. Oh, thank you. I'll call Marion right this minute. We can probably be there in an hour."

An hour and a half later the two women drove up in a silver Suburban that looked as though it had every bell and whistle offered by the dealer. Including a grid separating the rear end from the passenger end.

I was surprised when Marion climbed out of the driver's seat and Patsy introduced her. I'd been wondering what sort of Belvedere matron would buy a wolf puppy. I envisioned an earth mother type with beads and too much hair.

Not an earth mother. She was nearly as tall as I am and weighed forty pounds less. Her nails, foot and hand, were a matching shade of pink. Nobody was born with hair that precise color of silver gold.

Her fashionably rumpled slacks and shirt probably cost more than my winter coat, and her coral necklace might have decimated a whole reef.

The diamond solitaire on her left hand could deflect a laser.

Her makeup was perfect, but her eyes, once she took off her sunglasses, were red and swollen. She might project the cool, social image, but she was truly torn up. I felt a wave of pity even as I damned the woman for being a fool in the first place.

Then I got my first glimpse of Loba.

After the introductions, Marion handed me a canvas bag with 'Loba's Toys' embroidered across it in red.

"I brought all her toys," Marion said. "I've got her little beddy and her blankie in the back of the car." She turned away. "My poor baby."

"It's for the best, Marion, honey," Patsy said, and patted her arm. "Come on, honey, let's get Miss Loba out and introduce her to Dr. Maggie. "

Marion clipped the heavy leather leash onto her collar while Loba sat obediently in the back of the Suburban. Then she hopped down, walked around Marion, and sat in the sit-stay position obedience trainers demanded. Her eyes never left Marion's face.

"I have to admit she's gorgeous," I said to Marion.

She beamed.

Loba was dark Oxford gray, with a beautiful pelt that rippled in the slight breeze.

"She will definitely knock the socks off any male wolf she meets in Minnesota," I said. I didn't add that Loba might be too used to human beings ever to be allowed back into the wild. She might not even recognize her own kind.

"Come on, sweetie, come meet Dr. Maggie," Marion said.

I extended my hand palm down for Loba to sniff. She touched my fingers gently with her muzzle and wagged her tail.

I scratched behind her ears. She rolled her golden eyes in ecstasy. I scratched her chest between her front legs. She looked as though she'd flop over into an orgasm right there.

Then I hunkered down in front of her, and she laid her great head in my arms. "Who's a good girl, then," I crooned to her. Her tail wagged some more.

This was going to be a piece of cake. I could see why Marion was distraught. She was losing a creature that was probably as dear to her as her children and might be a great deal more affectionate.

Thirty minutes later Loba was happily installed in the biggest dog run and kennel at the clinic—the one on the far end. At the moment Loba was the sole occupant. We were having the last cold spell of the year, but with Loba's fur, she probably wouldn't feel the cold. The indoor cages, however, were climate controlled, so Loba could get inside if she wanted. "I promise I'll come down and play with you, girl, when I clean up your run."

When we shut the door on her cage and Marion walked away, Loba began to sniff, to groan, and finally to howl. It started low in the back of her throat and grew until she gave full tongue to a howl worthy of a werewolf.

Twice Marion turned back to speak to her, until both Patsy and I each grabbed an arm and dragged her back to the Suburban.

"I'm driving home too, Marion," Patsy said. "And the minute we get home I'm making you a peach daiquiri the size of Bermuda." She thrust Marion into the front seat, then she turned to me. "How are *you* doing?"

"Hanging in, but sometimes that blasted big bed feels as big and empty as the Pacific Ocean."

She hugged me. "Come riding with me. Call me and let's set up a date."

"Sure." I probably wouldn't. Being distracted on a horse is a recipe for disaster, and these days I got distracted too easily and too often.

I watched Patsy and Marion go. From the hunch of her shoulders I could tell Marion was crying.

Loba watched too. She'd come out into her run and was standing up with her front claws hooked into the metal fence that surrounded the run. No chance of her getting out of that, I thought. We'd once boarded a full grown cougar for a week while we drained his abscessed tooth. If he couldn't get out, nothing could.

"You'll do better if I let you settle down alone," I said. "Promise I'll come back this afternoon, pick up your poop and scrub your outside run. I'll scratch your belly and rub your ears then."

Loba dropped to the concrete and trotted inside. Good, she was 'denning up.'

That afternoon, Tonesha pleaded a sick headache and asked to go home early. "Wanda Jean's already left," Tonesha said. "We don't have any surgeries scheduled. It's real quiet."

"Okay, go. See you tomorrow. Hope you feel better."

A minute later I heard Tonesha's Saturn start up and lay rubber out of the parking lot.

I was alone.

I never minded being alone in the clinic. There is a subtle difference, however, when you know you'll be just as alone when you leave.

I'd force myself to read some articles in my office, try to concentrate on new advances in veterinary medicine, and ignore the thought of that lonely house waiting for me.

Instead, as sometimes happened, the minute Tonesha left, half a dozen clients showed up.

Misty Hardin's French lop-eared rabbit had to be treated for a nasty case of ear canker.

Dick Palliser brought in his bloodhound, Sable, with pin worms.

A pair of male cats had both developed cystitis and had to have their bladders drained.

A Jack Russell terrier needed its anal glands emptied, a nasty, nasty job. I nearly got bit and the dog screamed throughout the procedure.

Simple work, but time consuming.

It was nearly four o'clock when I finally closed the door on the last client.

Maggie's Militia, as Lanier Polman's fourteen-year-old daughter, Susan, had christened us after Morgan's death, was meeting at my house for dinner. At the moment, the rest of the group consisted of Lanier and Susan, Vickie Anderson, Eli and Heather Halliday, newly-qualified, newly married and now newly-pregnant.

For a couple of years we had tried to get together at my house for dinner every month or six weeks. They brought the food. All I did was provide the location.

Morgan had always been invited, but seldom joined us. He usually went to dinner with his golfing buddies on the nights we met. Since his death, the others had become much more conscientious about meeting every month.

Before I picked up the house and set the table, I had to tidy up Loba's run. No doubt she'd deposited some piles that would smell to high heaven by morning. I figured I'd slip her a few treats and scratch her ears, give the outside run a quick scrub with disinfectant, and head for home.

The door between the main clinic and kennel was soundproof so clients wouldn't have to hear animals making unhappy noises.

The kennels were set up the same way zoos and breeding kennels set up their enclosures. Along the back wall were five indoor enclosures surrounded by steel fencing. Each had its own door opening onto the access corridor. Animals could be fed by slipping food through a small panel cut into the fence that surrounded each indoor cage, and each concrete floor had its own drain so that it could be sluiced down daily.

Each indoor den had a door giving onto an individual outdoor kennel run surrounded by ten foot tall steel fence topped by an additional foot of barbed wire fencing canted to the inside.

If a sick or injured animal must be kept indoors, we could shut the door to its outside run. Once it was well enough to exercise, that door could be left open so that the animal could spend time either outside in the sun or inside in air-conditioned comfort in its own individual 'den.'

At the moment Loba was alone.

She didn't like it.

I heard her howl the moment I opened the soundproof door and stepped into the access corridor that ran along in front of the dens. The howl died in her throat when she saw me and changed to a serious growl.

Her nails clicked against the concrete as she trotted a long oval the length of both inside and outside enclosures. I had no idea how long she'd been at it, but she looked exhausted and miserable.

When I came to within five feet of her indoor cage, she stopped, bared her fangs and snarled. I froze. Then she wheeled and trotted back outside and into her pattern again.

The inside den area looked clean, but through the door to the outside I could see half a dozen piles of poop and runnels of urine. She'd obviously spent the afternoon marking the confines of her meager territory. By morning they'd be a mess and so would Loba.

Normally, Duane takes his bucket and mop and simply walks through the inside den and its canine inhabitant to the outside run, picks up the piles, sluices the urine and his wash water down the center drain, walks back through the den area and out into the corridor.

Loba wasn't a dog. I decided to sucker her into her den with some treats, sneak me and my mop and bucket past her while she was occupied, then shut the door between outside and den area behind me once I was outside. When I was ready to leave, I'd toss some treats to the far end of the outside run, and sneak past her and out while she was eating them. Simple.

Loba had seemed to like me earlier, but once she fully comprehended that she'd been ripped away from loving family and palatial surroundings, she had become truly pissed. Now *that* I could understand. I seemed to stay royally pissed. Preferable to self-pity, at any rate. I didn't doubt she'd take her anger out on anybody who got in her way. In this case, me.

The first part of my plan worked perfectly. Before Loba scarfed up her first treat I was through her den and outside with the door between us firmly shut.

Inside, Loba must have finished her treats. She threw herself against the door that separated us again and again, snarling all the while.

"I don't blame you, girl," I said as I worked. "Your whole world has crashed and you don't know why." She was as frightened as she was angry. "I don't know how to reassure you. Hell, I can't even reassure myself."

She'd ripped several of her chew toys apart in the four hours she'd been in the run. I left the remains untouched. They were in bits, but they were hers and they smelled of familiar places and beloved people.

I longed to comfort her, to hunker down as I had before and scratch her ears and her tummy, let her know that things would get better, that she'd eventually be with her own kind, maybe have pups. At this moment I didn't dare.

In any pack only the alpha male and alpha female breed. I had no doubt Loba with her veterinary-prescibed vitamins and her perfectly balanced meals was bigger than the females she'd encounter in the wild. I had been worrying that she wouldn't have the instinct necessary to fight for her place in the hierarchy.

No longer. This one wasn't just a princess. She was an empress in the making. Woe betide any courting male who tried to dominate *her*. God help the females who challenged her.

I had finished swabbing all but the last corner of the run when I heard the thunk from inside the office.

Loba had crashed against the inside of the door to the run so often that I really no longer registered the sound.

This sounded different. Almost a clang.

Then it hit me.

Somehow Loba had managed to dislodge the heavy bar that locked the kennel door from the inside. It had fallen into its hasp.

Suddenly I was the prisoner. Loba was locked in, all right. In with air-conditioning and fresh water.

I, on the other hand, was trapped in a concrete-floored dog run with no way to get that bar raised from my side.

Tonesha, Duane and Wanda Jean were gone for the day.

Eli would probably drive home from doing the pre-purchase exam and go straight to her cottage, assuming I had gone home from the clinic as well.

The sun was fast disappearing. The wind was rising. I hadn't bothered to wear a jacket, but the temperature must have dropped into the low fifties. My teeth started chattering.

Each outside run had its own door that gave onto the back lawn. Each was closed with a heavy padlock to prevent vandals and thieves from opening the doors and either chasing the animals out or hurting them.

Both Eli and I had keys to all those padlocks. We also had cell phones.

Mine sat on the front seat of my truck ten feet away in the parking lot. My key ring hung from the truck's ignition. The keys to those padlocks were on my key ring.

I couldn't climb the fence. The holes in the wire were barely large enough for my big toe, and on top of the fence three strands of barbed wire were set so that they leaned inside the kennel at a forty-five degree angle. Any animal that actually made it to the top of the fence was faced with the insoluble problem of that barbed wire.

The cougar hadn't managed to escape. I was older and much less agile. Beside, I didn't have claws.

Even if Loba wanted to help me, only a circus dog trained to do the trick could have raised that inside steel bar. It would have taken a big, strong dog—no Jack Russell terriers need apply, thank you.

The sun had dropped below the roof line of the kennel. I hunkered down against the brick wall to absorb what heat remained.

Sooner or later somebody would find me.

Loba had meanwhile continued to batter the door.

Suddenly I heard an ominous crack. The wood was starting to splinter.

# Chapter 32

## *In which Loba nearly wins the day*

If Loba managed to break through that door, all I had to defend myself was a bucket of dirty water and a mop with a wooden handle. Maybe I could jam it between her jaws until I could get inside and shut her out.

More likely I'd wind up jamming my forearm between her jaws while she chewed on it.

Better than my throat.

"Maybe Momma was right. I should have married a Delta planter and spent my days having tea parties. You hear that, wolf? You are making me question my vocation."

Inside I heard a thud as Loba sank to the concrete floor. Worn out, poor thing. Good.

"Nobody wants to hurt you. You and I have a lot in common. You've lost Marion. I've lost Morgan. You don't understand what's happened to you. Neither do I. We know we're miserable. You figure it's got to be somebody's fault. Me too."

Loba continued to pant. I leaned over to look through the slit.

I nearly lost my nose.

Loba snarled and tried to drive her canines through the small opening straight into my face.

I waited until I heard her thud onto the concrete once more. "So much for sweet talk. At least doctors get some appreciation occasionally. Vets are the Rodney Dangerfields of this world, I swear, wolf. The pay's lousy, the hours are crummy, and the conditions frequently suck. My patients have stomped, bitten, slashed, kicked, and generally smacked me around. Now you want to chew my face off."

Loba gave a great sigh. I heard the click of her toenails as I crossed the enclosure. A moment later I caught the sound of lapping.

"You go ahead and drink all you like, you blasted—critter—you. Right now I'd be happy to share that bowl with you. God, I am spittin' cotton."

I peeked through the slit again. Loba's head was buried in her water bowl. I quietly worked the handle of my mop through the opening. Maybe I could raise that bar before Loba finished drinking.

Without warning the handle was wrenched from my hands. The soggy mop hit me squarely in the chest and sent me sprawling. I heard the snap of wood, grasped the handle and yanked it out of the slit.

Or at least as much of it as remained. The jagged stob was now two feet shorter than it had been. Inside Loba growled, snarled, and tossed her new toy around.

"Drop it, damn you!" I slapped the door with the flat of my hand. "You could get splinters in your innards, you dimwitted hound!"

I kicked the door and yelped when my big toe collided with the wood. "Somebody get me out, dammit!" I stormed to the far end of the run. Where was Eli? Loba had been quiet for several minutes. Probably seeding her intestines with splinters that I would have to fish out under anesthetic.

I tip-toed to the door to the den and put me ear to the jamb.

Loba growled.

"You dad-dratted lupine bitch," I shouted."To think I felt sorry for you. You deserve to freeze in northern Minnesota. See how you get along with a bunch of wild wolves who haven't been carried around on silver platters. *I* am not a poodle. If one of us winds up needing stitches, it's going to be you and not me, you got that?"

"Maggie , what on earth are you yelling at? Come out of there."

I jumped and whirled. Eli stood outside.

"I saw your truck when I pulled into the clinic parking lot. I was going to go straight home when I caught a glimpse of that red shirt you're wearing, so I walked over. Come on out of there."

"Would you kindly tell me how? That dad-blasted wolf locked me in." I said. At that point Loba, who had no doubt heard Eli's voice, began to hurl her body against the inside of the door once more.

"What is she *doing* in there?" Eli asked.

"She is doing her dead-level best to tear through that door and then through me. She has been at it for the last hour."

"Maggie, where are your keys to the padlock?"

"Hanging from the ignition of my truck."

"Right beside your cell phone, no doubt."

"Don't start."

"How many times have I made you promise to keep that cell phone in your pocket at all times?"

"I thought I'd finish cleaning up Loba's run in five minutes."

"What if I hadn't spotted you in here? What if I'd gone straight home?"

"You or the girls would have hunted me up when I wasn't home to give you dinner."

Eli held up her hands. "It is kind of funny."

"Eli!"

Two minutes later I stepped onto the lawn in front of the kennel, took key and padlock from Eli and relocked the gate. "Now all we have to do is get Loba back where she belongs."

"Why bother?"

"She can't spend the night in there."

"I don't see why not."

"Because Duane will walk into that office to pick up his cleaning stuff for the kennels at six-thirty tomorrow morning and get the fright of his life is why not."

"You told me Lanier Polman said this thing was a sweetie-pie," Eli said as we started around to the back door of the clinic.

"It was. We bonded, or I thought we did. Ear scratches, tummy rubs, complete submission behavior."

"Your or hers?"

I considered decking her. "I knew she'd probably be upset after Marion left, but I figured if I just left her alone for a while, she'd settle down and accept the situation. She didn't seem to need medication to chill her out."

"Another miscalculation on your part. So how do we get her back outside, O Dances with Wolves?" Eli leaned against the wall. "Looks pretty hopeless to me."

"We could shoot her with the tranquilizer pistol, but I hate to take the chance. We haven't weighed her, so the dose would have to be guesswork. I'm already worried about the splinters from the mop she bit off."

"She did what?

"Didn't you notice I was only carrying half a mop?"

"Good grief," Eli said.

"Okay, how's this? I put food and tranquilizer into her dish, and while she's eating it, we lower a rope over her head from above and snub it up tight. Just like *Peter and the Wolf*. Then we open the door of the cage, race across, raise the bar to the outside, and slip back out into the office. Then we go fix dinner."

"Which *we* do you see as sneaking past her and lifting that bar?"

"You're faster."

"I'm also smarter. Somebody's got to go in that cage, pull up the bar and open the door. I promise you, *kemo sabe,* it ain't gonna be me. There's a twelve-foot-one-minute period when *one of us* will be locked in with a poodle-chomping carnivore harboring a grievance. It's your wolf. You do it."

"Fine. You just make damned sure you keep that lasso tight."

I broke up a tranquilizer pill, mixed it in with a can of dog food, and slipped it under the wire into the cage. I snatched my fingers out an instant before the wolf stuck her muzzle under the wire and snapped at them.

"Are you planning to wait until that tranquilizer takes effect?"

"Not if I can help it. Get ready with that lasso."

Eli stood on top of a small table beside the cage and took careful aim with the loop.

The wolf raised her eyes to see what was happening above her head.

Eli dropped the loop, pulled it tight around her neck, and snubbed it around the steel pipe that supported one corner of the wire. "Go, Maggie!"

I was on my way back, mission accomplished, when Eli yelled, "Come on, blast it! I can't hang onto her much longer! She weighs a ton."

I opened the door to the corridor.

Suddenly the wolf leapt straight up, twisted her body a hundred and eighty degrees in mid-air, and bit through the lasso.

It split as cleanly as though it had been sliced with a scalpel.

I screamed, jumped backward through the door and slammed it just as the wolf threw herself against it.

With no tension in the lariat, Eli teetered on the edge of the table she was standing on. "Help!"

I caught her.

Eli scowled at the bitten end of her lariat. "I don't know who you're billing, Maggie, but make damned sure you include the cost of a new rope."

"And a new mop."

Loba shook off the rope, picked it up in her teeth and trotted cheerfully into her outside run. She sank onto her haunches and began to worry the rope as though it were a particularly nasty copperhead.

"She should settle down now," Eli said.

"Right. She's happy. She thinks she's won."

Eli walked across the lawn toward her cottage. "Get yourself home, Maggie. And take a shower before you fix dinner. You smell like Loopy Loup."

# Chapter 33

## *In which Maggie makes an announcement*

"Maggie," Lanier Polman said when I walked in my kitchen door. "Where on earth have you been?"

At my heels, Eli said glumly, "You don't want to know," then she cheered up. "Actually, you do, since it's your fault."

I left them to it and ran up the back stairs and into my bedroom. I stripped off my clothes, showered, and called Patsy. "You owe me." I told her what had happened, then I hung up and called Sarah in Los Angeles. No need to tell her I was calling because I'd been scared of being savaged by a wild wolf.

"How are the wild fires and mud slides?" I said, then smacked myself on the forehead. Great way to start.

"No worse than the tornadoes in Tennessee," she replied. She sounded harried.

"Did I call at a bad time?"

"Actually, yes. I'm on my way to Thailand to scout locations. I have to pack and catch a plane to Tokyo."

"Is it safe?"

"A good deal safer than dealing with sick horses and nippy dogs the way you do. I don't think there are any man-eating tigers where we'll be."

"How about cobras and bamboo snakes and Maoist guerillas?" I asked.

"No guerillas. No *go*-rillas either. I'll probably be staying in a four-star hotel."

"Maybe I'll come visit."

"God no!" She must have realized how that sounded, because

she said in a more conversational voice, "I'll probably be working twenty hours a day." I heard her deep breath. "I'll be home for Christmas. Are you managing all right?"

"Sure."

"Things okay at the clinic?"

"Going great guns."

"And home?"

What did she want me to say? I'm miserable and lonely? That would do neither one of us any good. "I'm staying busy." I hesitated. "You'll be working twenty hours a day—more than I do. We're not that different, are we, Sarah?"

"I just have to please one director. Look, I have to run. Take care of yourself."

"I love you," I said, but to a dial tone. I scratched Bear's ears. "Well, that went well."

Lanier met me at the foot of my back stairs. "Sorry, Maggie." Then she grinned and spoiled the contrition all to heck. She was beginning to thicken around the waist a bit, but she looked beautiful and prosperous, not at all the waif I had met when she came to interview with Dr. Parmenter. She wore beautifully cut slacks and a silk shirt in a dark cerise that complimented her tan skin and streaked brown hair perfectly.

"You didn't tell me we were going formal," I said. I had tossed on clean slacks and a sweatshirt. "Whatever's in the oven smells good. Bread pudding?"

"Yep. Heather brought a big salad and Vickie brought Country Captain."

Country Captain is chicken cooked with rice, gravy, raisins and almonds. It's as Southern as spoon bread. Done by a good cook like Vickie, it's divine.

"I need to set the table," I said and started for the dining room.

"All done," said Heather from the doorway. "When you weren't here, we assumed you were out on a call, so we fixed everything." She eased her back. "I think I've about reached the limit of these maternity jeans. The stretchy panel in front refuses to stretch any more."

"Be thankful, Heather Louise," Vickie Anderson said. She lifted a glass filled with a suspiciously dark highball, and tossed her exuberant head of red hair. "You gestate only nine months. Horses are pregnant eleven and a half, sometimes longer."

"And elephants do a full two years," said Eli. "Tell Heather and Vickie why you're late, I dare you."

"I figured they'd all know by the time I got here, Doctor Mouth of the South."

"Maggie got trapped by the big, bad wolf." Eli giggled.

Lanier was hunting through my kitchen drawers. A second later she came up with salad tongs. These women knew more about my house than I did. "I am so sorry! I swear I've never seen Loba act like anything except a perfect lady."

"The poodle attack ought to have given us both a clue." I leaned against the kitchen counter. "It's not really your fault. Poor little bitch."

"Can you stand it one more day?"

"Sure, now that I know what I'm dealing with. I'll keep her on mild tranquilizers. Maybe I can even get back on speaking terms with her. Tell Marion she's doing fine. No sense in making the poor woman any more miserable than she is already."

After we had all finished seconds of Lanier's bread pudding, I clinked my glass. "Hush, everybody, I have a proposal to make."

The six heads turned to her.

"You all know Morgan wanted me to retire when he turned sixty-five this year."

"Yeah, but nobody thinks you'd have done it," Vickie said and refilled her wine glass. She'd brought a nice Reisling to serve with dessert.

I ignored her. "Eli and I have been talking about taking in a third partner for the last couple of years. So, I thought, maybe one of you would be interested in buying my half of the practice. Or two of you might want a quarter each."

The room erupted in noise.

"But, Aunt Maggie, what can you do if you don't work?" Susan asked.

I took a deep breath. "I intend to travel."

"For pity's sake, haven't you given up that idiotic retirement idea yet?" Eli snapped. Her mouth set in a hard line and her eyes narrowed.

I avoided her eyes and turned to others. "Anybody interested?

Heather, what about you? You're still working pickup at the emergency clinic, aren't you? You don't have a regular job yet."

"Actually, I'm pretty much working full time at the experimental station keeping records for Rick. At least until the baby's born, and then I'm going to try to be a stay-at-home mom for a year. Rick and I couldn't possibly afford to buy a partnership, but unless you're set on a woman, he might be interested in joining your practice as an employee to make some extra money. He loves his heifers, but it's kind of a dead end job."

"You've got the cart before the horse," Vickie said. "Seems to me we ought to try working some at the clinic. See if it's a decent fit. Maybe have Maggie work with us in our practices some. See how we do things."

"Good idea," Eli said. "If Maggie doesn't come to her senses and actually tries to go through with this nitwittedness, I'm the one who'll have to get used to a new partner."

"Eli, you'd work with Count Dracula if he could deliver a calf," I said. "Heather, do you think Rick would let me visit the experimental station? I haven't been down there in ten years."

"Sure," Heather said. "Rick loves to show off his girls. We're starting to artificially inseminate on Friday. You could come down and give us a hand."

"Well, Eli? Think you could spare me Friday morning for a couple of hours?"

Eli threw up her hands. "Why not?"

"How about the rest of you? Any takers?"

"Not me," Lanier said. "I have a thriving practice in midtown, thank you very much." She looked at Susan. "Maybe the kid, here, can actually go to college."

"I thought Daddy was supposed to pay for college."

Lanier stammered. "He—he is, but…"

"But he's never done one damn thing he was supposed to do since he dumped us," Susan said.

"Susan, watch your language."

"Why? Y'all say damn and hell and a whole lot worse."

"We're grown women, and we shouldn't. You are fourteen years old. You *definitely* shouldn't."

"It's a bad habit," I said. "When you're a vet like your mother…"

"A what?" Susan laughed, but there was no mirth in it. "I can't ever become a vet, even if I wanted to, which I don't."

"Okay, if you don't want to, but you're certainly smart enough," Heather said. "Lanier says your scores on the SAT are so high right now you probably won't have to take it again. Your mother probably won't have to pay for college anyway. You'll get scholarship offers out the wazzoo."

"Yeah, it'll help their affirmative action stats. Let's face it, I couldn't go to vet school. Attitudes may have changed, but not *that* much. Can't you hear the good ol' boys? 'Come on honey, roll faster, you can catch that cow.'"

"But you can *walk*," Heather said. "I've seen you."

"Pul-leeze," Susan said and rolled her eyes. "Okay, how's this? 'Come on, honey, let's see you hobble after that cow.'"

I glanced at Lanier. I half expected her to intervene. She had always been a good deal touchier about Susan's cerebral palsy than Susan had.

"Precious little wrong with your body," Eli chimed in. "Except your legs don't work that well."

"I don't think you'd want me doing brain surgery on you, Aunt Eli. Whoops! Little slip there—no more frontal lobe. Sorry."

To the best of my knowledge, Susan never spoke of her CP in front of her mother. She certainly had never allowed the bitterness show before. She tried to protect Lanier. Intellectually, Lanier knew she was not responsible for Susan's hypoxia at birth, but emotions override intellect when it comes to love.

I have good reason to know that.

Susan hit the arms of her wheelchair so hard it shivered, and a moment later her companion dog Pumpkin laid her head in Susan's lap in obvious concern. "Sometimes I get so mad at my body I just sit here and cuss it."

Lanier sat rigid. Her hands gripped the arms of her chair.

"Hey, kiddo," Vickie said, "I cuss my forty extra pounds every morning."

"You could diet if you wanted to, Aunt Vickie. Not much I can do about this. My theme song's *Whole Lot of Shaking Going On.*" Susan wore a smile more brittle than Steuben crystal.

"They're making breakthroughs in stem cell research every day. Surely they'll come up with some help for CP in the near future," Heather said.

"What do I do in the meantime? I ran my daddy off. Mom's stuck with me."

"Whoa!" Lanier nearly shouted. "Enough. Your daddy ran off because he was a juvenile jerk who wanted to play around. The baby daughter he left behind was barely a consideration."

"Sure, Mom. Keep that thought." Susan pushed her chair away from the table and spun so fast she ran over Pumpkin's toe. Susan wheeled off through the living room and down the hall. Pumpkin yelped, then ran after her.

A moment later the door to my guest bathroom slammed.

"I'm sorry," Lanier said as she dropped her napkin on the table and shoved her chair back. "I'd better go talk to her."

"Let me," I said. "I'm lousy with my own children, but I seem to get along fine with other people's."

"Lanier, believe me, as her mother, you'd be pouring oil on burning waters," Vickie said, then shrugged. "Or whatever."

I walked down the hall and knocked on the bathroom door, then knocked again. Then hammered.

"Can't I even go to the bathroom alone?" Susan snarled from the other side of the door.

"Sure, if that's what you're doing. It's me, not your mother. Open up."

"Go 'way."

"For Pete's sake, Susan. Open the door."

Pumpkin opened the door. Across the bathroom Susan sat in her wheelchair. Her eyes looked as though she'd been crying. "I can't believe I dumped all that bullshit on y'all."

"If you can't let it all hang out and feel sorry for yourself with us, who can you let fly to?"

"I started out to be funny, but it got out of hand."

I looked around. "I ought to put a chair in here." I sat on the closed toilet.

"Daddy Geoff did leave because of me. I don't even remember him. I haven't gotten a birthday card from him for five years. He's got another wife and some *undamaged* kids now. Mom won't ever find another man willing to marry her and take me on at the same time."

"First off, you're not that damaged. You can walk when you have to, you can use your fingers pretty well, and in a pinch you really can do most of the things that Pumpkin does for you."

"On a good day when the medicine's working."

"Granted. Fourteen is a rotten age. Don't let anybody tell you different. And fourteen when you *are* different can be hell."

"You know the worst? Everybody expects me to be some sort of angel, cheerful and happy. They'd all be horrified if I screamed or threw things or had a bitch fit in the middle of English class. Nobody is interested in the real me. Not even the special needs teachers. Dear little Susan, the invisible angel. Isn't she just the sweetest child? And isn't it just terrible she's in a wheelchair most of the time and talks funny and drops things?"

"You don't talk funny."

"I do, too. Not very funny, but funny. When I'm tired or having my period or mad I talk really funny."

"The kids laugh at you?"

"The boys ignore me, but the girls make every effort to include me. Makes them feel good about themselves. They're always nice to my face. I wish somebody would get mad at me or make snide comments. They treat me like a really expensive pet dog. Pat me on the head and consider me some kind of lesser species."

"Bummer. What do you plan to do about it?"

"What can I do?"

"Not play up to their version of who you are, for one thing."

"Then they'll have an excuse to dump me because I'm a bitch."

"Some of them will, but you might actually find somebody you could connect with."

"Aunt Maggie , what the hell—heck—do you know about it?"

I leaned over and scratched Pumpkin's ears. "When I was in high school I drove a big, yellow Buick convertible. The car was probably the only reason I got invited to join a sorority. One of the girls who joined the same time I did was paralyzed from the waist down. Polio was still a big threat every summer then. There weren't any of those fancy motorized wheel chairs. Mary Jane's weighed a ton and never would fold right. But I could get both her and the chair in my convertible, so I got stuck with taking her to meetings."

"Stuck?"

"Stuck. I didn't know her from Adam's off ox when we pledged. There was no more wrong with her mind than there is with yours, but she said everybody treated her like a mental deficient. And a saint. Hoo, boy, a saint she was not. God, what a temper. Nothing suited her. I took her complaints for a month. Then one day when I had the cramps and a sinus infection she hit my last nerve. I called her everything except a child of God. When I finally wound down I started to stammer an apology, but she was grinning.

"She said, 'I wondered how long you could take the real me before you blew up. I was really sick of waiting.' Said I was the first girl in that school or that sorority that had ever treated her as an equal. We were friends until I went off to college."

"What became of her?"

"She went to college, because a journalist, and a darned good one. Married. Moved away. We lost touch."

"So I should be a bitch at school?"

"I didn't say that. But you don't have to be the sunshine girl all the time. Screw 'em."

"Right. Screw 'em." Susan sniffled and reached for a tissue from the box on the back of the toilet. Pumpkin jumped up, pulled a tissue and handed it to her gently by one edge. She blew her nose. "Thanks, Pumpkin."

All of a sudden I had one of those blinding flashes. "Susan, what if you could do something most of them couldn't do?"

"Like what? Fall down?"

"I'm serious. Did you ever actually *ride* a horse?"

Susan made a face. "Get real."

"I am getting real. You know Patsy Dalrymple?"

Susan nodded.

"Patsy has her little fat fingers in half the charitable pies in west Tennessee. Among them is the Riding for the Disabled program. She's donated four of her old campaigners to them. They use the indoor arena at her boarding barn."

"I couldn't balance on a horse." Susan thought for a minute. "Could I?"

"Don't see why not. There are kids one heck of a lot worse off than you who ride. There's even one woman who lost both legs in an automobile accident and rides with artificial limbs."

"On a horse *I'd* have legs." She looked up with a frown. "What if I fall off?"

"There are plenty of teachers around to make certain you don't fall off."

"Would I just walk around on a lead line?"

"Depends on how fast you progress and what you want to do."

Susan turned her head. "My mom would never let me. She's chicken."

"Are you?"

"Heck, no." Susan raised her chin. "I'll try anything once."

"Good. Then I'll get Patsy to talk to your mother. At the moment Patsy owes me bigtime."

"How would I get to the stable or wherever they do the lessons?"

"They have a van to pick you up at school and drop you at home."

"How come you know so much about this?"

"I've looked after Patsy's horses for over twenty years. That includes the horses in the disabled program. So, shall I ask Patsy to call Lanier?"

"Yeah. That'll show those cheerleaders." She gave me a real smile. "Thanks, Aunt Maggie."

"*De Nada*. That's what aunt's are for. Now, are you coming back to the table?"

"In a little while. I get tired."

"I know you do, kiddo. Go hide out in the downstairs guest room for a while. Take a nap if you can."

"Okay."

"Fine. I'll leave you."

"Don't say anything to Mom about the riding, okay? I'm afraid she'll freak."

"You got it." I shut the door after her and went back to the table.

Vickie asked, "Is she all right?"

"Sure. She's going to rest a little."

"It was bad enough when she was little, but she's a teenager now. She's not just angry, she's scared," Lanier said.

"So are you."

"Terrified. What happens to her when she's grown? Or if I die? If she wants to have a home of her own? Babies?"

"She'll have them if she wants them bad enough. Butt out, Lanier. She's not engaged yet."

"And probably never will be."

"Don't bet on that." I made a mental note to call Patsy first thing in the morning.

I wanted to avoid Eli, so as she was saying goodbye to the girls, I high-tailed it out my back door and across the lawn to the clinic.

I half expected Eli to follow me, but she'd brought her truck, so she'd have to drive down my driveway to the fork, then turn left and drive up the short driveway to the clinic parking lot.

I had promised to say good night to Loba. I never forget a promise to an animal. though I don't seem to have a problem ignoring promises to the people I love. Otherwise I'd have seen that blasted

Mona Lisa at least once with Morgan.

We had dawn-to-dusk lights set on poles along the driveway and over the parking lots, so even if the moon had not been high, I wouldn't have needed a flashlight. Morgan's idea, of course.

I loved this place at night after the clinic shut down and the front gates were securely closed. They'd open to let the gals out, but nobody could drive through unless we unlocked them electronically from either Eli's or my house or from the clinic.

The fifty acres Morgan had bought when we couldn't afford peanut butter for dinner was now worth hundreds of times what he paid for it. When we moved into The Hideous House, we were out in the country. Now gigantic MacMansions were springing up all along the road. The house Morgan had built me, the clinic and Eli's cottage were all dwarfed by starter castles. If I should die before Eli, Nathan and Sarah could sell off a few acres and retire on the proceeds without ever encroaching on either the clinic or Eli's cottage and grounds.

The thought of someone tearing down my house made my blood freeze. But there's nothing stable except change, right? Who knew, after I retired I might even sell it myself to move to Africa or India.

That idea didn't appeal to me, as a matter of fact.

The night was cool, but felt wonderful after the close atmosphere of my house.

At least two bullfrogs drummed and thrumped down by the pond at the back of the property. Probably fighting over the ladies. I disturbed a mocking bird who whistled at me as I passed. The night insects kept up a continuing chorus of chirps and peeps.

Whoever said the country was quiet?

The light outside Loba's kennel revealed her curled up outside on the remains of what Marion had called "her beddie." I would tiptoe away without waking her.

Loba raised her head and stared straight into my eyes. In the reflection her pupils glowed blood red.

At that moment a bat swooped through the light in its nightly hunt for mosquitoes, and from somewhere back in the woods an owl hooted.

I shivered. *I don't belong here. Loba does. She should be padding silently under the trees and pouncing on field mice.* Would she learn to hunt for her food? Staring into those blazing eyes, I felt certain she would. "Goodnight, girl," I whispered.

Loba twitched her tail once against the concrete, the lowered her head and closed her eyes.

This was Pan's world—wild, amoral, with no regard for human concerns. In truth I was Pan's servant. I turned and half ran back to the safety of my lighted kitchen.

Bear, Teezy, and Bok Choy met me at the kitchen door. They eddied around my ankles and chattered at me. "All right, dad-gummit. You're not going to starve." I took a deep breath, opened a can of cat food and divided it among the three bowls. Bear and Teesy attacked their bowls. Bok Choy nibbled his fastidiously for a moment, then turned away to wash his paws.

I was leaning against the washing machine watching Teesy and Bear when Eli opened the back door without knocking and stalked into the kitchen. I jumped. "You scared me half to death."

"I want to talk to you."

# Chapter 34

## *In which Maggie eats crow*

Uh-oh. Ambushed in my own kitchen.

Eli's current border terrier, Sugar Pie, trotted in behind her and went immediately over to see whether the cats had left any treats behind.

"Maggie, don't let him do that," Eli said.

"It's all right, Eli."

"He's getting too damned fat as it is. That's why I brought him. He needs the walk."

"Want some iced tea?" I said, putting off the evil day as long as possible.

Eli sat at the kitchen table and folded her arms across her meager chest. Bad sign. "No, I do not want some iced tea. What possessed you to ask those women if they wanted to buy you out?"

"I should have waited, but..."

"If you stopped working and went off traveling full time, you'd lose your mind in six weeks."

"But maybe it's time for me to try something else."

"Lordy. What else are you suited for, woman?" Eli blurted. "Nuclear Physics? Driving a race car?"

She was starting to annoy me, largely because we both knew she was right. "There are plenty of positions for experienced vets in places like South Africa or India. I could go work at a national park somewhere."

"And what am *I* supposed to do in the meantime, while you are off finding yourself?" She sucked in a deep breath. I could see she was trying to calm down. "Ever since you found that damnable scrapbook, you've been feeling guilty…"

"Morgan wanted me to retire when he did. That would have been at the end of this year."

"You know he never meant you should retire totally. Cut back. He wanted a playmate for part of the time. Retiring was not some deathbed promise."

"Morgan didn't have a deathbed." I thought I'd been a brick since Morgan died on me. At one point, I'd worried that I hadn't loved him enough because I *had* been able to go on. I'd built a snapping turtle shell around my emotions. I had refused sympathy or pity because I knew I'd go to pieces if anybody offered them, but at least with Eli I'd expected a modicum of understanding. After all, she'd gone through the same experience when she lost Josh. Now here she was nipping at me like Sugar Pie nipping at a skunk.

The steel in my voice even surprised me. "Nathan's married and living on one ocean. Sarah's living on the other and traipsing all over the globe. Neither one of them is looking to provide me grandchildren any time soon, if ever, and working all the time, how could I see them anyway? Face it, Eli, I don't have any other family left."

I knew the instant the words left my mouth I'd screwed up.

When Eli gets mad, she yells. When she goes all the way to rage, she gets very quiet. That's when she's truly scary.

"I see," she said very quietly.

I could feel my shoulders tighten. "I didn't…"

"I know precisely what you meant, Margaret Parker Evans McLain. *Morgan* was the one who always called me family. I'm not at all certain now whether the words ever left *your* mouth. I do not, in any case, carry one smidgen of DNA from either the Evanses or the McLains. I am not *family*. Obviously, so far as you're concerned, I have never been family. Godmothers are *not* family. I am not actually Sarah and Nathan's aunt."

I opened my mouth to interrupt, but she raised both hands.

Anything I said would make it worse.

"I am close enough to run a business with, share land with, babysit your children, attend Nathan's stupid, boring Lacrosse and soccer matches with, share Christmas dinner with. But I am not *family*. I always thought I was a damned sight closer to you than to my chauvinist father and my stupid brothers. Obviously, I was wrong. You can sell your part of the practice to an orangutan without a by-your-leave. You want to be alone, Margaret? How about I sell *my* half of the partnership to some stranger and run off to Africa? You'll damned well be alone then." She stood up. "Come on, Sugar Pie."

I had to block the door physically to keep her from storming out.

Eli and I usually have one good fight a year. I always apologize, even if I'm not wrong. She never will.

In this case, however, I couldn't have been more wrong if I tried. I wasn't certain I could make it right.

"Sit down," I said.

"Move out of the doorway or I'll sic Sugar Pie on you."

"Gee, I might actually lose a toe. Sit, Eli, or I swear I'll sit you right on your butt."

She sat back but turned away from me. That little chin of hers could have carved a Christmas fruitcake, it was stuck out so far.

I sat opposite her. I tried to take her hands, but she pulled away from me, so I had to be content with putting my hand on her arm. Sugar Pie sat at her feet looking from me to his mistress with real distress on his funny little otter face.

I took a deep breath. "I'm sorry. I have said a lot of dumb things in my life, but that's about the dumbest. You know I love you. You're the sister I never had and the friend of my heart." I was starting to get teary-eyed. I hate it when I cry. It ruins my strategic position. Tonight, I was willing to sob my guts out if that's what it took.

"You said it. You meant it."

"I did not." I leaned back and stretched my legs out in front of me. "Shit, Eli. When you lost Josh, you stopped taking life for granted. You were what? Twenty-two, twenty-three? You learned early. Before Morgan died, I trusted life. I knew who I was, what I wanted to do and how good I was at it. I knew I loved Morgan and that he loved me back. I knew you were always going to be there. Morgan and you and I would totter into old age together. We picked each other for family, you and me, even before I found Morgan. That's closer than DNA could ever be."

"Then why did you say it?"

"Dammit, Eli, I'm tired, I'm half frozen, and I let my alligator tongue overload my humming-bird brain." I grabbed her shoulders and hauled her around so that I could look into her eyes. "You weren't serious about running away to Africa, were you?"

"You're not the only one who worries about the future."

"Eli, I swear to God, I won't do anything that doesn't make you happy. And you are my family forever and ever. Now you can slap me upside my head if you'd like."

She shook her head. "It's okay, Maggie. We're both tired. Let's leave it for another time, all right?"

She stood up as though she were an old woman.

I watched her and Sugar Pie walk across the lawn in the moonlight. For the first time since we had known one another, I felt I'd inflicted a hurt that would take a long time to heal, if it ever did. And I knew damned well that even after it healed, it would leave a scar.

For the first time I realized how much *Eli* had lost when Morgan died. He was my husband, but he was closer to her than any of her own brothers had ever been. Maybe it was time I stopped wallowing in my own grief like a hippopotamus in a mud hole and paid some attention to the other people I loved.

# Chapter 35

## *In which Loba leaves for her new life*

Thursday morning, Tonesha stuck her head into the room in which I was examining a highly pregnant Weimeraner. "There's this big truck outside with something about a sanctuary painted on the side. I guess it's the guys for that wolf."

I glanced at my watch. "I hadn't expected them this early. Tell Mr. Olafson I'll be right there." I turned to my client. "She's doing fine, Carly, but she's a youngster herself. We may need to do a Cesarean."

"When will I know she's ready?"

"Put her in her crate when you're not with her and give her a stack of newspapers. It's her first time, so she could be a little late, but dogs are usually right on the money sixty-three days precisely, so plan on bringing her in the day she's due to whelp, or if she starts frantically building a nest and looking anxious, whichever comes first."

"Thanks." Carly slipped the clip of her leather lead onto the dog's collar. "Come on, little Mo, baby. Let Mommy help you down."

I helped Carly lower the dog carefully to the floor and scratched her mouse-colored ears. "Ask Tonesha to give you a treat for her on your way out. I'll come with you."

Mr. Olafson from the wolf sanctuary was waiting for me at the reception desk. No matter how long his family had been in this country, his Viking genes had remained undiluted. He was completely bald, but wore a bushy red beard. He looked as though his hair had migrated from his skull to take root on his cheeks and chin.

He probably weighed about two-seventy, but at six feet five or six he wasn't fat. He wore threadbare jeans and a gray sweatshirt with the sleeves pushed up to reveal forearms bigger than my thigh. I put his age at something over thirty but under fifty.

He came forward and enveloped my hand in his. My calluses met his calluses. "Doctor McLain. Great to meet you!" His voice filled the reception room so full that even the dogs and cats went silent momentarily. "How's our girl?"

"Sleepy, and please, it's Maggie."

"Ah, and I am Nels. My son Lars is waiting in the truck. Where is she?"

"Right this way."

"Good. Need to get her settled and leave for Minnesota. Is it always this warm so early?"

"Don't give me that," I said. "The last time I was in Minnesota for a conference it was a hundred and five degrees, and your mosquitoes were carrying off small children."

By the truck, Nels's son Lars was a slightly smaller copy of his father with no beard and a long red ponytail. He grinned at me, but didn't say a word.

"Nice set-up."

"I kept Loba inside her den and gave her a dose of tranquilizer with her breakfast. I hope she can walk."

"Oh, don't worry. We'll get her into her cage, all right."

Lars nodded.

I opened the door into the inside kennel and stood aside for the two men. Loba slept quietly on her side with one paw protectively over the shreds of one of her toys.

"Can you take her toys with her?"

"Absolutely." Nels dropped to his haunches outside the cage. "Look, Lars, what a beautiful bitch. See the size of her." He grinned over his shoulder at me. "She'll make an excellent addition."

"If we can let her go free, Papa," Lars said.

"Why wouldn't you be able to?" I asked.

Young Lars turned soft blue eyes on me. "She may be too imprinted on human beings."

"We'll give her every chance," Nels said. "It may take a year or so to know for certain." He stood easily. "But then again it may work out perfectly."

"How do you go about it?"

"A pack won't generally accept a stranger. The she-wolves will view her as a threat and try to kill her or drive her off. So, we start a new pack. We have a couple of young males who just came into the sanctuary. We'll put her in one big fenced in area next to them where they can see one another, but not touch. Then, if that works, we'll try them on supervised visitation. If that works, we'll turn them into a single paddock."

"And if that works," Lars continued, "We'll turn them out into our twenty acre pen."

"Twenty whole acres?"

"Yep," Nels said. "If they work out together and can learn to hunt on their own, we'll take them up north where there's no other pack close, and let them go."

"Possibly Canada," Lars said.

"What happens if they don't work out?"

"Then we'll look after them and use Loba as a brood bitch."

I sighed. "I'd almost rather you kept her than turned her loose where she could get hurt."

"Now you sound like that Marion woman," Nels laughed. "Loba's a wolf. She deserves her chance to be what she was born to be."

"I'll still worry. Can I call you? Will you keep me up to date on her?"

"If you'll agree to pass on the info to that Marion woman so I don't have to," Lars said.

Nels twinkled. "My son tends to get annoyed with people who try to make pets out of wild animals."

"So do you, Papa." He turned to me . "That woman. . ." He shook his head.

"Go get the cage, son," Nels said. He hunkered down beside Loba's kennel.

"How does one wind up in the wolf rescue business?" I asked.

"My Norwegian granddad used to tell me horror stories about wolves when I was growing up in North Minnesota," he said. "If I'd really been bad, he'd give me the old baby-in-the-sleigh tale."

I shook my head.

"You know it, I betcha. People traveling home across the snow at night. A pack of wolves starts chasing the sleigh. They throw everything out to lighten the load so the horses can outrun the pack, finally, in desperation, they throw out the baby." He raised his eyebrows. "That was me, according to Granddad."

"I'd think you'd keep a safe distance away."

"I'm a zoologist by trade. Took an internship one summer at a wolf rehabilitation sanctuary. Saw what people do to wolves and stayed. It's grown since then."

Young Lars came back in carrying a large traveling cage one-handed.

"Remember," I said. "She's perfectly capable of waking up rarin' to go the instant you touch that door, and she'll probably go straight for your throat."

Instantly the two Vikings went into action. Lars pulled two sets of heavy gauntlets out of the traveling cage and handed his father a muzzle.

"That is a significant muzzle," I said. "The trick is how to get it on her."

"No problemo," Lars said.

"Should I—uh—wait outside?" I asked.

Lars eyed me. "Keep out of the way and you can stay."

Nels opened the cage, bent low so that he didn't tower over Loba, and drifted silently inside like a wraith. Amazing in such a big man.

Lars held the door shut.

Loba raised her head and peered at him bleerily.

He duck-walked to her, the muzzle ready in his hand.

As Nels positioned the muzzle over Loba's nose, she exploded. I yelped.

Loba would tear him to pieces.

I'd warned him Loba could be playing possum.

So fast that I wasn't even certain how he'd done it, he straddled Loba's body, grabbed the scruff of her neck with one hand, and slipped the muzzle over her nose with the other. With his weight pressing her down, he snapped the muzzle closed, and clipped a heavy chain lead to her collar.

She continued to scramble frantically under him.

Then he stood up with her in his arms—all ninety or so pounds of her. He held her around her waist with one arm and kept her hind claws away from him with the other.

Lars opened the door, and together, the two men slid Loba into her big wire cage and shut the door.

"That was *slick*," I said in awe.

Nels grinned at me. He had red claw marks down his forearms.

"Are you hurt?"

"She didn't break the skin." The two men swung the cage between them, walked out of the office and set it down on the tarmac while Lars opened the back of the eighteen wheeler. Cool air billowed out of the dark interior. "Now, if you'll get her toys, we'll give her some water. As soon as she's in the dark she'll be quiet."

By the time I returned with the few remains of beddie, blankie and toys I could collect, Loba was safely stowed in the back of their truck. They'd managed to get her muzzle off somehow. I was glad of that. I hate muzzles, even though I knew they are often necessary.

I handed Loba's bag to Nels. From inside the truck came strange scratching sounds.

"Want to see the rest of our loot?" Nels asked me.

"Sure."

Lars jumped up into the truck and reached a hand down and swung me aboard. I saw that Loba was lying down, but watching me intently.

"Oh, the babies!" I cried, and dropped to all fours. A pair of tiny cheetah cubs sat like bookends as close to the front of their cage as they could get. "May I?" I asked over my shoulder.

"Sure. They're real tame," Lars told me.

I wiggled my finger through the wire mesh and was rubbed vigorously by a pair of tiny whiskered faces. They still had long, fluffy kitten fur on their backs. The cubs didn't growl or purr—they trilled.

"Haven't located a zoo yet that wants them and neither did the people whose female produced them," Nels said. "So we took 'em. We'll either find 'em a zoo that needs 'em, or they'll live with us."

"What else?" I said and stood. From over my left shoulder I heard what sounded like castanets. I peered into the darkness. "I know that sound. You must have an owl."

"Hunter shot it. Only one wing. We're taking it to a wildlife program in Minnesota that will use it in an education program for children. Now that one I would not attempt to pet—not if you want to go back to your office with all ten fingers."

There were several other cages, all empty, and what looked like a couple of box stalls.

"They're for the musk oxen we're picking up in St. Louis. Turns out they've got a breeding pair. Speaking of which, we need to get going. It's a long drive to northern Minnesota."

"Surely you won't drive straight through again?"

"Surely we will," Lars said. "I drive, Papa sleeps. Then he drives, I sleep."

"I'd offer to fix you breakfast or something—"

"No, thank you."

Nels handed me a file of paperwork. "This is a copy of the bill of lading and the permit. We FedExed that woman the other paperwork."

"Okay." I walked to the back of the truck and prepared to jump down.

Then I hesitated. "Could I have a minute to say goodbye?" I felt my stomach begin to flutter and swore to herself I wouldn't cry. Hadn't this dumb wolf tried to kill me?

"You betcha," Lars said. "Papa and I will wait outside. Don't try to jump down without some help. It's a long drop."

Both men jumped to the tarmac and disappeared around the side of the truck.

I knelt beside Loba. Another goodbye. My life seemed filled with them. At least Loba was going toward happiness and not into an empty life. She'd find a mate, not lose one.

"Go with God, Loba. I can't believe I'll miss you." Loba slid forward on her belly. I put the palm of my hand flat against the front of the cage.

Loba gently licked it.

I lost it. I wanted to open that cage and drag Loba out.

"It would be wrong for you to keep her," Lars's gentle voice made me jump. "We'll teach her to be a real wolf."

"She just better be happy."

# Chapter 36

## *In which Maggie interrupts an orgy*

When I woke early Friday morning, I remembered I had agreed to help Rick and Heather artificially inseminate cows at the experimental cattle station in North Mississippi. When I heard the rain drumming on my bedroom windows, I prayed they'd cancel.

They didn't cancel, and I couldn't in all conscience back out on them, so I drove down to the station and along the gravel road in front that had turned to slippery muck. This was in a sense my first tentative step toward finding someone to take over from me when I retired—a sort of interview in place. I knew I liked Heather and had heard good things about her from the vets at the animal emergency clinic where she filled in, but I didn't know her husband Rick at all. I'd only met him once at Morgan's funeral. I wasn't sure I'd recognize him.

Obviously, he would never have been entrusted with managing the University's prize cattle herd if he hadn't been good with large animals, but that didn't necessarily equate to being good with clients.

I vacillated between excitement and trepidation. What on earth would I do if he should not only turn out to be the perfect person to take over from me, but should want the job right away and be able to come up with the money to buy into the partnership? If Eli were satisfied with him, I could retire at once.

I was reminded of that old saying, "Lord, I want to go to heaven—just not yet." I had to admit I wasn't ready either to fish or to cut bait.

I hadn't visited the cattle station for many years. I hardly recognized it. Perfect dark wood fences were freshly creosoted to cut down chewing from either cows or insects. A large, metal agricultural building had replaced the old wooden cattle barn.

Rick met me at the front door with his hand outstretched. "Hey, Doc, glad you could make it." He was about six feet two, lanky and long-muscled, and had deep brown eyes and a broad shit-kickin' grin that made me want to break out in a chorus of "Mamma, don't let your babies grow up to be cowboys." No wonder Heather fell for him. He led me into the front of the building, which was set up as an office and laboratory. Heather was hunkered over a big Gateway computer. She greeted me cheerfully, but her smile was for Rick. "What do you think of the place, Maggie?" she asked.

"Marvelous," I answered, and watched both of them swell with pride. "How many cows are we inseminating this morning?"

"Forty today, forty tomorrow morning. Heather's keeping a list of the flank numbers."

Rick led me through the door that divided the air-conditioned office space from the barn. Along the right hand wall twenty large black Angus cows swished their tails lazily as they champed the hay in the bins in front of them. Rick removed the sticks of semen in their neat glass tubes from a corner refrigerator, and asked cheerfully, "Want me to go first?"

"Absolutely. I'd like to see your technique. I don't do this often enough to be as good at it as you are."

I watched him artificially inseminate a couple of cows, then moved in beside him to do my share. The operation went quickly.

When we were finished, he grinned at me. "You been funnin' me. You're better than I'll ever be. Want to help me shoo these ladies out into the pasture and get in the next twenty?"

In a small holding paddock beside the barn another twenty Angus cows ate or chewed their cuds. Rick shooed the first group into the main pasture, then opened the gate that led from the holding pen into the stock area, and began to get the second twenty ready for insemination.

"How do you separate the ones we've done today from the rest we're doing tomorrow?"

"A couple of boys come in the afternoon to do the chores. They'll check the flank numbers and cut another forty into the side paddock. Piece of cake to get 'em in tomorrow morning. Want to see the rest of the place after we finish? We've got fifty acres in this pasture, plus the holding paddock. It's stopped raining."

"Sure. This is a very slick operation."

"I've kept records now for the last twenty years. Not me personally, of course. Heather and I have been here three years since we got out of school. She only works part time. The rest of the time she works at the emergency clinic."

Rick was happy where he was. Even though the herd officially belonged to the university, he definitely felt proprietary towards them. He probably wouldn't be interested in a partnership with McLain-Scheibler.

Heather might want to join us as an employee after the baby was born. We didn't pay as much as the emergency clinic, but the hours were better and her driving time would be less. We would all enjoy having a little one around.

Rick walked around to the side of the building and climbed into a four wheel ATV. A gun rack mounted on the roll cage held a rifle and two shotguns. Rick saw my eyebrows raise. "I am death on possums and rats. Last thing we need is Hanta virus."

I nodded, climbed aboard. Rick took off so fast I narrowly avoided whiplash. We sped, rolled and jounced all the way to the far end of the property, then did a wheely and headed back.

Suddenly, Rick jammed on the brakes. "Son of a bitch," he snapped. Across Rick's immaculate brown fence and up a slight rise, through scrub trees and underbrush, a ramshackle barbed wire fence listed crazily. On the far side peering down at us stood two of the grungiest long horn bulls I had ever seen. Both were black and white with at least a six-foot span of sharp horns. Both were caked with mud, beady of eye and two or three hundred pounds underweight.

"I told that fool to keep those two bastards in his other pasture. They stand there talking to my ladies and getting them all riled up."

"Who owns the property?"

"A guy named Barrows who lives in Olive Branch and runs a half-baked commercial operation. We've butted heads more than once. He's a real s.o.b."

He started the ATV again. Back at the office, he stormed, "Heather, honey pot, get Barrows on the phone for me. Those two damn bulls are up on the hill again."

He shut himself in his tiny office, I said goodbye to Heather with his angry voice reverberating in my ear.

"Had enough?" Heather asked.

"I'll be back tomorrow. Barring emergencies at our place."

"Thank you so much. Rick won't let me near a cow until after the baby comes." She blushed. "He thinks I'll break."

I watched Heather in my rear view mirror as I drove away. Those two were so in love, just at the start of their journey. *Please, Lord,* I prayed, *Let it be a long and happy one. Don't let it end too soon for them as it had for Morgan and me.*

Despite hints from Eli, I had so far avoided Morgan's office except to slip my expired passport from the pages of the scrapbook. I stopped at Kinko's on the way back from Rick's to get some new passport pictures, filled out the paperwork, and sent my old passport and a check for renewal. I would have enjoyed seeing the Mona Lisa with Morgan. Now it had become an obligation. Not the best possible mindset to start my travels. I always devoured books and loved music and art, but culture never gave me the immediate thrill I got from saving an animal's life.

That evening Nels Olafson called. "Loba's home and settling in."

"Good."

"She's used to being alone in her enclosure, so she's not missing the pack she never had. The two male adolescents next door to her are trying to bite at her muzzle through the fence and flipping over on their backs to offer their bellies to her. Characteristic submission behavior."

"How's she taking it?"

"Lording over both of them. Lars thinks we may actually be able to let them be together—under supervision, of course—in a couple of weeks."

"Let me know how it goes."

"Promise." Well, at least one creature was working out her new life. Maybe there was hope for me.

I slept badly. The only time I allowed myself to grieve was at night in bed. I had forced myself to stretch out across Morgan's side of the bed, but I still woke curled into a ball on my side cradling a pillow wet with tears. My head hurt.

I wanted to stay in bed with the cats, but instead I went to the experimental station. We should be through with the AI in an hour or so, then I could get to the clinic and do my regular job.

I arrived at the station just as Heather and Rick pulled up in Rick's elderly truck.

"Good," he said. "You can give me a hand herding the ladies in from the paddock."

Heather stopped in the office to boot up the computer and start the coffee. I trailed Rick.

The instant Rick opened the door between office and barn, I realized something was wrong.

Outside in the paddock cows bawled and stampeded past the doors.

"What the..." Rick ran toward the overhang where the ATV was parked.

I ran too.

Giant black shapes hurtled by, circled, ran into one another, crashed into the fences and the building like rifle fire.

"Holy crap!" Rick shouted and pointed.

At the far end of the pasture I could barely make out two black and white shapes with giant appendages sticking out from each side of their foreheads.

And giant appendages fully extended from the underside of their bellies as well.

As we watched, the marauders cornered cow after cow, mounted, flagged, dropped off and chased the next nearest female.

Not one of those females had ever been bred naturally.

No neat sterile pipette.

This was an invading army of two bent on gang rape.

Rick raced for the ATV. "Can you handle a shotgun?"

"You're not going to *kill* them, are you?"

"I'm damned well going to drive 'em away from my ladies. Can you shoot?"

"Certainly." I pulled one of the pump shotguns from the gun rack and jumped into the ATV beside him.

"Shells are in that box." Rick pointed between my feet.

Yesterday's ride had been a sedate spin in a limousine compared to this.

"Shoot over their heads."

I managed to load and press the shotgun hard into my shoulder. I pointed it high above the heads of the fleeing herd, and pulled the trigger.

Boom!

For an instant, the herd stood dead still.

Then they ran in the other direction.

All but the bulls at the far end of the pasture. They were too preoccupied to stop what they were doing.

Boom!

This time the smaller one swung his horns in our direction.

Boom! Boom!

Too close to ignore. Both bulls jumped down from their latest conquests.

Rick drove between them and the cows, herding them as expertly as though he'd been on a horse.

"Again! Keep it up!" he shouted.

Boom! Boom! Boom!

I broke open the gun and inserted more shells. The expended cartridges dropped at my feet or had bounced out of the ATV.

My shoulder hurt like hell. In the jouncing ATV, it was impossible to hold tight enough to avoid some kick when I pulled the trigger. I'd have a bruised shoulder. I might have a black eye.

What the hell. It was in a good cause.

Boom! Boom! Boom!

The cows peeled off to their left while Rick kept the ATV between the herd and the two bulls on his right. They were now running towards the front of the pasture.

Boom!

I spotted the hole in the fence. They'd trampled the wire on their side of the pasture, crashed through Rick's lovely board fence, and chased their first cows until they caught them.

They might have been at it since midnight.

The smaller bull took one long look over his shoulder, swung right and bolted for home. He tangled in the barbed wire and cantered off across his home pasture with fifty feet of barbed wire and locust wood fence posts trailing behind him like a bridal train.

The bigger bull turned through the gap in the board fence and took two steps up the hill.

Boom!

One minute he was running. The next he'd fallen flat on his side and lay with his head canted straight up where his horn had hooked into the dirt.

Rick stopped the ATV against the broken boards. To get past, a cow would have to jump over both ATV and passengers.

They wouldn't. They were already settling down as far from the scene as they could.

Rick leapt from the ATV and ran to the bull on the ground. I followed him. My shoulder and jaw screamed. My ears rang. I'd probably be half deaf for a couple of hours.

"Bastard's dead." Rick said.

"What? Dead? Did I shoot him?"

He leaned over and spoke directly into the ear that hadn't been close to the gun blast and shouted,"Not a scratch on him—well, a couple of barbed wire scrapes. No buckshot." He looked grim. "He screwed himself to death."

I saw his shoulders begin to shake.

"Hell of a way to go, though." Rick said, and bent double laughing.

A moment later we were both leaning against the ATV helpless with tears of laughter.

From the barn, Heather called, "Are y'all okay? What happened?"

That set us off again. I hadn't laughed, really laughed, since Morgan died. What a blessed release!

By the time we drove sedately back to the barn, Heather was standing waiting for us with her hands on her broad hips and a schoolmarm frown on her face.

While Rick cuddled her and told her what had happened, I went into the office to find a soft drink or water from the tap. I still held the shotgun open in the crook of my elbow. I could actually hear out of my left ear.

Gravel spewed outside, and a moment later a little bald man stormed in. A fringe of white hair stood up around his head like a Banty rooster's coxcomb.

"Where's my bulls?" he shouted. "Y'all done stole my bulls."

"Mr. Barrows, I presume?"

"Who the hell are you? Where's that damn vet, or whatever he calls hisself?"

I pointed. Barrows stormed past, slammed the door to the barn, and a moment later started shouting.

I followed.

"Y'all done kilt my good bull?" Barrows screeched.

I dragged Heather back into the office. "Go get us some cold Co'Colas, then sit down in here. Rick and I can handle this."

"I'll sue your ass, you see if I don't! I'll sue you, that wife of you'rn, the whole State of Mississippi, the county and the federal guv'mint! Them was prize longhorn bulls. Worth a mint! I'll have your hide, you killing my good bulls that 'a way."

Rick's earlobes were crimson. I stepped between them.

Barrows took one look at me and jumped back. "There, you see that woman threatening me with a shotgun? Call the po-lice. I'm gonna arrest every dad-burned one of you."

I casually moved the shotgun. "Mr. Barrows, I am so sorry for your loss."

Rick snorted.

"I do think you ought to sue, I really do."

"Say what?" Rick snapped.

"Well, Rick, he might as well. Of course, after the courts see your suit, they may not be all that interested in his."

"My—? Oh, yeah, my suit."

"What the hell you think you can sue for, woman? It's my bull done got killt. T'other'n gonna be plumb wore out for quite a spell, I reckon. May be too tuckered to climb a cow ever again." Barrows nodded with satisfaction.

"I am also a veterinarian. I can assure you he will recover his libido. I assume you purchased those bulls at the sale barn in Collierville?"

"What of it?"

"They'll no doubt have records of exactly how much you paid for them and when. They do depreciate, you know, when they get old. I assume you didn't insure them? No, I didn't think so. So you have no valuation other than your sale price."

Barrows opened his mouth, but I kept talking.

"Then there is the damage to the station's fence, and to the station's pasture from all the cows stampeding. There's no way to tell which cows your bulls bred, nor which cows will 'take' from your semen and which from the semen we used yesterday on a small group. The station has complete records on this herd for testing purposes for many years back. Your bulls could wreck twenty-five or thirty years of work. Quite a loss.

"Add to that the expense for drugs, time, and manpower to abort each and every one of the cows in this herd and rebreed them on their next fertile cycle. That will of course push the gestation period back and make the parturition date later, so the calves won't be as valuable. That will factor into the equation, as well as lawyer's fees,

fees for depositions, court costs. It does add up. You might as well countersue. Maybe the courts won't come down on you quite so hard."

Barrows's eyes had widened and his mouth—full of bad teeth and worse breath—had dropped open.

I smiled at him sweetly. "Now, I do think you'd better get your dead bull moved. He's still partially on Station land. We need to get our fence fixed. That shouldn't cost too much. Just the cost of boards, creosote and labor. We'll bill you."

"Now, you see here, girlie..." He glanced at Rick. "You and me's both gentlemen. We can settle this without bringing in lawyers and courts and women and all such, can't we?"

"Can we?" Rick asked Maggie.

"Possibly. My suggestion would be that Mr. Barrows remove his dead bull and put up some good fence so this doesn't happen again, and pay for the drugs and the new sticks of semen. You take care of your fence and the labor involved in aborting and rebreeding."

"What kind o' money we talkin' about?" Barrows asked.

Rick thought a minute, then named a reasonable figure.

Barrows started to jump up and down again, but thought better of it. He stared at me with loathing. "I'll write you a check."

"I think a cashier's check or cash might be better," I said. "Don't you, Rick?"

"You sayin' my check's no good?"

"Not at all. Just good business."

"Hells bells. Give me time to get my tractor to drag that carcass away and get that fence put back up. I'll be back." He started to turn away.

"Since we're gentlemen, Mr. Barrows," Rick said. "Let's shake on it." He stuck out his hand.

Barrows regarded it as though it were wired for electricity, then sighed and clasped it.

He dropped it a second later and stalked into the barn.

Rick watched him with aplomb until he heard the far door close.

Then he grabbed me around the waist, swung me off my feet and kissed me.

"Hey! I'm still holding a loaded shotgun. Put me down before I blow away one of your cows in the heat of passion."

He dropped me and loped to the office.

"Heather, honey pot, you got to hear this," he said with evident glee.

Before Rick could start his tale, my cell phone went off. "McLain."

"Maggie, thank God!"

"Patsy, what's the matter?"

"It's terrible! We've got half a dozen horses dying. My Marko's been down twice. You've got to come right this minute."

"Colic?"

Patsy sounded hysterical. "Nobody knows. Oh, God, Maggie, please come."

"I'm ten minutes away. I'll call Eli. She can bring down more equipment."

"Please, Maggie—Oh, don't let him go down!"

The line went dead and I sprinted for my truck.

# Chapter 37

## *In which an idiot causes a tragedy*

On my way to Patsy's barn, I called Eli and asked her to bring every bit of equipment she could find to treat colic. If we had to do surgery, they'd have to move the horses to the clinic—possibly to several clinics.

But first, we had to try the old reliable remedies.

"Don't forget the Pepto Bismol," I said. Seconds counted in colic cases. If things were actually as bad as Patsy said, none of the horses would be able to survive the four and a half-hour trip to the vet school and hospital facilities at Mississippi State. Starkville was still a long drive away, even with the new four lane highway most of the way.

I pulled into the Dalrymple farm road so fast I nearly lost the truck on the curve and ended up in the ditch that ran along beside the board fence. I slammed on my brakes in the parking lot among a bunch of crazily parked SUVs and trucks. Recently Patsy had begun boarding and training horses for a few friends. The owners must already have been notified and come running.

Patsy met me at the door to the stable. Her hair fell around her plump little face in sweaty orange tendrils. Her baggy shorts were drenched and so was her t-shirt. "Maggie! Thank God." She grabbed my hand, pulled me into the stable and toward the double wash racks across the broad center aisle.

The stable hummed with activity. Big warmblood jumpers who obviously wanted to lie down in their stalls and roll until their bellies ceased to hurt were being pushed and prodded up and down the center aisle by grooms, trainers, riders and parents of riders.

Marked Fox, known as Marko, Patsy Dalrymple's three-year-old Hanoverian stud colt, leaned drunkenly against the wood paneling that lined one side of the wash rack. He was solid black except for a white sock on his right hind foot. His wet pelt gleamed like black tar.

Big Mike, head groom, leaned his three hundred pounds against Marko's shoulder in an attempt to keep him on his feet. Another groom played a stream of cold water from the wash rack hose over the colt's body.

Ignoring the water that soaked me too as I leaned against the colt, I pulled back his lips. "God, Patsy," I said. "How long has this been going on? His gums are nearly white." That meant shock, poor blood circulation, and agonizing pain in his gut. This was not like a normal colic. It definitely wasn't founder. The stud colt was putting weight on all four of his feet. The illness had come on too quickly and too severely. Besides, most cases of colic were individual. A whole barn of colicky horses argued some kind of poison.

Paul Nelson, Patsy's partner in the training operation, came up at that moment. "We noticed it about six-thirty this morning. We've got five others sick, but they're all adult horses. He's the youngest and by far the worst."

"Paul, why'd you wait so long to call me?" I asked.

"We thought we were looking at some kind of herb poisoning from the pasture, although Mike and I couldn't find anything except clover. That might make them salivate, but not this." He ran a wet hand over his thick gray hair. "We tubed them with mineral oil, washed them down with cold water, and kept them walking. They've had as much Banamine as we dared give them. None of them has an elevated pulse in the ankle, no temperature either. We thought we could handle it. Obviously we can't. What the hell is it?"

"For a while we thought we had it licked," Patsy said. "The others seem to be getting better." She leaned her forehead against the colt's shoulder. He shuddered. "Maggie, for the love of God, do something!"

I caught Paul's eye over Patsy's head. He shook his head. Even Patsy must know in her heart that there was nothing to be done except to put the colt down. Big as he was, he was still a baby without the physical or psychological resistance the mature horses had developed.

He was in agony. It was unconscionable to let that agony continue.

"Patsy, honey," I said. "Look at me."

Patsy took a deep breath and raised her eyes to my face.

"You know what I have to do."

Patsy dropped her face in her hands. "Do it, Maggie, do it quick." Her voice rose, "I can't stand to see him this way."

At that moment Eli raced in. She took one look at the stud colt and put her arm around Patsy's shoulder. "Come on, Patsy, you don't want to watch."

Patsy jerked away. "Yes, I do. I must. I brought him into the world, Eli, I have to see him out of it."

More death. I couldn't get away from it.

"Eli, go help the others. They're not as bad off. I'm thinking Pepto might be the best thing. Massive doses. They've had everything else. Patsy? You're sure you want to watch?"

"Go, Eli."

I reached for my vet bag. Behind me I heard a massive groan. Shod hooves scrabbled for purchase on the wet concrete.

Then came the crash. "I couldn't hold him up, Patsy," Mike said.

Patsy dropped to her knees beside the colt. "Maggie, put him down, please, please!"

I put my hand on Patsy's shoulder and said quietly, "No need, Patsy, honey. It's over."

"No." Patsy bent over the black head and sobbed. The others stood around helplessly. After what seemed like an aeon, I watched Patsy square her shoulders, rub her fingers over her eyes and sniff. "Mike, help me up."

"Yes, Ma'am."

"Go get the tractor and pull him out back where the others can't see us." She turned to me. "Maggie, you've got do the necropsy right this minute. I'll help."

"Oh, Miss Patsy, no," Mike said. "Let me."

"It's my job, Mike. You have live horses to help. Maggie and I have to find out what's causing this before we lose any more of them. Now, you go get that tractor."

"Find out how Eli's doing," I said. "You have a right to assist at the necropsy, but I'll be damned if I let you watch us tie him up and drag him out of here like a side of beef."

Patsy's jaw tightened and the loose skin under her neck quivered.

"Don't argue. Go. Mike will call you when I'm ready." I gave

Patsy a shove toward the main part of the barn, then nodded at Mike. "Let's get to it."

"Right. Poor Miss Patsy."

"We better make sure there aren't any other 'poor's' tonight."

Lashing the colt's legs together, attaching the ropes to the tractor and pulling the corpse out to the area behind the shavings pile where it would be hidden from the barn was hellish. Eli would keep everyone else away, but the others knew Marko had died. That would raise the panic level.

Before we had the ropes off the colt's legs in the paddock behind the barn, Patsy trotted out with her head high and her chin stuck out in front of her. "What are you waiting for?"

I was already gloved, and I held the heavy scalpel I would need to cut through the horse's abdomen and lay the vital organs out where I could see them and take samples.

"Wait," Patsy said. She sank onto the ground beside the colt, cradled his big black head in her arms and rocked back and forth. I had never actually heard a woman keen before. I wanted to kneel beside her and add my voice to hers. Grief upon grief. If only I'd been able to keen like that for Morgan instead of holding all my grief locked away...

After a couple of minutes, Patsy sniffed, laid down the youngster's shining head, stood up and took her place beside me. "Now."

Necropsies were dirty and stank, but Patsy didn't bail out. She stood beside me as I opened the horse's abdomen. A moment later I was on my knees, my hands carefully lifting the horse's caecum. "Sweet Lord. Look at this. I've never seen anything like it."

"It's all red and swollen. Shouldn't it be puffy and white?" Patsy asked.

I sliced into the caecum. A mess of mineral oil, oats, and hay lay wadded inside. I ran my fingers over the inside walls. "It's covered with ulcers. Some of them must have been bleeding for hours."

I picked up a handful of the contents and rubbed them between my palms, while I narrowed my eyes and stared at the mess. I caught my breath. "Patsy, run back to the barn this minute. Tell them not to feed—not one scrap, nothing, not until I get there."

Patsy looked startled.

"For the love of God, Patsy, run."

Patsy ran on her stubby, pudgy middle-aged legs as though she were closing in on first at the Boston Marathon.

I pulled specimen bottles from my kit and began to take samples of the mess I had uncovered, and then slices of liver, heart, lung and intestines.

I was concentrating so hard, I didn't hear Patsy behind me until I heard Paul's voice. "What is it?" He sounded winded. Patsy was gasping.

"What?" Eli came up and dropped beside Maggie. "Lordy, what in the Sam Hill?"

"This is alfalfa, isn't it, Paul?" I asked as I showed him a pulp of wet hay.

"Right. We only feed alfalfa hay. Need to get as much nourishment into these guys as we can. Puts a bloom on them like nothing else."

"Did you recently buy some from a new source?"

He and Patsy stared at one another open-mouthed. "Yeah. We were running low until first cutting this year. Dan and Patsy don't grow alfalfa, so we buy it. Our usual guy was out, so we bought a load of last year's cutting from a guy from up the other side of Jackson just to tide us over."

"Have you been feeding it long?"

"Mike?" Paul shouted. "Didn't we start feeding that new alfalfa this morning?"

"We been using the last of that second-cutting from the fall. Ran out after supper last night, so yeah, I guess so."

"Maggie?"

"Look at this," I held my gloved hand out for Eli.

"I don't see any—Lordy, yes I do."

"What, for God's sake?" Patsy asked.

"Blister beetles."

"Blister beetles? What are Blister beetles?"

Paul bent over the mess in my hand. "I've heard of them out in Oklahoma and Colorado."

"Patsy," I said. "Blister beetles look like little grey and black lightning bugs. Ever hear of Spanish fly?"

"Sure. Isn't that supposed to be an aphrodisiac?"

"It's really a massive and deadly genito-urinary tract irritant. If you got a grain of it, you might not die—although you could—but you'd pray to God to take you."

"And horses have much more primitive genito-urinary tracts than people," Eli said.

"Patsy, you and Paul can't blame yourself for Marko's death. Eating one whole beetle would be enough to kill him. His fate was sealed at breakfast this morning."

"The others? Are they going to die too?"

"At this point and with a gallon of Pepto in them, maybe not. They were lucky. They're all mature horses. They probably ate a wing or a feeler."

"It's that deadly?"

"It's that deadly. Blister beetles seem to prefer alfalfa. If it's cut properly, there's little chance they'll get baled up with the hay. Any man who grows the stuff should know that."

I glanced up at a rumble from the back of the group. Big Mike looked as though he were swelling. His dark face was suffused with blood, and the whites of his eyes seemed dangerously swollen. "Where's he live, Paul?"

"The man who sold us the stuff? Why?"

"I'm gonna go kill him is why."

"Not right this minute," I said. "We need you here."

"Maggie, I asked the guy about blister beetles," Paul said. "I've never heard of a single instance around here except for alfalfa imported from out west, but I did ask the question as a matter of course. Mike heard me, didn't you? The guy swore to me he'd cut his hay with a sickle bar and not a straight baler. Said there couldn't possibly be any blister beetles in the bales."

"Let's see if he was telling the truth. Mike, would you put a tarpaulin over Marko? Weight it down so the coyotes don't get it until y'all can bury him in the morning."

Jack nodded.

Every human head in the barn turned toward us as we came in, although nobody stopped walking or cooling down his charge. Paul climbed into the hay loft and tossed down a bale. I cut the wire holding the bale together and separated the flakes of hay carefully. "Somebody get me a bucket and a strong flashlight."

Even with the flashlight, the bugs blended in so well with the alfalfa that it took all our eyes to spot the first one. Once we did, we found dozens. Some were in pieces—a wing here, a thorax there. Many, however, were intact.

"That son of a bitch." Paul said. "I'll help Mike kill him."

"What good will that do? You'll both be in jail. The main thing is to get him down here to pick up his hay. Tell him you found mold or ranunculus, anything but blister beetles."

"Then what?"

"Call your lawyer. He's probably insured. So sue his ass."

The whisper of "poison" and "blister beetles" ran through the stable.

Eli and I checked the other horses. All seemed to have passed through the worst. I called everyone together and showed them the beetle carcasses. "Call us if anyone looks like they're getting worse," I said. "We'll be back first thing tomorrow morning. I want to be here when that bastard comes to pick up his hay."

Eli and I pulled into Patsy's parking lot before seven the following morning, and left our trucks where the logos didn't show. Better the nitwit didn't see there were vets on the premises.

Behind the barn, Mike was using the backhoe to dig Marko's grave.

From the looks of them, neither Patsy nor Paul had slept last night. For the first time since I had known her, Patsy looked her age and more. The stubble on Paul's cheeks was gray.

"Well?" I asked.

"The others are better."

"Thank God. What about the guy who sold you the alfalfa?"

"He's due any minute. I gave him Hail Columbia."

"But not about the blister beetles?"

"No. Ranunculus and mold. You can handle the blister beetles thing."

"We gave all the horses a small bran mash this morning with some Pepto swished around in it," Patsy said. "I never thought they'd touch it, but they ate it right up."

"How are *you*?" I asked.

"Mad as a hornet. My Dan says he'll sell a thousand acres to pay the lawyers if that's what it takes to get this devil."

The crunch of gravel heralded the open-sided truck. The truck looked respectable, although the engine was noisy. The logo on the side read, "Top Class Alfalfa."

"Hey, y'all," said the man who climbed down from the truck. "Don't see how none of my alfalfa could 'a had no mold."

He had little piggy eyes set too close to the bridge of his nose, a beer belly, too many brown teeth for his mouth, and an ominous circle in his breast pocket that denoted a tin of chewing tobacco. He didn't seem to have any in his mouth, but if he should attempt to spit, I'd deck him. His truck, however, was clean and swept free of leftover bits of hay. Truth to tell, he probably didn't look any different from most of the hay farmers. There would have been no overt reason for Paul not to trust him. I was reading into his face what I knew about his business.

A pair of helpers climbed down from the bed of the truck and slouched over to the barn. "Can I drive on around and down the aisle like I did when I brung y'all the hay?"

Paul nodded. I suspected he didn't trust himself to say anything.

As soon as the truck was positioned, the men began to toss the bales down from the hayloft and stack them in the back of the truck.

"Did you bring the money I gave you?" Paul asked. His voice sounded strangled. I could see that he'd bunched his hands into tight fists.

"How many bales y'all done used?"

I laid a hand on Paul's arm. The muscle jumped under my fingers.

"We used two and we'll be keeping three," I said.

"Lets see, five bales at five dollars a bale is twenty-five less I owe you."

I held out my hand. The man carefully counted out bills from a roll he carried in his hip pocket. His men were through loading and stacking in about ten minutes. As the man got ready to climb into his truck, I said casually, "Those three bales are evidence."

"Evidence?"

"Evidence of the infestation of blister beetles that killed a valuable stallion yesterday and sickened five other horses to the point of death."

"Wha?"

"You lied to me, you s.o.b.," Paul snarled. "Those bales were *full* of blister beetles." He advanced on the man with his fist raised. I grabbed his arm.

"Naw. Ain't no way. Not my hay."

"Remember, you use those little red metal tags on your hay wire? It's your hay, all right. You'll be hearing from my lawyer. I suggest you contact your insurance company about settling."

For a moment, I thought the man would turn truculent. Then, he decided to run instead. He jumped into his truck and backed out so fast he nearly ran over Mike and Eli.

I turned to Patsy. "I just had a thought. That idiot is not above selling that load to another horse barn. Get on the phone. Call everybody you can think of in the area. Warn them. Fast."

Patsy's eyes grew round. She raced into the office.

Later that afternoon, I got a call from Patsy. "You'll never believe this. That horrible man took that load of hay down to the sale barn and sold it for a dollar a bale."

"Blister beetles won't kill cows. They have all those stomachs."

"That not the awful part. When he was leaving, he asked Dave, 'what in hell are blister beetles?'"

# Chapter 38

## *In which Vickie dumps Herb*

Eli and I were always deeply saddened whenever we lost a patient, but losing Marko, another of Patsy's prize youngsters, brought the loss of Sarah's Pride to the forefront of my mind. For a moment I thought of calling and telling Sarah about Marko's death, then I thought better of it.

Besides, she was somewhere in the Far East. She called me at least once a week, but said she was on the move and never knew for certain where she'd be. I had a number to call in case of emergency. Someone at the Los Angeles end would track her down if I really needed her.

I finally made an excursion to the grocery Sunday afternoon and came in about four in time to catch my ringing phone before the answering machine picked up. It was Vickie Anderson, and she sounded panicked.

"Herb's just been served with a restraining order and divorce papers," she said. "Oh, God, Maggie, it never occurred to me the sheriff's deputies would work on weekends. I expected him to be served at work on Monday."

"Calm down," I said. "Is he still there?"

I heard her draw a ragged breath. "He roared off in his precious Jaguar. The deputies stayed until I got a locksmith to change the locks. It cost a fortune on Sunday."

"Have you called your boys?"

Vickie's two sons were currently at LSU, one in pre-med and the other just starting undergraduate school.

"We talked when they were home for spring vacation last month."

"Listen to me," I said. I had visions of Herb driving that Jaguar into the side of the house or blowing Vickie away. "Can you tell the people at your subdivision gate that Herb is not to be allowed in?"

She caught her breath. "I guess I can show them the restraining order. But, he's got a card that opens the back gate, and there's no guard on duty there. His card will have to be cancelled, and they can't do that until Monday." Her voice dropped to a whisper. "I never thought I'd say this, but I'm scared."

"Of course you are. Pack a bag as fast as you can, get in your van and drive over here. You can tell the boys where you are after you're safe."

"Maggie, I couldn't…"

"Of course you can. Do it."

The moment I got off the phone, I dialed Eli's answering machine, told her the bare bones of the situation and asked her to come to my house as soon as she could.

Eli and I have always done our best to keep our personal lives separate. We don't just drop in on one another and expect to be fed or included in parties or evenings out. Eli is Sarah and Nathan's godmother, but she was never required to attend Nathan's soccer matches or Sarah's piano recitals.

She usually went anyway.

Since Morgan's death, we shared our evening meal together a couple of times a week, but I didn't go to her house without being invited, and she didn't come to mine. She and Shep kept asking me to join them for the theater or their jazz evenings, but I didn't want them to feel either guilty or obligated now that I didn't have Morgan to squire me. Besides, without Morgan to share the experience, going out was pure purgatory.

But when it came to the needs of our mutual friends, we could always count on one another a hundred per cent.

Vickie had never discussed her rocky marriage with any of the Militia, but she had kicked Herb out half a dozen times. She'd never before gone so far as to serve him divorce papers.

Eli arrived five minutes after Vickie.

Vickie's hands shook. She'd obviously been crying. I packed her off to the downstairs guestroom to settle in and call her sons. When she came back ten minutes later, I handed her a glass of iced tea.

"You want a drink? You could use one."

She shook her head. "Alcohol's done enough damage to this family. Thank God neither Jason or Adam drinks so much as a beer."

She sank onto the couch in the den and leaned her head back. She looked as though she'd been dragged backward through a knothole.

"You want to talk about it?" I asked.

She sat up, sighed, and set her iced tea on the side table. "I swore the last time Herb got himself a girlfriend that if it ever happened again, he was out of my life." She avoided our eyes. "She wasn't the first."

We knew that. Shoot, everybody in west Tennessee knew.

"He'd always say he was going golfing on Saturday afternoon. Since Jason and Adam were old enough to understand about sex, they've called it 'golfing.'" She managed a smile. "Not where Herb could hear them, of course.

"I was planning to wait until Adam finished his first year at LSU. Nobody should have to deal with freshman year and a nasty divorce at the same time. Jason went along. As a senior, he can look after his brother." She sighed and reached for her drink. "I swear, I feel as though I'd swallowed the Sahara desert.

"The night before they went back to school, they told me to divorce him and find somebody decent, that they didn't want him in their lives any longer." She shook her head. "He'll blame me, but he's the one who drove them away. They see the drunken rages and the women." She sighed and squared her shoulders. "So I've spent the last month getting my financial ducks in a row in case Herb reneged on his agreement about dumping his current woman. Both the boys are on full scholarships, and they inherited some money from my father and mother, so they're all right whatever happens in any divorce settlement. I've changed my will to cut out Herb and benefit them, made them the beneficiaries on my insurance, made them custodians of my limited power of attorney and my living will, and set up a living trust for them that excludes Herb in the event of my death. The house, the cars, the practice—everything we own is already in my name for what Herb always called 'tax reasons.' Then Friday morning I cancelled all the credit cards and put every cent in our joint accounts into new accounts in my name only. And got a new lock box for all the papers, also in my name only."

"Wow," Eli said softly.

"My lawyer talked me through it. Herb has never contributed much to the bills, although he made the down payment on the house.

He probably has a fortune in some Cayman Island account, so I'm not being all that mean to him. He doesn't even own his precious Jaguar. I do."

Eli caught my eye. Vickie made a lot more money than either of us ever did, but then she did a great deal more grooming and boarding for a much richer clientele.

Vickie could barely hold her head up during a scrappy supper of U. S. Senate bean soup, a salad and French bread. The minute dinner was over, I sent her off to bed.

"I should go home," she said.

"Indeed you will not! New locks or not, Herb could break in and blow you away."

"He's my husband, Maggie, he wouldn't..."

"Just like he wouldn't give you a black eye on Thanksgiving last year?" I asked.

Her eyes widened. "You knew?"

"You should have had him arrested."

"I know, but the boys..."

I blew out my breath. "Go to bed, Vickie. We'll talk tomorrow."

As I closed her door, I said, "Keep this closed if you don't want three cats in bed with you."

Ten minutes later Eli and I were eating Angelfood Swiss Chocolate ice cream and drinking decaf in the den. It was barely eight o'clock, but felt like three a.m. We decided Eli and I would mount guard on my house until we were certain Herb wouldn't bash in the front gate.

As the opening credits for the new A&E mystery rolled, the telephone shrilled. I snatched it up. "McLain. Oh, hi." I hit the switch to turn on the speaker.

Lanier Polman asked, "Is Vickie with you? I've been calling the house and all I get is the answering machine."

"She's here and probably asleep by now. She was whipped."

"Herb called me in a rage looking for her. That's how I know what happened. I can't believe they'd deliver divorce papers on Sunday. I guess they figure they can catch people at home on the weekends."

"So Herb is looking for her?" Eli asked.

"Is that Eli? Yeah. He sounds half crazy. One minute he's raging, the next he's blubbering about how sorry he is and how he'll never do it again. As if."

"Has she ever gone this far before?" Eli asked.

"Never. When she found out the latest mistress was some twenty-two year old intern at Herb's brokerage house, she told him unless he cut off the affair quick and clean, she'd kick his butt out. Two weeks ago, the mistress herself called Vickie to ask her to 'get out of the way' so she and Herb could be together." Lanier laughed. "So Vickie obliged."

"I'm glad she's been talking to you," I said. "She hasn't said a word about any of this to Eli and me before tonight."

"But you're the ones she came to when she needed help," Lanier said. "Your front gate is locked, isn't it?"

"Absolutely. If Herb drives his Jaguar through, he'll total it," Eli said and took a big spoonful of ice cream.

"When Geoff and I were divorced, we didn't have a pot to pee in. Vickie's clinic makes one hell of a lot of money. Her lawyer gave her good advice about protecting it from Herb."

"How do we protect *her*?" I asked.

"Tell her she's welcome to stay with Susan and me as long as she likes."

"She's welcome here as well," I said. "But she ought to be able to live in her own house without worrying she's going to be attacked."

"I'm sure by tomorrow he'll have calmed down. He'll probably call you too looking for her."

When the phone rang twenty minutes later, I picked it up, not remembering the speaker was still on.

"Let me speak to my wife."

"Good evening, Herb," I said pleasantly.

"I know she's there."

"No, you don't, but as a matter of fact she is. She's asleep, and I don't intend to wake her."

"Goddamit, Dr. McLain, put her on the goddam phone. I can't even get in my own goddam house to get a clean shirt."

"Can the profanity. Leave me the number at which you can be reached. When Vickie wakes up tomorrow morning I'll give it to her. If she wants to call you, she can. Go buy a shirt and some clean underwear at Wal-Mart. They stay open all night."

"You can't do this. I'm on my way over there now, and if you don't let me speak to her I'll break your goddam door down."

"Herb, the front gate at the road is closed. I have no intention of punching you in. If you try to break through it, you'll have half the deputies in the county down around your neck, not to mention that pretty Jaguar of yours will be wearing half a ton of wrought iron. If I were you, I'd call my doctor for a prescription of Antibuse and check myself into a rehab facility. At least you'd have a place to sleep tonight." I hung up.

"My," Eli said. "How forceful you sounded, Big Mama."

"I wish Morgan were here."

"You did fine on your own." Eli said.

"I'm shaking." I went to the kitchen and came back with the loaded Glock .25 that Morgan bought me for my birthday five years earlier. "Just in case Herb really acts a fool," I said, laid the gun on the side table, picked up my bowl of ice cream and turned back to A&E. "Now, what have I missed?"

# Chapter 39

## *In which Vickie works with a large animal*

Monday morning Vickie looked a bit better as she downed her third cup of high-test coffee and ate her second sweet roll at my kitchen table.

"I'm not calling him back," she said when I told her about Herb's call. "I'm not going into the office either. I called the emergency clinic and got a substitute for the day."

"What happens if Herb shows up?"

"My secretary is supposed to call nine-one-one." She leaned back and ran her hands through her wonderful red hair. "I'm being a coward, I know. I've got to face him sometime."

"Well, you can't hide at home and you can't hide here once the front gate is open," I said. "Remember how we talked about seeing how the other half worked? I'm on my way out for the morning. Come along. You can give me a hand. See how you like the large animal side of veterinary practice after all these years with puppies and kittens."

Vickie froze. "Horse or cow?"

"Horse. I've already got the stuff in the car."

On the drive to Nelly Youngblood's farm, I told Vickie, "It's a simple semen collection. You know how to do those."

"No I don't. I may have done one or two twenty years ago."

"Nelly has a maiden Rhinelander mare that hasn't gotten pregnant. She wants to try one more time by inseminating artificially. All we have to do is collect the stallion, and inject the semen into the mare's cervix. Piece of cake."

Vickie fell silent.

I felt like a toad for throwing this at her, but it was an excellent chance to see if she could work out as a partner. At McClain-Scheibler she might concentrate on the small animal side, but if she should buy my half of the practice, she'd be expected work with both large and small animals.

Nelly Youngblood ran a small breeding and training operation with a single Rhinelander stallion. She had five mares of her own and shipped semen all over the United States for people who wanted to use her sire.

She was only about five foot three, but exuded the generalship of a six foot tall four star general. Her breeding barn was immaculate. I introduced her to Vickie, and handed Vickie my case containing the artificial vagina. Vickie took it as though it contained a nest of scorpions.

"Just us three, I'm afraid, to do it," Nelly said. "The mare popped her follicle this morning, so we have to do this quick if we intend to catch her."

"Why artificially inseminate?" Vickie asked.

"She's hell to breed. She'll tease perfectly to the stallion, then try to kick his head off when he comes down to her."

"Lovely," Vickie whispered.

"So I use an old mare who'd stand for gang rape as a jump mare. I've already got both mares scrubbed and tails wrapped, and the stallion scrubbed as well."

"In school we used padded sawhorse, not a real mare," Vickie whispered as Nelly walked away from them down the aisle.

"Same thing. The stallion jumps her, and when he goes to breed her, you stick the artificial vagina in front of him so he penetrates that and ejaculates."

"Who, me?"

"Would you rather handle the stallion? Nelly's going to hold the mare."

"How big is he?"

"Nearly eighteen hands high, and broad as a pool table."

"I'll take the artificial vagina."

"Thought you'd say that." I pointed to the cylindrical leather case. "I've got it all set up. Just go down to the wash rack, fill it with warm water, and we'll get to it."

"Why did I let you talk me into this?"

"Come on, Vickie, you did this stuff once upon a time in vet school. Get over it."

Vickie squared her shoulders and walked off to fill the AV tube at the washrack while I checked the stallion.

"This thing is heavy when it's filled," she said. She carried it back to me by its handle like a suitcase. Filled, it wasn't much smaller in diameter than the duffel bag in which it was stored.

"Okay? You know what to do, right?"

Vickie nodded, but her eyes were terrified.

"Bring out the mare, Nelly. Think we ought to tease her to him one more time?"

"Wouldn't hurt."

The mare was broad and heavy, but not tall. She walked up to the stallion's stall, turned her back to him, squatted, urinated, and flipped her tail.

He began to nicker low and seductively. At the same time he bounced around in his stall.

"Okay," Nelly said and walked the mare up to the front of the stable.

"Ready or not, here I come," I said. I opened the stallion's door, looped the heavy stainless steel chain of his breeding shank over his nose, gave it a couple of yanks to get his attention, and brought him out.

Vickie squeaked, but she held the artificial vagina up where she could reach him the minute he mounted his mare.

He pranced down the aisle nickering. The mare nickered in return.

When he lifted his body to cover the mare, Vickie closed her eyes and stuck the artificial vagina where he couldn't possibly miss it.

He gave one loud 'hunh,' dropped to the ground and backed up a dozen paces.

"What the heck?" I said.

The mare continued to tease and nicker. Vickie peeked under the stallion's belly. He was still erect and ready, but he adamantly refused to come up to cover the mare. He danced back and forth in total frustration while I held onto the steel shank for dear life.

"He's never done that before," Nelly said. "Something's the matter."

"I'll put him back in his stall," I said. "Maybe he's sore. Has he been bred much lately?"

"No more than usual. I can't understand it," Nelly said. "He's been bred artificially before. Never bothered him."

"Is it something I did?" Vickie asked in a small voice.

"Don't see how. You were right in position. He seemed to hit the end of the A-V, stop, then back off."

"Let me see that thing," I said.

Vickie handed me the A-V.

"It's certainly full of water. It ought to be tight enough." I walked over to the washrack. "Let's start from scratch." I unscrewed the cap that held the water in place and turned the AV over to empty it. I couldn't help laughing. "Vickie, what temperature water did you use?"

"Warm."

"Not warm enough. It's already down to tepid. He must have thought he'd penetrated an iceberg."

Nelly began to laugh. "Poor baby. No wonder he backed off. I swear I have never seen such a look of complete consternation on a stallion's face in my life."

"I'm sorry," Vickie said in a small voice.

"No big deal. I'll just bring old Jasmine back out while you fill that thing with hot water. One thing about stallions, they're ready to go any time there's a receptive female in the neighborhood."

This time the stallion took his time approaching the mare. He sniffed and nibbled at her hocks, bit her flanks gently, rubbed his neck against her back. A real romantic.

Then he lifted his body above her head.

Vickie kept her eyes open this time, and as he came toward the mare she thrust the AV straight at him with grim determination.

Thirty seconds later his tail flagged and he backed off the mare.

"Good boy," I said and walked him back to his stall. "Good job, Vickie. You see, you survived."

On our way back to the clinic, Vickie sat silent. "I really screwed up. It's been much too long since I did that."

"Don't worry about it. We got it done. The mare's been inseminated and hopefully is in foal. The stallion's happy. The only one who missed out is the jump mare."

"I know how she feels."

I glanced over at her.

"I've spent the last fifteen years of my life being an occasional jump mare. Herb wanted his cookies. He didn't much care whether I got mine or not."

"Sorry."

"Thank God there are alternatives."

"Not nearly as much fun."

"As good sex? Not on your life. As lousy sex? I'll take the alternatives in a heartbeat."

I'd never made love with anybody but Morgan. I ached for his touch, physically ached. I missed the way he'd casually kiss the nape of my neck as he walked by me in the kitchen, the way I snuggled against his chest in bed. Not only sex, but the warmth of a familiar body, a familiar scent.

If I did find someone else, I wouldn't be committing adultery, for heaven's sake. But it would feel like a betrayal.

Even with no basis for comparison I knew there could never be any better sex than we had enjoyed. Still, I refused to admit to Vickie that Morgan had been my one and only. Not cool. Very old-fashioned. "Celibacy is a bitch," I said.

# Chapter 40

## *In which Maggie delivers an unusual baby*

Memorial Day weekend, Eli decided to have a party and invite Maggie's Militia and any husband or boyfriend who might be hanging around. I suppose she felt she had something to celebrate because I hadn't mentioned retirement for a couple of weeks.

Even Shep Fischer decided to drive up from Destin, Florida. He had sold his house in Colonial Acres and moved into a condo in Florida six months earlier.

Now he spent his days fishing or hanging out in the bars in Destin. Eli tossed her head and said she didn't think he wanted to marry her a bit more than she wanted to marry him.

"As long as he's involved with me, he can accept all those casseroles and dinner invitations from the widows who are after him and not have to commit to anything."

I told her I wasn't too sure of that.

"He's too lazy to get married," Eli replied. "Born rich, got richer. Never hit a lick at a snake."

I was delighted that Shep drove up for the party. He was the closest thing I had to a brother and the only male in my life at the moment. I missed him the way Eli missed Morgan.

The heat had not percolated from simmer to parboil yet, but it was eighty-five degrees, and Eli had brought out fans to keep the air moving.

By the time I arrived, Shep and Eli had already set up the six-foot picnic table and arranged lawn chairs and chaises longues under the trees.

"I will never fry another chicken as long as I live," she said to me as I reached for a handful of potato chips.

"Darlin,'" Shep answered. "Nobody fries chicken like you."

Eli lifted on tiptoes to kiss his cheek. "Bless your heart. Now, go drain the cucumbers, butter the bread, and start making the cucumber sandwiches."

I set down a big bowl of potato salad beside the chicken.

"I used that new bowl with the ice around the outside. Wouldn't want to give anybody ptomaine. The ice cream is finished, but still in the beater container. Shep, honey, you got the watermelon iced down?"

Shep pointed to a large cooler by the back steps. "I must have thumped a dozen of those suckers before I found one that sounded right."

"I've heard that's an old wives tale," I said. I arranged napkins and paper plates and plastic utensils under cloths where the bugs couldn't get to them.

"You just wait until you eat it before you doubt my judgment."

Eli and Shep had moved the big propane bug killer from the horse pasture to her yard. "That is the ugliest thing I have ever seen," Shep said.

"Hush. It works. I am not getting West Nile or malaria for any old picnic," Eli answered. "Lordy, it is hot."

"Eli, you keep saying you're going to put in a swimming pool. I wish you'd go ahead and do it," I said.

"Me, too," Shep said. He dropped a plastic bag of ice on the bricks of Eli's patio to break it apart, then scattered it in the ice chest that held the beer and soft drinks. "Miss Maggie, come on in the kitchen and help me make cucumber sandwiches."

We worked companionably on Eli's counter and her small kitchen table. Shep buttered the bread, I assembled the sandwiches and cut them into triangles.

"Why do you care whether Eli puts in a pool?" I asked. "You have the entire ocean."

"The ocean is filthy these days, hadn't you heard? And full of sharks. I would prefer to go to my grave with all five of my appendages intact."

"Five? Oh."

"What's this about your retiring? Gonna come join me in Florida?"

"Given my choice of Florida or the guillotine, I'd choose the guillotine."

"Plenty of available widowers."

"And even more widows after them. If I ever considered another man, which I don't think I would, I'd prefer a twenty-five year old body builder with the brain of a newt and the stamina of a goat."

"We have those too if you can afford them. Seriously, you're not really think of retiring, are you?"

"Seriously. Keep your voice down. Eli gets hysterical whenever I mention wanting to see the Mona Lisa."

"I don't doubt it."

"Besides, who are you to talk about retirement? For you retirement isn't a change, it's an extension."

"Yeah. I hate it. Reach me that other loaf of bread, will you?"

I tossed the bread to him. "You're serious. Why do you hate it?"

"I never knew I had a territorial imperative until I sold my house in Memphis and moved to the condo in Florida. It's mine, all right, at least the inside of it is, but it's just a glorified apartment with a view of the Gulf."

"But you hate yard work."

"I hired somebody to do that up here." He handed me another stack of buttered slices. "All the women I know who have moved down there keep bitching about having to find a new hairdresser, a new gynecologist, a new dentist. Well, sweetheart, I have a beard, most of my hair, a prostate, and all my own teeth. So I have to hunt up new sources too. And the grocery store doesn't carry Bumble Bee Tuna. How can you live in a place that doesn't carry Bumble Bee Tuna?"

I laughed and slid another stack of sandwiches onto Eli's good ironstone platter. "So what do you plan to do about it?"

"I've already done it," Shep said with satisfaction. "I close on the sale of the condo in Florida next week, and a week later I move into my new house up on Pickwick Lake."

"You're kidding. That's less than two hours from here."

"Am not. It's a planned community, so I won't have the yard work, but cottages look like old-fashioned farmhouses with front porches and picket fences. They're sitting in the middle of the woods with a view of the lake and their own boat docks."

"What about all that Florida golf?"

"Let me tell you, Miss Maggie, when you golf the way I do, eighteen holes a day is the path to frustration, high blood pressure and sunstroke. Besides, I miss *seasons*. Perpetual summer punctuated by the occasional hurricane won't cut it." He dropped his eyes. "And I missed y'all."

"Does Eli know?"

"Miss Eli does not know, and you are not going to tell her, you hear?"

I raised my hands in a gesture of submission. "I promise."

"She'd say I told you so."

"She did tell you so."

"That's why I'll tell her in my own way." He turned my shoulders so that I looked him square in the eye. "Maggie, sweet thing, you have to trust me on this. You do not want to retire and move someplace else among what the Bible calls 'the alien corn.' You sure don't want to die among strangers in a strange land."

"I don't plan to die anytime soon."

"We never do, do we?"

I knew he was thinking of Morgan.

"Maggie, you don't want to give up your life's work for somebody else's agenda."

I felt my face go red. "Eli put you up to this."

Shep raised his eyebrows in angelic innocence. "Why, no."

"I don't believe you." I stood up. "I know Eli is sneaky, but you, Shep?"

"Honey, I been telling you the God's honest truth."

"Right." I picked up the loaded platter. "You finish the sandwiches. Put them in the refrigerator. We'll replenish as needed."

Outside, I covered the platter of sandwiches and placed it beside the chicken. Everything was ready. Now all we needed was people.

"Yoo-hoo," called a cheery voice.

I looked up. "Sweet sufferin' Jesus."

"Lordy," Eli whispered. "How's she balancing on two legs?"

Heather toddled along with Rick steering. She wore a sprigged cotton maternity tent stretched way beyond its limits.

"I hate my husband," she said without preamble.

"You'll hate him more when you're in labor," I said equably. "But you'll forget it eventually."

"Honey pot," Rick said, "Let me get you a chair."

"The tallest, straightest you can find," Heather snapped. "Then you can help me sit down in it."

"When are you due?" Eli asked. "Next week sometime, right?"

"Our baby girl is due two days from now," Rick said proudly.

"If I don't pop by next Wednesday morning," Heather said, "they'll induce. I have heard that's real fun."

"Learn this mantra," I said. "I want my epidural. Practice saying it loud and often."

"I'm going natural," Heather said. "At least I hope I am. The doctor's not so sure he won't have to do a Cesarean."

"Everything's fine," Rick said.

Heather gave him a milk-curdling look. "Oh, sure. Fine. Rick's dragged me to the hospital twice. They pat me on the head, tell me I'm having Braxton-Hicks contractions and send me home. Then every time I lie down the little monster starts doing the rumba. I need to be near the bathroom, Eli. I have to go every fifteen minutes."

"Has your mother come down to help?" I asked.

Heather raised her eyes. "We're not telling either set of grandparents I'm in labor until the baby is born. My mother would barge right into the delivery room, and I don't want anybody there but Rick."

"Afterwards, I'll call both sets. It'll take Heather's parents three hours to get down here. They farm about fifty miles east of Nashville."

"And Rick's folks have to drive from Little Rock."

"So we'll at least get to hold our own baby," Rick said.

"When my sister had hers," Heather said, "My mother wouldn't let her near the kid. I'm breastfeeding, so I'll get to hold her then."

"You're sure it's a her?" Eli asked.

"Unless the doctors missed something on the ultra-sound." Heather squirmed and tried to get comfortable. "At least my ankles aren't swollen and my blood pressure's still normal."

Lanier's van pulled up behind Rick's truck. As the side door opened, Rick walked over to see whether he could help Susan. She waved him off and pushed the lever that lowered the elevator on which her wheelchair rested.

"We're used to this," Susan said. "I can do it by myself."

The big yellow Labrador jumped out behind her and stationed himself at the right hand wheel of her chair.

"Is this Pumpkin?" Rick asked and rubbed the shaggy ears. "I've heard a lot about you."

Pumpkin wriggled with pleasure.

"Why is he named Pumpkin?"

Susan grinned. "The first time I saw a picture of him—long before he was trained—he was a little orange ball. I named him Pumpkin right that minute."

"Now we're only missing Vickie," Eli said and glanced over at me. There was no need to mention who else we were missing. My mother told me after my father died, that getting through all the special occasions, the holidays with their traditions, that first year was the hardest part of her widowhood. So maybe next Memorial Day's picnic would be easier. I sure as shooting hoped it would.

"Vickie swore she's coming," I said.

"Alone?"

"Please God alone," I whispered.

Vickie's Explorer rolled up. She wasn't alone.

"Lordy, she's taken Herb back," Eli said.

But when the doors opened, Vickie was followed by two beautiful young men who towered over her.

"Hope you don't mind. Adam and Jason leave for LSU tomorrow. They're just home for the weekend."

Sarah and Nathan had been grown and living away since college, but watching Vickie with her two and Lanier with Susan, I suddenly wished I could teleport my two children from wherever they were spending Memorial Day, if only for a few hours.

"Delighted to have them," Eli said. "Introduce yourselves, guys. There's beer, but whichever one of you is still under twenty-one, stick to soft drinks." Eli pointed to an ancient oak that shaded a large area in the evening sun.

"We don't drink," said Adam, the taller of the two.

"Good." I turned to Vickie. "So?"

Vickie lifted her chin. "Herb's being as big a horse's patoot as I thought he would be about the property settlement, but all he can do is flounder and swear."

"No threats?"

"The boys took him out for breakfast yesterday and told him how the cow ate the cabbage."

"Good. I wouldn't want those two giants as enemies. Lord, they are gorgeous!"

"Herb did pass down his handsome genes. Let's hope they got their discipline and responsibility genes from me."

Everyone including Heather ate enormously, and sank into deck chairs semi-comatose. Vickie's sons left for another party after Lanier and Susan offered to drive Vickie home.

I caught the longing in Susan's eyes when the boys drove off. They were both too old for her, of course, but they were male, they were handsome college boys, and they were going dancing. That must hurt.

I don't know how many times I'd watched my Sarah traipse off to dances dressed in everything from jeans to formal gowns. Please, God, I thought, let Susan find a knight in shining armor who sees beyond the wheelchair and takes her to the prom.

I moved my chair over by Susan's wheelchair. "How's the riding?"

Susan's face was as luminous as the moon. "Aunt Maggie, it's wonderful. When I'm on Mariah, I've got legs."

"Mariah? Patsy's old Mariah?"

"She's not that old. She's not sway-backed or anything, and she moves so smoothly I don't have any trouble hanging on." Susan smiled. "I know she belongs to Mrs. Dalrymple, but in my heart I think of her as my horse."

I felt a frisson of anxiety. I knew another girl who loved a horse that deeply. I didn't want that kind of tragedy to happen to Susan. She had enough tragedy. She needed joy.

"Mrs. Dalrymple says Mariah's the mother of your daughter's horse," Susan said as though she'd been reading my mind. "I've heard Sarah was a really good rider."

"She was. I'm glad you're enjoying the classes."

"I never knew Mrs. Dalrymple before. She's a really super lady. Did you know she can ride?"

I broke out laughing. "Susan, when Patsy and I were both young and a whole lot lighter and more flexible than we are now, Patsy could ride the hair off any horse that moved."

"You too, Aunt Maggie?" Now Susan's eyes really shown. "I didn't know you rode horses."

"I couldn't until Patsy taught me after I got married. She and I used to go trail-riding when we could work out our schedules."

"But how could you give it up?"

I opened my mouth, then shut it again. "You know, that's a very good question. Maybe Patsy and I ought to do more of it."

"The kids at school are actually jealous of me."

"Good for you."

A pair of bats glided through the light and swooped down just over Susan's chair. "Oooh, get away!"

"They won't hurt you."

"Rick, I need to go to the bathroom again," Heather said. Rick unfolded from the grass, set his beer bottle down carefully, and slipped his hand under her arm. She popped up like a champagne cork out of a bottle.

"Want me to go with you?"

"I can still pee by myself, thank you." She waddled off.

He watched her. "You don't think she'll fall up the steps, do you?"

"I promise, if she's not back in five minutes, I'll go check on her and give her a hand up if she needs one," Eli said. "Get a grip, Rick. She's not going to calve right here on the lawn. How many calves have you birthed, by the way? A hundred?"

"She's a human being. She's *my* human being, and that's my baby."

"Human babies, especially first babies, take forever to be born after labor starts. Chill." Although five minutes had not passed, Eli meandered to her back door and went in.

A moment later she came back and stood on the top step. "Uh, Rick, Heather's water just broke."

Rick took the steps in one bound. "Heather, honey?" he called.

"She's locked herself in the bathroom," Eli said. "Maggie, you come and talk to her."

I squeezed past Rick and tried the door to Eli's powder room. Locked. "Heather, honey, you okay in there?"

I heard a wail. Rick tried to push past me. I'm certain he planned to knock the door down. "Back up," I said. "Let me handle this. Go stand over there by the refrigerator."

"But..."

Eli grabbed his arm and pulled him back.

I leaned against the door. "Open up, Heather. It's just Maggie."

"I've ruined the party! I knew I shouldn't come."

"You haven't ruined anything. Can you reach the door to open it?"

"I've made a big mess."

"Messes can be cleaned up. Unlock the door."

I heard a movement, then a click. I also heard Rick behind me, but Eli had him well in charge.

Heather sat on the john with her shoulders hunched. "I was feeling great. I haven't had so much energy in weeks. I scrubbed out all the kitchen cabinets and cleaned the refrigerator and..." She squeezed her eyes shut and caught her breath. A moment later she relaxed.

"Whoa. That was a doozie."

I dropped to my knees in front of Heather. "How long have you been having contractions?"

"I didn't think they were contractions," Heather wailed. "It was just like menstrual cramps. Like those Braxton-Hicks things they kept sending me home for."

"How far apart?"

"I don't know. I wasn't keeping track. Maggie, I'm so sorry."

"Now you *are* being an idiot. Babies come when *they* choose. You'll never be as out of control in your life as you are right now. Rick and I will lift you into your truck so he can drive you to the hospital. This time I guarantee they'll keep you."

"But..."

"Heather, this is your first baby. You probably won't be out of your first stage of labor for hours. Can you stand?"

"Of course I can stand." She made it halfway. "I'm not helpless—oh, shit!" She grabbed her belly. Her eyes widened, her fists clenched. "This h-h-h-hurts."

"Heather, don't you dare push! Remember your breathing exercises from birthing class? Practice. Puff, damn you, puff!" I pulled out the whole linen closet full of towels and laid them on the floor in front of her. "Come on, sweetie. Let Maggie help you sit down." I had visions of sliding her along to the steps and out the back door. She had gotten into the bathroom, so she must fit through the door, but at the moment, I wasn't too sure.

"I weigh a ton."

"Shut up." I got an arm under Heather's legs, half pulled her off the toilet and propped her on the floor. "Keep your knees up and tight together and don't you push."

"I'm okay."

"For the moment. What's your doctor's number? "

Heather gave it to me and I passed it to Eli. A moment later she stuck her head around the doorjamb. "Your doctor says he'll meet you and Rick at the hospital. He says don't worry, you have plenty of time."

"Maggie, I'm scared."

Of course she was scared. I remembered how I'd felt when my water broke with Sarah. It was as if my own body had turned on me. I had to find the right words to say, not that I thought she'd pay a whole lot of attention.

"You are simply the latest in a long line of female mammals who have been doing this for millennia. Before my Sarah was born my very wise doctor told me to stop intellectualizing and pay attention to my instincts. If you were a cat or dog you *could* be having a litter. I'll be right back with Rick and Shep to help move you."

"Don't leave me!"

"Heather? You okay?" Rick called.

I walked out onto the back steps.

"Her water broke?" Vickie asked.

"Not only that. She's in real labor."

"Good grief," Shep said.

"Say what?" Vickie added.

"We've called her doctor and I think Eli's calling nine-one-one. Heather's progressing faster than she should be for a first baby. She's been ignoring the contractions most of the day."

"Poor child's probably still got hours before she delivers," Vickie said.

"I don't think this baby read the rule book. The contractions seem to be coming about every two minutes. I think she's already starting second stage labor. If the EMTs don't get here fast, we may have to deliver it."

"Maggie, we're vets, not obstetricians," Lanier added.

Another long wail sounded from the house. "Oh, hell," I said.

Eli said from behind me, "We can't get her upstairs to my bedroom. The kitchen table's not nearly big enough, and there's no room to work around it. Can we get her to the clinic?"

"I don't think we can make it that far."

"How about the picnic table?" Vickie asked. "She'll be on a firm surface with plenty of room."

"Eli, you got a box of OB gloves in your pantry?" I asked.

Eli nodded. "Probably half a dozen boxes."

"Bring a whole box. And your emergency bag. We need Betadine and alcohol and soap and water and a suction bulb and scissors and God knows what all. Shep—Shep, honey, you look like a deer in headlights. Eli's always got a stack of newspapers a yard high beside the fireplace. Bring them out here and lay them on the picnic table. I've read they're more hygienic, God knows why. Vickie, you and Lanier clear everything off the picnic table."

"Can't we leave her where she is?" Shep asked.

"You've seen Eli's powder room. There's barely room to turn

around. We'll never be able to work on the floor on our knees. Susan, drive your chair over to my house. There's towels and blankets and sheets in the downstairs cupboard inside the back door. Can you get over the stoop to reach them?"

"Sure."

"Shouldn't somebody boil water?" Shep asked from the top step.

"If it will make you happy. Get the newspapers and then go help Susan." I turned towards the highway. "If that damned ambulance would get here we wouldn't have to do all this."

The door to Eli's powder room opened into the room rather than out into the hall. Rick had to lift Heather's torso to give Eli and me room to push it fully open.

"Hey, baby girl, how you doing?" I asked, dropped to my knees and took Heather's hand.

"Maggie, I am so sorry," Heather wailed. "I spoiled the party. I shouldn't have come."

"But what a special attraction. Okay, we have to get you out of here."

"Help me up." Without warning Heather's back arched. She gripped my hand hard enough to bring tears to my eyes. "Ow, ow, ow!"

"Whoo, whoo, whoo," Rick puffed.

"Shut up, you bastard!" Heather shouted. "This is all your fault."

After several false starts that ate up an agonizing amount of time, Heather managed to struggle to her feet with Rick's support.

"Maggie, I can't move. It feels like I've got a basketball hanging out of me."

"Okay. Rick, can you pick her up and carry her?"

"Sure. Come on, honey lamb."

"Don't you honey lamb me, you... Oh, shit!"

I suspected Rick's back would ache for days. As he struggled down the back stairs with Eli leading him and holding Heather's feet, Heather snarled, "If you ever do this to me again, I'll kill you!"

Rick turned agonized eyes to me. I shook my head. "That's mild. Just wait until she's ready to deliver. Don't take it personally. You should have heard what I said to Morgan. She won't remember it. Come on. Carefully, on the table."

Rick laid Heather gingerly on the pallet of newspapers.

Eli handed around obstetrical gloves. The gloves were intended for cows and horses, so the clear plastic reached all the way to our armpits. Then she handed me a pad orange with Betadine.

"Soap and water's fine," I said. "Or better nothing at this stage."

Susan wheeled up and stopped so sharply I was afraid she'd tip over. She could barely see over the linen and blankets on her chair. Eli took them and began to prop them under Heather's head and back.

"Shep, take Susan back over to my house and stay there," I said. "We're going to need Eli and Vickie and Lanier to hold Heather's legs and give her something to brace against."

"Right."

I glanced at Susan. Her eyes were the size of soup plates. I smiled at her. "You've seen plenty of puppies and kittens born. This isn't any different."

"I want to stay," Susan whispered. "Can I?"

"No way," Shep said and grabbed the back of her wheelchair. "We'll be at Maggie's."

"But Moooommm."

Shep was already loping to my patio door.

"Rick, you and Heather had birthing classes, didn't you?"

"It wasn't like this."

"Didn't they show you how to sit behind her and prop her up?"

"Uh-huh."

"Do it."

"You heard her," Heather snarled. "Get back there *now*, dammit."

Rick peered down at his sweet little bride as though she'd suddenly sprouted six fire-breathing heads.

"Now!"

"Where is that ambulance?" Vickie asked.

I stripped off Heather's sodden panties.

Without instruction, Lanier and Eli had positioned themselves on either side of Heather, who now sat semi-recumbent with her knees in the air and her legs spread.

"Hang on to those legs," I said. "I'd just as soon she didn't kick me in the mouth."

Heather gave an inchoate choking yelp.

"It's okay, baby," Rick said soothingly and patted Heather's shoulder.

"You put that hand down where I can get to it, buster, you're going to draw back a nub."

Eli dried Heather's face with a towel.

"Oh, God, I'm going to make a mess!" Heather bawled.

"Okay, Heather, I'm going to check your cervix," I said. I looked and stood up so fast I nearly clipped Lanier in the chin. "The head's already crowning. I'll need to turn it."

Heather growled and pushed.

I gently turned the baby's body. "Thank God it's not breech." No way could we have done what my wonderful LPN Taisie did when Sarah was born. Heather was too far along to get up on her hands and knees and rock.

"Okay, kiddo," I said. "A couple of more good ones and all I have to do is catch." I was amazed at how calm I sounded. Actually, my adrenaline was pumping so hard I'm surprised it wasn't spewing out my eyeballs. I glanced up at Eli. She smiled a tight little smile and nodded almost imperceptibly. She knew I was scared. But I couldn't let Heather or the others know.

Heather squalled, "Here we go again!"

"Heather, honey, if Rick lifts you up more, can you hook your hands under your knees?" Eli asked. "That'll give you something to hang onto while you push."

"Rick!" Heather commanded. He rolled her farther up. She hooked her hands under her knees. They slid off immediately. "I'm all sweaty."

Vickie wiped her palms and legs and grasped her hand. "Better?"

"Yeah. It's starting. Grrrrr."

"Heather, honey, bear down, grit your teeth, yell your heart out. Cuss Rick," Eli said.

"Damn straight. Oh, sheee-ut."

"Oh, yeah, baby," I whispered. "Come to Auntie Maggie."

Heather yelled obscenities that Rick probably had no idea she knew. He hung on gamely, although I suspected his hand would be sore for a week. Heather didn't have enough leftover energy to chomp on it.

I squatted down in a position I hadn't assumed since I played catcher on my high school softball team. "One more. Almost there. Gotcha!" The baby girl's shoulders popped free and a moment later the entire baby slid into my hands. I grasped her and held her upside down. The baby coughed once, then mewed like an angry kitten and squirmed.

"Lay her on Heather's chest with a bath towel over her," I whispered. "Eli, you got the suction bulb?"

Eli began gently to suction the baby's mouth and nostrils. Once covered with a towel on Heather's tummy, the baby settled down at once.

"Don't cut the cord until it stops pulsing," I said. "We've still got to deliver the afterbirth."

Heather's hair clung to her skull; sweat dripped down her cheeks. She gazed down at the bloody, soapy little creature on her chest in wonder. She touched the baby's downy head gently and began to count her fingers.

I glanced up at Rick. He stared at his daughter as though someone had hit him right between the eyes with a two-by-four. How Morgan would have loved to see Sarah and Nathan born! Damn the doctors who had wanted to make birth sterile instead of joyful.

"Hey, little critter," I said. "Welcome to the world."

From somewhere down the road came the sound of an approaching siren.

Eli's head snapped up. "Well, finally," she said, as the red and white ambulance careened up the driveway and rocked to a stop by Eli's side porch.

"Over here! You took your sweet time getting here."

"Sorry, ma'am. Memorial Day traffic. Hey, y'all had the baby already?"

"You can take over," I said. "From here on, it's your problem."

"Who delivered it?"

"I did," I said.

"You're shaking," Eli said. She took my arm and led me toward her back stairs.

"Damn right. What if something had gone wrong?"

"You'd have handled that the best you could." She glanced over her shoulder. The EMTs were preparing to load Heather and the little girl onto a gurney for transport. Rick still held Heather's hand, but she no longer threatened to bite it off. She had eyes for nothing except the small miracle in the EMT's arms.

"I didn't really take a good look at the baby," I said.

"Lots of black hair."

"That'll fall out," I said.

"Give me a minute." Eli went to Rick and touched his arm. He seemed to wake from a dream. "Go with them. We'll bring your truck to the hospital."

"Huh? Oh, yeah. The truck." His face softened. "Aren't they beautiful?"

He didn't wait for an answer. Two minutes later the EMT ambulance, Rick, Heather and their new baby girl raced off into the evening.

"You're welcome," Eli called after them.

Vickie gave me a high five, bloody gloves and all. She was crying.

As a matter of fact we were all crying. I grabbed Eli's hand. "What if that had been Sarah or Lisa having a baby? Bringing a new life into the world is scary stuff."

"The cycle goes on," Eli said. "God, I am getting downright maudlin."

Even if by some miracle Sarah or Lisa did decide to present me with grandchildren, they'd never know what a wonderful man their grandfather had been. "I don't know about y'all," I said, "but I could sure use a drink."

# Chapter 41

## *In which Maggie meets some angry buffalo*

Rick and Heather asked Eli and me to be Margaret Elizabeth Halliday's godparents. Of course we accepted. They planned to call her Meg, not Maggie, but she was still named after Eli and me.

I decided to clean out Morgan's closet on the Fourth of July. Independence Day. I made Eli stick with me while I did it.

I had secretly been perusing those brochures Morgan had collected, and frankly, the thought of going alone to a country where I didn't speak the language bothered me. I asked Eli if we could close the practice for a couple of weeks and both travel to Europe. She simply snorted at me and went back to work.

Eli didn't know about my new passport.

I made an appointment with an agent at a local travel agency. Vickie had worked with us several times, and seemed to be re-learning to handle large animals. She thought selling her practice might be the only way to get Herb to agree to the divorce settlement. Eli still wasn't happy thinking about having someone buy me out, but she did agree that adding Vickie to our existing practice might be a good thing. That was a good first step.

When Rick called me at dawn one hot Tuesday morning in August, my first thought was that something was wrong with baby Meg.

"No, she's blooming," Rick said. "Growing like a jimson weed. We're having the christening the first week in September. Y'all are godmothers. You have to be there."

We chatted for a few minutes while I tried to figure out why he'd called me. Finally, he took a deep breath and asked, "What do you know about buffalo?"

"I've treated a few. A couple of my clients raised beefalo for a while until they found out there's no market for the meat. Why?"

"One of the people I know from the cow station just drove home from a sale in Houston with three buffalo. He wants me to come check them out. Could you ride along? I don't know a damned thing about buffalo."

"Let me check my schedule. I'll call you back."

"How's ten sound?" I said when I got him. He agreed.

I drove down to the cattle station and met him. When I climbed into his dusty pickup, I asked, "Who is this guy and why on earth did he buy buffalo?"

Rick turned south drove the back roads to I-55. "He owns a convenience store and gas station at one of the lesser interchanges on I-55. He says he's been looking for something besides gas and hot dogs to attract customers."

"So he picked buffalo? Is the fool suicidal?"

"He won't admit it, but I suspect he was drunk as a skunk when he bought them at a sale in Houston and hauled them home."

"Does he have the first notion what he's dragged home?"

"Nope. Me neither. That's why you're here."

"Do you know whether these are cows or bulls?" I asked Rick.

"We're about to find out," Rick said as we pulled into a service station beside the interstate.

The buffalo might not yet have attracted paying customers, but a couple of elderly gentlemen lounged around on the front porch of the small grocery store. A posthole digger thudded out of sight in the back.

The store was the sort of country mom and pop grocery store that served sausage biscuits in the morning, sandwiches at lunch, and fried chicken at night from its buffet counter. A sign on the door read "We take W.I.C. and food stamps. Se Habla Espanol."

I would be willing to bet they also ran tabs for everybody in the neighborhood and were paid when the crop came in or the social security check arrived. The place was freshly painted and spanking clean. Even the big front windows gleamed. I guessed there'd be more brands of chewing tobacco and snuff inside than there were brands of candy bars, and more cases of beer than cola.

Out of sight around the far side of the building came the bawl of annoyed buffalo. The scent of their bodies had wafted all the way to the gas pumps in front of the store.

"My eyes are watering," I said. "It's the methane. For heaven's sake, don't light a match anywhere near them or we'll all be blown to kingdom come."

"Y'all the vets?" A skinny would-be cowboy shoved off from the building and came over to us, only taking time to spit a stream of tobacco juice out of the right side of his mouth.

"Jimmy Joe," said an aged black man who sat on top of the outside cooler. "Mr. Pete'll skin you alive he catches you spittin' on his clean concrete."

Jimmy Joe ignored him. "Mr. Pete's around back supervising. His crew's nearly 'bout finished with the pen for them things. I'll go git him."

I walked up to the elderly black man and nodded. "Seems to be quite an event."

The man grinned. He was missing most of his teeth, but managed not to lisp. "Mr. Pete'll do *some* foolishness when he's in the drink," he said. "But this foolishness done took the cake." He shook his head. "I done tole him you can't keep nothing that big in no little pen."

"How big is little?"

"Four-five acres. He gonna build 'em a run-in shed for bad weather too."

His bright eyes turned dull and shifted away from me. That was the signal that Mr. Pete must have been walking up behind me. I turned and smiled. His small features huddled in the center of his round face like the holes in a bowling ball. He had small blue eyes, a pug nose, and a cherub's mouth with pink, moist lips. He had a spherical body and thighs so round that he swayed from one foot to the other as he walked. He was perspiring and wiping his bald skull with a red bandanna and grinning.

"I do declare, I done got two of you. Will wonders never cease."

"We came to see your ladies," I said with an answering smile. "Where are they?"

"Y'all come right on with me." He trundled off around the corner of the building toward the bawling.

An eighteen-wheeler stock trailer stood back of the store. I noted it shivered slightly every time one of its occupants shifted or stamped. Through the slats I could see three great brown woolly shapes lifting their heads to bawl their umbrage.

"Y'all come on. Ain't they the finest things you ever done see?

Folks gonna be driving near into the ditch to get up here to show their little 'uns the great American buffalo."

"Mr. Pete, how long have they been in the trailer?" Rick asked.

"Got 'em home yestidday afternoon 'bout supper time."

"And you drove straight from Houston?"

"Yessir. Bought 'em at the stock sale, loaded 'em up and started for home right away."

"Were you *planning* to buy buffalo?"

"Not a-tall. Took the trailer down there to get me some Santa Gertrudis straight out of Mexico. Then I saw them gals and I just had to have 'em."

"Maggie," Rick whispered. "They've been in that trailer for two days."

I walked over to the new paddock and left Rick to talk to Mr. Pete without interference. The black gentleman had come around the other side to stand by me. I offered my hand. "I'm Maggie McLain."

"Sam Jones, ma'am. Folks 'round here call me Uncle Sam."

"Where did you learn about buffalo?"

"Spent some time in the prison farm in Memphis a long time ago when I was young and stupid. Had to take care of them buffalo they got in that herd down there in the park." He shook his head. "If that didn't scare a fool straight, wouldn't nothing but a bullet do it. Mr. Pete don't know what he's done got hisself into."

"Have you told him?"

"I tried." He pointed to the seven-foot tall metal fence posts that were driven into the ground to form the perimeter of the buffalo pen, and the diamond wire mesh stretched between them. "He thinks them flimsy posts and that fancy horse wire gonna hold a buffalo, he got another think coming."

"That's all he's using?"

"He did have sense enough to hang that gate from six by sixes set in ce-ment. Every one of them posts ought to be six by six and set the same way."

"With construction steel fencing instead of horse fence," I said.

"Yes, ma'am."

"I'll tell him."

"He ain't gonna listen."

"We can but try."

I walked back to Rick, who was waving his arms in exasperation.

"Now, don't have a cat fit," Mr. Pete said. "I'm gonna turn 'em out in a little minute."

"That fence will not hold a buffalo," I said quietly.

"Sure it will."

"I promise you, they will go through it like a hot knife through cold butter."

"Pshaw. Will not." He grinned gently. "Not gonna need to go anywhere nor want to once they see that clover and lespedeza I got in that pasture. Already got a stack of hay rolls in the back for 'em too once the first frost hits. They'll think they done landed in hog heaven and won't never go nowhere else."

"I pray you're right," I said.

"Now, I was just telling this young man here, they told me down in Houston one of these ladies was pregnant. Trouble is, I lost track of who's who. I need to know which one of 'em is gonna calve."

I stared at him in confusion. "How do you expect us to check? You don't have any pipe stocks in that pasture we could run them into. They have to be checked one at a time."

"Shoot, I know that." He looked Rick up and down. "I figured one of y'all could climb up on one side of the trailer and one on t'other, then one can reach in and hold up the tail while the other hangs over the side and feels for a calf."

I choked.

"I was trying to explain to Mr. Pete here his idea would be both dangerous and ineffective," Rick said.

Mr. Pete snorted. "Oh, come on, son. I guess a big ol' boy like you could climb on down into the trailer with 'em, I mean they're sweet as pie, but it's kinda messy in there right now what with the manure."

"Not to mention the tempers of three buffalo who have been cooped up for thirty-six hours."

"Well, what the Sam Hill did I get y'all out here for anyways if you can't do a simple little job like testing them buffalo."

Rick started to speak, but I held up a hand. "Mr. Pete, there are only two ways that I can see for you to find out which of your buffalo is pregnant. The first is if you come out here some morning and find one of them suckling a calf."

"Shoot! That's no good. I got to know now so I can look after her right."

"Then the only way you're going to find out is if she whispers in your ear."

"Well, hell's bells."

The rangy man slouched up at that point. "Mr. Pete, we got the gate hung. Pasture's finished. You can turn 'em loose."

"Don't you do it, Mr. Pete," Uncle Sam said.

"Shoot, Sam, I know what I'm doing. Now, folks, y'all wait 'til I get them buffalo unloaded into the pasture, then we can lasso one at a time so you can check them."

He turned away without waiting for our reply, climbed into the cab of his eighteen wheeler and started the engine.

"Maggie, what do we do?" Rick whispered.

"Get into your truck, turn it around to face the road and get ready to floor it if you have to."

"You mean run before he turns them out?"

"No way. I wouldn't miss this for the world."

The eighteen wheeler drove slowly through the wide open pipe gate and fifty feet into the pasture. Mr. Pete climbed down, but left the motor running. "Okay, boys," he said. "Close that gate and let's get that tailgate open. Y'all stand behind the doors. Wouldn't want nobody hurt while they're investigating their new paradise."

I noted that Uncle Sam had already taken shelter behind a shiny red crew-cab pickup truck.

The man who had been finishing the gate and the cowboy who had met us at the front of the store shut the gate behind them, and with Mr. Pete's help, they hauled open the doors of the stock trailer. For a long moment nothing happened. The buffalo had room to turn around in the trailer, so they weren't forced to back out. I could see them jostle for position once they realized their prison gates had been thrown open.

Then they leapt down from the trailer almost as a unit.

"Holy shit! Look at the size of 'em," said the fence builder.

"Beautiful," Mr. Pete shouted. "Just beautiful."

"Oh, Lord preserve us," Uncle Sam shouted from his place behind the truck.

The buffalo dropped their huge heads and began to crop the late fall clover. Mr. Pete climbed back into the cab of his truck while the two men closed the tailgate and climbed in beside him.

Rick and I watched him turn the rig carefully in the pasture. The ground was dry except around the water trough, so there was little chance of his bogging down.

As they reached the gate, one of the men jumped down and

opened it, then shut it after the trailer drove out.

Mr. Pete climbed down and sauntered over to Rick and me with a beatific smile on his face. "See there. Told you so."

*Crack*! Mr. Pete spun to see his fine new six by six slowly topping toward the ground and carrying one end of the gate with it. The largest buffalo, the one that had obviously shoved her shoulders and head against it and split it like a sapling, gazed down at it while she considered her next move. Her sisters, however, did not hesitate. They crashed straight into the fence beside the gate, and flattened it, posts and all. Then all three galloped around the building toward the road.

"Rick," I shouted. "Get this truck started. We've got to turn them to the right or they'll wind up on the interstate."

Rick drove out onto the country road and slammed on his brakes. His truck was nearly long enough to cover both lanes. One buffalo attempted to turn into us, then decided on the line of least resistance. All three bolted down the road away from the interstate.

"Glory! Stop 'em before they get killed!" Mr. Pete screamed as he and his helpers hauled themselves into the bed of Uncle Sam's truck.

Uncle Sam pulled up beside Rick. "Want me to follow 'em?"

"Heck, yes. We'll call the cops."

The buffalo were rounding the first curve in the roadway, and so far had not deviated from the blacktop.

"For heaven's sake, don't lose 'em!" I shouted. Then I called 911 on my cell phone.

"What is the nature of your emergency?" The voice sounded cool.

"I'm at the corner of I-55 and Jayce Road chasing three buffalo who are headed east. Call the highway patrol, the local cops, the sheriff and anybody else you can think of to get in front of them and set up roadblocks."

"Ma'am, is this a joke? There are rules..."

"Lady! Do what I'm telling you before somebody gets trampled. Then start calling people along the road, tell them to get their children and their dogs inside and stay inside themselves. I am not, repeat not, joking. Four tons of buffalo are stampeding down Jayce Road."

"Ma'am, could I have your number?"

"This is Dr. Margaret McLain." I gave the dispatcher my cell phone number. "Alert the sheriff and the highway patrol *now*."

"Yes, ma'am."

"Rick, turn around and get back on the interstate headed toward Jackson.

"We're just going to leave them?"

"No way. We're going to see a man about a buffalo."

# Chapter 42

## *In which Maggie saves several creatures of the bison persuasion*

I called the 911 operator again. "Can you patch me through to one of the officers who's setting up the barricade?"

"Yes'm." The girl sounded excited. Probably more fun than she'd had in years.

"This is Sheriff Sims. Is this Dr. McLain?"

"Sheriff, Sam Jones is following the herd in a red dually. He knows about buffalo. And if you can find a couple of gentle cows, the buffalo may follow them into somebody's pasture and settle right down. Watch your squad cars. I warn you, buffalo can jump as high as a horse and they can bash straight into you. You do not want that, believe me."

"We'll have to shoot them."

"No, you will not shoot them, dammit. Listen to me. Get those cows. I'm on my way to talk to a man who knows all there is to know about buffalo cows and has the fences to hold them inside if we can get them to him. If we can coax them back into their stock trailer and drive them to him, I'm sure I can convince him to keep them at his place until Mr. Pete can build a safe enclosure for them. They're not dangerous, for pity's sake."

"We can't risk any of the public getting hurt."

"You won't risk a darned thing if you listen to me and Sam Jones. These bison weren't raised on the plains. They're not used to running. They're fat and out of condition and probably worn out by now. All they'll want to do is rest and eat. Think of them as big woolly cows. You know cows?"

"Raised a few. Never had a stampede."

I thought I detected laughter beneath his words. Good. The funnier he thought the situation, the less likely it would turn tragic.

I gave him particulars. "Rick, take the next exit, go north and take the second dirt road on your left. Sheriff, I'll call you. Don't you dare hurt those buffalo."

Ten minutes later we pulled up in front of a tidy yellow farmhouse with green shutters. Rick honked, and I climbed out as a gray-haired woman in jeans and a T-shirt came out the front door and down the steps. "Why, what on earth? Dr. McLain, haven't seen you for a coon's age. Did Jedediah call you?"

"No, Lorena, this time I need *his* help. Where is he?"

"Finishing up a piece of pie in the kitchen," came a bass voice.

"Hey, Jed, we've got an emergency. Do you still have your holding pens for your buffalo?"

"Sure do. Got rid of my buffalo cows, but shoot, I still got old Ranger."

"Good." I turned to Rick and introduced him. "Jed and Lorena got into the beefalo business ten years ago. I treated their buffalo."

"Yeah, and got out five years ago," Jed said. "Figured I'd lost enough money."

"Then he got into emu," Lorena said. "Got out of that three years ago along with everybody else who had a lick of sense."

"Half the poor souls who'd invested in birds simply opened their gates and turned them loose." Jed shook his head. "It's bad enough to hit a deer on the highway at night, but an emu? Probably scared a few drunk drivers into staying sober for the rest of their lives."

"Jed'll probably go to raising something like deer next."

"Now, Lorena, there's plenty of folks in New Zealand making a killing farming deer."

"You try it, Jedediah Blackwell, and you won't be the one making the killing, I will."

"But you still have Ranger?" I asked. I turned to Rick, "He's Jed's buffalo stud bull."

"He's just a big old pet. Couldn't sell him for love nor money, didn't want to slaughter him. My grandkids would kill me. They love the old fool. Y'all come on around back and say hello. Y'all can tell me what's cooking on the way."

"I've got biscuits in the oven," Lorena said. "I'll come soon as I take 'em out."

I told the buffalo story as we walked around the house and back toward the big yellow metal barn behind it.

Jed shook his head. "Mr. Pete must 'a stuck his entire head in a bottle of bourbon to do something that stupid. I've been by that store a million times. Never stopped. I can see why he'd like to have some kind of attraction. But buffalo?" He shook his head. "Don't know what I can do to help." Jed pointed past the barn. "Say hello to Ranger."

The paddock in which Ranger grazed was constructed strong enough to contain the average African elephant. Where Mr. Pete had used ordinary metal fence posts, Ranger's paddock was constructed of eight-foot tall six-by-sixes set in concrete, and the wire was heavy steel construction fencing.

"Wow," Rick whispered the instant I saw Ranger. "Now *that's* big."

Ranger trotted around his pasture like a happy puppy. Instead of tossing a Frisbee, however, he was tossing a five-hundred-pound tractor tire. He caught the rim on one of his horns, tossed his head and threw it back over his shoulder to land eight to ten feet behind him. Then he'd trot around and do it again.

"Come on," Jed said and unhooked the heavy chain that held his gate closed. "He's just a big ol' pussycat."

"No thanks," Rick said, then whispered to me, "I don't know about you, but I don't have a death wish."

"Aw, come on. He loves people."

Jed walked toward him. We followed warily.

Ranger lifted his head, spotted company, snorted and trotted toward us, the truck tire momentarily abandoned in favor of more interesting company. He stopped four feet away.

"Come on, Maggie," Jed said. "Just scratch behind his ears and he'll love you for life."

I inched forward, reached across his horns, and scratched. Ranger sighed. He obviously loved the attention.

As a matter of fact, he loved it so much that he felt it was his duty to reciprocate. He gave me a fond little nuzzle.

His forehead connected with my rib cage with the force of an anvil.

I bounced off the fence and made dying fish noises while I tried to gulp air back into my lungs and stay on my feet.

Rick moved behind Jed. Ranger blinked in hurt surprise. I could feel his breath against my chest. His huge head and hump towered over me.

"Nice Ranger," I gasped. "For God's sake, Jed, tell him not to snuggle."

Jed poked Ranger in the side. "Go on, Ranger. You git now."

Ranger blinked again, then deciding that he might get into trouble if he tossed *me*, he wheeled, trotted back to his tire and gave it one long throw for good measure.

"Can we leave now?" Rick asked.

When we were safely back on the other side of the gate, Jed said, "Sorry about that, Maggie . He's a little near-sighted."

"Now you tell me."

As we drove away from Jed's place ten minutes later, Rick said, "Maggie, if it wasn't for you knowing everybody under the sun, those buffalo would be dead meat right now."

He was probably right.

"You can't just up and retire." He shook his head. "You're not gonna be much help walking around some museum when crap like this happens."

"Eli…"

"You know stuff Eli doesn't, and she knows stuff you don't. We need you both. How's she gonna manage without you?"

"She has Shep."

"He's not a vet. Y'all been friends and partners too long, Maggie McLain. Don't go doing something dumb. Morgan left holes in other people's lives too."

My short ride-a-long with Rick lasted most of the day and gave me plenty to think about. Eventually, the three buffalo cows were enticed back into their trailer with the assistance of a couple of Jersey heifers and some sweet feed.

An entourage consisting of the stock trailer, Sam Jones's red dually, Rick's truck, and assorted law enforcement types and general hangers on made the trip to Jed's place without further incident.

After Jed settled the buffalo temporarily in a paddock that would probably have contained Godzilla, Lorena fed our entire entourage homemade peach pie and iced tea.

As we turned back onto the interstate and headed for home, Rick said, "Mr. Pete's lucky he only got a citation for loose livestock. Poor man looked like a deflated balloon."

"Thank God for Sam Jones. He knows how to take care of them. When I left him, Mr. Pete was talking about maybe getting him fitted out with some kind of Wild West costume."

"You're kidding."

"Nope. And Sam seemed delighted with the idea so long as he could have a six-shooter."

"May I never see another buffalo as long as I live," Rick said.

"I don't want to see any more loose livestock as long as I live," I said. "Goat, emu, or buffalo. They all get into trouble the minute they get loose."

"And usually they're the ones that end up dead."

Rick and I had barely reached the Tennessee border when his cell phone rang. I picked it up for him.

"Oh, Maggie, thank God," said Heather's voice. She sounded frantic.

"Is the baby all right?" I asked, and Rick nearly put the truck into a ditch.

"The baby's fine, I'm fine. It's that Barrows man and his bull again."

"What now?"

"He swore he'd keep him up and build a decent fence. I don't know what he calls decent, but..."

Rick pulled off the road into the parking lot for a rest stop. I handed him the cell phone. He listened to Heather while his face got redder and redder. He clutched the wheel so hard his knuckles were white. He said, "He knows damned well that once a bull gets out of an enclosure, the best thing to do is sell him, because he's going to keep doing it." He glanced at me. "Do you have to go straight home?"

I called the clinic to tell them where I was. Tonesha said Eli was handling the walk-ins. Everything was quiet. "Nothing waiting for me at home. I'll ride with you."

Rick drove like a madman. The gravel road in front of the station was blocked by a patrol car. On the road beyond, the lights of half a dozen patrol cars strobed.

Rick pulled to the side of the road. We both grabbed our bags and raced toward the closest barricade.

"I'm Dr. Rick Halliday," Rick told the state policeman at the barricade. "I'm in charge of the station. This is Dr. McLain. My wife called me about a bull."

"He's down there." He pointed past the ambulances.

I had to hurry to keep pace with Rick's long legs.

"Oh, God," I whispered, as I realized what I was looking at. A purple SUV stood upright in the center of the road. From the back it looked undamaged. As I came closer, however, I saw the front was bashed in, the windshield in pieces.

Mr. Barrow's longhorn bull lay on the shoulder of the road. His head was covered in blood. He was unconscious, but I could see his sides move. He was breathing. Someone—Rick's men, probably—had lashed his legs together with heavy rope.

With Meg strapped into a carrier on her back, Heather ran toward us and flung herself into Rick's arms.

He hugged her and baby together, then thrust her away. "What the hell happened?"

"Fool kids done killt my good bull." Barrows detached himself from the group of uniformed sheriff's deputies and slouched toward us.

"Your bull nearly killed them, you mean," Heather snapped. "And he's not dead."

"Not yet."

Three young men huddled in the back of one of the squad cars. I peered in at them. They were all three spattered with blood. One turned frightened eyes up to me. His teeth were chattering.

The doors of both ambulances slammed simultaneously with an echo like a rifle shot. A moment later they tore off with sirens blaring and lights blinking.

I felt sick. I gestured at Rick. "Who's in the ambulances?"

"Couple of fraternity punks, is who," Barrows said. "Drunk as a passel of skunks on bootleg hooch."

"Please, Mr. Barrows," I said and started toward the bull. "Heather? You sure the bull's tied securely? I'm not interested in connecting with those horns if he wakes up."

"He's safe."

"Hey, didn't nobody give you permission to treat my bull!" Barrows said.

I stopped and turned to face him. "You are without a doubt the meanest, dumbest piece of work I've seen in a good many years as a veterinarian. Now, do you want two veterinarians who are *here* to treat your bull? Or wait until we call your vet, assuming you have one? Or do you want to leave him on the side of the road to die?"

"Ain't no woman never talked to me thataway."

"Pity. Oh, the heck with it. I'm treating that bull whether you like it or not."

"Better not send me a bill!"

I shot him a glance. "Come on, Rick. Let's get the blood cleaned up." I dropped onto my knees beside the bull. "What on earth happened here?" I asked a highway patrolman hovering close by.

"Those five young morons left a party in Collierville last night after midnight and drove down into Mississippi to find a bootlegger. He sold them a quart of tequila out the back door of a juke joint. They were heading back to the party when they got lost. They were driving flat out down this road to get to the highway when..."

"When they hit my damn bull."

"Mr. Barrows," I said. "Hush up right now."

"Heather says sometime last night that bull of his jumped his *unrepaired* fence again," Rick glared at Barrows. "Then he broke down mine..."

"Didn't neither," Barrows said and spat into the gravel. "Jumped it clean."

"When the bull started chasing my cows this time, they ran from him, straight through the hole he'd made in the fence and right onto this road."

"Dear God. How many dead?" I asked and looked around for more carcasses.

"That's the thing," the patrolman said. "When they saw the car heading at them, the cows peeled off to the sides. That stupid bull plowed straight ahead. The kid in the back seat said the driver saw him and slammed on his brakes. Skidded all over the road, but managed to keep the car upright."

I looked behind me at the two long streaks of black in the center of the gravel.

"Apparently, *el toro* here saw the SUV as a rival for the affections of his lady friends. He charged. Horns went straight through the windshield when he rode up over the hood."

"Oh, no."

"Go take a look." The patrolman grinned. "It's worth seeing."

I walked over to the SUV, peered in the side window and gasped.

"Yeah." He grinned. "Horns grazed the driver, missed the passenger in the front seat, and rammed into the back seat. An inch to the right and it would have gone straight through the driver and impaled the kid in the center back seat like a shish-ke-bab."

"How are the boys?"

"The three in the back are over there, scared sober and sick as dogs. The blood belongs to the bull. That was the driver and the front seat passenger in the ambulances. Paramedics think they each have a couple of cracked ribs from the air bags, mild concussions and the worst hangovers of their young lives. If this doesn't turn them teetotal, nothing will."

"Where are your cows?" I asked Rick.

"I thought you might have to help with the roundup, but apparently freedom wasn't all it was cracked up to be. My boys have already driven them back into their pasture. They're fixing the fence now."

"Uh, doc," Barrows said. "Might some of your boys give me a hand getting ol' Ralph here back into my pasture?"

For a moment I thought Rick would deck the man. Then he shrugged. "Sure. I'll call 'em." He turned to me. "It looked a lot worse than it was."

I looked in the SUV's window one more time on my way by. Stuffing and tattered upholstery protruded from the hole in the front seat around the hole the bull's horn had made, but the hole itself was as neat as a bullet hole.

An inch or so to the right, and that horn would have been every bit as deadly as a bullet.

The young deputy who had let me through the barricade grinned at me. "Lucky little bastards, weren't they?"

"What's Barrows's liability?"

"His bull was loose, but this is a semi-private road, and those kids were drunk and driving well over the speed limit. I'm ticketing everybody. Let the judge work it out."

On the way home I thanked God that no matter what stupid things Nathan and Sarah had done when they were the age of those kids, neither one of them ever got mixed up with drugs or alcohol. So far as I knew, that is. The line between stupid teenaged behavior that causes an end to teenaged lives and stupid teenaged behavior that turns into a prank is very thin. Kids can cover up and act independent as long as they escape the consequences of their actions. The minute they get into real trouble, however, they turn into children seeking sanctuary with Mom and Dad.

Let Rick hug his little Meg and pray for her safety. I said a silent prayer for Sarah and Nathan. The world is never safe even for those of us who are careful.

# Chapter 43

## *In which Maggie makes travel plans*

I walked into the Paradise Travel Agency in Memphis shortly after a solitary lunch. I'd spoken to one of the agents, Olivia Overton, on the phone, and when I shook her hand, she said, "I was sorry to hear about Morgan."

"You knew him?"

"I have booked and cancelled lots of flights for him."

"My fault. This time I promise I'll carry through."

"So where do you want to go and when?"

I stared at her. "I'm not sure. Where did Morgan want us to go?"

"We're not talking Morgan, Dr. McLain. This is *your* trip we're planning. Have you ever been abroad?"

I shook my head.

"Got a passport?"

"Brand new."

"Have you ever considered joining a tour group? I always recommend that for someone who's never been overseas before."

"With a bunch of total strangers?"

"There are groups that cater to all age groups, all economic levels, even hobbies. Would you be interested in joining a *Jack the Ripper* tour to London?"

"Good grief, no."

"It is getting late in the season. September is a wonderful time to go to Europe, but much past that the weather can be tricky." She smiled at me. "Unless you go to Spain or Majorca. Look, how about I get together a packet of brochures on tours to the British Isles. That way you won't have to worry about the language barrier. As a single woman, you're sure to get a place, although you'll have to share with a roommate to avoid paying the additional single supplement."

"I had a roommate my first six months in vet school," I said. "She was in engineering, I think. I don't even remember her name. We hated each other."

"You have a business partner, don't you? Ask her to join you."

"She won't close our practice for that long."

"Then, I'm afraid it's either pay the single supplement or share." She became all business. "I'll make you up a big packet and send it to your home. You can go over it, call me with any questions you have, the let me know what you decide. There are some marvelous tours at Christmastime."

"Christmas away from home?"

"Plenty of people would pay their last dime to avoid Christmas at home. Too many memories, too much family."

That hit me. God, if I could just avoid Christmas at home this year... I wanted to see the children, but not under those circumstances. I didn't think I could bear to put up a tree, decorate the house, act as we've always acted, but without Morgan. "What kind of Christmas tours?" I asked.

"Skiing in Switzerland or Austria..."

"That's out. I don't slide down mountains."

"Tours to the South of France or the Middle East."

"Nix on the Middle East. And I don't speak French."

"Then how about a Dickens Christmas in London? Museums, shopping, lots of good theater. You'd stay in marvelous places. I have one that starts a week before Christmas, spends New Year's in a castle, and flies home on January second. A small group. I think it would be perfect for your first trip."

Christmas in London. A completely new tradition to take the place of the big Christmas tree, the big dinners on Christmas Eve and Christmas Day, the presents. Sarah and Nathan could start their own traditions in their own homes. And the English spoke English. I'd been an English major in college until I switched to science.

Christmas in London sounded better and better.

I could afford that single supplement. I was too set in my ways to share happily with a strange woman.

"Book it," I said, and started to hyperventilate.

On my way back home, I had to pull into a Starbuck's for a decaf latte to keep my hands from shaking.

Now all I had to do was to tell my children and Eli that Christmas as they knew it was off.

"Okay," Nathan said when I told him about the trip. "But I want quid pro quo."

"What sort?"

"Come to Lisa and me in Connecticut for Thanksgiving."

I did not want to spend Thanksgiving with Nathan's in-laws. I knew them only from the wedding. They seemed nice enough, but I had the feeling they felt Morgan and I didn't quite measure up to what they considered appropriate for their daughter's family.

I didn't really know Lisa, although she seemed very nice. She was a hotshot corporate attorney, beautiful, brilliant, and dressed like *Sex in the City*, whereas I wasn't certain who Manolo Blahnik was, exactly. To tell the truth, she intimidated me. "I couldn't possibly get a flight this late."

"Let me worry about that," Nathan said. "Come Monday and stay until Sunday."

"Fish and house guests go bad after three days."

"Mothers don't. You and Lisa need to get to know one another."

"Her family is eastern seaboard rich, Nathan. A pair of her shoes costs more than my entire wardrobe. Her mother wears sable."

"Then go buy some clothes. I'll pay for them."

"I can afford my own clothes, thank you. I tend to prefer L. L. Bean and Land's End to Bergdorf Goodman is all."

"You're a doctor. You don't have to live up to anybody else's opinion."

Well, of course I did. I wanted Nathan's in-laws to be delighted with me for his sake. There was an awkward silence, then I said, "Eli will barbecue me if I leave her to handle the practice alone over Thanksgiving."

"I'll talk to her. You'll be closed Thursday and Friday. Won't she be spending the weekend with Shep anyway?"

Damn. Trapped. "All right, but I arrive Tuesday and leave Saturday. Deal?"

"Deal. Oh, and Mother, think seriously about having Christmas the way we always do."

The minute I hung up from talking to Nathan, I called Patsy. "Did I or did I not say I'd get my own back on you for sticking me with Loba?"

"You did." Patsy sounded suspicious.

"How about we both drive down to Hernando and have lunch at Timbeau's on the square? They have great spinach salads."

I spent ten minutes hunting for a parking place on the square in Hernando. Court must be in session. The neo-Georgian courthouse in the center lorded over the steamboat gothic storefronts around the square in a sorry attempt to look as though it had been built before the War of Northern Aggression. In reality, I was almost certain General Grant burned its predecessor down on his way either to or from the Battle of Shiloh, I never could remember which.

Grant seemed to have a vendetta against Southern courthouses. Patsy, who was big into genealogy, said Grant's arson made tracing Mississippi family records in Grant's path before 1860 darned near impossible.

Over lunch I told Patsy about my trip to Connecticut for Thanksgiving with Nathan's in-laws. "I do not want to embarrass Nathan."

"Don't be ridiculous. You're a professional woman, a doctor, and a banker's wife. You act as though you are some country mouse who doesn't know which fork to use at dinner."

"The point is that down here everyone *does* know me. I *do* have a reputation. I am who I am, and if somebody doesn't like it, who cares? I haven't been shopping for anything other than jeans for two or three years. I like my lifestyle, but it's not the lifestyle that Nathan's parents-in-law live. Yes, I want to fit in—or at least not fit out. If that's stupid and shallow, then it is. I don't have the right clothes or the right jewelry. Lisa's people are Connecticut rich, Cape Cod rich."

"Well, I'm Mississippi rich and I think you look fine." Patsy speared a fat shrimp off the top of my salad.

"Hey, cut that out!" I leaned forward protectively. "Down here you can't tell country rich-rich from dirt poor without a program. Your Dan wears Wranglers, work boots, plaid shirts and a John Deere cap everywhere but to church."

"So do I." Patsy stuck out her left hand. "It's easier to tell about the wives." She waggled the six-carat diamond ring on her fourth finger. "Darned thing looks like a Zircon. I wear it out to impress my friends and when I go to New York or Paris or someplace. It's insured, but Dan would kill me if I dropped the thing in a bucket of horse liniment." She grinned. "Want to borrow it?"

"On me they *would* think it was a zircon. Ordinarily, I like what I look like—a hard-working, country vet."

"To tell the truth, you're downright dowdy. When was the last time you had your hair cut? You're gray as an old possum, too." Patsy forked half a piece of bacon into her mouth and eyed me. "Those hands look like you been digging ditches."

"That's a damned sight too much truth."

"I am telling the truth so you know what we got to fix before you go." Patsy buttered a piece of French bread. "We got two weeks before you fly to New York. That's plenty long enough. Let Patsy handle things."

"Patsy, don't go off half-cocked."

"Full-cocked, honey." She put down her fork and signaled to our waiter. "Dahlin', put these things in some take-out boxes, would you, please?"

"I'm not finished," I said.

"Yes, you are. You can have the rest of that for dinner tonight. Now, pay the check while I collect the takeout boxes. We'll drop your truck at the clinic and take my car to Memphis."

"Where?"

"Shut up and come. First we fix you, then we fix your clothes. Don't worry about jewelry, you can borrow mine. And my sable coat."

"I wouldn't dare be responsible for your jewelry, and I couldn't fit into your sable coat."

"Of course you can. It's cut long, and you're a whole heap thinner than I am."

After we dropped my truck, Patsy headed for Memphis. I had forgotten how harrowing driving with Patsy could be. Patsy could barely see over the steering wheel of her Suburban, and kept up a running commentary on what I should wear in Connecticut so I wouldn't look like a hick.

Patsy peeled off I-55 just past the turnoff to Graceland. As usual the parking lot was full of cars, and there was a line waiting in front of the wrought iron gates to the mansion. After Patsy managed to avoid hitting anyone running across the wide street, I finally felt safe opening my eyes.

Twenty minutes later, Patsy did a two wheel drift into the parking lot of Mona's Spa in East Memphis.

"I can't afford this place."

"My treat." Patsy trotted inside, closeted herself with Mona, the owner of the Spa, came out of her office to introduce her to me and give me the schedule of my appointments for the next two weeks, then dragged me out and shoved me into the car before I could say more than two words.

"I go there all the time," Patsy said. "You could certainly afford it once a month. You make plenty of money. What do you have to spend it on?"

"How much is all that going to cost?"

"Bad manners to ask. Next, hair. We may be able to take care of that today." She glanced at me. "God, I hope so. When was the last time you had a hair cut?"

"I've been letting it grow."

"Letting it go, you mean. Dragging it back from your face like that into a rubber band makes you look like an aging gay ballet master." She shook her head, sped across two lanes of traffic and turned left at a yellow light that turned red before her front bumper cleared the intersection.

I gasped. "That one was puce," I said.

"Nonsense. Pale lemon. Here we are." She pulled into the parking lot of a salon so chic even I recognized the name. "Come on."

"I should never have called you. You're on one of your darned crusades." By the time I got to the door of the salon, Patsy had already gone inside and closed the door in my face.

I went in after her.

"May I help you?" a stunningly beautiful brunette behind a tall reception counter asked.

"Uh, I'm with Mrs. Dalrymple."

"Oh, of course. She said to wait right here. Just have a seat."

I picked up a brand new copy of *Vogue* and perched on a faux French chair upholstered in Prussian blue watered silk. I spent the next ten minutes staring morosely at anorexic fourteen-year-old girls dressed in bizarre finery and made up to look fifty. "Here she is."

I looked up. Patsy stood in front of me with her hand outstretched as though pointing out a bloody wreck.

The tall young man beside Patsy was every bit as anorexic as the young women in *Vogue*. "My God," he said. He strode over to me and dug his fingers into my hair. He ripped off my rubber band.

"Ow."

"Oh, definitely color. All over. And short—tons and tons of layers." He stuck his index finger under my chin and lifted my face. "Wonderful cheekbones. Too much nose, of course, but that adds character. Amazingly unwrinkled for her age, wouldn't you say?"

I felt like somebody's prize heifer. Did the animals also understand the buyers who assessed their futures as beef or brood? I wanted to scream, "Not to the slaughterhouse!" I kept my mouth shut.

He drew back. "Come with me, sweetie. Patsy, darling, go away this minute and don't you dare come back for two hours."

"I'm going shopping for you, Maggie," Patsy said. "You can take everything home and try on there. See you." She disappeared.

"Young man," I said as he led me away, "I'm not your sweetie, nor are you mine. How about you try calling me 'Doctor?' It's never safe to antagonize a woman who uses a scalpel."

Three hours later I dropped Patsy's accumulation of shopping bags in my kitchen and walked over to the clinic. As I came down the hall, Tonesha looked up from her magazine and said, "Woo-eee! Look at you. You look hot!"

Eli and Wanda Jean stuck their heads out of contiguous examining rooms.

"My God," Eli said.

"Hey, great color," Wanda Jean said.

"The man practically shaved my head," I grumbled. "I look like a mahogany newel post."

"Ten years younger is how you look," Eli said. "Think he'd do mine?" She ruffled her curly silver hair.

"You dye your hair and I quit," Wanda Jean said.

"Me too," Tonesha said. "But you could do with a new cut. Yours is kind of old ladyish."

"Thank you so much," Eli said. "Call Patsy and ask her to make me an appointment, or he probably won't see me for six months."

"Done." Tonesha picked up the telephone. "Since we're spiffing up, how about we buy some new couches for the waiting room?"

Eli slammed the door on her and I scooted out the back.

# Chapter 44

## *In which Maggie discovers she's still got it*

I stepped off the plane at LaGuardia and made my way to the luggage area without seeing Nathan. I felt like an abandoned child. God, I hated cities, New York most of all, although after my Christmas tour, I might hate London worse.

I scanned the crowd until the maw of the luggage carousel disgorged my gigantic suitcase. Patsy had forced it on me because it was the largest Louis Vuitton made and could hold all the clothes Patsy had conned me into buying.

"I'm only staying Tuesday through Saturday," I had told her.

"You'll have to change at least twice a day and maybe more. Here, take my Judith Liebman evening bag." She produced a small apple covered with jet, and with a ruby clasp curled up like a worm.

"Patsy, that thing couldn't hold a handkerchief, and it's probably worth ten thousand dollars."

"A bit more, but who's counting. Now if you won't take my diamonds, take some of the good costume jewelry. See, these jade earrings will go perfectly with that green dress."

I put my foot down over the sable coat. I bought a new black cape, and wore my new red parka that I'd get a damn sight more wear out of in the coming years.

So here I stood in my parka and my new haircut, my semi-footlocker at my feet, and no sign of my son. I had no directions to his house in Connecticut, and it was too late in the afternoon to call his office. I dug out my cell phone to call him. He was probably stuck in traffic.

"Mother! Hell, I'm sorry. Got stuck in an accident. This your bag?

Come on. Before we get home it'll be time for dinner. Lisa's dying to see you."

I closed my eyes as I hugged him and drank in the smell of wet wool and after-shave. He felt so big. How could he be my baby?

We drove away in Nathan's gray BMW.

After I brought Nathan up to date on Eli and the people at home, Nathan asked, "Are you really planning on retiring? Totally, I mean?"

"Has to happen sooner or later. You don't approve?"

"It's your life, of course, but I don't think *Dad* would approve."

"Morgan is the very reason I'm getting out. We agreed that when he retired, I would, or at least cut back. I found a scrapbook..."

"Uh-oh. The scrapbook."

"You knew about it?"

"Sure. It's been a family joke for years."

"Nobody let me in on it."

"You shouldn't be in on it now. I should have taken it home with me after Dad died."

"Why? There's so much of Morgan in it."

"Too much."

"Nathan, why did nobody ever tell me how important it was to him to travel?"

"He wanted to show *you* the world, is how he used to put it. I don't think he cared so much for himself, but you're pretty insular, you know, Mother?"

I bristled. "I am not insular. I had eight years of college, buster, which is more than you have."

"I don't think looking down a microscope at bacteria is necessarily a culturally broadening experience."

I took a deep breath. "Okay. Maybe I am a little insular. That's why I plan to travel." I lapsed into silence against the plush leather seats. Several times Nathan started conversations. Several times I let them drop. We didn't seem to have much to say to one another.

Two hours after we left La Guardia, we turned off into a street of comfortable big houses with bigger lawns than I would have thought feasible this close to the city.

"Here we are," Nathan said. "Home at last." He turned into the driveway of a mock Tudor house that looked more real than mock. It was also a bit larger and a heck of lot more imposing than my little two story Georgian.

"My goodness," I said. "You are doing well."

"We both are." He pulled around the back of the house into a triple garage and shut off the engine.

Lisa met me in the kitchen with an air kiss, and a "Welcome, Mother McLain."

"Lisa, honey, please don't keep calling me Mother McLain. It sounds like a cure for piles. Call me plain Maggie."

Lisa blinked, uncertain whether to laugh. "I'll try, Mo—Maggie."

She led the way through a thoroughly decorated house, emphasis on 'decorated.' I didn't see one rocking chair or one sit-around that might have been inherited from Old Aunt Hattie. Maybe Lisa didn't trust her taste.

Upstairs, however, the decor was more relaxed, as though Nathan and Lisa had spent all their money on the public rooms. My bedroom held a king-sized bed and had its own palatial bathroom with separate tub and shower.

The toilet was shut away in its own tiny room so small I doubted I could turn around to flush the thing.

"Now, this is your closet," Lisa said, opening the door to a closet half the size of my bedroom at home and fitted with the latest in designer closet furnishings. "I know you must be tired. If you'd like to unpack later, we could have dinner now."

"Fine," I said. I shucked my parka. Thanks to Patsy, I wore well cut navy slacks, a navy sweater from J. Crew, and real flats, not boots or sneakers.

The dinner consisted largely of dishes that had probably been prepared by the nearest gourmet grocery. "I'm afraid I'm not much of a cook," Lisa said. "We both work so late, mostly we just eat take-out." Now that I could understand.

"Morgan and I did the same thing when we were getting started," I said. I drank water, although I would cheerfully have killed for some iced tea. "How about I make us some iced tea?"

"Oh, I didn't think—I mean, we don't drink iced tea except in the summertime." Bless her, Lisa was as uncomfortable as I was.

Nathan and Lisa drank wine. Over a very nice chocolate mousse, I said, "I expected a Golden Retriever, or at least a Siamese cat."

Nathan said, "We're home so seldom it really wouldn't be fair to have a cat or a dog."

Another familiar echo. Morgan and I hadn't acquired our own pets until McLain-Scheibler was in its first brick building. "How about a gerbil?"

Nathan laughed. After a moment, so did Lisa.

"When we have time and children, I promise you at least one Golden Retriever," Nathan said.

"If I have to make a choice, I'll take the grandchildren. But I'd rather not deliver them." I segued into the story of young Meg's birth on the Fourth of July.

Nathan said over decaf mocha latte, "You're on your own tomorrow. We both have to work, unfortunately. I tried to take off, but no such luck. We thought you might like to ride into the city for the day. It's an easy train trip. I'll leave you the BMW and directions to the train station. We thought you'd probably like to do some Christmas shopping? Maybe hit the Metropolitan Museum? Tomorrow night it's just us. There's a little Greek restaurant about two miles from here—great souvlakia."

"Sounds lovely," I said and tried to remember the last time I'd had souvlakia.

"Then Thursday we're having Thanksgiving dinner with Mother and Father," Lisa said. "Very informal."

"Friday you're on your own again, I'm afraid," Nathan said. "Although I'll be home early. We've got a big do on Friday night at the Club."

"I'm happy to look after myself Friday night," I said. "Don't worry about me."

"Oh, no, Moth—uh, Maggie! You have to come. Nathan's getting an award. He solicited the most sponsorships for the golf tourney. It's a big honor."

"What's the dress code? Short or long?"

"Why, either one I suppose. Dressy." She blushed. She really was a pretty girl. And a nice one, maybe, if I got to know her better. "Of course, if you didn't bring anything…"

"I'll manage. Thanks to Patsy Dalrymple, I brought enough clothes to stay for a month." Lisa raised her eyebrows and I laughed. "I promise I won't."

"I didn't mean…"

"I know you didn't. Hey, it's okay. I'm really looking forward to a couple of days in New York on my own. I might even check that place Patsy told me about in Times Square where you can get cheap tickets. Maybe see a matinee."

Lisa let out her breath. "I told Nathan you'd enjoy yourself. He was afraid you'd just stay here and mope."

"Nope. No mope I."

"You don't leave until two Saturday afternoon," Nathan said. "So Saturday it's just you and me. Lisa's busy. Besides, I wanted some time for just the two of us."

Wednesday morning I dutifully drove the BMW to the train station, picked up a schedule so that I wouldn't miss the train back, and rode into the city. Nathan had left me an excellent city map.

The air was cold but clear. I was toasty in my parka and gloves until I walked into Bloomingdales and began to sweat, but whether from the heat of the store or the crush of so many people I had no idea. I bought Eli a new black leather handbag, and Sarah a pair of gold earrings and a cashmere sweater. I had both sent to Memphis.

I fought my way deep into FAO Schwarz until I found a wonderful stuffed cow half the size of a newborn calf. Perfect for little Meg's first Christmas, although she wouldn't be able to enjoy it for months. I had it sent home as well. Getting on an airplane was bad enough without Christmas packages to be opened and inspected.

I walked up Fifth Avenue, spent an hour wandering through the Metropolitan and ate lunch in the courtyard there, then wandered up to the Central Park Zoo. Although the town teamed with tourists in town to watch the Thanksgiving's Day parade, the cold had kept most casual sightseers away from the zoo. I wandered among the animals happily and struck up conversations with the keepers, who were happy to stop working to talk to me.

I sank onto a bench outside the big cat enclosure. This should have been a wonderful day. New York at Christmas!

But without my arm tucked through Morgan's as we strolled, I felt as though I were doing chores, and not pleasant ones either. Having Morgan beside me, turning to him to point out something funny or beautiful or interesting made even the most mundane excursions happy ones.

What on earth made me think I'd enjoy traveling alone? Did I have some crazy idea that Morgan's ghost would be looking over my shoulder commenting on the Mona Lisa or the Pyramids? Hell, I'd given an entirely new meaning to the term *guilt trip*. *Face it, Maggie, you're alone. Morgan is dead. Not passed away, not transported to a higher plain. Dead.*

I thought I'd been handling my life extremely well under the circumstances. Bull hockey. I'd been marking time, waffling, wallowing in self-pity. Morgan would have been ashamed of me. Whatever life had in store for me from here on in, it was time I got on with it. That would truly honor his memory.

I plunged back into the crowds to catch the train back to Nathan's in time for a long nap and a hot bath.

The three of us ate a heavy Greek meal, listened to a bouzouki band and watched belli dancers until ten-thirty. The meal was wonderful, the band was great fun, and the dancers were stunning. They had the added attraction of being so loud that conversation was next to impossible.

Thanksgiving I put on the green wool dress that fit me beautifully, although it looked as though it had only two seams. Patsy said that was the mark of an expensive dress, which this one definitely was.

When I came downstairs, Nathan said, "Mother, you look great."

I sat in the back of the BMW on the forty-minute drive to the Bigelow house where Lisa's parents lived. When we rolled in through the gates and up to the house, I saw where Lisa's taste had come from. This house looked like the Tower of London and was about the same size. The whole neighborhood oozed wealth. I doubted one full-time gardener could keep up with the manicured grounds.

In my years as a veterinarian, I had learned that the woman in dirty jeans braiding the mane and tail of a junior jumper gelding at five thirty in the morning might well be the wife of a Fortune Five Hundred CEO. Wealth as such didn't intimidate me.

But second generation Connecticut money was different from Delta money. These people would probably find Patsy Dalrymple crass and loud, although she was probably richer than they were. They cared about the way things—and people—looked to others. Patsy didn't give a damn.

I swore to remember Patsy's admonishment. "Speak when you're spoken to, stick to the weather, and try not to sound like a yaller dog democrat. Those folks are probably so republican you'd start a riot."

My heart sank when I saw at least a dozen cars—Rolls, Mercedes, Jaguars, and the occasional lowly Cadillac, pulled up in the Bigelow's graveled forecourt.

"Nathan, I thought it was just us," I whispered as we walked up the broad stone steps. "Why didn't you warn me?"

"Because I didn't know. Put on your corporate face, Mother. You did this for years with Daddy. Why do you act as though you've never done it before?"

"Not with your in-laws I haven't. The only time I met them was at the wedding."

I tried to grasp the names as I grasped the hands of the other guests. Most were my age, with the exception of a couple of sulky teenagers who would no doubt prefer to be anywhere else and were some sort of cousins to Lisa.

I watched them evaporate across the broad hall into another room and shut the door behind them. "Video games," Nathan whispered.

"We've all been dying to meet Nathan's mother," said a woman who looked as though she'd been stuck in a wind tunnel and had barely escaped with her life. She was bone thin, and her unlikely champagne hair was teased far back from her lineless forehead to complete the wind tunnel effect.

"Botox," Lisa whispered as the woman turned away. "Takes away the lines, but paralyzes your eyebrows."

I accepted a fragile glass of sherry. No doubt it was superb sherry, but it puckered my mouth.

"Tastes like battery acid," said a male voice behind me.

I turned to meet the black eyes of a very tall, very thin man with a shock of white hair and the leathery skin of an outdoorsman. He wore a navy blazer and gray flannel slacks, neither of which he had bought off anybody's peg.

"I don't think we're supposed to think that," I said.

"Nuts. Give me a Heineken any day."

"I'm a Diet Coke girl myself."

"You're Lisa's mother-in-law?"

"Maggie McLain." I stuck out my hand. He shook it and held on a tad too long.

"I'm Jack Ashton. I'm her uncle on her mother's side. I didn't make it to the wedding. I was out of the country."

"Nice to meet you."

"How'd you get roped into this funeral? These parties are always incredibly stuffy."

"As you say, I'm Lisa's mother-in-law, and I'm visiting. Couldn't very well leave me home."

"When do you leave?"

I laughed. "Isn't that the question you're not supposed to ask guests?"

"If it is, it's stupid. You stuck with that thing at the club tomorrow night?"

"For my sins."

"Too right."

"That's an Australian expression, isn't it?"

"I sailed in New Zealand some."

"A sailor?"

"In my younger days. Now I gunk hole on the occasional Saturday when there's not enough wind to turn over in."

"I've never been on a sailboat, and certainly not in the Atlantic Ocean. It sounds wonderful."

"Come back in the summer and I'll take you out for a weekend."

I started to say I worked all summer, but then I stopped. Maybe I wouldn't be working this coming summer. I'd be free to go sailing with this man if he were serious. A weekend? In today's mores among people like this, what would I be letting myself in for? Did he mean simply sailing or something else? When I dated before I married Morgan, the guys always *tried* to get you in bed, but they never actually *expected* you to go. Casual sex is an oxymoron in my book. The whole idea of dealing with the man-woman dynamic after all my years of monogamy scared me pea-green.

"Down south we say 'y'all come see us.'" I said with what I hoped was a sophisticated smile. "We generally don't mean it."

"Up east I say 'I'll take you sailing' and mean it."

I felt a hand on my arm. "Dr. McLain, Nathan says you're a veterinarian."

I nodded and looked into the anxious eyes (and immobile eyebrows) of the woman with the champagne hair.

"Oh, that is so marvelous." Her hand was tipped with coral talons that I could swear were the color I'd refused. "I just have to talk to you." She drew me away adroitly and lowered her voice.

"It's about Glenda of O'Maugh." Her voice dropped to a whisper. "When I tried to breed her, they told me she goes—you know—crosswise." She made a crosswise sawing motion with her hand. "And now she's out of season."

I took a deep breath. "Who is Glenda?"

"Oh, so silly of me. Glenda's a Glen of Imaal terrier. They're very rare in this country."

"I've never seen one, but I know what they are. They used to turn the spits in the Irish pubs, didn't they?"

The woman nearly shivered with delight. "Yes, that's it." She dropped her voice again. "And Glenda's—you know—doesn't go straight up and down from her little bottom, it's crosswise. We own the male too. We left them together and they tried, but the male couldn't—you know—get in, and it hurt poor Glenda terribly. She cried and cried."

"And now she's out of season."

"Yes. Is there an operation to—you know—straighten her out?"

"You'd have to ask your own doctor, Mrs. uh, but I doubt you'd have to go that far. You can have her artificially inseminated the next time she comes into season. The pups may have to be taken by Cesarean section, but then again, she may whelp without a bit of trouble. That's not an uncommon difficulty with some of the smaller dogs like Corgis."

"Oh, you are wonderful!" The lady trilled. "Niles, Niles, darling! Come over here. Dr. McLain says we don't have to have Glenda straightened out, we can just artificially inseminate her."

Every one in the room turned to stare.

Two minutes later I was the center of the party.

"Dr. McLain," said a florid man in an extraordinary maroon jacket and regimental tie, "I've had my Bouvier's ears clipped, but one of them refuses to stand up. We've tried taping and shots and vitamins. My vet's given up hope. You have any suggestions?"

I told him the British no longer allow cropped ears. More and more Americans were leaving ears natural even on Dobermans. "You might consider getting the other one to flop. Then at least they'd match."

"I could still show at Crufts," he said, and laughed.

"I don't see how magnets can have any effect whatever on a pulled suspensory ligament," said a tall woman—they were all thin—with sun-roughened skin that spoke of too many hours in the hunt field. "He's an Irish Draft-thoroughbred cross gelding," she said. "My vet wants me to buy this horrendously expensive magnetic machine thingy to use on his leg. How can it be strong enough?"

"There have been anecdotal successes," I said. "But if it really is a torn suspensory, I'd suggest sending him to Cornell or Rude and Riddle in Lexington, Kentucky. They do miracles. Listen, I really shouldn't be diagnosing another doctor's patient. Talk to your own vet, please."

"I will, and thank you so much."

I was discussing a case of recurring cystitis in a year-old male Siamese cat when the butler announced from the far end of the room,

"Dinner is served."

"Thank God," I whispered. I hadn't realized Jack Ashton had been watching me. Now he swooped down and captured my arm. "Need a bodyguard?"

"Do I ever." Not Morgan's arm. Oh, how I wished he'd been here. He'd have laughed his head off at me and my impromptu consulting practice.

"I had Lisa move the place cards. You're between Colonel Mendoza and me. He's deaf, never says a word to his dinner companions. And he doesn't own a dog."

"Bless you," I said. "I feel like the urologist who went to a cocktail party and wound up discussing prostates with every male in the room."

I fell asleep in the car driving home, and only woke when Nathan woke me.

"Upsy-daisy," he said as he opened my door.

I stretched and touched his cheek. "I used to have to wake you up and carry you upstairs, remember?"

"Now it's my turn."

"If you don't mind," I said as I dragged up the stairs, "I think I'll sleep in and mooch around here tomorrow rather than going into the city."

"Won't you be bored?" Lisa asked.

I shook my head. "Not for a minute."

The following evening after a day spent blissfully reading a murder mystery I found on the bookshelf in my room, I slipped into my black cocktail dress, closed the clasp on Patsy's ten thousand dollar evening bag, and tried a few steps in Patsy's strappy Jimmy Choo sandals.

"Thank the Lord I've got these big ole peasant feet," Patsy had said. "These things cost as much as a pair of handmade riding boots, and they've got no more leather in them than a set of reins."

I swung my black cape over my arm and walked downstairs.

"Mom, you look spectacular," Nathan said.

I blinked back tears. He hadn't called me Mom since he went away to college at seventeen and turned me from Mom into Mother.

"Lisa's the spectacular one," I said. She wore a strapless red silk satin cocktail dress and had tossed her hair casually up. I assumed the diamond studs in her ears were real. She looked like a rich young up and comer's rich young up and coming wife.

"You're not so bad yourself," Lisa said, as she straightened her husband's black tie and patted his satin lapel.

"I'll bring the car around to the front," Nathan said as he walked back through the kitchen.

"You really do look stunning," Lisa said. "I —" she took a deep breath. "I've been terrified of your visit."

"Me, too," I said. "Afraid I'd be a pain?"

Lisa's eyes grew wide. "Oh, no! What you do is so important, and Nathan looks up to you. I feel like such a schlump when you're around."

"Whatever for?"

"You're so good with people, for one thing. I mean, you had all those stuffy old fogies eating out of your hand yesterday. Even the colonel said you were a 'fine figure of a woman.'" She laughed. "All I do is write up corporate contracts. What's that in the scheme of things? I'm always so uptight for fear I'll screw up, and you're so sure of yourself and so easy-going. You've intimidated me from the first moment I met you."

I threw back my head and laughed. "I'm terrible with people, Lisa. I've been scared to death I'd do something to make you and Nathan ashamed of me. Believe me, you do not know from intimidated."

"You're just saying that."

"The hell I am." The horn honked. "Come on, Lisa. Let's go knock 'em dead."

After the dinner and the awards, Nathan asked me to dance. "I don't dance very often, you know, son," I said. "Not at all since your father died."

He took my hand and dragged me to the dance floor. As they began to move, he whispered in my ear, "Then you need to start dancing again. You haven't called me 'son' since I left for college."

"You grew up. Remember, you wanted me to call you Nathan. That's when you stopped calling me Mom. I like Lisa, Nathan. I wasn't certain until this visit, but I am now."

"Good, because she likes you. You intimidate her."

"God knows why."

"You intimidate most people."

"Not your father."

"No, he was proud of you."

"I haven't been the best wife and mother."

Nathan drew back and looked down into my eyes. "Where'd you get that idea?"

"I was always somewhere else."

"Yeah. Making a living, saving lives—that kind of unimportant stuff. Dad was there when you weren't. Your 'tag-team' parenting worked pretty darned well. Dad was almost the only father we knew who actually spent time with his children. Half the guys were either divorced and saw their kids for a couple of hours on the weekend, or spent every waking minute locked in their offices or traveling. When you'd have to go out on a call at night, we called him DOD—Daddy-on-Duty."

"How come I never knew that?"

"It was our secret." He sighed deeply. "He was so proud of what you do. He bragged on you whenever your back was turned."

I laughed, although I knew both Nathan and I were on the verge of tears.

"May I cut in?" Jack Ashton slipped his arm around my waist.

I stiffened. "This is the first time I've danced in years, and then I danced with my husband. He made me look good."

"Relax. I have no intention of ravishing you right here on the dance floor."

I felt my cheeks flush. "Don't try. I know self-defense."

"I'll bet you do. When can we go sailing?"

"It's winter. An open sailboat…"

"Not exactly open. She's a forty-six foot C and C out of Kennebunkport."

"Oh. Wow. That's not a boat, it's a ship."

"Technically, she's still a boat. How about Christmas? We wouldn't even have to set sail. Just sit in the harbor and listen to the burblers keeping the ice at bay."

"I'll be in London at Christmas."

"London, England? For God's sake, why?"

"I'm taking a tour." At this point I wasn't sure I wanted to go through with the trip, but I was stuck with it.

He laughed. "London at Christmas? That is no way to travel. Listen, if you want to go somewhere, let me take you to Africa."

"You've been to Africa? Where?" I asked eagerly. "The big preserves? Olduvai? Ngorongoro? The Serengeti? All those places I see on NOVA?"

"All of the above. Plus the Okavanga Delta and South Africa."

"I've always wanted to go to Africa," I said. "It's too expensive. We never could afford it. I'd love to hear about your trips."

"Look here, let me help you plan a trip this spring."

"I couldn't..." Then I stopped. Why couldn't I? Why not spend just a little more money than seeing that damn Mona Lisa on seeing something I truly *did* want to see? If I could convince Eli to go along, I'd have somebody to enjoy the trip with. It wouldn't be Morgan, but it would be a friend.

"Think about it," he said, as he whirled me away in a waltz.

I would, but not about going with Jack Ashton. My word, I wasn't ready for that. I might never be ready for that. In my mind, I was still married to Morgan.

That night I thought of what Jack Ashton had said. Was going to London at Christmas truly nuts?

The following morning, I packed, stripped my bed, dragged my suitcase to the kitchen, and made certain I hadn't left anything of value, including Patsy's purse.

I was finishing the comic section of the paper when Nathan walked in. He was wearing jeans and a ski sweater.

"Hey, I was going to bring that thing downstairs for you," he said.

"I have a regular chiropractor's appointment. You probably don't."

"I'm driving you into the country for breakfast. This is the busiest shopping day of the year, so no way are we going near Manhattan."

"Is Lisa coming?" Nathan had said we were to have the morning together, but after my rapprochement with Lisa, I thought she might have changed her mind.

"This is Nathan's day," Lisa said. She looked as though she'd barely waked up, and still wore robe and slippers. Her hair was uncombed, and her face devoid of makeup. For the first time, she seemed vulnerable, a kid. One of *my* kids.

She came to me and hugged me. "Please come back. Next time maybe you and I can do some things in the city, see a couple of plays."

"I'd like to come back."

"Uncle Jack would like it too." Lisa laughed. "He's smitten."

"He's very nice, but let him know it's too soon for me."

"Divorced twenty years ago. No children. Semi-retired. Let me know when you're ready and I'll give him a heads-up."

After goodbyes, a drive through the crisp winter morning, and a big breakfast at a log inn, Nathan turned the BMW toward the city.

"We'll go the long way," he said. "We'll be seeing you again in a month, remember?"

I took a deep breath. "I don't know how long I'll be here between planes. You don't really have to come see me."

"On your way to London?"

"Right."

Nathan pulled off onto a lay-by, cut his engine and turned to me.

"As to that…"

"Uh-oh."

"I know this is your first Christmas since Dad died."

"And the first since I found that scrapbook."

Nathan rolled his eyes.

"Just listen," I said. "It's time your generation started your own traditions. My London trip gets me out of the house at Christmastime, and lets you off the hook."

"You're assuming we want to be off the hook."

"You can have your own tree, dinner with the Bigelows, even go skiing or whatever people do up here in the frozen north. All without worrying about your poor old gray-haired mother pining away by herself in Tennessee." I spread my hand. "Perfect, no?"

"No." He took my shoulders. "You cannot do it. I will not allow it."

"Nathan, let go of me. Since when do you allow me to do—or not do—anything?"

"Mother, you are being a—I don't know—a twerp! The only place I want to be this Christmas is in Tennessee at my own home place with what's left of my family. I do not want to go skiing, and I sure as hell don't want to spend Christmas day with the Bigelows who have more stuffing in them than Eli's turkey." He slapped the steering wheel. "I can't believe Eli is letting you do this. She'll be stuck with the practice for the entire time you're gone."

"She's not *letting* me do anything, Nathan. She's being very accommodating. I've got Vickie Anderson to cover for me while I'm gone. She's probably going to take over my half of the partnership sometime next year."

"No way. It ain't happening. For God's sake, Mom. For a bright woman, sometimes you can be so dumb I want to sock some sense into you. Dad wanted the *two* of you to do those things."

"That would be my choice too, but it's not possible. Nathan, don't you see? I've got to break some old patterns while I still can? The life Morgan and I had was the only life I ever wanted or ever expected. Since he died I've been floundering. Maybe I'll decide to come home, settle down in the same place and do the same job, but maybe I won't. I have to find out, can't you see that?"

"Okay. Travel. Semi-retire. You and Eli go kicking off someplace fun next spring or summer, by all means. But not this Christmas." He started the car, looked out the driver's side, and melded into traffic without another word.

After ten minutes, I ventured, "You really want to come home for Christmas? You and Lisa?"

He snorted. "What have I been saying?"

We didn't speak while I checked in, nor until there was a single person in front of me at the security gate. Then I said, "Okay. You win."

"Thank God," he said. He hugged me and kissed me. I clung to him until the security guard said, "Lady? We got a line here."

"You may not be able to get tickets," I said as I passed through the metal detector.

"We've already got 'em." He waved me out of sight.

Twenty minutes later as the plane circled La Guardia and banked to the west, I said out loud, "Oh, God, what do I tell that poor travel agent?"

# Chapter 45

## *In which Christmas is back on*

The first thing I saw when I arrived home Saturday night was the frantically blinking light on my answering machine.

"Oh, please, Lord, not now," I said. I longed to ignore the calls, but when I saw that there were a dozen of them, I decided I'd better be responsible and listen to them, even though I wasn't due back on duty until Monday.

I dragged Patsy's Louis Vuitton suitcase up the stairs and into my bedroom, then I sank onto the bed where Teesy, Bear and Bok Choy were keeping vigil for me.

After twenty minutes of cuddling they settled down. I picked up the telephone to listen to my messages.

The first message was from Lisa, saying how much she'd enjoyed my visit.

Ditto from Nathan.

The surprising one came from Jack Ashton. "I know you said Southerners don't mean their invitations, but I'm ignoring that. Does 'y'all come' extend to lonely sailors from Maine?"

Oh, good grief! No, I had already explained to him that Southerners never meant it when they said *y'all come,* nor was I interested in joining him in the middle of the Atlantic Ocean.

The next call was from Sarah. At the same time I'd talked to Nathan, I'd put a message on her answering machine saying I wouldn't be home for Christmas. I'd hoped to intercept it before she got back from the far east and heard it. No such luck.

"Please Mom, say you're not planning on spending Christmas in London. I want to come home. I know Nathan does too. You don't have to do anything—no tree, no decorations, no Christmas Eve party. We want to be with you this year of all years."

Whoa! Had somebody replaced my daughter with Stepford Sarah?

Next call. "Mother, please call me. Where are you? I know you haven't left for London yet."

I erased Sarah's other calls without listening to them and called Sarah at home. "Sarah?"

"Mother, where have you been? "

I started to tell her about Christmas, but she interrupted. "You just can't go to London for Christmas this year."

"If you'd listen a minute, I've cancelled my trip. Christmas is on as usual."

"Thank God. I meant it about not doing anything about the house or the food. We'll do it all when we get there."

I assumed she meant Nathan and Lisa too. Then she said, "Maybe this isn't the right time, but could I—I mean, I want to bring somebody with me."

That had never happened. "Man or woman?"

"Man." Sarah's voice had taken on an uncharacteristic softness. "His name is Evan Stornberger. He's the second unit assistant director on the Thailand picture."

"You met in the jungle?"

"In the hotel bar, actually. I want to introduce him to all of you."

"Is this serious?"

She actually *giggled*. My Sarah.

"Then of course he must come. Small problem. I still haven't cleaned out your father's office, so you'll have to use the downstairs guestroom. I'll ask Eli if he can stay with her."

"It's not like we haven't, I mean..."

"Not here, kiddo."

I heard a baritone whisper in the background.

"All right. Eli's house."

"Is he there? May I speak to him?"

"Dr. McLain? This is Evan Stornberger. If it will be an imposition for me to come at Christmas..." He had a pleasant light baritone voice with no accent at all. That probably meant he was from the mid-west.

"We'll be delighted to have you. There's plenty of room. Plenty of chaos as well. Does chaos bother you?"

"I have four brothers and sisters. Chaos is my middle name. Here's Sarah again."

"Can you pick us up at the airport or should we rent a car?"

"Somebody will pick you up—me or Eli or Nathan. Let me know when you're arriving. We'll worry about cars when you get here, okay?"

"Thanks." I think she started to hang up. I certainly did, but with the phone halfway to the cradle, I heard her say, "Oh, Mother?"

"Yes?"

"I've missed you."

After we hung up I sat for a long time at the kitchen table just scratching Bear's ears.

Sarah bringing a man to Christmas? A Hollywood type? Was he responsible for the new kinder, gentler Sarah?

More times than I can remember, I'd wished I could kick my grown daughter out of the den the way a mother bear did and forget her. Bears didn't even recognize their offspring after they turned five, but Sarah and Nathan would be my babies so long as they lived. Every triumph would be my triumph, every hurt would be my hurt.

Maybe Sarah was finally growing up.

As soon as her office opened the next morning, I called Olivia Overton, the travel agent, sent her a check for my cancellation fee for the London trip, apologized for doing it to her again, and promised that I would indeed book some more trips with her in future.

I don't think she believed me.

# Chapter 46

## *In which Loba has pups*

"Thank God you've come to your senses," Eli said. "The very idea of flying to London, like as not through a blizzard, then freezing your buns off just to shop at Harrod's." She filled my soup bowl with another ladle of vegetable soup. "Here, have some more baguette. It'll be dry as a bone tomorrow morning. We have to finish it."

"I want to do Christmas as usual."

"You sure about that?"

"Absolutely. Christmas is the time for friends and family, even if this year there's one less family member. We can hoist a glass of champagne to Morgan."

"If you say so, but don't knock yourself out. Shep can come down from Pickwick and do some work for a change. The least the man can do is hang the lights on the Christmas tree. What about the Christmas Eve dinner? Want to move it to my house?"

"Christmas is on Friday, so Nathan and Lisa are coming Wednesday night. I haven't heard from Sarah and her new boyfriend yet, but they'll have to be in by Thursday evening, possibly even before Nathan and Lisa. I hadn't told Maggie's Militia the Christmas Eve party was off yet, so I suppose everybody's still planning to come. I'll call and make sure. You're positive it's all right for Sarah's boyfriend to use your guest room?"

"As long as he doesn't mind my flagrant cohabitation with Shep."

"This Evan and Sarah would probably prefer flagrant cohabitation in the guest room. I'm sure they're sleeping together, but with Nathan and Lisa across the hall, another happy couple making love downstairs would probably leave me suicidal."

Eli picked up my nearly empty soup bowl, took it to the corner, and set it down on the floor. Sugar Pie, who had been lying quietly on her feet, bounded over and began slurping the dregs.

"Did you even ask if I was finished?" I said.

"Were you planning to lick the bowl?"

"Sugar Pie can do that."

"Besides, you have to save room for brownies," she said and pulled a pan out of the oven. "Still warm."

They were wonderful—nearly like fudge and filled with pecans. I was reaching for my second square when Eli asked, "What do you want to do about Christmas breakfast?"

"There's where I draw the line. They can go out to MacDonald's for all I care. I'll have the makings for breakfast, but I'm damned if I'll get up and fix a fancy meal Christmas morning. I've always hated doing it, and this year I refuse."

"Okay, okay. You do exert your independence over the oddest things, Maggie."

Except for the presents I bought in New York and shipped home, I bought all my presents on line and avoided shopping. I stayed busy nonetheless.

I vaccinated all Patsy's horses, drew new Coggins tests to make certain they were negative for Equine Infectious Anemia, and wormed them. I did the same at Nell and Bernadette's barns, plus kept my share of office hours to handle the small animals.

I was floundering in routine, routine, routine. It was always like this in December and January, but this year the days dragged by. The weather was wet and dreary, never quite cold enough to freeze the drizzle into black ice on the roads, but the sort of interminably gray dankness that settled into my bones and my soul like a pall of dead roses.

The nights were also interminable. I vacuumed the guestroom at two in the morning and relined several kitchen cabinets with fancy vinyl shelf paper. I ran all the television sets all over the house to keep me company. Anything to avoid the silence.

I let the answering machine pick up my calls at home. The Monday before Christmas, the phone rang, and I heard a voice say,

"Maggie? It's Nels Olafson."

I grabbed the phone. "Nels? Is anything wrong with Loba?"

He laughed. "She and her three pups are fine."

"She had puppies?"

"Last night. Couple of days early. Thought you'd like to know."

"Is she all right? How was the labor? What sexes are they?"

"Whoa! She's fine. They're fine, two boys and a girl, one gray, the other two probably black. She's denned up, but she seems to be caring for them beautifully. We're leaving her alone as much as we can."

"I'm so glad. Thanks for calling me."

"We thought we'd name the little girl Maggie. Merry Christmas. Got to go."

I said to my three cats, "Even a wolf can make a new life. How come I seem incapable of it?""

# Chapter 47

## *In which Mariah needs surgery*

Five days before Christmas, my private line rang at two a.m. I was scrubbing the ovens in the kitchen. When the answering machine picked up, I heard Patsy's voice.

"Maggie, pick up. Now."

"Patsy?"

"Maggie, Mariah's colicking. Bad. We've tubed her and filled her full of mineral oil and walked her. I think she needs surgery. It could be a flipped gut. She's not a young mare."

I sat down hard at her kitchen table. "Can you make it to Mississippi State? They're the closest vet school."

"Can't you do the surgery?"

"I can if I have to. If you are afraid to risk the trip, Eli and I can call Wanda Jean at home and do the surgery tonight. But if you think you can get her there, go. Let them do the surgery. They have more doctors on staff and better recovery facilities. As you say, she's not a young mare."

"You don't mind?"

"Mind? This is a horse's life we're talking about, Patsy. Of course I don't mind. Call them right this minute, get her loaded into your trailer, and drive like hell."

"Thanks, Maggie."

"Call me and let me know how she is." Doubts struck even as I hung up the phone

Had I done the right thing? What if the mare was too bad to endure the four-hour drive to the vet school? Could I have done the surgery?

Then Susan's shining face flashed into my consciousness. If anything happened to Mariah, Susan would be devastated. She deserved the best chance.

Churning with leftover adrenaline and wide-awake, I set up the stepladder beside the naked Scotch pine I'd bought that afternoon and unpacked the Christmas lights. The previous Christmas Morgan had meticulously replaced each light in its separate slot in the original cardboard box from which the string had come. I sank down on the sofa and simply stared at them. I'd never put a light on any of our Christmas trees, including the first one. That had been Morgan's job.

Almost every day I discovered more evidence of his care for us all. When he was alive, he and I didn't often see one another or talk on the telephone during the day. We were both working. Sometimes we didn't see one another at all until I fell into bed. He'd been dead nearly a year now, and so long as I kept doing my job I could almost convince myself that everything was the same, that he'd be there when I crawled into bed.

Then I'd discover something like the Christmas tree lights and I'd feel as though I'd been kicked in the stomach. My sense of loss seemed to grow with each new discovery of his small kindnesses.

I don't know how long I held the boxes of lights on my lap before I stood up and began to unwind them. *Get on with it, Maggie. Getting on is what you do, as Eli said so many years ago.*

The lights would never be put away neatly again. I didn't have the patience. Morgan used to watch me fiddle with them and fume, then he'd take them away from me, kiss me on the forehead and do them himself.

I shut the cats into the utility room, ignored their plaints, and climbed the ladder with the first string. From here on in, the tree was my sole responsibility. I had to find a way not to hate doing it.

I found *Holiday Inn* on one of the old movie channels, turned the volume up too loud and sang along. Morgan used to say my voice could single-handedly destroy Karaoke, but tonight I wanted the noise.

"Might as well put on a few ornaments," I said. They, too, were immaculately arranged, from the cracked sand ornaments the children had made in kindergarten to the ornate German glass ornaments that Morgan had begun to collect fifteen years ago. I do not believe in ghosts or visitations, but that night I felt as though Morgan were looking over my shoulder, shaking his head whenever I put two red balls too close together.

By the time I festooned the last curl of red brocade ribbon down the side of the tree, my shoulders screamed, but my spirits were higher. I climbed down from the ladder, turned on the lights and sat on the sofa to contemplate the tree. "Not bad," I said.

The room was a wreck. Boxes lay on chairs and sofa, floor and coffee table. Everything would have to be cleared away before I picked up Sarah and Evan.

I glanced at the telephone. Patsy should be pulling into Starkville right about now if she drove as fast as she normally did. Pray God Mariah had survived the trip and would survive the surgery.

For Susan's sake, for Patsy's sake.

And for my sake.

I stood close to the exit gate at the airport trying to catch a glimpse of Sarah's dark gold hair. I saw a gloved hand waving from the back of a group of what must be Japanese tourists waving Graceland banners.

"Mother!" The voice was certainly Sarah's. I stepped forward with my arms open.

Sarah both hugged me and actually made physical contact with my cheek. When I stepped back I saw that she was glowing. "Mother, this is Evan Stornberger. Evan, my mother."

"Dr. McLain."

"Maggie, please." I had been trying to picture an assistant second unit director with no success. I had finally settled on scruffy and artsy.

I'd been wrong. Evan Stornberger wasn't handsome, but he had a craggy face with broad cheekbones and piercing blue eyes. His tan might originate in a tanning booth in Beverly Hills, but it might be from the actual jungle.

He wore a well-trimmed dark beard streaked gray at the corners of his mouth and short hair that looked as though it might be receding from a broad forehead.

Sarah would be thirty on Christmas. Evan Stornberger must be at least ten years older. He was taller than Nathan, and where Nathan had inherited his father's chunky build, this man was beanpole thin, but moved with the muscular grace of a runner or a swimmer.

Both Sarah and Evan wore starched jeans, turtleneck sweaters, and navy blue blazers. Evan caught my glance at his clothes and smiled. It was a good smile, I decided, open and not condescending. "We're not planning to put on a vaudeville act, Dr. McLain. The outfits are sheer accident."

"Maggie. Dr. McLain makes me feel a hundred."

"Will do." He guided Sarah toward the escalator with a hand in the middle of her back. Both Sarah and Evan had checked immense leather duffel bags stuffed to capacity. There was also a large cardboard box that had obviously been opened and resealed by security. "Presents," Evan said.

"Do you want to go home, or ride around town and show Evan the Mississippi River, or have something to eat?" I asked Sarah.

"Home," Sarah said. She walked behind the truck, then stopped. "Mother, the registration on your truck should have been renewed in August."

"Huh?" I looked at the sticker on the license tag. It *did* say August.

"You could get a ticket. Why didn't you send the packet in to the registration bureau?"

"They must not have sent me one. I've been so busy..."

She took a deep breath. "No problem. We'll take care of it for you while we're here."

Evan stowed the duffel bags on the rear seat of the truck and barely had room to squeeze his long legs in. Sarah climbed into the front and laid her arm along the back of her seat. He reached for her hand. A moment later as I was starting the car, she said, "When did you have the oil changed?"

"I beg your pardon?"

She pointed to the sticker sat the upper corner of my windshield and then at my dashboard. "You're way overdue. And I'll bet you haven't had the tires rotated either."

"Whoa! Sarah, hold up," I said.

She turned to look at Evan. "My father took care of the cars."

"I got it *washed* yesterday." I felt my face flame.

"It's okay. We'll take care of the tires too."

"Sarah, I'm not totally helpless without your father."

"I know you're not. But when you've been looked after the way you have, it takes a while to get used to looking after yourself."

No guilt dumping. Just a straight statement of fact. I nearly wrecked the truck when I turned to stare at her.

"When are Nathan and Lisa arriving?" she asked.

"This evening. Nathan's renting a car, and doesn't want us to meet him, Christmas schedules being what they are. Your father's car is still in Eli's garage, so you have transportation too."

"We'll swap the day after Christmas. You take Daddy's car, and we'll take the truck to the shop."

"Like hell you will," I yelped. "Nobody touches my truck."

"It needs service. I promise we won't break it." She sniffed. "Still smells like eau de equine."

"I like eau de equine," Evan said. "Better than eau de bovine. Eau de sheep never did appeal to me."

Sarah laughed. I laughed too. My Sarah seemed more relaxed and at ease with herself and with me than she'd been since before Pride's death. I decided that if Evan broke her heart, I'd cut his out and feed it to him. If he had this effect on her, then I hoped he'd marry her. Soon.

I caught Evan's eye in her rear view mirror. I could swear he winked. I dropped both of them at the house, told Sarah where to find the keys to Morgan's BMW, all gassed up and scrubbed within an inch of its life, and drove back to the clinic. I didn't have to go back to work. So far as I knew there weren't any patients scheduled, and the boarding kennel was closed for Christmas. This would be the first time Sarah had been in the house since Morgan's funeral. She needed the time to acclimate.

After that business with the truck, I also felt like a ninny.

"Well?" Eli called from her office. Tonesha and Wanda Jean and Duane had all left for the holidays and wouldn't be back until Monday. "What's he like?"

"He's very attractive, seems to like her, and is at least ten years older."

"Ex-wives? Children?"

"Eli, I just met the man." I plumped myself down in the chair opposite her. "Sarah…she's changed, or at least I think she has. She seems more relaxed, not as quick to take offense."

"Sarah mellowed? Now, that I will have to see."

That evening before the four of us went out to dinner, Eli settled Evan in her guestroom and presented him with a key. "My friend Shep Fischer will be driving in tomorrow morning to stay here as well," she said, "so if you run into a soigné gray-haired gentleman carrying a highball, ignore him. He belongs."

We went to a moderately priced steakhouse. Over Evan's protestations, I paid the check, which made me blink. Probably cheap by Hollywood standards, but more than I'd spent on meals in the last month.

"What does a second unit assistant director do, actually?" Eli asked over the avocados stuffed with crabmeat.

"You know those scenes in the jungle where the bad guys are creeping through the underbrush to ambush the hero, and overhead you can see the monkeys screaming and running away?"

Eli nodded.

"I direct the monkeys."

"You do not," Sarah said, with a proprietary pat on his arm. A nicely muscled arm. "Well, he does, but he also directs the extras in the underbrush. The second unit is frequently off in Prague or Zamboanga or somewhere while the main unit—the one with the stars and the story—is on a soundstage in London or Toronto. In another couple of years Evan will be directing his own pictures."

"Maybe. Maybe not," Evan said. "I'm never out of work, and I make a good living. I don't have the talent or the drive to be Spielberg or Lucas, or even Jean-Luc Goddard. I'd like to direct nice small pictures. What most people don't understand about the business is that successful small pictures with low production costs frequently make much more profit than the blockbusters."

I buttered another roll. I knew I shouldn't, but the bread in this place was exceptional. I wondered where they got it. "I want a happy ending. I get enough tragedy in real life. I prefer fantasy."

"I'd like to direct comedies, but they're much tougher than drama. It's easy to get the timing on a death scene right, but timing a comic love scene takes real skill."

"How about television?"

"Maybe. I've had a couple of offers. Now, sitcoms—that's grueling. But the money's excellent if you have a hit."

Sarah sat quietly through this exchange watching Evan as though every word that fell from his lips was a pearl.

She was obviously head over heels in love. I felt a pang. Did he love her back or was she riding for a broken heart?

# Chapter 48

## *In which Maggie has a close encounter with a steer and has doubts about her choice of profession*

Patsy left a message on my answering machine that afternoon. "Mariah's surgery went well. Dan's driving me home. I expect to sleep for twenty-four hours."

Nathan and Lisa's flight was delayed, so we had all gone to bed before they drove up in their rental car. Sarah didn't even get up to greet them, but I did. Then I went back to bed. It was two a.m. Christmas Eve morning. I prayed we'd have a quiet day.

As if.

Four hours later, I grabbed the telephone before it could wake up the children and heard J. L.'s voice. "It's Christmas Eve," I moaned. "Can't this wait until tomorrow?"

"Maggie, do you think I would be calling you if it could wait? One of my prize bull calves run into a tree sometime last night and broke off a stob in his shoulder. We need to get it out and clean and stitch the wound right now."

I came awake instantly. "How big is the stob?" In the south a stob can mean a length of wood that impales anything from somebody's foot to a forty foot fishing boat.

"Damned thing's sticking three feet in the air. Won't take you no-time. We'll have him up and waitin' for you."

The stick had to be removed before he drove it deeper into muscle or bone. Untreated, the wound would fester. The calf would die.

It was still dark outside. I could sneak out the back, do the job at J. L.'s, and be back with hot doughnuts before anyone caught me. Sarah would not approve of my taking a call on Christmas Eve, but

J. L. was an old and valued client.

J. L. had a bunch of cattle and did well out of them, considering the size of the twenty-year-old Georgian mansion that sat smack in the middle of his property, not to mention the miles of expensive white PVC fences surrounding it. He had a B. A. from Williams and an MBA from Vanderbilt.

We don't raise cows in the south the way they do in Texas or Montana. First off, we think in terms of cows per acre rather than square miles per cow. We graze them on rich grass and clover in the summer and hay them in the winter with bales of hay we've raised ourselves.

Being more often under the eye of the stockmen, however, doesn't keep cattle from getting into the damnedest situations. In my experience cows are dumb, ornery, and will do nearly anything to prevent your keeping them alive and in one piece.

I drove too fast and prayed I wouldn't run head on into another truck doing the same thing. Luckily, I only had to slam on my brakes once to allow a fat possum to cross the road in front of me. Apparently, J. L. and his wranglers had managed to move the calf only as far as the small holding paddock before I arrived. It covered about three acres on the top of a small rise. Across the fence the rest of the herd watched in a bunch, no doubt glad they weren't 'it.'

A small clump of maple and oak at the corner of the paddock stood stark and leafless. At some point a big old maple had fallen over and lay on its side perhaps ten feet from the others. From the position of the riders, J. L. had been using that tree as a barrier to the calf's movement in that direction.

J. L. and two of his hands were waiting for me. Ramirez was a big, quiet, dark bachelor. I had seen him bulldog a steer. The steer never had a chance.

Jesus stood only a few inches taller than Eli, but was built like a fireplug and wore a perpetual grin. Both men were both top wranglers and worth every dime J. L. paid them.

As I started to open the door of the truck, J. L. walked his horse toward me. For the first time I saw the calf.

Calf? The thing was a half grown bull the size of a Toyota. Jesus grinned at me and called, "Hola, Dr. Maggie, we nearly got him."

Ramirez had snubbed his lasso around the horn of his saddle. The other end was looped around the neck of the calf.

Ramirez's quarter horse was backing up and sitting on his

haunches to keep the line taut, despite the youngster's best efforts to free himself.

"Y'all let me know when you got the back half too," I said.

Thirty minutes later the score read *"calf: four, cowboys: nothing."*

"Hell and damnation!" J. L. shouted as the calf slipped down in the mud on his side and tossed the lasso free again. "I'm gonna shoot the sumabitch!"

"I might have been able to if I had the capture pistol," I said to J.L., "but you swore you'd have him secure by the time I got here."

"Hell, woman, don't rub it in." He spun his horse and trotted past me to keep the calf from bolting back towards the herd. "Once we get him down, Maggie, you ready to shoot him with something to keep him down?"

"Absolutely."

Their next attempt was successful. As Jesus pulled his lasso taut around the steer's rear ankles, I jumped out of the truck and landed in a patch of mud so slick I had to catch onto the side view mirror to keep my Wellington boots from sliding out from under me.

I leaned over and drove the syringe full of tranquilizer into the calf's shoulder. "Gotcha!" I said. "He should be out in about a minute and a half."

At that point all hell broke loose. The calf kicked straight back with his bound hind legs and caught Jesus right in the crotch. "Madre de Dios!" Jesus howled and grabbed for his groin with both hands.

Thereby releasing the rope binding the calf's rear legs.

The calf surged to his feet and tossed J. L. on his butt in the mud. Ramirez's horse couldn't hold on alone. His line tore free and dangled from the calf's neck. "Uh-oh," I whispered. The calf now had a needle and syringe hanging out of his left shoulder, and the stob sticking up out of his right. He looked for all the world like a fighting bull after the picadors have been at him. He was obviously every bit as angry.

"Maggie, run for the trees," J. L. whispered. *"Now."* He inched his hand down along the ground toward the line that still hung slack from the animal's neck.

The calf lowered his head and pawed. I spun and ran.

Ahead of me I saw the dead log. If I could get on the other side of that, he'd slow down until the tranquilizer took effect. He couldn't jump over it. He'd have to go around the end.

Somehow I managed to leap the log and keep running.

I glanced back just as the steer cleared that log with the ease and grace of a Grande Prix show jumper. I never knew cows could jump like that. Hell of a time to find out.

The maple tree had grown up into several trunks, all meeting close to the ground. The space between the trunks formed a "v" that looked wide enough for me to pass through. I prayed it wouldn't be wide enough for the steer.

I planted my right boot into the crotch of the tree and prepared to jump.

Then three things happened at once.

My boot stuck in the angle of the tree so that my stocking foot came straight up out of it.

The steer's forehead connected solidly with my rear end and launched me out the far side of the tree. And my right boot flew off and smacked me on the back of the head.

All my life I've heard about accidents that knock people right out of their shoes. Until that moment I had never believed it was possible.

I glanced back over my shoulder just as the calf stared at me with surprised brown eyes and passed out with his nose against my boot.

"Maggie, my God, Maggie, are you all right?" J. L. slid his hands under my armpits and hauled me to my feet. "Can you walk?"

"I can limp, thank you. Jesus, would you mind bringing me my boot?"

I thanked God for the mud and the wet grass. It was embarrassing enough that J. L. and the others witnessed me sailing through the air and out of my boots. I would have been a darned sight more embarrassed if they had realized that steer had literally knocked the pee out of me. The entire back of my jeans was wet.

I cleaned and stitched up the calf, dropped my Wellington boots on the floor of the truck, and laid a plastic bag on the driver's seat of my truck so it wouldn't get wet.

"Come on up to the house," J. L. said, "Let me check you out, give you a little Laphroaig."

"It's too early for me, thanks."

"Me too, but I ain't just been butted in the ass by a bull calf."

"J. L., I will probably freeze in this position in about thirty minutes. I need to drive back to the clinic while I can still get out when I get there. A little horse liniment ought to limber me right up."

The truck jounced and slid to the pasture gate over the mud and wet grass. J. L. and his horse opened the gate for me.

I could feel my rear end swelling. By the time I got back to home it would be sticking out far enough that you could safely rest a pot of geraniums on it.

And it hurt. I hurt. Not just my body, but my pride. I knew better. I should have waited until I was certain J. L. and his boys had the calf under control. I could have caught my *foot* in the crotch of that tree, not just my boot. I could have broken my wrist when I fell.

I had done a stupid thing and I had paid for it. The whole cow community would know about my ignominious launch before New Year's day. By the time I told the story myself a couple of times, it would sound pretty funny even to me.

But it wasn't funny.

Ten years ago I wouldn't have been so casual. For that matter, ten years ago I could run a whole lot faster.

Suddenly retirement had precious little to do with traveling.

I drove all the way into Collierville, picked up two dozen hot doughnuts at the drive-through so I didn't have to get out of the truck, drove home and coasted the last few feet into my garage.

Now, if I could just sneak up the back stairs and climb into the shower…

"Mother," Sarah said from the open door of the guest room. "Where on earth have you been at this hour?"

I held up the doughnuts. "Breakfast."

She walked out into the hall and stared at me. "That's not all. You are covered in mud! You're filthy." She sniffed. "And you're starting to smell. You've been out on a call, haven't you?"

I shrugged. "It was an emergency out at J. L.'s."

"What kind of emergency? How did you get in such a mess?"

"Tell you later." I wanted a hot shower. I did manage not to limp or whimper on my way upstairs. When I climbed out of my massage shower twenty minutes later, I felt fairly normal until I caught a glimpse of my naked rear end in the mirror.

My right cheek was imprinted with an almost perfectly square bruise from the calf's forehead.

Not big enough to pot geraniums, but I could probably manage a pansy or two.

# Chapter 49

## In which Maggie settles an argument

"Perfect Christmas weather," Nathan said as he kissed me good morning.

"Lisa's still asleep." He grabbed a doughnut and poured himself a cup of coffee. "What's it like having a houseful of family again?"

"Morning Nathan," Sarah said from the doorway. Evan stood behind her. He and Nathan introduced each other, and Sarah poured two cups of coffee.

"What're you up to this morning?" Nathan asked. "Lisa and I thought we'd maybe catch a matinee, get out of Mother's hair until the party tonight."

"What movie?" Evan asked.

"I don't know what's playing."

Nathan reached for the morning paper, and the telephone on the kitchen cabinet rang.

I raised a hand to tell him not to answer it, but too late. He spoke, listened, and handed the phone to me. "It's some guy about a crazy horse."

"I'll take it upstairs. Hang up when I answer, will you, Nathan?"

Upstairs I listened to Orville Pinchow rant and finally beg.

"I can't give my granddaughter a horse that's gone crazy," he said. "Maggie, I know it's Christmas Eve and all, but you got to come out to my place and check this mare over. Please."

I pulled on work clothes and boots, then limped down the back stairs and into the kitchen.

"Sorry, guys. I have to go out. Shouldn't take long. Do whatever you're going to do without me."

"What about the party tonight with the Militia?" Nathan asked.

"Everything's done. I just have to put the roast in this afternoon. I'll be back long before that. An hour at most."

"If you're really only going to be gone an hour or so, why don't you take Sarah with you?"

"Good idea," Evan said. "You haven't really had a chance to be alone, you two," he said. He kissed her on the cheek. "Go."

As we drove out the driveway, I said, "You haven't ridden along with me for years."

"I wanted a chance to talk to you too, Mother," Sarah sounded serious. As a matter of fact, she sounded exactly the way Morgan used to when he sat down to lecture me about something. I felt my shoulders tighten.

"Before we leave, Nathan and I need to sit down with you and get your life back in order."

"My life is in perfect order, thank you very much."

She shook her head. "We could be stopped by the police right this minute because the registration for the truck is out of date." She pointed to the sticker above the driver's seat. "It is also nearly four thousand miles past the date for its regular service. Now that Daddy's not here..."

"The truck is working fine, thank you." I flipped on the radio. "We can talk later. I want to hear the Nine Lessons and Nine Carols from King's College at Cambridge."

My mother told me that sooner or later positions are reversed—parent becomes child, child becomes parent. I wasn't ready for that yet.

"When was the last time you balanced your check book?" she asked.

I stamped the gas. The truck slid around a ninety-degree corner and barely avoided taking out somebody's mailbox. "My checkbook is none of your damned business," I snapped. I hadn't balanced it at all since Morgan died, actually. "I know how much money I have, thank you, and my accountant will continue to do the taxes the way she has for years." She started to say something else, but I interrupted. "Not now. I have a crazy horse to treat."

"Here we go. I warn you, Orville's a character." I turned off the highway and drove down a long gravel drive toward a medium sized horse barn.

Orville yanked open my door before I could open it myself. As I climbed out, I said, "Hey, Orville, what's all this about a crazy horse? Oh, this is my Sarah, home for the holidays. I don't think you've ever met."

"Told you, this filly's for my granddaughter's Christmas. You think I'm gonna put a kid on a horse that tried to kill me?"

"Where is she?"

"In the covered arena." Orville swept his Stetson off and pointed to an angry bruise and knot on his forehead. "I'm too old to let some damn two-year-old filly dump me in the dirt. Woman was broke to death on Friday, and today she tries to kill me." He led the way down the broad hall of his barn.

"Orville raises cutting and reining horses," I told Sarah. "Wins the futurity in Jackson three years out of four."

"Yeah. I'm too old to be breaking horses, so I sent her down to Jim Bob Buckram a couple of months ago to knock the rough edges off her. He told me she was broke to death when I picked her up last week."

"Jim Bob doesn't lie," I said.

Orville sighed with exasperation. "That's what I have been trying to poke into that pea brain of yours, Maggie. I rode her down at Jim Bob's before I loaded her, and got on her the minute I brought her back home.

"That filly never put a foot wrong. I swear, the woman could turn on a dime with no more'n my little finger on the reins and nine cents left over. She got cow in her ain't been touched yet." He shook his head. "Last Friday I left for a cutting horse show in Dallas. Got back last night late and came down here first thing this morning to exercise her one more time before Christmas."

"What happened?"

"I knowed something was wrong the minute Sanchez put her halter on in her stall. When he tried to groom her, she commenced to roll her eyes and paw the ground. I smacked her a good one on the shoulder. Damned if the woman didn't turn around and bite me!" Orville pushed the sleeve of his sweater up. "Lookee there." He pushed up his sleeve and showed me a bruise on his forearm.

"Anyhow," Orville continued, "I smacked Miss Bar Girl right on her pretty bay nose."

"How did she react?" I asked.

"She acted real surprised," Orville said. He sighed and looked at the beautiful blood bay filly braced on all four legs in the center of his covered arena with real pain in his eyes. "Kicked the stew out of the skirting boards behind her when I tried to saddle her."

"What do you expect *me* to do?" I asked.

"I thought maybe you'd give her a little tranquilizer, quiet her down so you could check her over."

"Orville, if she's got a brain tumor or epilepsy, there's no way I can tell in a casual exam."

"Just try is all I ask, Maggie. For my granddaughter."

I sighed.

"One week not being rode ain't enough to turn a dead broke filly into a raving maniac," Orville said. "I figured she'd settle down once I was in the saddle. She's so darned pretty I knew Christin would fall in love with her. I had the boys hold her hard while I climbed up on her."

"What happened when you got into the saddle?" Sarah asked. I was surprised. I expected her to be—or at least feign—complete lack of interest.

"Honey," Orville said, "I used to ride bulls when I was young and stupid, and you don't have to do that but eight seconds to get a halfway decent score. I don't think I made five seconds on that filly. Next thing I knowed, I'm flat on my back in the dirt trying to suck some breath back into my lungs, and she's bucking all the way around the arena."

"So how'd you get that goose egg on your forehead?" I asked.

"I tried to catch her as she went by. Stirrup caught me right acrost the eyebrow."

"What'd you do to her?"

"Not a damn thing. Not her fault she's crazy. Figured I'd wait until you stuck some good stuff in her to calm her down before I tried to ride her again." He sighed. "If it weren't for Christin, I swear I'd sell her for fifty cents."

Sarah and I walked over to the filly's stall. A neat bronze plaque over the stall read "Miss Bar Girl" in fancy English script. All the stalls had similar plaques, illegible from this angle.

The filly stopped chomping her hay and came over to nuzzle me —not nip, just nuzzle. I bent down and blew gently into her nostrils, so she'd know I was a friend.

"She's beautiful," Sarah said and stroked her nose.

I barely breathed. Had Sarah even touched a horse since Pride's death?

Orville puffed up. "Red as a sunset, a pure foundation quarterhorse.

"She doesn't act crazy to me," Sarah said.

Sanchez called from the end of the arena, *"Senor, telephono. Es Senor Jim Bob."*

"Jim Bob?" He turned to me. "You figure out how to stick that filly with something to calm her down while I go have a 'Come to Jesus' meeting with ole Jim Bob about what the hell he thinks he's doing sending a crazy filly home with me." He stomped off, hesitated, and said over his shoulder. "Come on, Miss Sarah. You look like you're half froze to death, besides, you'll keep me from saying some cusswords you oughtn't to hear."

"Go on, Sarah," I said.

"After southern California, this is like being inside a refrigerator." She followed Orville.

"Sanchez," I said.

*"Si, Senora Doctor."*

I pointed to the mare, *"Malo al caballo*—uh—last week?"

He shook his head. *"No malo, Senora Doctor."* His eyes were frightened.

"Anybody here—shoot—anybody *differento—hermano*?" I couldn't remember the word for man, only for brother.

"Me and Ramon." His eyes shifted away from her.

"Who else?"

Sanchez's eyes shifted.

"Tell me, please."

"*Mi amigo* Esteban—help— bring in horses last night, but he no hurt..." He was whispering, looking over his shoulder toward the hall down which Orville had disappeared to the telephone.

"Okay, easy." I held my hands up, palms facing him, the universal signal of "calm down."

At that point the horses to the right and left of the blood bay filly stuck their heads out. The horse on the left was a deep sorrel—the color of dogwood leaves in October.

I glanced at the horse on the right, then walked over to her to stroke her nose. A second later I began to chuckle. "Damn. I'd bet Orville a thousand dollars I know what made his filly go nuts."

I turned to Jesus. "Quick, now. Get this filly right here out of her stall, throw Orville's saddle on her and bridle her up. Hurry, before he gets back from the telephone."

"*Senora Doctor?*"

"Sanchez, *ayuta* me. And quick."

Ten minutes later Orville stalked back into the arena trailed by Sarah. They both stopped so quickly that Sarah ran into Orville's back.

I continued loping the blood bay filly quietly around the arena with nothing but my index finger on the reins.

"Lord all mighty, woman," Orville said. "Whatever you done give that filly, I want some for my wife."

I slid her to a halt beside him and hopped down. "Here, Orville, you try her."

He thought about it for a second or two, then he pulled himself into the heavy western saddle and picked up the reins. Sarah and I watched him work the filly for ten minutes. I looked at Sarah and winked, then mouthed,0 "Tell you later."

Finally Orville trotted back to me and dismounted. "Damnation, I gotta go call Jim Bob and apologize," he said. "Is she safe for Christin or is she going to go nuts on me again the minute the drugs wear off?"

"I didn't give her any drugs."

"Then how in hell?"

"Anybody can do it, Orville. All you got to do is whisper the right name."

"Huh?"

"Orville, the filly next to Miss Bar Girl. What's her breeding?"

"She's a half sister to Miss Bar Girl. Name's Miss Bar Queen." He stared at me for a long couple of seconds, then I saw the light dawn. "Sanchez! Ramon! Y'all get your illegal alien butts out here this minute!"

The two men came running. Sanchez was grinning sheepishly, but Ramon, who couldn't have been more than eighteen, was quaking.

Orville pointed to the row of stalls along the wall. "Who brought those horses back in from the pasture last night?"

Ramon pointed at Sanchez.

"Who else?"

"*Mi amigo* Esteban. He don't read too good."

"Esteban must have mixed up the stalls last night," I said. "They're half sisters and dead-ringers. He put Miss Bar Girl in Miss Bar Queen's stall and vice versa. Orville, honey, you hauled a totally unbroke two-year-old filly out of her stall, tied her up, threw a forty pound saddle on her back, stuck a cold metal bit between her teeth and plumped your two hundred plus pounds smack in the middle of her back. It's a miracle you're still alive."

"Dang." Orville pulled his Stetson off and slapped it against his leg. "If you hadn't come out here, Christin would 'a lost her Christmas present. Woman, you can *not* retire on us. Without you, who the hell's gonna protect all them supposedly dumb animals from real dumb-asses like me?"

# Chapter 50

## *In which Maggie has an epiphany*

Orville tossed the reins of his filly to Sanchez and walked across the arena with us. As we passed by his office, Ramon called out, "Telephono."

"If it's Jim Bob, tell him I'll call him back." Orville grinned at me. "Got to figure out how to cook all that crow I got to eat."

"No, senor, for Doctor Maggie."

"Oh, nuts," I said. "Sarah, you can wait in the truck. I won't be a minute. Probably Eli asking me to pick up something at the grocery."

I was wrong.

When I climbed into the truck, I said, "Mike Rasmussen's Percheron stud, Big Jake, is down in his stall. Mike thinks it's probably a mild impaction. We'll have to stop by there on our way home."

Sarah sat up. "Should I call home? We promised we'd be back before lunch."

"We will be. A little mineral oil and a shot of tranquilizer and Jake'll be fine." I turned the truck around, leaned out my window and yelled, "Merry Christmas!"

She sat quiet for a few minutes, then said, "Mother, you had no way of knowing you were right about those two fillies."

"It was logical."

"You weren't wearing a hard hat either. How many times did you drum into my head that you never get on a horse—any horse — without a hard hat?"

I didn't want to hear it. "It worked out, didn't it?"

"It might not have." She didn't have that accusing tone I was used to. This was what my mother used to call 'more in sorrow than in anger.' I'd have preferred anger.

She was right about the hard hat, drat her. I had been cavalier because I was showing off.

"You could have broken a hip or cracked your skull open back there."

"You could have gotten bit by a cobra in Thailand," I snapped. "Did it stop you? Or me from worrying about you?"

"It's not the same thing."

"It is too." I pulled up to a four-way stop and motioned for an eighteen-wheeler to come across. Poor bastard, working on Christmas Eve. At least he didn't have to listen to his children bitch at him.

Having seized the reins of this conversation, I had no intention of putting the spotlight back on *my* failings. "You better hope Evan will look after you the way Morgan looked after all of us. Otherwise, you're going to have to give up your cute little trips to Thailand and Katmandu and Zamboanga, unless you intend to take any stray baby you may have along with you in a back pack while you're scouting locations in the jungle."

I floored the truck. We spun gravel and narrowly avoided the ditch on the side of the road.

We didn't say a word to each other the rest of the trip.

Mike was waiting for me outside his barn. When I realized Sarah had no intention of getting out of the truck, I left the keys in the ignition so she could run the heater and the radio if she liked. I grabbed my bag and followed Mike down the hall to Big Jake's stall.

Big Jake had been my patient since he was four years old. I'd wormed him, vaccinated him, treated him for diaphramatic tympani, and even once for a mild impaction. We had grown old together. Now he was over thirty.

He still looked young and strong, although he'd been semi-retired for the last six years. Mike gave him a small band of broodmares to bully and herd in his very own pasture, and at night he came into a palatial stall fit for a king his size.

This afternoon, however, he was obviously in great pain. He lay like a small black mountain in his stall. His dark maw had long ago turned gray. So had the hair around his ears and eyebrows.

"What have you been feeding him?" I asked Mike as he opened the stall door to let me in.

"Same as usual. Oats, hay, pasture."

"You think his gut's impacted?"

He shook his head. "Not any more. I felt of his pulse in his ankles, Maggie. It's stronger than what it should be. Can't you give him one of those shots like you did when he was a youngster?"

I shook my head. "This isn't diaphramatic tympani, Mike. He could be foundering."

Ponies and draft horses are prone to founder, the layman's term for laminitis. But not generally in December. Usually founder occurs during spring when the grass is fresh and green and the horses gorge on it after a winter of dry hay. The gut begins to produce poisons, and those poisons travel throughout the body. The body pumps blood to its vital organs—heart and lungs—and leaves the extremities like the legs and hooves to look after themselves as best they can.

Only they can't. A horse that founders badly may even slough an entire hoof wall because of lack of circulation. Even a mild case can so distort the coffin bone in the sole of the foot that it rotates down and leaves the horse lame for life, even if he survives.

In an old horse like Big Jake, and definitely a horse that was too miserable to stand, the prognosis wasn't good.

Mike knew that. I knew it. I suspect Jake knew it.

I felt my heart sink. Another loss at Christmas time, even if only the loss of an old friend like Big Jake, was almost more than I could bear.

I went to work at once, pumped him full of antibiotics and electrolytes and saline solution and painkillers.

"We need to get him on his feet," I said to Mike. "If he can't walk, we need to keep him standing until we can get his hooves into buckets of ice water."

"Don't look good, does it, Maggie?" Mike said as he stroked Big Jake's neck. "He's done been a good ole horse. Be like losing a friend."

I blinked back my tears. Wouldn't do Big Jake any good for me to cry. I took a deep breath, straightened my shoulders. I was still smarting from that blasted cow butt. "You go get your tractor and some heavy rope. This time I think we're going to need them."

"Uh-huh."

"We'll try to force him to stand, then slide the ropes under his belly and snub them to the posts at the corners of his stall. If he starts to go down again, we can winch him upright with your tractor. It's a long shot, but it's all I've got."

He nodded. "I'll go get the tractor."

He ducked out of the stall, and I heard the thud of his feet down the aisle toward the front of the barn where his big tractor stood.

I'd pulled off what Mike Rasmussen thought was a miracle once before.

Today I was fresh out.

Big Jake was going to die, and there wasn't a damn thing I could do to prevent it. I didn't want Sarah to see me put him down. I prayed she'd stay in the truck.

As if to prove me wrong, Big Jake surged to his feet and stood shivering with pain. But he stood.

I had to check his heart sounds and his gut sounds and his lung sounds while he was standing. Then I had to pick up his hooves one by one so that I could test the soles for signs that the coffin bone had begun to rotate downward.

I leaned against Big Jake's side with my head toward his tail and placed my stethoscope just forward of his loin.

That's when he fell on me. He didn't sit down on his butt the way he had when he had the tympani. He collapsed flat out on his side.

Mike couldn't hear me yell for help and neither could Sarah.

Big Jake and I might die here together before anyone realized there was a problem. Sarah had already berated me for taking chances. She and Nathan had lost Morgan last year at Christmas as much as I had.

I would not die on my children.

I kept thinking that I had a hundred bucks worth of rib roast in my refrigerator. If I died it would spoil. Crazy.

I wriggled, managed to pull my face out of the shavings in Big Jake's stall, and tried to yell for help, but all that came out was a croak. I could hear Mike's tractor start up. If I could just shove Big Jake over a few inches…

I pulled my right arm out from under him, balled my hand into a fist and began to hammer his ribs. "Get off me, horse. I know you hurt, but for the love of God, get off!"

He groaned and fought to roll away. I squirmed a few inches forward before he subsided once more and trapped my legs and hips again.

I was having trouble catching my breath. I closed my eyes and saw stars. I couldn't pass out. My face would fall back into the shavings and I'd suffocate.

"Mom! Oh, God, Mom!"

Sarah's voice. It seemed a long way away.

"Grab his halter," I croaked. "Pull!"

"Sweet Lord, Maggie," Mike added his voice to the mix. Big Jake strained away from me. A moment later I felt Mike's callused hands grasp my free wrist—absolutely the wrong thing to do if Jake had fractured my spine, but at that point I didn't much care. I wanted out of there fast.

I felt as though I were being stretched on a rack. Big Jake rolled forward and back, steamrolling a ton of horse against me. I could hear Sarah's gasps and sobs.

"Leave me, Mike," I gasped. "Help Sarah with Big Jake."

He didn't ask questions. He went.

What seemed like an eternity later, Big Jake rolled onto his chest. I dragged myself into the corner of the stall. If he stood up, he wouldn't have any idea where those hooves of his would land. I didn't want them landing on my head.

He surged upright as I covered my head and rolled into a ball.

Sarah and Mike jerked me to my feet. Sarah threw her arms around me. "Mom! Dear God, Mom!" She started to drag me around Big Jake toward the front of the stall.

I could stand. My legs felt like over-stretched rubber bands, but they *felt*. As a matter of fact, as the blood surged back into them, they burned as though they'd been dipped in kerosene and set afire.

Sarah put her arm around my waist. "Come on! He could go down again any minute." I let her pull me out into the aisle where Mike grabbed hold of my other side.

"Guys, guys, I'm fine," I said. As blatant a lie as I ever told. "Mike, Sarah, we've got to snub those ropes crossways under his belly to the stall supports. He mustn't go down again."

"Leave him, Mom," Sarah was sobbing. "You're hurt."

"Not hurt. Quick, Mike."

"Hell, I'll do it," Sarah said. She shoved me at a hay bail and grabbed one of the heavy lines from Mike's tractor. "Don't you dare move."

"Sarah, be careful," I wheezed. I leaned back against the wall behind me and took deep breaths. No stabbing pain, so I hadn't punctured a lung. I poked my ribcage. Sore, but not agonizing. I struggled to my feet in time to see Mike and Sarah slip the last bull line under Big Jake's belly and take several wraps around the six by six at the back of his stall.

"There," Sarah said. Then she turned and saw me. "I told you to sit down and stay sat! We have to call an ambulance."

"I'm okay, Sarah, really I am. No broken ribs, nothing but a few bruises. Go on back to the truck. I'll be there in a minute. I promise I'll be out in a minute. I need to speak to Mike."

She looked from one of us to the other. "One minute. You don't come out, I come in and drag you, clear?"

"That's some girl you got there, Maggie," Mike said. "She got here before I even heard you. Scared the pee out of her, I'd guess."

"Mike, I've done all I can do," I said as I stroked Big Jake's nose. "I don't think it's going to be near enough. Do you want me to take care of it?"

He ran a hand down his grizzled face. "We got him on his feet. I'll keep an eye on 'em. I'll stay up with him tonight. If he ain't no better by mornin', well, I've got my forty-five. Won't be the first time I've had to put a horse down."

"No! You'll do no such thing."

"Maggie, tomorrow's Christmas."

"If I have to come out on Christmas morning to give him a shot of barbiturates, I'll do it. He deserves to die peacefully and with dignity. We all do, dammit. Don't you dare put him down yourself. You promise?"

He signed. "Yeah, all right. What're the odds we can save him? I don't give a hoot whether he's sound or not."

"Best guess? At his age? Eighty-twenty against us." I touched Big Jake's forehead and then Mike's arm. "Call me at the crack of dawn. Let me know. I'll come." I stroked the horse's shoulder. "He's a dear old boy."

I managed to walk out of the barn without limping and with my head held high.

Sarah sat in the driver's seat of the truck with the motor running. "You are not driving, Mother. I ought to take you to the emergency room."

"I'd wind up sitting in a room with sixty people with communicable diseases. I'm not hurt now, but I'd sure as shootin' have pneumonia by morning. I've got a roast to put in the oven."

As we drove toward home, Sarah said, "You could have been killed twice today."

"But I wasn't."

"You can't keep doing this." She glanced at me and I saw her eyes were brimming with tears. "You're all the family Nathan and I have left, Mom. For the first time in my life, it looks as though I might actually find a good guy to marry and have kids with. They'll already miss out on the best grandfather they could ever have had. I don't want them to miss out on the best grandmother too."

# Chapter 51

## *In which Maggie announces her decision*

I popped that rib roast into the oven the minute I saw Sarah, Evan and Nathan and Lisa off to the movies. I had sworn Sarah to secrecy about the Big Jake incident, and although she offered to stay and help with dinner preparations, I really wanted the house to myself.

I dragged myself upstairs followed by three cats at my heels. They knew I was in pain. Times like this I was glad that we had put in a whirlpool tub when we built the house. By the time I was pruny, I felt passable, although when I looked at my rump in the three-way mirror I could see more purple than pink. Long sleeves would hide the scrapes and scratches. A hot patch in the middle of my back would keep me moving. I lay down for an hour with all three cats pressed hard against me, and when I dragged myself out of sleep, I thought I really could get through the party.

Most of the preparations for dinner had already been made. I turned the lights on outside and on the tree, put out ice, checked to see that the table was set and that the serving dishes were ready.

Then I made the trifle. It takes a quart of whipping cream and is so rich that I usually don't dare to make it except at Christmas. I had considered not fixing it this Christmas, but that was part of our lives through the years with Morgan, and should remain part of our lives without him.

By the time the children came back, I was dozing in my recliner in the den in front of the fire with the cats. The four of them were arguing amiably about the movie. Evan thought it was pretentious, and Sarah agreed with him. Big surprise. Lisa and Nathan liked it.

They rummaged around in the kitchen searching for drinks and snacks until I called, "You mess up my food and you don't get any supper."

"Mother?" Nathan came into the room with a lite beer in his hand. "I figured you'd be over at the clinic."

"We're closed."

"You need any help with dinner?" he asked.

"All done. Shoo, scat. "

"Then I'm going to grab a nap," Sarah said. "I don't suppose you'd agree to Evan's joining me?"

"You're right. I wouldn't. Sorry, Evan."

"No problem."

Sarah made a face at me and shut the door of the guest room behind her. "Us too," Nathan said. He took Lisa's hand and led her up the back steps. "You can't stop us. We're legal."

Evan sat on the sofa across from me with a tall glass of what looked like cola in his hand. "If you want me to go to Eli's and leave you alone, tell me. I won't be offended."

I shook my head. "Glad to have you." I leaned forward. He grinned.

"This is where Sarah and Nathan say I get the third degree, right?"

"Does that bother you?"

"Your Southern third degree can't come close to my Iowa mother's third degree."

"Tell me about yourself."

"Unto the third and fourth generation?"

"If you know back that far."

"Fair enough." He took a deep swig of cola.

"One ex-wife," he said. "No children, no alimony. She sells real estate and makes more than I'll ever make. But I make a decent living and I like what I do."

"Where does Sarah fit in?" I asked.

"I want to marry her, have babies, the whole schmeer."

"So you came this Christmas to ask me for Sarah's hand?"

He gave me an answering grin. "Sarah talks about you all the time. I wanted to meet you. See if you and Sarah were as much alike as I guessed."

"Alike? Sarah's Morgan's child. We've never been on the same wave length, not since..."

"Since her horse died?"

"You know about that?"

"I know her side of it. According to her, you weren't there when she needed you."

"I wasn't, but I had no way of knowing about Pride. Sarah thinks I've failed her all her life. Every time we have a fight, she reminds me that I walked out in the middle of her piano recital at the good part of Clair de Lune to stitch up a basset hound that had been hit by a car."

"About the horse?"

I told him the story of Pride's death.

"In her heart, she knows it wasn't your fault."

"News to me." When I set my diet cola down on the table beside me and started to stand up, I caught my breath.

Evan reached for me. "You're hurt," he said. "Let me help you."

I pulled myself erect. "Just a little stiff. I'm fine. Now, I have to go check on dinner."

"What can I do to help?"

"Not a thing. In my kitchen I do not play well with others."

"Understood. I'm going over to Eli's to get ready for dinner."

"Have a drink with Shep. You'll like him." After he left, I called Patsy to find out about Mariah. I left a message on her answering machine asking her to report on the mare's progress. I assumed I would have heard bad news. That must mean Mariah was still progressing satisfactorily at Mississippi State.

I nearly lost it when I counted the places set for dinner. One less than last year. But Morgan used to say that nothing could hurt Christmas, and that lives well lived should be celebrated, not mourned. "So, love," I whispered. "We'll celebrate."

Susan and Lanier arrived first that evening. Susan looked very grown up with her long caramel-colored hair in a French twist. She wore a long red velvet dress with a scoop neck that showed a pair of burgeoning breasts. In a couple of years, she'd be as beautiful as her mother. Pumpkin was enduring a big red bow on his collar.

The only other person who wore a skirt was Nathan's Lisa, who had put on a long tartan wool skirt with a white ruffled blouse.

The rest of us all wore dressy pants and fancy sweaters.

"The house looks great," Susan said to me. "Look at all those presents under the tree."

"My mother used to say that everybody should get three presents for Christmas—one good present, one funny present, and one sentimental present. It's not what's in the boxes that counts, it's having plenty to open."

"Maggie, the stuffed cow you sent Meg is wonderful," Heather said as she handed Meg to me. "I already use it to prop her up."

"And she's sleeping through the night, Thank the good Lord," Rick said. He carried in the bag of stuff that accompanied Meg everywhere she went.

Susan rolled over to me and took my arm. "Miss Patsy brought Mariah home from Mississippi State yesterday," she said.

"So soon? I thought they'd at least keep her through Christmas weekend."

"They said she was healing fine, but Miss Patsy is still worried about her." She turned her head to take in the crowd and saw Sarah. "Can I go tell her about Mariah?"

I started to say no, then nodded.

Pumpkin ignored Bear, Teezy and Bok Choy, who retired to the top of the refrigerator. When Eli arrived with Sugar Pie, the two dogs investigated one another's smells, then settled down amicably by the fire. They were old friends.

I sent Nathan down to the far end to Morgan's place. "You'll have to carve the roast," I said.

He looked startled.

"That is the nature of things, my dear. One day your son will take over from you." He leaned over and kissed me. I had made up my mind that under no circumstances would I cry or wax maudlin. After we were seated, I gave the usual Episcopal prayer, "For what we are about to receive, the Lord make us truly thankful." Then I lifted my glass. "To Morgan."

They echoed my toast.

"Now, Nathan, how about some roast beast?"

After we had all been served and had begun to eat, Lanier asked Evan, "Are you being indoctrinated to our Southern customs?"

"Is this where I get hazed?"

"You have to eat hog jowl and black eyed peas on New Year's Day for good luck," Susan said.

"Jowl? As in cheek?"

"You got it," Lanier said.

"Thank God we'll be back in California before New Year's."

As I passed the gravy boat, I said, "I found out today Evan's a farm boy."

"Absolutely." Evan smiled at Sarah. "We've got a big Amish community in our area. My audition film for USC was a documentary about the Amish way of farming with draft horses."

"You, too?" Sarah said.

"Sarah, aren't you ever around animals at work?" Susan asked.

"No way. I go hunting for locations—houses, office suites, sometimes cabins or forests—searching for the perfect venue for a scene." She shrugged. "Sometimes the scene only last six seconds, but the director still has kittens if it's not right."

"Sometimes it winds up on the cutting room floor," Evan said.

"But the search can be gratifying. Evan and I met at the hotel bar in a little town in northern Thailand. He was shooting the jungle and I was hunting for the perfect grungy office suite." She smiled at Evan.

Nathan cleared his throat and stood up. "Listen up, everybody, I have an announcement to make." He stood. "Mother, thank you for not running off to London. Christmas would really be screwed up otherwise."

A chorus of 'hear, hears' answered him.

"I know that you've been talking about retiring. Everybody is against that, as I'm sure my Dad would have been under the circumstances. But you do need a vacation. So does Eli. Something you would really like to do."

"Damn right," Shep said. "She ought to marry me and run away to Hawaii."

"In your dreams," Eli said.

"So, if I may continue," Nathan interrupted, "I am presenting you two with an early Christmas present, one that you have to make use of during the coming year. I've even set up tentative reservations for you, and asked Vickie to stand in for you while you're gone." He reached behind him, and picked up an envelope from the seat of his chair. "It's a tad warm from my rear end, but open it anyway."

"Nathan, what have you done?"

"Open it."

I glanced at Eli, who shrugged. I tore open the envelope and read the contents. I laughed and handed the letter to Eli.

"A wagon train?" Eli said. "You've booked us on a wagon train?"

"Absolutely. This is only eight days—nice and short for a start. You spend four days learning to drive a team of draft horses, then you and the rest of the group including chefs and outriders, drive the Oregon trail for four days."

"Nathan, this must have cost a fortune," I said.

"Actually, it didn't, but that's not the point. The point is that you and Eli, not you and some bunch of strangers, are going to get away this summer to do something that you will actually enjoy, and you can't cancel for any reason other than four broken legs, two apiece. You have to swear before this august company here assembled." He glared at me. "I mean it. You and Eli. Swear."

I grinned at Eli. "Okay, we swear."

"We swear," Eli said.

The table broke into applause. All except for Sarah.

I stood and clinked my glass. It was now or never. "Okay, I know you didn't believe me when I started talking about retirement. I'm not sure I believed myself. Now I do. I'm quitting."

I closed my eyes against the din. The chorus of no's and don't be stupid and no, you're not's echoed around the table. Then I heard Sarah's voice override the others. "Mother's right. It's time she retired."

"Are you nuts?" Nathan said to his sister.

"Shut up, Nathan. If she doesn't quit now, she could be badly hurt." She glanced at me.

I shook my head and tried to telegraph, *Don't tell them about Big Jake*. "She could teach at one of the vet schools," Sarah concluded.

"Maggie," Eli sounded grim. "Don't do this to me. Not tonight."

"Eli, we've talked about it all year. I won't walk out until we're set, but I'm definitely leaving. I want to go out on top, not when I'm doddering. Now, let's have some dessert."

I should write a book on how to kill a party in one sentence. From festive, the atmosphere went to grim. Except for Sarah, whose chin practically hit the ceiling every time she glanced at her brother. Conversation died.

Susan had two helpings of trifle, although Lanier raised her eyebrows. "Susan, there's rum in that trifle."

"Not enough to matter." She giggled.

"Oh, I don't know about that," Rick said. "I'll need a couple of cups of Maggie 's coffee before I dare drive home."

"We all will," Vickie said. "I for one may never eat again." They were trying to regain the atmosphere. It wasn't working. I should have felt good about my announcement. Instead I felt glummer than I did when I lost a patient.

I poured coffee and Nathan handed the cups around.

"How come you didn't eat any trifle, Aunt Maggie?" Susan asked.

"Too many calories. Besides, if I drink alcohol, I turn purple and foam at the mouth."

"No, you don't."

"Well, I definitely won't get out of bed before noon tomorrow."

"On Christmas morning? That's crazy. Pumpkin and I get up real early."

Lanier groaned.

Then the telephone rang.

"Mother," Sarah grasped my arm, "Let the damned thing ring for once. They can call somebody else."

After three rings, the answering machine in the kitchen kicked in.

"Maggie , please be there. Please, please, answer, this is Patsy."

I bolted for the kitchen.

"Patsy? Patsy, honey, what's wrong?" I asked.

"I know it's Christmas. I wouldn't call, but I think she's going to die."

"Mariah? But Susan said Mississippi State cleared her to come home with you."

"She was doing great. Now all of a sudden, she's down in her stall and rolling around again. Maggie, for the love of God, Mississippi State's closed for the holiday. You're my only hope. You and Eli have to open her up again, find out what's wrong. Please, Maggie."

I took a deep breath. "Get her in the trailer. We'll be ready by the time you get here." I dropped the phone back into its cradle and shoved the kitchen door open. "Patsy's mare's colicked again. She's on her way. We'll have to operate."

Susan gasped. "Oh, no, please, not Mariah."

"I've had wine and trifle. Give me that coffee," Eli said as she shoved into her coat. "I ought to be okay to do the anesthesia."

"What do you want *us* to do, Maggie?" Vickie asked.

I glanced at Susan's terrified face and kept my voice calm. "People, we are going to need some help getting that mare onto the operating table and prepped for surgery."

Everyone stood but Sarah.

"Sarah, get off your butt, get your coat and come on," I snapped. "Evan, you too."

Sarah blinked and opened her mouth, then shut it again. Evan pulled her up. "Come on, my love, time we went to work."

I headed for the front door. "Rick, sorry to kick you out, but you and Heather get Meg and go home."

"We'll stay," Rick said.

"She's right, Rick," Heather said. "She's got plenty of help. She doesn't need to be worrying about us."

"Maggie, you sure?"

"Absolutely. Merry Christmas." I turned to the front door. "Come on, we've got less than twenty minutes to prep and scrub."

# Chapter 52

## *In which Maggie sees the truth*

In the paddock parking lot behind the clinic, Nathan, Evan, Shep, and Dan Dalrymple, Patsy's husband, unloaded the mare from Patsy's trailer. Watching the horse inch backward down the ramp was painful. She could barely walk and was dripping sweat despite the winter chill. I immediately gave her a shot to lessen the pain as we walked her into our operating theater.

The surgical table stood upright in the center of the room under a bank of bright lights. The men walked the mare up to the side of the table, and Vickie and Lanier strapped her tightly to it. Then Eli gave her the shot that would put her out.

As she began to slide down in her restraints, Eli hit the motor to rotate the table so that Mariah lay on her back with her belly up. Nathan and Dan tied her legs up to winches, then I raised the table.

At the head of the table, Eli pulled down the three separate hoses, one for oxygen, one for xylozine, and one for Ketamine. She checked the gauges to make certain there was plenty of each, inserted a long needle into the mare's neck, and put a mask for anesthesia over her nose and mouth.

"We'll have to go in through the original incision and see what's happening," I said. "There's no time to call Wanda Jean in. Vickie, are you sober enough to assist?"

"Hey, I didn't have time to eat more than three bites of trifle," Vickie said.

"How about I help you set up, Mom?" Nathan asked.

"You haven't assisted me in surgery since you went off to college, Nathan."

"I can do it," Lanier said. "I'll set up the heart and blood pressure monitors."

"Nathan, son, you can shave her belly. Not much hair has grown in since the last surgery, but we ought to get it off." Nathan nodded, turned on the heavy duty electric trimmers and worked his way carefully over the mare's belly.

I pulled on scrubs, tossed a set to Vickie and Lanier and started scrubbing at the sink in the corner.

"She'll have to be scrubbed with antiseptic after Nathan shaves her," Eli said.

"I can do that," Evan said.

"It's okay, Evan, I can handle it," Nathan said.

"All non-essential personnel out," I said.

Dan practically pushed Patsy through the door into the hall.

"Vickie, you about ready?" I asked.

"One minute."

"Instrument trays set up?"

"Gotcha covered," Vickie said. "More coming when you need them."

"Vitals? Lanier?"

"Strong."

"Eli?"

"We're all set."

"You go, girl," Vickie said and took her place beside me at the side of the table.

"Let's do it." I slipped my mask up over my nose and mouth and picked up a scalpel. "Okay, folks, let's see what we've got here."

"This is one hell of a mess," I said. I dropped my bloody scalpel on the table already piled with used instruments.

"It's all stuck together in there," Lanier said. "I've never seen anything like that before."

"Happens sometimes," Eli said. "Even after the most successful colic surgery, everything inside gets gummed up twenty-four hours later."

"Irrigate," I said. "Did you add the Heparin to the solution? We don't want blood clots on top of everything else."

"Absolutely," Vickie answered.

Blood spurted up onto my chest. "Damn!"

Vickie clamped off the bleeder before I even had time to ask her.

"We'll have to resection the bowel," I said. "There's been some more necrosis."

"Aye, aye, captain," Vickie said. I glanced at her. This was definitely a large animal and Vickie was certainly enjoying herself. *Damn,* I thought, *so am I.*

But I'm probably going to lose this one, too.

Vickie leaned over and wiped my sweaty forehead.

I glanced up. Through the window in the surgery door I caught a glimpse of Patsy Dalrymple. "Lanier, go talk to her."

Without a word, Lanier went out, but left the surgery door half open so that she could hear me if I hollered for her.

"Is there any hope at all?" Patsy asked. She was trying to see around Lanier. Lanier tried to block her.

"If there is," Lanier whispered, "Maggie will find it. She's a great cutter."

"But what caused this? Did Mississippi State do something wrong?"

Lanier shook her head. "Keep your voice down, Patsy." She moved Patsy farther down the hall toward the back of the clinic so that Susan couldn't hear. She continued whispering. "They did a great job. As a matter of fact, if they hadn't done such a good job the first time, Maggie wouldn't have any chance at all of saving Mariah. She's not a youngster, but she's strong. No way to predict this. That's why we have to go back a second time so often."

"Usually the horse dies, doesn't it?"

"I'm afraid so. Maggie's doing everything she can, but it may not be enough."

"How can I tell Susan?"

Lanier closed her eyes. "Don't tell her anything yet. If the time comes, I'll talk to her."

"I know you'll all do your best, and if nothing works, do what's best then too. Tell Maggie to use her own judgment."

"Go home, Patsy. We'll call you."

"Dan and I are staying. Period." Patsy squared her shoulders. "Someone has to look after Susan."

I heard the whir of Susan's wheelchair in the hall behind Patsy.

"I'll stay here with her." Sarah's voice. I looked up to see Sarah at the door behind Susan in her wheelchair. Evan stood at her shoulder.

"Maggie," Vickie called me back to my job. I cut into the bowel and prayed.

"Don't close the door," Susan said to her mother. "I want to see."

"Susan, honey," Sarah said, "Come away. You don't really want to look..."

"Leave me alone! She's my horse!"

I heard Lanier gasp and looked up. Susan had pushed herself up out of her chair. She stood in front of the open surgery door. She began to collapse, but Sarah and Evan grabbed her and held her upright.

Sarah was sobbing. My Sarah. Susan's face was tight with effort and despair.

"Lanier," I whispered. "For the love of God shut that door."

I had no idea how long we'd been at this. My hands had taken on a life of their own. They no longer needed my conscious brain to function.

I lifted my head to try to catch my breath through the surgical mask and saw the faces of Susan and Sarah staring in the small window from surgery to hall. They shouldn't be watching this—this charnel house. This wreck of a horse I was probably going to lose on the table.

I felt Vickie slap another scalpel into my hand.

Animals seemed to accept dying as a part of life. For me, death was the enemy. I hated that instantaneous transformation from living body to dead carcass. Why else is spirit called 'anima?' Because it animates every creature in life and deserts us all at the moment of death.

I felt personal failure every time I lost an animal or put one out of its suffering. If I were better, smarter, cleverer with my hands, faster, stronger...

I never had the chance to fight Death for Morgan. It was my greatest defeat, but I'd never even entered the battle. Ever since Morgan's death, ever since I'd found that scrapbook, I'd felt like a failure. I was so tired of battling an enemy who would ultimately defeat me. The best I could hope for was victory in some minor skirmishes.

"Okay," Vickie said. "Now how do we keep everything from gumming up again? Mariah won't survive a third operation."

"Lanier?" I asked.

"Vitals are good, all things considered. She's a fighter, I'll say that for her."

I looked down at the veins along Mariah's intestines. Still throbbing. The diaphragm. Still pulsing. She was a fighter, all right.

With Morgan behind me, I'd been a fighter too. He'd had the faith, the hope, the strength to risk everything on me when I'd hung back. Now I had to trust myself, take the risk.

And I damned well would. I'd battle Death for Mariah and the people who loved her. I would not give up.

I took a deep breath and turned to Lanier. "We're going to try the longest possible shot. Otherwise, Mariah is definitely going to die."

"Go for it," Eli said.

"Bring me a fresh gallon of K-Y Jelly," I said.

Lanier ran to the storeroom next door to the operating theater and returned with a gallon bucket. She pried open the jar and set it on the surgical table next to me.

"We use this stuff to lubricate everything from vaginal specula to thermometers," I said. "How about we see if it'll lubricate innards?"

I dipped both hands into the jelly, picked up a glob, reached into the horse's abdomen and sloshed it in and around every organ. I slid my hands over liver, intestines, and caecum, replenishing my supply from time to time.

Then I stood back and looked at the mess I'd made. "Okay, we've resectioned the gut and removed the dead tissue. We've gunked her up with enough lubricant to oil the wheels of commerce. Either it works, and she lives, or it doesn't, and she dies. That about it?"

"You got it," Eli said. "How you holding up?"

"I'm still here." I took a deep breath. "Vickie, you want to close?"

"Sure."

"You did good," Eli said.

"I tried."

"Then let's stitch this sucker."

Eli elevated the oxygen.

After Vickie closed, we manipulated the pulleys to slide Mariah onto the gurney, then maneuvered the still-sleeping mare into the padded recovery room. We lowered the gurney so that it fitted into the floor and locked it into place. We propped her up against bales of hay to aid her breathing, slipped out and shut the door behind us.

I should have felt exhausted. Instead I felt elation. Mariah might still die, but I hadn't quit on her.

I ripped off my bloody gloves and glanced down at my hands.

No sign of a tremor.

Eli grasped my shoulder. "Go to bed. We'll straighten up here and watch over her until she comes out of it."

"Or doesn't come out of it," I said.

"She's alive. Her vitals are good. You're not a bad cutter," Eli said. "For an old broad."

"Maggie Mac," Lanier said. "You da *woman*!" She and Eli exchanged a high five.

"Yeah." I slapped Eli's hand, then raised my fist toward the ceiling. "Take that, you bastard!"

"Huh?"

"Never mind." I eased my back with both hands, stripped off my bloody top and tossed it into the corner. "Vickie, Lanier, thanks for staying. Lanier, you ought to take Susan home."

I walked down the hall and into the reception area. "Evan? I didn't expect to see you here."

"How's the horse?" Evan whispered. Sarah slept cuddled against his chest.

Susan lay with her head on the arm of her chair, finally so worn out she'd fallen asleep. Pumpkin slept at her feet.

"Won't know for another couple of hours. If she stands up by herself, shows no sign of pain other than post surgical, eats a little hay, and poops, then she may come out of it all right."

"And if she doesn't?"

"She doesn't. Nothing more we can do for her except make sure she doesn't suffer. Why don't you go to bed? I can steer Sarah to her bedroom."

Sarah stirred and stretched. "I'm awake." She allowed Evan to pull her to her feet.

Patsy slept on one of the couches under a horse blanket. Dan stretched in one of the chairs with his head on his hand. "Patsy," I shook her shoulder.

"Huh?"

"She's out of surgery. Go back to your own house."

"I want to stay."

"Come on, Patsy. Shoo. Think you can drive safely?"

"I can," Dan said, instantly awake. "What do you think Mariah's chances are?"

"She's alive. We should know more by morning. You have family all day tomorrow. I'll call you as soon as we know something."

Patsy yawned. "I'm as stiff as a poker. You ought to buy some new couches."

"Lanier, take Susan home. She must be worn out."

"No, Mommy," Susan said sleepily. "Have to stay."

"Come on," Eli said. "We can bed you and your mother down on the sofa bed in my den. It's closer than Maggie's and there isn't but one step up from the driveway."

"Noooo," Susan said, but she allowed Lanier to roll her out the back door of the clinic. Pumpkin trotted along behind her. Some time during the night he'd removed the red bow. I didn't blame him.

"Vickie," I asked. "How about you?"

"I'm staying right here, thank you very much." She pulled a cushion out of the seat of one of the chairs, tossed it on the floor, and sat down beside it.

"You should be home. Your boys…"

"Know where I am. Go, Maggie. I'll holler out the back door if there's any change."

Eli yawned and took Evan's arm. "Come on, cowboy, your bed's at my house, remember?"

"Not even after I've decided to make an honest woman of Sarah?"

"Not even."

He kissed the tip of Sarah's nose. "See you in the morning."

She mumbled something, walked across the lawn and into our house. She shut the door of the guest room without even a goodnight.

I lay down on the couch in the den and pulled the afghan over my shoulders. If I went upstairs to bed I'd never get up. I'd check on the mare in a couple of hours. No sense taking off my clothes.

I meant to fall asleep immediately, but my tired brain and bruised body wouldn't let me. Finally I gave up, picked up a down jacket from the hook in the back hall and walked out to the deck. I stretched out on the chaise longue and covered myself with the jacket. I didn't dare fall asleep out here or I'd wake up in the morning with hypothermia or pneumonia.

"Mother?"

"Sarah?" Her voice jerked me awake.

"What on earth are you doing out here? You'll catch your death."

"I just stretched out for a minute. I thought you went to bed."

Sarah pushed her sleeves into a down parka and sat on the step beside me. "I never watched you do major surgery before."

"Were you grossed out?"

"I thought I would be, but I wasn't. The way you all worked together so smoothly—it was like a female football team with you as the quarterback."

"I threw a few Hail Mary passes tonight, believe me."

"Will Mariah live?"

"I don't know."

"Susan will be devastated if she dies."

"Yes, she will." I didn't want to think about that. I knew Sarah was remembering Pride's death and what it did to her. To us. So I changed the subject. "Your Evan's a nice man. Did I hear something about marrying you?"

"Yup. Mother. I have to tell you something."

"Okay."

"If I'm going to marry Evan, I have to get some things clear between us. All my life I resented not being at the top of your list of priorities. I wanted you to put me before any of the animals."

"I did. I do."

"You don't understand. I actually wanted you to walk away from them for me. Because human beings are more important, aren't they?"

I slipped down to the step beside her, leaned back against the foot of the chaise and took a deep breath. "I don't feel that way. If God gave us dominion over the animals, he also gave us responsibility to go along with it. We're the ones with the big brains. If I can help them, I must."

"Pride's death wasn't your fault." Her voice was so low I could barely make out the words. After he died, Sarah had never mentioned his name again.

"Sarah, why did you give up riding?"

"If you don't care about something, you don't hurt when you lose it."

"But you did care."

"I thought I could stop caring. I couldn't." She dropped her head. "I'm so scared of losing everything and everyone I love. And now there's Evan. How do you bear that constant fear when you have children?"

"You grit your teeth and pray."

"I'd want to lock my children in a padded cell. "

I laughed. "And raise such emotionally healthy kids."

She grinned at me. "How do you know what you're doing is right?"

"Good grief, Sarah, you don't." I put my arm around her. Instead of pulling away as she normally did, she cuddled against me. How long had it been since I'd held her this way? I didn't want to let her go, not back to California, not to marry Evan, not to chance having a baby or going to the jungle. But I'd keep my mouth shut and send her out into the world with my fingers crossed. After a moment, I lifted Sarah's chin and brushed a strand of hair off her cheek. "Why do mothers and daughters always seem to hurt each other?"

"You got along fine with Gram."

I snorted. "Your grandmother went to her grave disappointed that I was a veterinarian and not a country club wife."

"She was proud of you."

"Oh, no she wasn't. Once when I was just starting out, we were setting the table for Thanksgiving dinner and I was telling her about a really brilliant piece of surgery I'd pulled off. Know what she said?"

Sarah shook her head.

"That's nice, dear, but the dessert spoons face the other way."

Sarah laughed.

We sat on the step with my arms wrapped around Sarah just the way I used to when she was a very little girl. "So many stars up there. I can almost smell the dawn."

"I was wrong. You mustn't retire," she whispered.

"I know. Tonight when I was deep in horse guts, I decided I could never give up such a glamorous profession."

"You could cut back. Come to Los Angeles to visit. Hire some help. And there's the wedding. We ought to have it out there where all our friends are."

"I promise I won't get ticked off if you have to go running off to Thailand again."

"Please be careful, Mother."

"I will, Sarah, I promise. You be careful too." I felt warmer than I had since Morgan died, even in the chill of Christmas morning. *Don't die among the alien corn,* Shep had said. He was right. I belonged here, doing this job for as long as my eyes could see and my fingers hold steady.

"Maggie!" a voice called from the darkness.

"That's Vickie," I said.

Sarah beat me to my feet and pulled me up.

"Maggie, come quick!"

"Oh, damn," I whispered and ran toward the clinic. I could hear Sarah hard on my heels and see my breath in the cold air.

As I reached the back door of the clinic, Eli ran down the steps of her house dragging on a jacket. Zipping up his jeans one-handed, Evan pushed Susan's wheelchair at breakneck speed with the other while Pumpkin and Lanier raced to keep up.

I followed Vickie into the clinic and turned toward the recovery stall.

"What is it?" Susan cried.

I put a hand against my heart. I had to stay calm. I'd be the one to put Mariah down.

Vickie stood aside to let me look in the window of the recovery stall.

"I'll be..."

"What is it?" Susan begged. "Tell me, please, please."

"Evan, help her up. Let her see."

Evan lifted Susan to her feet and supported her to the window. "Oh, oh, oh," Susan said and burst into tears.

"Mother?" Sarah asked.

"Take a look."

Sarah looked. "Mother, she's up." She laughed. "She's up."

"That's not the best part," Vickie said. "She's still groggy, but she's nibbling hay. And look, Maggie, look there in the back of the stall."

I looked. In the shadowy far corner of the stall steamed a small but respectable pile of fresh manure. "Hallelujah!"

"You got your Christmas miracle," Evan said and wrapped his arms around Sarah.

"Can I please, please go in?" Susan begged. "Just for a second?"

"There's a step up into the stall," I said.

"I'll help you," Lanier said.

Susan turned to her mother. "I can do it myself."

I caught Lanier's eye. She looked stunned. I wanted to tell her their relationship had changed at that moment, but she'd find out soon enough.

I opened the door to the stall. Susan lifted first one foot to the platform, then the other.

I could hear Lanier breathing heavily behind me. I squeezed her hand.

Susan stood erect and held out her hand. "Good girl," she crooned.

Mariah raised her head from her hay and stretched her velvet nose forward to touch Susan's hand. Then she went back to her hay.

Evan caught Susan as she tried to turn around. "Whoa, there, *podner*."

"She knows me, I know she does," Susan said. Tears streamed down her cheeks, but her face glowed.

"You did it, Maggie," Vickie whispered.

"*Maggie's Militia* did it. Hell of a team." I glanced at my watch. "It's nearly five in the morning."

"Christmas morning," Vickie said.

"I'm starved. Anybody want breakfast?" I asked.

Eli raised her eyebrows. She remembered I'd sworn not to cook Christmas breakfast.

"Can we come back to see Mariah afterwards?" Susan asked.

"Don't see why not."

"Then okay."

"Looks like Nathan and Lisa are already up," Eli said. "The lights are on in Maggie's kitchen. Come on, everybody. Let's see what we can find to eat."

I hung back. "I have to call Patsy."

I listened to five minutes of effusive thanks from Patsy, then walked across to my back door. I opened it a crack, heard the noise, saw too many happy people in too small a space trying to fix breakfast, and walked around to the front door.

I held the chimes on the wreath to keep them quiet, slipped in and turned on the Christmas tree lights. I could hear the babble from the kitchen.

"Who cleaned up after last night?" Vickie said.

"Nathan and I." Lisa's voice. Nice girl. Nathan had done well. Evan was nice too. Maybe God had sent him to Sarah to ground her as Morgan had grounded me. I peeked into the living room. Sugar Pie and all three cats lay in a heap in front of the newly-made up fire. Pumpkin stayed in the kitchen with Susan.

"Well, come on, Nathan, set the table," Lisa said. "Evan and I can't do this alone."

I had started back toward the front porch when the phone rang. Everyone stopped speaking. Would I answer it?

I closed my eyes. Until that moment, I'd forgotten Mike and Big Jake. Somehow God always balanced one miracle with one disaster. I picked up the phone in the front hall. "McLain," I said.

"Doc?" Mike's voice. I sat down on the deacon's bench by the front door and dropped my head into my hand.

"Yes, Mike? Should I come?"

"Yes ma'am, but not 'til this afternoon or tomorrow mornin'." He sounded positively chipper.

I felt my heart lurch.

"I spent all night sticking Big Jake's feet in icewater. Couple of times he tried to fall, but them ropes held him up. This mornin' his temperature's down and his gut sounds normal." He snorted. "Plus he has made him a big ol' pile of crap. Shoot, he tried to bite me a minute ago when I stuck his front hoof in another bucket of icewater."

I closed my eyes and leaned against the wall behind me. "You realize, he may be lame for the rest of his life."

"Damned if I care."

"I'll be out to see him after lunch." I said goodbye, hung up the phone, and realized I was surrounded.

"How is he?" Sarah asked.

All I could do was nod.

She let out a big sigh of relief. "I'm glad."

"I'll see him this afternoon after we open presents."

"Mind if Sarah and I ride along?" Evan asked. "I have a warm spot in my heart for Percherons."

Sarah smiled and took his hand.

"Oh, Lord, the eggs!" Lisa said and scampered back toward the kitchen. Everyone but Eli trailed her.

Eli sat on the bench beside me.

"I'm not quitting," I said.

"You had me worried a couple of times, but I had faith you'd come to your senses eventually."

I stared at her open-mouthed. "Well, I'm glad one of us knew I was staying."

"I think your idea about asking Vickie to join us is worth pursuing. I want some time off too, you know. You're not the only one who gets tired."

I patted her arm. "There's no excuse for the bad times I've put you through this last year, Eli. I'm sorry."

"Morgan *died*, Maggie. That's a pretty good reason."

"Not one *he* would have approved of." I peered out the front window. "Are those snowflakes?"

"Can't be."

"Want to bet?" I laughed. Behind me the kitchen had descended into chaos. Nathan and Sarah and Lisa and Evan were all talking at once. I heard glassware break followed by an oath from Nathan. Chaos. Nice, familiar, happy chaos.

I wrapped my arm around Eli's shoulders. "I think this is the place where some adenoidal tyke says something about God blessing us every one."

# Afterword

Every veterinarian I know is an incorrigible raconteur. The tales in *All God's Creatures* have been manipulated a bit to protect both the guilty and the innocent, but in essence they're true. The characters, however, are completely fictional.

The majority of admissions to schools of veterinary medicine these days are women. One of my female vet friends says that when the men realized that veterinary medicine was not nearly as lucrative as people medicine, that the hours were worse, the conditions often horrendous, and the patients seldom appreciative, many decided to become M.D.'s instead of D.V.M.'s. M.D.'s only have to treat one species. Veterinarians are expected to treat aardvarks and zebras with equal facility.

So many people told me stories and helped with *All God's Creatures*. I apologize to anyone I have forgotten to thank.

Thanks to the School of Veterinary Medicine at Mississippi State University. It is one of the finest schools in the country and produces exceptional veterinarians. I have taken advantage of their services to help one of my own fillies. I have used them as a location for several stories, not because the stories took place there, but because it's the school with which I am most familiar.

My thanks to Phyllis Appleby, Barbara Christopher, Patricia Potter, and Kenlyn Spence for their inestimable critiques.

Thanks also to Bobby Billingsley, Peggy Gaboury, Jimmy Langley, James Luttrell, Louise Maddox, and Sandra Chastain, animal people all, who contributed stories.

Thanks to Elizabeth (Eli) White for graciously lending me her name.

Thanks to veterinarians Bruce Bowling, Laurie Dilworth, Andy Livingston, Melissa Poole, Ruth Wilburn, Khaki Wright, and other vets who talked to me. They never sent me away empty when I begged them for new stories.

Thanks to Elizabeth Burgess, R.N., M.A., who talked me through the birth of a human baby. I don't remember much about my own experience.

My special thanks to Cindy Weis, equine practitioner and raconteuse extraordinaire, who looks after *my* horses so well. Cindy not only spent hours jotting down stories about her experiences, but also looked over portions of the manuscript to make certain my procedures and wording were correct. I have enough unused stories from Cindy for a whole new book.

My deepest thanks to Debra Dixon, who helped me find my voice, and Deborah Smith, who edited brilliantly.

What I got right I owe to these people. Whatever I got wrong is on my own head.

Most of all, thanks to the animals that enrich our lives. May we always be worthy of their affection and their trust.

# Carolyn McSparren

Carolyn's grandfather held her on a horse when she was two. That moment began a love affair with horses that has continued all her life, even when she lived in cities where the only horses she saw were either pulling carriages through the park or maintaining crowd control.

Although she longed for her own horse when she was a teenager, her parents couldn't afford to buy or keep one, so she set her dream aside. She decided to become an English professor at some obscure college and write murder mysteries. Surely then she'd be able to afford her own horse.

Instead, Carolyn went to graduate school and earned her master's degree from the University of Memphis, then became a developer of continuing education programs in business. She wrote technical manuals and marketing pieces on such stirring subject as Statistical Quality Control, about which she knew as much as she did about quantum physics. Those years of writing on demand, however, honed her skills as a fiction writer and self-editor.

During that time, her daughter fell as much in love with horses as Carolyn had. Carolyn bit the bullet and bought Megan her first horse—not a very fancy horse but a good guy nonetheless. A year later she owned three horses, including a mare in foal. She finally came back to riding.

Over the years she's known many veterinarians, farriers, trainers, riders, dog and cat fanciers, and general animal people, all of whom love to tell stories.

The editors of BelleBooks heard some of the stories and decided they deserved to be shared. Thus *All God's Creatures* was born.

*Excerpt from Carolyn McSparren's story in SUMMER AT MOSSY CREEK*

# LOUISE and JACK

*by Carolyn McSparren*

Ida Hamilton Walker stuck her head around the kitchen door and said in a frazzled voice, "Louise, we're running out of potato salad."

"Here." My daughter Margaret handed her a Tupperware bowl straight out of the refrigerator. I would have dumped the salad into a crystal bowl, but didn't suggest that. This was Margaret's first foray into the world of Southern post-funeral feasts, so I refrained from correcting her. I doubted those Visigoths eating me out of house and home in the living and dining rooms of Aunt Catherine's little cottage would notice.

I'd only *bought* the ham and the turkey, of course. Half the town had descended on Aunt's house with food the minute they heard she had breathed her last. They brought everything from sweet potato casseroles to homemade coconut cakes. They filled Aunt's refrigerator and mine as well.

Good thing, too. Unlike Moses, I couldn't call down manna from heaven, and after Aunt's funeral, practically the whole town of Mossy Creek came back to her house to chat and eat.

And eat some more. I swan, you'd think it was a church picnic instead of the aftermath of a funeral for a ninety-two-year-old woman. But she had wanted a great big party, and I was glad to help her get her wish.

She was actually my great aunt, and one of my few remaining relatives. I'd been run off my feet arranging the viewing at the funeral home, picking what she was going to wear into eternity, and organizing folks to meet and greet during the viewing at the funeral home before they moved her to the church for the service.

Her old lady friends had demanded an open coffin, and I wasn't prepared to put up with their complaints if I closed it. Lying in state, Aunt looked like a generic "aged crone" from Madame Tussaud's gallery of waxworks, but that was unimportant. She was long gone from that body. She would have been the first to agree that if the empty husk that was left gave pleasure to her friends, it was fine with her.

I also had to get folks to stay at both her house and mine during the actual service and the trek out to the graveside. According to Amos, the Police Chief, thieves actually read the obituaries. Then while the family is away burying old Uncle Victor or whoever, the thieves break into the empty house and steal everything in sight. Talk about tacky.

Despite being the chief mourner, I'd spent most of the last three days in Aunt's kitchen and on the telephone. Thank heaven for my Garden Club. They'd pitched right in with flowers and food, made sure the house stayed presentable, and saw to it that every dish and bowl was labeled and entered so that it could be returned to the right person with a thank-you note. Plus somebody was always available to greet folks who came by either the house or the funeral home.

I've heard men boast that a girl only becomes a woman when she loses her virginity. Typical. As though that frequently uncomfortable and bloody encounter with a male is the defining moment in the female life.

A girl truly becomes a woman when she is first initiated into that cadre of women who keep every sort of ceremony humming from behind the scenes. They are seldom appreciated, except by one another. They are the Marthas who spend most of any event around the kitchen stove and the sink.

*Read more of this and other stories in...*

**The MOSSY CREEK HOMETOWN SERIES**
**is available at www.BelleBooks.com**

# The Mossy Creek

## MOSSY CREEK

*Book One*

The first book in the series introduces a mayor who sees breaking the law as her civic duty and a by-the-books police chief trying to live up to his father's legend. We've got a bittersweet feud at the coffee shop and heartwarming battles on the softball field. We've got a world-weary Santa with a poignant dream and a flying Chihuahua with a streak of bad luck. You'll meet Millicent, who believes in stealing joy, and the outrageous patrons of O'Day's Pub, who believe there's no such thing as an honest game of darts. You'll want to tune your radio to the Bereavement Report and prop your feet up at Mama's All You Can Eat Café. While you're there, say hello to our local gossip columist, Katie Bell. She'll make you feel like one of the family and tell you a story that will make you laugh — or smile through your tears.

# Hometown Series

## REUNION AT MOSSY CREEK

*Book Two*

This time they've got the added drama of the big town reunion commemorating the twenty-year-old mystery of the late, great Mossy Creek High School, which burned to the ground amid quirky rumors and dark secrets. In the meantime, sassy 100-year-old Eula Mae Whit is convinced Williard Scott has put a death curse on her, and Mossy Creek Police Chief Amos Royden is still fighting his reputation as the town's most eligible bachelor. There's the new bad girl in town, Jasmine, and more adventures from the old bad girl in town, Mayor Ida Hamilton. And last but not least, Bob the flying Chihuahua finds himself stalked by an amorous lady poodle.

*Also available from BelleBooks*

# The Mossy Creek

# SUMMER IN MOSSY CREEK

*Book Three*

It's a typical summer in the good-hearted mountain town of Mossy Creek, Georgia, where love, laughter and friendship make nostalgia a way of life. Creekites are always ready for a sultry romance, a funny feud or a sincere celebration, and this summer is no different. Get ready for a comical battle over pickled beets and a spy mission to recover hijacked chow-chow peppers. Meet an unforgettable parakeet named Tweedle Dee and a lovable dog named Dog. Watch Amos and Ida sidestep the usual rumors and follow Katie Bell's usual snooping. In the meantime, old-timer Opal Suggs and her long-dead sisters share a lesson on living, and apple farmer Hope Bailey faces poignant choices when an old flame returns to claim her.

# Hometown Series

## BLESSINGS OF MOSSY CREEK

*Book Four*

The good-hearted citizens of Mossy Creek, Georgia are in a mood to count their blessings. Maybe it's the influence of the new minister in town, who keeps his sense of humor while battling a stern church treasurer. Maybe it's the afterglow of Josie McClure's incredibly romantic wedding to the local "Bigfoot." Or maybe it's the new baby in Hank and Casey Blackshear's home. As autumn gilds the mountains, town gossip columnist, Katie Bell, has persuaded Creekites to confess their joys, troubles, and gratitudes. As always, that includes a heapin' helping of laughter, wisdom, and good old-fashioned scandal.

*Look for Book Five of the Mossy Creek Hometown series coming in June 2005*

## A DAY IN MOSSY CREEK

Everyone's special
in their own way.

# KASEYBELLE

## *The Tiniest Fairy in the Kingdom*

by Sandra Chastain

*Book One in the* Everyone's Special
*Southern children's series*

KaseyBelle saves her friends from an angry giant and learns that it's not the size of her wings that makes her special, but the size of her heart.

*Also available from BelleBooks*

# SWEET TEA & JESUS SHOES

Come sit on the porch a spell. Let's talk about times gone by and folks we remember, about slow summer evenings and lightning bugs in a jar. Listen to the sound of a creaky swing and cicadas chorusing in the background. Let's talk about how things used to be in the South and, for some of us, the way they still are.

"Sweet Tea and Jesus Shoes is a joyful and endearing collection of nostalgic stories which are sure to win the hearts of readers everywhere." —Phyllis George, Miss America, TV Personality & Businesswoman

Sweet Tea And Jesus Shoes

Deborah Smith, Sandra Chastain, Donna Ball, Debra Dixon, Nancy Knight, Virginia Ellis

"The warm tones in this compilation of anecdotal reminiscences and personal essays beckon readers to pull up a chair and listen to tales of life in the South. Told with humor and honesty from the perspective of traditional and not-so-typical Southern Belles, the stories piece together a literary quilt of eccentricities in Southern living. The authors share their voices, memories, family secrets and personal disappointments. From tales of the familial tension between Smith's cleverly named "Mamaside" and "Daddyside," to Dixon's yarn about an aunt so mean her stare could "peel paint off the sides of completely weathered barns," the stories are creative and observant. Readers looking for proof that every family is just as off-kilter as their own will particularly enjoy this read. It's about living and loving and learning, regardless of which time zone you call home."
—*Today's Librarian*

*Look for Book Two of the Sweet Tea series*
*coming in 2005*

# MORE SWEET TEA

*Also available from BelleBooks*

*Novels about a very different kind of Southern family*

by *NYT* bestselling author

# DEBORAH SMITH

*WaterLilies Series*

Forget everything you believe
about the mysteries of the ocean.
Remember everything you love
about the mysteries of the heart.

## ALICE at HEART

*Book One*

"This book just knocked me out. Absolutely magical and, in my mind, a real masterpiece. Kudos to Deborah Smith for producing something so fresh and so perfect."

—*Susan Elizabeth Phillips*

# DIARY of a RADICAL MERMAID

*Book Two*

Glamour, mystery, romance, humor and webbed toes are all back in full fin as rambunctious mer-socialite Juna Lee Poinfax invades the dignified coastal world of the Bonavendier clan. Determined to chronicle Mer life for her on-line journal, Juna Lee instead dives into Lilith Bonavendier's latest scheme to awaken the "inner mermaid" in an unsuspecting distant relative. World-famous author M. M. (Molly) Revere — who writes the mega-successful Water Hyacinth series, about a group of children who are secretly mermaids — is a shy, plain-footed young woman with nothing but vague clues to her extraordinary family link to the mer world. After Juna Lee — working for Lilith — lures the likable Molly to the Georgia coast, both Molly and Juna Lee find themselves in the middle of trouble. Mer-hunk Rhymer McEvers has come to Sainte's Point Island to hide his three remarkable nieces from their mysterious and possibly murderous mer-father — a man who may be more myth than reality, but dangerous either way. Molly has to face the reality of her heritage while falling in love with the enigmatic Rhymer and helping him protect his nieces from a danger so amazing even the Water People can barely believe it.

*Also available from BelleBooks*

## The Mossy Creek Hometown Series

Available in all fine bookstores and direct from BelleBooks

**Mossy Creek**

**Reunion at Mossy Creek**

**Summer in Mossy Creek**

**Blessings of Mossy Creek**

*Coming in June 2005*

**A Day in Mossy Creek**

## *Other BelleBooks Titles*

(for details see pages 264-271)

**KaseyBelle:** ***The Tiniest Fairy in the Kingdom***

by Sandra Chastain

Book One in the *Everyone's Special* children's series

---

**Sweet Tea and Jesus Shoes**

*Coming in early 2005*

**More Sweet Tea**

---

*WaterLilies Series, by bestselling author*

Deborah Smith

**Alice at Heart**

*Book One*

**Diary of a Radical Mermaid**

*Book Two*

BelleBooks

770-384-1348

P.O. Box 67 • Smyrna, GA 30081

BelleBooks@BelleBooks.com

visit our website: www.BelleBooks.com